M~~e~~dicine

Other Titles by Derek Armstrong

■

The Game
An Alban Bane Thriller

"Reality TV, a murder, a cantankerous detective with a touch of House MD ... compels us to keep reading, and his prose style keeps us chuckling." —*Booklist*

■

The Last Troubadour
Book 1 Song of Montségur

"Armstrong's action-packed second novel." —*Publishers Weekly*

■

The Last Quest
Book 2 Song of Montségur

"Wit and wisdom ... a wide-screen Technicolor adventure for spiritual grownups."
—Bestselling author Lon Milo DuQuette

■

The Persona Principle
with Kam Wai Yu

"Bound to increase in importance."
—*Entrepreneur Magazine*

■

Blogertize—A Leading Expert Shows How Your Blog Can Be a Money-Making Machine

"Any business can profit from these principles."
—*Profit Magzine*

Author Of *The Game* And *The Last Troubadour*

DEREK ARMSTRONG

LARGO, USA

M A D i c i n e

For information, contact Kunati Inc., Book Publishers in both USA and Canada.
In USA: 6901 Bryan Dairy Road, Suite 150, Largo, FL 33777 USA
In Canada: 75 First Street, Suite 128, Orangeville, ON L9W 5B6 CANADA,
or e-mail to info@kunati.com.

F I R S T   E D I T I O N

Designed by Kam Wai Yu
Persona Corp. | www.personaco.com

ISBN-13: 978-1-60164-017-8   EAN 9781601640178
FIC000000 FICTION/General

Published by Kunati Inc. (USA) and Kunati Inc. (Canada).
Provocative. Bold. Controversial.™

h t t p : / / w w w . k u n a t i . c o m

Library of Congress Cataloging-in-Publication Data

Armstrong, Derek Lee.
MADicine / Derek Armstrong. -- 1st ed.
p. cm.
ISBN 978-1-60164-017-8 (alk. paper)
1. Pharmaceutical industry--Fiction. 2. Medicine--Research--Fiction. 3. Genetics--Research--Fiction. 4. Viruses--Fiction. 5. Satire. I. Title.
PS3601.R575M33 2008
813'.6--dc22

2008011608

Dedication

As always, for Kam.

In memory of my mother, Anna.

1

Site F, California

Doctor Alistair Begley felt the rise of sweat under his Armani shirt as he drove out of Site F.

The dark road sliced an arc through towering pine and fir. He slowed as his headlights splashed the last exit sentry post.

He drove into the circle of cold mercury vapor lights. A cheerful orange billboard with yellow lettering dominated the security trap: Braxis, A Better Life for Everyone.

Begley hated that lying sign. He might have believed it eighteen years ago when he was the newest Braxis brainchild, but now it just increased his sense of urgency. It should have read: Braxis: A Better Life for Some, To Hell With the Rest.

The fat tires of his Porsche Carrera S crunched newly graded gravel. He felt queasy as he stopped beside the steel and glass booth.

He thought of his grandkids. He could do this—for them. "Calm down, Begley," he whispered. He fixed a smile on his face and pressed the window button, grateful for the cool autumn night air and the soothing sound of crickets.

"Morning, Fletch," Begley said, proud that he could remember a third-shift guard by name. He handed the man his security card, the key that would start the gates opening.

Fletch smiled back as he swiped Begley's card. "Morning, Professor. Kinda early?" The electrified gates began to open.

Begley forced a laugh and hoped it sounded genuine. "I've been round the clock for seventy-two." He ignored the tickle in his nose. Midnight departures were enough to make any sentry cautious, although Fletch wouldn't question Begley's zeta clearance. After all, he helped create this "better life."

"Headed to LA?"

"September fourteenth. My grandson's birthday."

Fletch leaned closer to his monitor. From his car, Begley saw his own face on the screen, a lower mileage Ali Begley, graying around the temples, grinning white teeth a stark contrast to skin as dark and wrinkled as a California raisin.

Fletch handed him back his card. "How old's your grandson?"

"Four," Begley said.

"You sure you can drive all the way to Long Beach? You look tired, Professor."

"Should make it in three hours." Still, Begley wasn't so sure himself. The stress of the last few months had permitted little sleep.

He glanced at the hermetically sealed case on the seat beside him. He would stay awake. Too much relied on his alertness.

"I had some java before I left." He sniffed but resisted the urge to rub his nose.

"Coming down with a cold?" Fletch sounded nervous.

Begley hoped the overdose of directly injected histamine suppressors and Amantadine would be enough to get him through this post, but he could feel the perspiration, cold on his forehead. He forced a laugh and leaned out the window. "Now, Fletch, you know better."

"Well, you're the doctor."

Begley slipped his Porsche into first gear and peered over the curving sweep of the dash at the towering barbed wire gate and tire barrier. The first gate was barely five yards from Fletch's booth, but the second gate and the tire barrier were thirty yards further. If he timed it wrong, he would be trapped in an electrified cage.

He trembled, not just a shiver, but a deep quiver that started at his tailbone, pressed into the leather of his seat, and ended in damp, shaking fingers wrapped too hard around the steering wheel.

Irrational, prehistoric fight-or-flight instinct nearly shut down his rational mind. He reached over and touched the cool metal of the case on the passenger seat. The numbing cold of the refrigerant inside made the case feel electric. He snatched away his hand.

He did not have the luxury of a failed attempt. It was no longer just a matter of conscience, or even of his family's safety.

In that frosty case was death. And hope. A new world. Or a devastated one.

Fletch waved an ear thermometer in his hand. "Sorry, Professor. You know the rules."

"Sure. I wrote them." Begley leaned out the window, but kept his foot on the vibrating clutch.

The guard stepped out of his booth and pressed the thermometer into Begley's ear.

It beeped.

"You're burning up!" The guard stepped back as if Begley had shoved him, his face paling in the blue glow of the fence lights.

Begley dropped the clutch and slammed the accelerator. The roar silenced the night birds as fat tires spun and gravel sprayed the shocked guard and the booth. The Porsche slewed, swinging wildly as three-hundred-and-fifty horses screamed. The first gate blurred by. In his mirror, Begley saw Fletch struggling with his holstered gun, but now the car was too far down the gravel to make a target. The guard ducked into his booth.

The amber lights flashed on the gates, waves of warm pulsing light, and the gates began to close. Begley shifted and felt the raw power at his back, the rocket-like thrust. He might make the gate, but the spikes of the tire barrier, sharp, tire-hungry teeth, rose out of the steel grate across the road.

Begley sneezed but kept both hands on the wheel and deliberately steered off the gravel to avoid the tire barrier. He doubted his sports car, even with four wheel drive, could survive the steep dip into the car trap, a precipitous concrete ditch on either side of the tire spikes, but there was a chance he could jump from bank to bank if he hit at the right speed. He hit fourth gear, said a quick prayer, and then he was soaring, his gut cramping with fear as his tires left the ground. He cried out as the case flew off the seat and slammed into the ceiling liner. He forgot to lift his pedal, and the engine snarled as the wheels spun without resistance. The wind was knocked from him as the car landed with an alarming bang, the force transmitted through his steering wheel. The car shuddered, bounced off the grassy slope, then slid sideways. There was another metallic clang as his fishtailing back end churned up grass and dirt.

He slewed back on to the gravel road, then almost back off again. He shifted down as a blind corner swept up. He took it fast, slid again, but accelerated into the spin. The Angeles Crest Highway was only five miles away. The blur of trees to his left was not as disconcerting as the precipitous black canyon to his right. He felt the ominous thumping from the rear end. Suspension or tires, maybe both. The vibration became a shudder.

He pressed the accelerator to the floor and clenched the wheel. The Jeeps would already be in pursuit, so he poured on all the speed he could manage without flying off the precipice to his right. If he could reach the public highway, he might make it because Administrator Gies would never call the police. He would send the twins.

As he drove, taking the corners hard, he reached for the handle of the tossed case, hoping the hermetic seals were intact. He lost control on another hairpin as the steep road hugged the low mountain. As he eased off, the car slid sideways for a moment, but he managed to regain the back end in spite of the menacing pounding and thuds.

He sneezed so hard he almost lost control again, but ahead saw a single pair of headlights and knew he was getting close to the highway. The Porsche felt loose, sliding in the back end more than it should.

He wouldn't make it far, but now he felt sure he could reach the highway. For the sake of his grandkids. For the sake of everyone's grandkids. Braxis had to be stopped.

He almost missed the turn, swung erratically as he carved an arc on the narrow roadway, nearly swiping trees on the passenger side. He came around the bend and slammed on the brakes, and the car quivered. The case was thrown off the seat again and the Porsche bounced to a stop.

A swath of asphalt crossed the dirt road.

Begley slumped in the seat, clenching the wheel, breathing too hard, his throat burning. Bursts of pain stabbed at his half-closed eyes. His rapid breathing turned into a long hacking cough. He closed his eyes, concentrating, willing himself not to be sick.

He turned the case on the seat and dialed the combination on the metal case. He knew he shouldn't open it. If the shatterproof vials had somehow leaked, the hermetically sealed case would slow the spread—if he didn't foolishly open the lid. His hands trembled. He had to know. He flipped open the lid.

"Merciful God."

The twelve triple-sealed vials were intact.

He sneezed again. How long did he have before the Jeeps arrived?

Begley unbuckled the seatbelt and reached into the passenger seat foot well. He fished around, found his medical bag and pulled it back on the seat. He had prepared three hypos back in his lab, and now he plunged two vaccine syringes into his deltoid. The burning sensation told him the dosage was too high, but all that mattered now was getting to LA. Alive. He pumped another dose, and then some Amantadine.

He had no time to change the tire. They'd be on him by then. He'd have to try to flag down a car. Yes, he might infect them—a small price to pay.

He knew now that he would be one of the fatalities. His immune system was exploding in a viral firestorm. The fevered glow blossomed into a heated burn, still manageable, but only for a few more hours. He thought again of Zoë and Dorsey. Nothing else mattered.

He sneezed into his hand and blood splattered his palm. He snatched the envelope from his suit pocket, laid it inside the shockproof case, snapped it closed, and spun the combination locks. He slapped the label on the case: Doctor Ada Kenner, Emerging Viral, NCID, Centers for Disease Control. Just in case. He had sent all the data by secure email to both Ada Kenner and to Alban Bane, although it was likely the Braxis firewall had intercepted the encrypted attachments.

He sniffed, shivered, blinked several times. Tears were hot on his face. Too late. Too late for him. But not for others.

The inside of his car lit up as headlights reflected in his rearview mirror. They were on him already.

He fumbled with the door release. He could run. Run into the forest, into the gloom. With his fever and the sneezing he wouldn't last long. The twins would come on their long, loping legs. They would be on him like grinning wolves.

He prayed, then, mumbling the Lord's Prayer out loud. An avowed atheist, the unbidden prayer frightened him more than his own certain death. His rational mind cringed. It was the thought of the twins rather than the virus that brought the prayer. In Begley's rational world, there was no room for a God, but in that moment he knew for a certainty there was a Devil. The Devil's own twins would be in those approaching jeeps.

Then, coming down the highway was another car.

Begley grabbed the case, threw open his door, and jumped to the middle of the lane, in front of the oncoming car. Brakes squealed and Begley was close enough to smell tire smoke as the driver tried to avoid the idiot on the highway. Begley's last thought was of Alban Bane.

2

Flight 411

Around the time Alistair Begley ran the gatehouse at Braxis, TV camera crews and photographers with whirring cameras followed a striking man with a tartan umbrella and patched Red Sox baseball cap to the security gate at London Heathrow. Crowds gathered, wondering if he was an American telly star. There was something familiar about his jocular appearance: red hair tumbling from under the dirty cap, the T-shirt that read "I had tea with the Queen" stretched taut over a wide chest and impressively rippled abs, and the big laconic grin that never seemed to leave his handsome, freckled face. He had to be some kind of celebrity.

Alban Bane turned, doffed his lucky Red Sox cap, and said, "Sorry, lads, lassies and leachies, I'll miss your harassment." *Like hell I will.*

But the British tabloids weren't about to give up; they loved to hate Bane. They crowded around the small queue at the metal detectors. The Batty Scot, some called him on the pages of their rags, others The Loco Yank, depending whether they saw him as American or Scot, inevitably with pictures of a smiling baseball-capped Bane, fencing off cameras with his tartan umbrella.

"Director Bane, one more question!" a stout woman correspondent from *The Crime Gazette* shouted.

"Why not save me the trouble and make something up? You will anyway, lassie."

Some of the reporters laughed. Others thrust microphones at him. Bane was always good for a sound bite.

"Are you consulting on the Manchester bombing, sir?"

"I'm just here for a visit, lassie." He pointed at his T-shirt. "Had tea with the Queen, see?" He put up his sense of humor like a starship shield, deflecting the too-smart journalists.

Ms Stout from the *Gazette* wasn't about to be deflected. "Has anyone taken credit for the bombing, Bane?"

"Her Majesty didn't tell me."

A gaunt, balding man from *The Times* squeezed to the front of the crowd. "How do you like being the director of the World Advance Response Taskforce?"

"Aside from the name, I like it fine." Bane flipped open his badge. "How'd you like to work for an organization called WART? Ach, it's damned embarrassing."

"WART's last Interpol audit revealed more than half your agents are women."

"Is that a question?" Bane glared at the journalist, a scowling woman.

"Yes. Is there a reason you favor women?" The scowl intensified, as if she dared him to say something politically incorrect.

"Women are smarter than men. Although there are exceptions, lassie." Two or three male journalists laughed.

Bane slipped around the metal detector and flashed his badge at the gate guard.

"Sir, I have to ask you to check your weapon." The guard said it quietly, as if afraid Bane might take offence. Both of them ignored the shouting journalists.

Bane patted his belt holster. "Dinee worry, lad. I'm in first class. The seats are wide enough for my holster."

"But, sir—I know who you are sir, but—but, only the air marshal is armed."

Bane read the guard's nametag, then handed him a holographic authorization card. "Alec, read and learn."

Alec the guard obviously recognized many of the signatures or names. He handed the card back. "My apologies, sir. Not even the MI-6 are allowed to carry on International flights."

Bane shrugged. "MI-6 sleep with their guns. Very phallic. Me, I carry because this card says I have to. Damned stupid rule."

"Blimey, sir, if it were anyone but you, sir. See you all the time on my telly."

Bane gave an exaggerated sigh. "Aye, it's great to be me."

The guard stared at him, probably trying to decide if Bane was serious. Finally, he smiled. "I'll have to let the air marshal know. Follow me, Director, sir." The guard escorted him to the boarding gate, past the waiting passengers. Alec the guard whispered to the gate attendant, who nodded and took him personally on board to meet the air marshal.

The marshal was an unsmiling woman, short and muscular, with major happy jugs that very nearly spilled out of her plain suit. Her abrupt scowl told him he was in for a rough ride. She examined Bane's authorization, her flecked brown eyes lively but revealing no emotion. She stood close enough that he could smell mouthwash and soap. Female cops and marshals were never to be taken lightly, happy jugs notwithstanding.

"I suppose there's no arguing with this, Director Bane," she said, her English slightly accented and her voice low and clipped. She handed him back the authorization card. "I am Marshal Claire Racine. I'll be back in economy." She flipped open her jacket. "And my gun is bigger than yours, so behave."

He laughed. "I think I'm turned on."

"Your reputation for being politically incorrect is obviously justified." She smiled. "But this is my plane. You are nothing but a passenger. Understand?"

"Didn't see your name on the tail, but I like the idea of riding Air Claire."

"I know of you, monsieur. In France, we call you the *plaisantin*."

"I'm known as 'the Joker'? That explains the giggles in Paris." He shrugged. "There's no known cure for my mouth. Doctors have tried."

She didn't smile. "What's in the bag, sir?"

He grinned. "Condoms, facemasks, bullet clips, forensic kit, satellite phone, titty magazine—"

"Facemasks?"

"Carried them ever since SARS."

"Paranoid, sir?"

"Always."

"Plaisantin." She sighed, then glanced at her watch. "We're boarding in a moment."

"I'll shut up."

"That would be good." She tilted her head to one side. "I'm not going to like you, am I?"

"Probably not. No one does." Not even my daughters, he thought. "But I like you, Claire."

She sighed. "Take your seat, monsieur." She turned and strode rearwards.

Bane couldn't resist watching her angry, clenched buttocks—for just a moment. Then, he settled into row three in first class, an aisle seat, closed his eyes, and went back to concentrating on work, on the latest emergency.

The panicked call that cut short his investigation in Manchester had come from the aloof Professor Begley. Begley had been Bane's main contact at Braxis Genetics, a company perenially under investigation by various federal agencies and in trouble with Bane because of their associations with terror groups. Its list of shareholders included numbered companies owned by the elusive Emerson Bartlett. Begley was a master at diversion, and revealed nothing in his last phone call.

"You must come, Director. It's life or death." Begley had sounded alarmed.

"You've heard of the police? The FBI?"

"No. They follow rules."

"Meaning I don't."

"Right."

"I'm a busy man, Begley. Give me more to go on. Your boss fired you? Your wife left you? You killed someone? World coming to an end?"

"Sunday morning, at the Holiday Inn, Bane. You need to be there. Thousands of lives are at stake. Maybe millions."

"Oh—world coming to an end. That's what they all say."

"Khan's involved."

Bane sucked air through his teeth. "Chaudhry Shujaa Khan? The man who sells nuclear weapons to terrorists? That Khan?"

But Begley had already hung up. There could be no question of not following up with the strange call from Begley after a name drop like that.

Bane dozed in his seat, but his eyes opened when someone knocked into him. A tired strawberry blonde woman loomed over him, trying to cram a too-large carryon into the bin over his head. She lost her balance and dropped the bag. Bane caught it, lightly, and sprang up to help her.

"Thank—" The woman's smile faded, her eyes fixed on the gun on his belt as his jacket fell open. She stepped back into the aisle, pulling her son with her.

"I'm a cop," Bane said. Not strictly true, but easier for her to understand. When she didn't relax, he flipped his badge discreetly.

"WART?"

Bane tried not to roll his eyes. He pocketed his folio, snapped the bin closed.

"That's so rad!" her young boy said, pointing at his gun.

"Ssh!" Bane buttoned his jacket to hide the holster. "Our secret, okay?"

The boy nodded, not blinking.

"My son," the woman said warily. "I'm Monica McCarthy. My son, Jacky."

Bane loved kids more than anything in the world, but he knew that Jacky's sparkling eyes meant no sleep on this flight. He yawned. He had endured twenty hours on the site of Britain's worst terrorist bombing. The children were the worst, and Jacky's smile reminded him of just how horrible the scene had been.

The child's doll, lying in the rubble, the little girl's hand clinging to it. He saw bits and pieces of a hundred corpses, but the child's doll, and that little clinging hand would stay with him in his nightmares for months to come. Thank God there had been no journalists to witness his tears. And now, six hours later, staring at this little five-year-old boy, the tears gathered again, unshed behind tired eyelids. At least Jacky didn't cling to a doll.

He knew by Jacky's big too-cool-for-school eyes that the boy wouldn't give him a moment's peace on the flight. Bane decided to pre-empt. He pressed his finger to his lips, to reinforce his "ssh" and said, "I'm undercover, Jacky. Keep this to yourself."

"Are you like James Bond?"

"Better looking and funnier."

"Wow!" Jacky wasn't about to let him alone. The boy sat on the seat opposite the aisle, staring at him. Too loud, he said, "Can I see your gun?"

Oh hell. Every passenger in first class froze, as if someone had shouted, This is a hold-up! All the passengers in first class stared at him, expressions varying from outright terror to shock to recognition.

The turmoil was immediate. Some passengers crowded around him asking for autographs. Others ran for the flight attendants. In moments, everyone knew he had a gun, even back in economy.

Bane stared at young Jacky. "Way to keep a secret. No inviso-ring for you."

The passengers seemed even more agitated; some whispered, one person had tears on her face.

They've got to get me a private plane, Bane thought. He had requisitioned a plane six times, all to assurances one was on order, complete with all the 007 bells and whistles, but months later he still flew commercial.

He sighed, then held up his arms and raised his voice: "Hello fellow passengers and crew. In the interest of getting us airborne, and avoiding the usual boring questions and gossip, yes, I am Alban Bane. Yes, I have a gun. But don't worry, I am supposed to have it. Ask anyone. Be warned, I sometimes arrest people who ask me stupid questions. So, any questions?" No one said a word, including Jacky. "Good, then I'm going to close my eyes and go to sleep."

His butt barely hit the seat cushion.

"Sir, come this way, please." The pilot stood over him, red-faced. He sounded as if he was nasally congested.

Bane sighed. "Yes, captain."

He followed the pilot to the galley near the entrance to the cockpit.

The captain was a tall, beefy man with wide red cheeks. He sneezed, covering his nose with his hands. Bane noticed two things. The man had a terrible cold, nose red and eyes puffy, and he chewed his nails. Great. A nervous, sick pilot. He remembered the Parameter Watch Notice from the CDC and found himself fishing in his coat pocket for an N-95 filtration mask. He held the mask in front of his face.

"Are you being funny?" The pilot pointed at the mask.

"Nope. I get no sick leave at work."

"I didn't appreciate your speech, Director Bane." Nasal congestion didn't make him sound less angry. "I'm considering having you deplaned." He sneezed.

Bane slipped the elastics mask clips over his ears. "I can be a pain in the ass."

The pilot sneezed again, catching snot in his hand.

"Bad cold, captain?"

The pilot sneezed again.

That's all I need, Bane thought. He could face a half dozen thugs with guns, but faced with a microscopic bug, he ran for a mask.

"In case you haven't heard, there are drugs for that."

"Smart mouth. I don't like a smart mouth." His throat was raspy.

"Being Director of WART has certain privileges. One, I can't be bumped by annoying pilots. Two, I carry a gun everywhere. Three, I can have a smart mouth, and no one can gag me. I plan to sleep. Hopefully, you don't."

The pilot slammed the cockpit door. Funny how many people slammed doors in Bane's face. His old buddy Arm forced him to take a "Smart Ass IQ" test online, and Bane scored over 200, which meant King of all Smart Asses.

As Bane returned to his aisle seat, he felt every eye in first class on him. No one spoke and that was fine by him.

"That was waaay cool!" said Jacky as he sat.

Bane smiled behind his mask.

"Can I have one?" Jacky pointed at the mask.

"Sure, kid." He handed the boy a mask and Jacky slipped it on. He had one friend on board, at least, and certainly not Jacky's glaring mother. A nervous white-haired woman sat by the window next to Bane. She looked pointedly out the window and said nothing to him.

Good. Now he could sleep.

Once they made it airborne he dozed, but haunting images of a headless doll and a bodiless hand invaded his peace almost immediately. He was jostled hard from the aisle and woke instantly. Instinctively, his dopey mind triggered alert and his hand went straight for the grip of his revolver. He released, took a long breath, and glanced over his shoulder.

The pilot ducked through the curtain to economy and stared back at him with bloodshot eyes. He seemed angrier and sicker. His damp face glistened.

"Eat your chicken, Jacky," his aisle neighbor Monica said. She pushed the uneaten tray of food closer to her son.

Jacky had his mask shoved up on his forehead. "Mommy, it tastes pukie."

"Just eat it," she snapped.

The flight attendants had obviously not wanted to wake Bane for mealtime, probably afraid of what he might say. He had a hundred airline-food jokes.

Jacky looked at Bane, a sudden smile on his face. "You like puke food, Mr. Secret Agent?"

Bane winked. "I'm more like a detective, Jacky. But it looks yummy."

Mommy Monica gave him a cold *I don't need your help* look.

"Are you sure you're not a spy, Mr. Spy?" Jacky sounded disappointed.

"Sorry, little man, I drink beer not vodka martinis." From Jacky's smile, he obviously understood the 007 allusion.

"My daddy's a fireman."

From Monica's sharp look, Bane understood all. She was divorced. The missing wedding ring, the paler band of skin on her finger, and her sudden teary eyes told him it was recent. Jacky's boast had hurt her. "What's your mommy do?"

"Mommy's just a lawyer."

"Just? *Just?*" Bane hated lawyers. They were lower than the journalists who plagued him; someone was always suing him for something or other: libel, killing their baby, putting so-and-so in a wheelchair. But instead he said, "Do you know, Jacky, that lawyers are the most important people on earth?"

Jacky's mouth made a small *o*.

Jacky's mom mouthed "thank you" and smiled.

And in that moment, the captain returned up the aisle and headed towards the flight deck. The faint salty-puke smell reached Bane, even through the microfilters of his disposable mask. The captain coughed as he reached the cockpit door, a heave that made his shoulders shake. His shirtsleeves were rolled up to reveal damp black fur and his underarms were dark with sweat stains.

Jacky pointed. "Who's flying the plane?"

"The other pilot," Monica said.

Bane didn't like the look of the man. He seemed sick and feverish, and that meant contagious in the jet's re-circulated air. Worse, this man was flying their damned plane.

Barely a moment passed, and the cockpit door slammed open once more. The pilot marched quickly to Bane's seat.

"This is my plane," he said.

Bane folded his arms. "Yes sir, I know."

"I could lock you up."

"Where? In the head?" Bane smiled.

"My authority is total here, you know." The smile was almost a leer.

Bane saw Jacky make a "nutcase" sign with his finger and the boy pulled his mask down over his face. "Captain, either you're high on cough syrup or out-of-your-mind sick. Either way, I'm tired."

"It's my plane!" He laughed.

Monica looked frightened as she hugged Jacky close. Bane had been around enough nutcases and psychotics to know the pilot had, at the very least, a rage problem, but probably something much more serious was going on.

"Your plane. Got it." It was a little unnerving to realize their pilot was not just sick and angry but possibly a madman.

The pilot jerked around, his movements clumsy and occasionally spastic. Bane saw the hard ridge of tense neck muscle. Again, the pilot slammed the door.

Monica's eyebrows lifted in a "what gives?"

Bane shrugged. He popped two aspirin from his coat pocket. He was trying to cut back on the ASA, lately down to six or eight a day.

The plane vibrated and dipped and Jacky grabbed Monica's hand. His round face scrunched into a little Jack-o-lantern mask of fear, his wide, blue eyes unblinking and dry, and his lips drawn into a taut line.

The cockpit door opened and the pilot walked past Bane's seat yet again, through the curtains and into economy. A moment later he re-appeared, hand still trembling, his face furrowed in a scowl. The captain knocked Bane's shoulder as he passed. He paused at the door and glanced back. His eyes blinked a rapid staccato as he stared at Bane, he coughed once, then entered the flight deck.

Bane stared at the door. What was going on? He knew fear-induced psychosis when he saw it; he'd been around more psychotics than the average practicing psychiatrist. This pilot couldn't stay in his seat. He was wildly out of control and an out-of-control pilot was no more reassuring than a surgeon with shaky hands.

An attractive brunette attendant started to clear the trays and wagged her finger at Jacky. "You didn't eat your snack, cutie."

Jacky looked up at her, his lip trembling into an attempted smile. "I'm not cutie. I'm Jacky! And it's pukie!"

"Is this your first flight, Jacky?"

He nodded.

The flight attendant swayed, expertly holding Jacky's tray without spilling a drop of his untouched Coke as the plane dipped into turbulence. "Well, it's the safest way to travel. Did you know that, Jacky?" She turned away as she sneezed. "Excuse me!"

The plane bounced hard.

The attendant's face remained locked in a facsimile of a smile, nearly losing her tray. She recovered expertly and rushed forward to the galley.

Bane glanced out the window. The sun was setting, a sunny-side up egg yolk in a Teflon-gray sky. Jacky leaned across his mother and pressed his face to the glass.

"Mommy! What's that, mommy?"

The plane lurched again. Turbulence. Monica obeyed the Fasten Seat Belt sign and shoved her son back in his seat, clipping on the belt.

The attendants rolled serving carts back to the galley, securing them in their bays. They appeared crisp and professional, but they hustled.

"What's going on?" Jacky asked.

Monica snugged her son's belt. "Nothing, boo. Just a little bumpy air."

"How can air be bumpity?"

"I don't know, Jacky."

Jacky looked at Bane. "Same way trees wave around, Jacky," Bane said with a shrug.

"Oh." He smiled. To his mother he said, "I need to pee."

"Can you hold it, boo-boo?"

"Nope." Jacky was only five, so there was no point arguing. Bane, a veteran of two five-year olds knew that.

She unhooked his belt and her own.

"You'll have to sit down, ma'am!" The attendant shouted it from her fold-down seat by the galley. Monica pushed Jacky back in his seat and buckled him in, ignoring his complaints. She belted herself in as the plane bumped again, seemed to sway, then dipped sharply.

Bane winked at Jacky. "Try crossing your legs." Jacky crossed his legs.

The brunette attendant picked up the handset by her station. Her face flushed, she pressed the button and hesitated long enough for Bane to hear her fast breathing on the speakers. "Please remain seated and fasten your belts. Make sure your carry-ons are secure, please."

Bane knew this was not a turbulence alert. In those scenarios, they always told you what was going on, and it was almost always from the pilot.

Then he heard it. A long rumbling, almost hollow sound. He felt it vibrate through his shoes and in his seat. He reached out, leaned over the white-haired lady next to him and touched the window. He felt it jump under his hand.

"What is it, mommy?" Jacky sounded really terrified this time.

"Nothing, boo-boo. This happens all the time."

The hell it does, Bane thought.

Monica grabbed her son's hand too hard.

"Ouch, Mommy."

She loosened her grip but held on. Bane knew all her maternal instincts screamed at her to protect, protect, protect ... and Bane's survival instincts had kicked in too. He wanted to unbuckle and pound on the cockpit door.

A long shudder rippled through the plane. He heard something like a clunk, metallic and distant. What could be wrong?

The shudder continued, then another clanking sound.

The plane tilted, sudden and hard, so steep that Bane's belt snapped taut.

"Mommy!"

Jacky's cry pierced the sudden roar of voices screaming all around them. An overhead bin opened and bags tumbled out. A hard-edged attaché case hit a businessman in the head and he slumped forward, blood splattering his seat.

A young Asian girl, maybe two years older than Jacky, slid down the aisle. A woman clung to the girl's ankle. Bane reached out and grabbed the woman's flailing arm.

The tilt of the plane was nearly vertical now, and Bane held on to the woman. She held her daughter and whimpered. Bane's grip was so tight it must have cut off the woman's circulation. His own lap belt cut into his waist as the seat and belt took the weight of a man, woman and child.

Monica pushed Jacky's head down to his lap and held him there. She leaned over him, both arms extended, her terrified eyes locked on Bane.

"Mommy! Mommmmmmiiieee!" Jacky shrieked.

The plane tilted further, steeper and steeper, like an out-of-control rollercoaster, except the plunge didn't end.

The woman flopped in his grip, like a game fish on a line, but he held on to her, his eyes fixed on hers, trying to be reassuring. He saw the fear of death in her face.

The screams rose in intensity.

Bane was falling out of the seat. The belt held him. It cut into him, it hurt, but it held.

An alarm shrieked through the plane.

Monica prayed "Hail Mary, full of grace ..."

A deep volcanic rumble snatched away her "amen."

Bane clung to the woman's ankle and stared at her young girl. He forced a smile as her terrified eyes stared back at him. The eyes grew wider but fixed on him, and he knew that the girl was beyond terror. Bane nodded and winked once. "It's all right, sweetie," he shouted over the screams in the cabin.

He found himself thinking of his own daughters, safe in their boarding school, and how much they had been through with the loss of their mother to a killer, with the kidnapping last year—and now the loss of their father? And he found himself praying too. But that just angered him. Furious that he would think of praying for help, he reeled in the woman and her girl, hand over hand, pulling them up and up even as the plane tilted steeper into a howling plunge.

3

Firenze, Italy

Even as Bane fended off journalists at Heathrow, Doctor Ada Kenner dodged her own nuisance. In the graceful city of Firenze, animal-rights protesters swarmed her as she stepped out of the white marble archway of the Grand Hotel. She recoiled from the fiery crowd and the record September heat wave. The protestors shouted variations on, "How many monkeys did you kill today?" Everyone in the crowd wielded signs with similar themes: Braxis tortures animals! The red typography was cleverly designed to resemble dripping blood against a picture of a dissected rhesus monkey.

Ada felt a slow burn of anger—her virology research didn't involve experimentation on animals, and she was a vegetarian and avowed animal-lover (two dogs, three cats, one parrot)—but she gave her best smile, and tried to push through the pickets and cameras.

She held the brim of her precious Biltmore Fedora, determined not to lose it in the crowd. It had been her father's hat, always too loose on her, but it went with her everywhere, a reminder of the great man. Cameras clicked as she pushed through the crowd. What must she look like? She'd probably see herself in tomorrow's papers, or on CNN, a short-haired, athletic, dark-skinned woman in unfashionable jeans and an even less fashionable hat.

Ada heard another crescendo of protester chanting; thank God, the mob had a new victim. This time, the crazies swarmed Doctor Ernest Gies, her old Harvard professor.

The frail man disappeared behind sign-wielding activists. Ada heard him shout, "We save lives, we don't—"

A woman's shriek cut him off. "Butcher! Animal killer!"

Ada felt a pang of anxiety, and started back through the crowd to rescue her teacher. A pro-wrestler look-alike security man cleaved through the crazies like an icebreaker, followed by Professor Gies.

Gies grabbed Ada's elbow on the way by. "This way, kiddo."

She yielded to the pull from her professor and mentor, and together they ran along the banks of the Arno river, forgotten, as yet another hapless scientist exited the hotel. A few protesters stayed with them until they veered through the Piazza dei Giudici, and pressed on to the crowded Piazza della Signoria, by which time Ada was drenched with sweat, her loose shirt and khaki shorts clinging to her like Spanish onion skin.

"It's good to see you, kiddo," Gies said, slowing now, comfortable in the anonymity of a crowd of tourists. He released her arm. They paused in the shade of the grand reproduction of Michelangelo's David, ignoring annoyed tourists with cameras who tried to wave them aside. "And what are you doing here?" He leaned and kissed both her cheeks. "This is a Braxis-only event, kiddo." He winked. "I won't ask how you got in." He pointed at her forged badge.

"I need you," she said simply.

"So, you're here just because you missed the old curmudgeon? I always knew I was irresistible."

The venerable Harvard professor had changed. His sense of humor was as dry as his paper-brittle skin. It was good to see him, but his appearance worried her. He seemed to have aged fifteen years in the last few months, his bloodshot eyes framed by a nest of worry lines.

"It's important. And you didn't return my calls," she said.

He studied the flow of tourists. "Not here, kiddo. I know a quiet bistro."

Ada sensed intrigue in his hushed tone and furtive glance. When she had arrived in Florence, the fairytale city enchanted her, taking her back to her honeymoon so many years ago. Only the protestors had spoiled the day. Now, as they walked quickly through streets touched by the gold of a setting sun, the ancient city seemed less like a magical place where old friends might laugh over Chianti, and more like a city of conspiracy, full of lurking protestors and skulking scientists.

The bistro was empty when they arrived, and the waiters gave them looks that said, *this is Firenze, we don't eat until the civilized hour,* but Gies bribed their way in with a wad of crumpled Euros. The comforting aroma of basil made her stomach rumble and they ordered Su Pane Frattau—a crisp bread with tomato-basil sauce—and a bottle of Chianti.

Gies didn't bother with "Do you like your new job?" or "What's it like working for your ex-husband?" He swirled his glass of wine, staring at her through the vermillion liquid, and jumped straight to business. "What are you tracking, Ada?"

Ada sipped wine and studied his tired eyes. "What makes you think I'm tracking anything?"

"I read your Parameter Incident Watch."

"Those notices only go to health officials, hospitals and law enforcement."

"I consult with the FBI from time to time. Your notice was interesting, Ada: 'To all agencies and departments, report all incidents of violent rage, aggressive pyschopathy or sociopathy not attributable to context.' That's the gist, isn't it?"

She set down her wine glass. "So you can guess why I needed to see you, professor?"

His lip twitched as if he attempted a smile then changed his mind. "You've only been CDC coordinator of Emerging Viruses for two weeks. What makes you think your 'syndrome' is viral?"

She broke off a piece of bread and munched. Gies had changed, that was clear. It was not just the fatigue. His move to Braxis Genetics was almost a betrayal of his principles. After the loss of one of his sons to violence, Gies had morphed into a dark mutation of the old, smiling professor, like a butterfly transforming back to the caterpillar.

"I'm concerned," she said, at last. "I'm analyzing a vector of violence that cannot be attributed, an increase in unmotivated violence of seven hundred and thirty-two percent in five American cities."

"And violence in America is so unusual?"

"Nearly every case was an upstanding citizen, happy family person, even a Baptist minister who went on a rampage through his flock at Sunday services. Tell me that's ordinary."

He folded his age-freckled hands on the table. "Slow down, Ada. I don't want to hear incidental babble. I taught you better than that. Biochemistry? Physical pathology?"

She nodded. Same old cranky Gies, always stopping her, correcting her. "Of the ones left alive—"

He held a finger. "No. You're jumping ahead, again."

Sure, teach, she thought. But she smiled. At least Gies listened; when she had tried to explain all this to Devon—her boss and ex-husband—he had shooed her out of his office with a "Send me a report." When she had told him she was flying to Florence, the city where they had spent their happiest few weeks, he had just sighed and said, "Surely you've got lab work to do?" Now, as Ada studied her old teacher, she was struck by how similar Devon and Gies were. She had adored them both at one time, but the infatuation had been misplaced. Neither had vision. Neither of them trusted her.

"Elevated white blood counts and SED rates in the attackers," she replied to her teacher, finally. "Symptomology includes violent sneezing, fever, migraine headaches that sometimes lead to violent psychosis. Then explosive hemorrhaging from nose, mouth, ear canal and eye sockets."

His eyebrows lifted, and he leaned forward. "The hemorrhaging wasn't mentioned in your Parameter Incident Watch."

"I sent out a separate notice."

"You've ruled out hemorrhagic fever—Ebola, Marburg?"

She refilled their glasses, her hands shaking. It felt good to be critiqued by her old professor. "Yes. Hemorrhaging is only apparent from the skull pan, and no rashes. Liver inflamed, but no other organs involved."

"So you conclude?"

She sipped her wine. Was he testing her, prompting her, helping her? "Probable—some type of immune firestorm."

"Based on what, Ada?" She could almost hear the unspoken: Tch, Tch, I taught you better than this. Shame on you, kiddo. "Bullsizzle. Unless you have more than this, it's too early for such an extreme hypothesis."

"I don't have much more."

"On the basis of this, you issued your Parameter Incident Watch, costing taxpayers millions? And named the dizzy thing?"

Dizzy? Ada had forgotten how Doctor Gies never swore. Dizzy probably meant damn. "Yes. My computer modeling indicates the vector has jumped to multiple cities in less than nine days."

"And this name you gave it?"

"I'm profiling it based on symptomology."

"But MADS? Just because of your tenuous link to dementia, sociopathy and violent psychotic breaks?"

"I'll admit my twisted humor at work. It stands for Mitochondrialencephalopathic Acute Degenerative Syndrome."

"Very creative."

"We have to call it something."

"I'm disappointed, kiddo. Where's the science?"

"I'm playing the investigator, not the scientist. Lives are at risk."

"You think. Or you just have a series of psychotic Americans. Not so uncommon in these paranoiac times. We fear terrorists, bird flu and higher taxes. It's no wonder family men and preachers go mad."

"Hundreds in a few weeks?" She controlled a sudden stab of anger. Gies was no different from Devon. "Various autopsies have revealed encephalopathy. It's the cause that eludes us."

"You came all the way here to Firenze, to a private Braxis conference, to pick my tired brain? Oh, bad choice of words given your prognosis." But he didn't smile at his own humor and his shoulders drew up with tension; his eyes darted back and forth between Ada and the view of the road.

She slid to the edge of her seat and leaned closer. "I couldn't get you to return my calls, remember?"

"Until yesterday, I was in protocol. I don't even collect messages."

"What are you working on?"

He laughed and finally a glimpse of the wily old professor emerged. "I'm in the private sector, now. Sworn to secrecy. I signed a dozen documents threatening life and limb if I breathe a word. To even consult with you requires signoff from our CEO personally. I'm afraid you came a long way for nothing, kiddo."

She reached out her hand. He shivered when she touched him. "I don't believe you have nothing for me. You're plugged into everything. Everywhere. Everyone." His hand felt cold and sandpaper rough. He pulled away his hand and sipped his wine.

"Your curiosity and imagination always got you in trouble." He rubbed the loose skin hanging off his emaciated face.

This time she couldn't hold in her anger. "At least I don't work for the private sector. For Domergue." She couldn't help the dig. Her mentor's move to Braxis still baffled her. In Harvard he had instilled a very real disdain for pharmaceutical and genetics companies. He used to say, "It's where the money is, folks, but not the brains," over and over. Ada could only assume money won out over Gies's brains.

"Domergue's okay, as greedy corporate CEOs go. He may be Satan incarnate, but Braxis is breaking through on a number of fronts. He gives me an unlimited budget. I can do a lot to save ..." He trailed off, as if he had said too much.

"To save … what?" She fixed Gies in her gaze. "Certainly not animals, that's clear from the kooks over there."

"Nutcases. They follow Braxis events, picket our gates, raid our labs," Gies said. "Whackos. Do you know that fizzing group broke into my lab? Freed a hundred subjects, dogs and monkeys mostly."

She did know, which was why she was here in Italy. In tracking the vector, the incidents seemed to spread out fanlike across America, starting a few weeks ago in LA, where Gies worked. She smiled. "How did they get in?" Ada couldn't picture it. A half dozen masked protesters breaking into a highly secure facility? Braxis guarded its secretive facilities with armed guards, electric fences and biometrics. It was one of the reasons she distrusted Braxis: the secrecy, the rumors of shortcuts, the billion-dollar profits, buzz about unsanctioned testing on human subjects in Colombia and the company's willingness to go to court rather than to allow the Centers for Disease Control to inspect their labs.

"Very complicated. They got themselves hired by Braxis as highly qualified grad students. Worked for months first. Then—" Gies sounded disgusted.

"They believe in their cause."

"Dangerous fanatics. Every one of those animals was infected."

"With what?"

He made a zipper motion in front of his lips.

"Of course you called the CDC for containment?"

"Of course not." Gies frowned. "Our security team—you saw that big guy back there? He's an ex-navy seal." His hand shook. "His extermination team killed every single animal. All accounted for."

"Braxis." Ada said it like a swearword. "I've issued dozens of non-compliance orders myself when I worked in level-four oversight. Sloppy science and secretive facilities. And Colombia." Ada remembered the shockwaves in the viral community when the stories circulated about the Colombian Free Vaccine Program from Braxis. It turned out to be a thinly disguised unsanctioned human trial that led to hundreds of body bags, although without the Colombian government's cooperation, the CDC could do nothing. The World Health Organization sent people who found no evidence and were ushered quickly out of the country.

"Colombia was bizzle!" Gies sagged back in his chair. "And there's no sloppy science in my labs."

Bizzle? Ada had to remember her seventies slang, an affectation of her old professor. Bizzle meant Bull. He took swearwords and replaced everything after the first letter with "izzle"—just like some seventies geek. Angry, she said, "No, you're just careless with animals."

"I'm not the only one careless with animals."

Ada's body went rigid. She couldn't believe he'd said that. Twelve years ago it had been Ada who had been careless with a mouse in her lab, infecting herself and her unborn child with LCVM. She saw the apology on his face, but it was too late. Her baby was born legless; her marriage had broken up.

"You've got to help." She tried to keep the harshness out of her voice.

"I can't."

"Then point me to someone who can."

"Always Doctor Idealist."

She squeezed his hand. "Give me something, Ernest. Anything. This thing scares me."

He straightened his shoulders, gave her a smile. "You have to put aside the emotions, Ada. I tried to teach you that. They get in the way of our work."

She nodded. "I never could detach that far."

"I know." He leaned forward. "Go see Begley. Doctor Ali Begley."

"Who's that?"

"He works with me at Site F, near LA. Tell him I sent you." Gies pulled away his arthritic hand. "He's more like you, Ada. The idealist."

Her satellite phone vibrated and played the Star-Spangled Banner. Embarrassed, she glanced at the call identity, a government-issue satellite phone number, but not in her directory. She pressed the phone to her ear. "Kenner."

"Doctor Adalia Kenner," said a low, husky female voice, slightly accented. Asian? She didn't recognize her. "I'm responding to your Parameter Watching thingy."

"Go ahead." She kept her voice formal, despite a tingle of anxiety.

"I am Nam Ling, okay? I work with Alban Bane."

Ada frowned. *Bane*. She knew that name. He was a notorious publicity hound, but by all accounts a man who had saved the world a time or two—according to American newspapers—but only by trampling on the rights of everyone.

"One moment." She covered the mouthpiece. "Excuse me a moment, Ernest?" She left her beloved old professor to nurse his wine and moved quickly to the powder room. She sat on a plush stool in front of a mirror, staring at her own tired features. Why did the woman staring back at her look so scared? Of course she knew why.

"Nam, I don't know you. Can you identify yourself, please?"

"I'm sorry. I'm a special agent of WART."

"Wart?" For all her fatigue and worry, Ada laughed.

Nam didn't sound amused. "World Advance Response Taskforce. WART." Her voice carried a weight of sadness. "I called, doctor, because a man, this mister Gary Merrick—father of three, six-figure income, volunteer at his Church—he builds a bomb out of chemicals available at the local mall and blows up a building in Manchester."

"How many hurt?"

"No one hurt, doctor. One hundred and thirty-three dead."

How could she sound so calm in the face of such horror? Ada closed her eyes. "That's horrible. But why are you calling me?" She already knew it must have something to do with her Parameter Incident Watch, but what?

"Our Mister Merrick, he was a doctor too, and he was, they say, a happy man, and the only thing that changed was he caught a flu-bug. Then he becomes Mister Suicide Bomber. Stable family man. No history of anythings suspicious. His wife says he not suicidal, not at all."

"I see." Ada found it difficult to respond. "You're trying to—to tell me—" She stopped. When she issued her Parameter Incident Watch, it was inevitable there would be phone calls like this, simply because her notice was very broad, but the horror took hold of her.

"The man, this doctor, smiling right up to the end."

She clenched the phone. Smiling up to the end. It didn't mean anything. She didn't know anything. Her job was to track trends, to identify emerging viruses, not smiling suicide bombers. Only one out of every nine hundred emerging trend watches ever had substance. Most of the time, they turned out to be coincidence and her boss—her ex-husband boss—was the first to point this out to her.

Ada said, "As a precaution, Agent Nam Ling, I recommend the investigators borrow hazmat suits. The British equivalent of the local health unit should have them."

"Is too late, now. I called you after. Director Bane was there as an observer only, but he's coming back now." She sounded tired. "He asked me to call you, see? To ask how serious your watch is, yes?"

"It's a precautionary. Remember SARS? A seventy-two year old man from Beijing spread it to passengers on a flight to Hong Kong. The virus killed hundreds."

"I know about SARS." Nam sounded eerily calm. "Director Bane, he asked me to call you. To meet him."

Ada opened her eyes, surprised to find her eyes watery, verging on teary. She couldn't stop thinking about the numbers of dead in Manchester. In her business, she dealt with numbers. But—one hundred and thirty-three?

"I'm in Italy."

"Florence. I checked, yes. I'm sending a plane to get you, okay?"

"I'll have to ask my boss."

"This is done, Doctor. Please hurry."

"Director Bane wants me in Manchester?"

"No. In LA. He's flying there now." For the first time, Ada caught a sense of distress in Nam's voice.

"Why LA?"

"To meet Doctor Alistair Begley."

Ada held her breath for a moment and stared at the frightened woman in the mirror. Braxis—again. Alistair Begley—the very same man her old teacher had asked her to go see.

One hundred and thirty-three dead. Coincidence? Maybe, but alongside the other responses to her Parameter Watch Notice—the Seattle Shooter (another family man), the last three school shootings (good kids), a mass-murder in St. Louis (a well-loved preacher with a gun), and a hundred other coincidences—it meant the world had gone mad, or her theory had substance. She hoped it was a mad world. Because her watch notice pointed to devastation.

Near Site F, California

Shemar stood on his brake pedal. "What the hell?"

His lovingly restored '66 GTO muscle car dove in response to the brakes, and the harsh smell of burned linings was pungent. Had he hit the madman? The man had jumped in front of Shemar's car, waved his arms and his briefcase, then covered his face as the GTO slid. Shemar glared at the man. Not only had he taken a layer of rubber and brake linings off Shemar's precious car, he had scared him half to death. But the man waved now, his face harshly pale in the headlights. The old man limped around the front of the car—had Shemar hit him?—and was at the door before Shemar could think to squeal off.

The Angeles Crest Highway, scenic and bustling during the day, was nearly deserted in the middle of the night, although Shemar did notice a pair of nearly identical Jeeps pulling up behind the man's Porsche. It was just past midnight and the distant glow of Los Angeles was eerie rather than comforting, washing out the tapestry of stars over silhouetted pine.

Shemar thought about leaving the hiker. Let the people in the Jeeps give him a ride. He didn't need some whack-job in his car. But the man drove a Porsche and dressed well, the passenger door was already opening. Besides, Shemar felt like being the good Samaritan today; he had made his first script sale, to none other than Abbey Chase, a hack producer of reality television and true-crime flicks. She'd probably destroy his story, but he was too high on the day to care. She had even invited him to a party at her exclusive mountain resort, partying with the Who's-Who of Hollywood. He hadn't expected a hitchhiker on the way back from the party—maybe the guy was on his way back from the party himself—but it didn't feel right to blow past the dude on the best day of Shemar's twenty-six-year life.

"My luck, he's some psycho killer," he said out loud, but he kept his foot on the brake.

The hitchhiker was in his fifties or sixties.

"Thanks for stopping." The man coughed as he slid in. He covered his mouth quickly, though Shemar felt a light spray of spittle.

"No spare?" Shemar asked, wiping his mouth.

"No light. Can't see a damn thing. I was going to walk to one of those emergency phones. Then I saw you coming."

Shemar slammed the accelerator and roared back on to the highway, his heart still racing. "And you thought the best way to hitch was to jump in front of a speeding car."

The hitchhiker sneezed and snatched a handkerchief from his breast pocket. "I'm mighty sorry."

Shemar took a good look at the man, clinging to an aluminum case. He was impeccably dressed and his pasty pale face was accentuated by white hair. The man sneezed one more time. "A big excuse me."

Fall cold. That's all he needed. But his mother had always said, "Take the bad with the good, Mar," explaining her own version of karma. So by her philosophy, the good was his first Hollywood script sale, all eleven hundred and fifty-dollars of it; and now the bad—he might get a cold; a small price to pay to the Hollywood muse.

"I'm Shemar."

The man coughed. "Doctor Begley. Alistair Begley." He sneezed again, a deep belching blow that sent shivers through Shemar. Bad cold. Damn his urge to be a good Samaritan.

The man flew into a fit of coughs.

"You holding up, Doc?" he asked.

"Holding up? Oh, yes, I'm fine, thanks."

"You coming from the blow-up?" Shemar said.

"Blow-up?"

"Party." Obviously the good doctor was not one of the hundreds at Abbey Chase's mountain retreat. Many were still back there, dancing to live bands, making deals with producers and directors.

The doctor bled from the nose and there was so much blood it ran down his chin and neck. "Doc, looks like you need a—doctor." He laughed, trying to keep it light.

"My sinuses are prone to bleed."

Shemar speeded up. He couldn't dump this man on the side of the road, but he wanted him out of his car. The trees flew by in a smudge of monotone. Bends swept up too fast and the fat tires squealed.

The doctor coughed again.

In spite of reckless speed, Shemar glanced across at the doctor. "Bottle of water in the glove box, Doc. You a medical doctor?"

"Viral geneticist." The doctor coughed.

The mention of viruses inspired Shemar to lower his window, hoping it would blow the cold germs to the back. "What brings you up the mountains? House call?"

The doctor tried to laugh, but it only brought on more hacking. So they settled into an uncomfortable silence, listening to the rumble of the old 389 big block engine as they swept down the mountain highway. The engine was music to Shemar's ears. Not a "sensible car," Shemar's mama would say, with oil prices heading for the stars, but the GTO was his baby.

The hacking cough and nose bleeds continued and Shemar worried about blood on his restored seats. He had spent all of last summer working at Wal-Mart, saving enough to reupholster the interior of his baby.

"Cover your mouth, Doc?"

"Sorry—" The doctor heaved.

Oh hell, there go my seats, Shemar thought.

The sickly sweet stench of vomit filled the car.

"Crap." Shemar lifted his foot off the accelerator. Beside him, the doctor hunched over, retching. "We gotta get you to a hospital."

"I am so sorry—" the doctor coughed again. "I have made such a mess." And then he convulsed. Shemar realized he had drifted into the oncoming lane, corrected, but then looked sideways at the doctor as he felt the seat vibrate.

"Doctor, you all right?"

There was no answer, just more retching sounds, and Shemar stopped the car.

"Doc?"

Something wet splattered Shemar's cheek. At first he assumed it was more spittle, or even vomit. He wiped it away with the back of his hand, then turned on the dome light. Blood.

The doctor groaned.

"Goddam!" Shemar shouted. He felt suddenly wet.

He unbuckled and flung open his door. His shirt was sprayed with blood. The seat was shiny and wet—his newly upholstered seats! The doctor thrashed and bucked, half on the seat, half in the foot well. There was so much blood. Had he slit his wrists?

But there were no wounds on the doctor. The blood hemorrhaged from his nose and mouth. Streamers of blood even seeped out of his ears.

Shemar backed out of the car.

Long ribbons of blood flowed in place of tears down Begley's cheek. He clawed at the seat, scrambling to get out.

The doctor convulsed one more time and spilled onto the road.

5

Over the Atlantic

Alban Bane hung from the safety belt of his first-class seat, wet with sweat, his facemask clinging uncomfortably, his breathing labored. Filter masks weren't made for acrobatic exertions such as hanging upside down, supporting the weight of a mother and child. He desperately wanted it off his face.

There could be no doubt they would die if someone in the cockpit didn't act soon. He focused on his immediate goal, to save the mother and child. He had to believe the plane would right itself. If not, there was nothing he could do. The feeling of helplessness was new to him, and it made him queasy.

As he dangled, he found himself thinking again of Mags and Jen, his grown-up daughters. They lost their mother to rape and murder when they were toddlers, but none of them—Bane included—ever got over it. Bane's job brought him in touch with his own mortality on an almost daily basis, something his daughters never let him forget. Four years ago, when one of Bane's suspects kidnapped Mags and held her hostage in a terrifying game of death, she had changed. She hated her father then. Still hated her father now that she was focused on getting into lawschool. They had fought over that, too. "A lawyer, Mags? You want to be the first lawyer with a nose ring?" He hated lawyers almost more than he despised criminals—to him they were much the same thing. And now he might die with her hating him. How would she react when the news splashed grisly pictures of the airplane, scattered across many acres of crash site? Would she regret her fury, cry for him? Or spit on his grave?

Bane faced death every time he went into the field. Those close to him called him suicidal. But the truth was, it made Bane feel alive to face his fears and conquer them, to offer his angry resentment of life—a life that had taken away so much of what he loved—at the altar of law enforcement. And it might not seem like it, but Bane was always in control. His life was in his own hands, even if the probability of scraping through was infinitesimal.

Here, he had no control. There was nothing at all he could do to "scrape through." He'd been shot, nearly bled to death, lost a finger to a madman, broken many ribs, plunged into an icy cold well in a haunted mansion, faced a psychopath's knife—but always he scraped through, barely alive, sometimes wishing he wasn't. Here on flight 411, he would live or die by another's actions, and nothing he could do might prevent that. And it pissed him off. His daughters would hear about his death in the news. The last headlines would be his sarcastic jabs at journalists—"Director Bane crash lands after 'tea with Queen' "—or his daughters would hear about it from their aunt or the Dean of the University, and Jen would cry and Mags would just swear and stomp off, and then they'd be truly alone. Alone, as they were right now. Because Jen had made it clear the last time he called that he was never around. "No, Mags won't talk to you, Pops. She's worse than ever. She told me to tell you to eff off."

Bane never felt regret, not for anything; he never gave himself the time to feel that way. He reacted to the murder of his wife by spending twelve years hunting her killer. He pursued the kidnapper of his daughter until he found her, even though it cost him his job and nearly his life. He never had the time for self-pity. Now his life didn't exactly flash by as he hung upside down on a plane about to crash, but his last fight with his daughters did. How could he leave them now, when they had no one else? They had heard about his near-death so many times on the news that maybe it would be a relief to finalize it.

The helplessness brought out a fury he had never felt before. For once he couldn't do anything.

He clung with both hands to the ankle of the dangling woman and her child. Very bad. Adrenalin and panic gave him the extra strength, allowing him to hold on even as the plane lurched again. His forearms burned from the strain. The screams had become whimpers, lost to the shriek of jet engines. The mask on his face heated up, drenched with sweat now, and it was hard to swallow. If he had a free hand, he would have ripped it off his face, and to hell with bugs.

It seemed hours later when the plane lurched violently upwards then slowly—too slowly—climbed back to horizontal. Bane hung on to the woman, fearful of another dive. The wail of alarms from the cockpit drowned out the whimpers of the passengers.

Finally Bane released the woman's ankle, badly bruised from his grip. She looked back at him from the aisle floor, face streaked with tears, clutching her daughter.

He unbuckled his belt, wobbly as he stood up, braced in case the plane went into another dive. "Sit here, Ma'am," Bane said. He helped her stand. She was in shock, pale, trembling and near-hysterical, but she clung to her daughter. He gently pushed her into the seat and buckled her in. He tussled the child's hair. "Hold on to Mommy."

He bent quickly over the man who had been struck by the briefcase, judged the wound superficial, then ran for the cockpit door. He pounded on the door.

"Won't do much good," said Marshal Claire Racine, stepping close behind him. She tapped his shoulder. "I have the key." She seemed oddly serene. Her jacket was off, but she was sweat-free and breathing normally, which was more than Bane could say of himself at that moment. Her flecked brown eyes darted to one side, silently instructing him to step aside.

Bane complied. "The pilot was acting peculiar."

"I'd say so," said Claire, fitting the key.

He handed her a sterile mask. "Wear this."

"Why? Because it looks pretty ridiculous on you."

"I always wanted to be a doctor."

"Funny."

"He's contagious."

She fit the mask. "I saw what you did."

"Oh?"

"The girl and the mom. Thank you."

"Won't the Air Marshal's union object?"

The door opened before she could withdraw the key. The pilot burst out of the dimmed cockpit, knocking aside both Claire and Bane. Bane registered the rage in the captain's face, the slick of perspiration and the sickly smell of stale vomit as he flew past. And the eyes. Bloodshot didn't begin to describe the red inflammation in the man's pupils. Bane could have sworn he saw red tears, too. Was the man bleeding out of his eye sockets?

Bane quickly surveyed the cockpit. The co-pilot had the plane, though he was covered in blood and sweat.

"Jim tried to down the plane!" the co-pilot shouted. "Took both of us to restrain him!" The navigator sat in the pilot's chair, his hair matted with blood.

Bane strode quickly after the pilot, although some of the more foolish passengers had unbuckled and stood in the aisles to brush off air sickness, too dazed to comprehend they were still in danger. The pilot, already well down the aisle in economy, knocked two women and a businessman back into their seats then veered into the second galley. By the time Bane worked his way through the cabin, the galley was empty.

Claire, right behind him, pointed at a narrow door with a Plexiglas window. "Elevator."

Bane admired her composure, already rethinking her suitability for WART. Like most women law-enforcers, she had that sense of utter fearlessness. He pushed the button, and slowly the elevator re-appeared.

They both squeezed in to the tiny lift. At any other time Bane might have been aroused by the close body contact.

"I know Jim," Claire said, shifting away from him, her voice muffled by the mask "He's a good man. Family. Never an odd moment."

"The whackos are always family men. It's almost a golden rule. And everyone has odd moments, Claire."

He kneed open the door as the lift stopped in the hold. Both Bane and Claire had their guns in hand as they emerged back to back, facing outwards.

Bane instantly holstered his gun. "That's something you don't see every day," and he pointed.

Claire gasped, then immediately re-asserted control. Definite WART material. She stared, calm now, at the bloody pilot.

"Death by golf club?"

Sounding eerily calm, Claire said, "I'm not even sure how that's possible. Can someone actually do that?"

"If they were insane." He couldn't help it. "Or nuts about golf."

"Not funny."

"My way of dealing, Claire."

Thankfully, the pilot was turned away from them, slightly, sparing them the worst of the nightmarish vision. The pilot had apparently taken two golf clubs from a golf bag in the luggage area, pressed one against each eye, then...

"He impaled himself," Claire said, her voice so cool she might have just said, "Good morning."

They stared at the dead pilot, and for once Bane had nothing to say. For some reason he thought of the ceramic doll and the child's hand in Manchester. How fragile life seemed in that moment.

On Turtle One

Ada Kenner imagined Nam Ling as a scowling, tough construction worker look-alike; instead, Nam was a wisp of a girl with a smiling Asian face, perfect smiling teeth and a completely shaven head. At first, Ada thought she was a teenaged boy, then slowly realized she was a woman. She wore tight jeans and a plain black jacket that revealed nothing noticeable in the way of breasts, and she carried no purse. Her only ornament seemed to be a long string of amber beads coiled several times around her muscular wrist. She was a miniscule knot of muscle. Every fiber of her ninety-five or so pounds was hard and taut, veins pressing hard against her dark skin. Her fragrance was noticeably woodsy and appealing, like sandalwood, yet Ada felt certain she wore no cologne, just as she eschewed makeup. Dangling from her belt was a barbed chain, coiled like a whip, but with handles on each end, like nunchucks. It seemed to be the only weapon she carried.

"*Namaste*, Dr. Kenner," Nam said, and she folded her two hands in front of her chest and inclined her head. "I'm Nam Ling." She reminded Ada of a Buddhist nun, all smiles and no hair, and somehow instantly trustworthy.

Ada was at a bit of a loss. Did she return the bow? Instead she held out her hand, and Nam surprised her with a too-firm, dry handshake.

"*Namaste?*"

Nam's eyes crinkled as her smile widened even further. "It is a greeting of deep, deep respect."

"Oh." Ada couldn't tell if she was being mocked but guessed not. Nam seemed genuinely warm. "I didn't know you were coming with the flight, Agent Ling."

"I am to be your protector, Doctor." Again the white-white smile and cocked head. "Bane says you very important, yes?"

"Do I need protection, Agent?"

"I believe so, yes. Not taking chances, hmm?" Still smiling. "This way, please, Doctor."

She led the way out on to the sticky hot tarmac and Ada was surprised to see armed soldiers in unfamiliar black uniforms. The soldiers hustled them across the tarmac to a low-slung black airplane.

"This is Bane's new plane. Turtle One."

"Turtle?"

"Because we carry everything with us, you see?"

"Aha." Ada smiled. There was something endearing about Nam.

The soldiers boarded with them and closed the hatch, slinging machine guns on straps, an ominous gesture that impregnated the air-conditioned cabin with tension. Confused, Ada followed Nam into the main cabin. Everything smelled new, although the private jet was not particularly luxurious, just comfortable and office-like.

"Settle wherever you like."

Ada moved to a cluster of giant black leather captain's chairs that circled a small conference table. The chair enveloped her and when Nam sat opposite her the agent seemed childlike in the immense seat. She tucked her small legs up in a lotus posture. The engines were already whining and in a moment they began to taxi.

"No safety tips from the flight attendants?"

Nam just smiled.

Ada chewed her lip. No point in probing Nam for information during takeoff. She settled back to study the small cabin. Judging from the long body of the craft, this "meeting room" was less than a quarter of the cabin space. She wondered what lay behind the bulkheads, and she heard a substantial murmur of voices. Many people back there, she felt sure. The forward cabin was elegant and functional but not plush. The seats were certainly comfortable, but this was no executive jet. It had a distinctly official personality, almost military.

As if understanding her curiosity, Nam pressed a button on the arm of her chair. A flat-screen monitor slid out and up. The arm opened to reveal a phone handset and keyboard. "State of the art everything, Doctor."

"How interesting." Ada couldn't resist a yawn. "I'm sorry. I've hardly slept in weeks."

"From here, with the right password, I can access any law enforcement database—even the CDC system, see?"

"Fascinating." If that was an invitation to network into the Centers for Disease Control mainframe—an implied, "get to work"—Ada was too exhausted to oblige. The jet thrust pressed Ada hard into the seatback.

"Short take-off capabilities," Nam explained, still smiling her quirky, infectious best.

"Yes, I see."

Far faster than a commercial jet too, it seemed, for only a moment passed before Nam unbuckled her lap belt. As lithe as a cat, she ran—she didn't seem to walk, and her slowest stride was something of a jog—to the bulkhead door.

Ada caught a fleeting glimpse of a dimmed room lit with glowing red LEDs and banks of monitors. Dozens of people worked at keyboards, all seated in rotating chairs with seatbelts.

Ada picked up the handset in the arm of her chair. She dialed Devon at his home, pleased that she had a good reason to call him in the middle of the night, and even more delighted when Devon's new live-in bimbo answered. "Give me Devon," Ada said without a greeting.

She heard Devon in the background, "What? Who? Oh, hell." Then he was on the phone, exaggerating a yawn. "A.K. Do you now what time it is?"

Ada hated when Devon called her A.K. That was what they called her in the office but it didn't feel right coming from him. "I assumed you and your latest fling would be up all night."

He said nothing, probably shocked. She came across as a bitter, jilted ex-wife, something new to him. She must be more tired than she thought. "I'm sorry, Dev. But you had me virtually kidnapped in Europe."

"A.K. I don't think I approved your trip in the first place. This was just a good excuse to get you back to your lab." He sounded pissed. That was always good. She got her way when he was pissed.

"Dev, I seem to be on my way to LA, not Atlanta. You know something about this, I assume?"

Devon laughed, but it sounded nervous. "I had no choice, A.K."

"Don't call me that. Doctor Kenner is fine. Ada if you must."

"Fine, Doctor Kenner." He sounded suddenly furious, his voice clipped and curt. "I've promised Director Bane your full cooperation."

"That's nice of you, Devon."

"A.K.—Doctor—there's more at stake here than our normal jibs and jabs."

"I know that. I've been trying to tell you that for weeks." And it took a total stranger, this Director Bane, to convince you. Bastard.

"Then why so cranky?"

"How did this Bane convince you? You're the director."

"Funny. You never call me Director." When Ada remained stubbornly quiet, he admitted, "He mentioned terrorism."

"Oh, come on. You're not that simple-minded. The Feds think everything's related to terrorism. Don't be stupid."

"IQ of 162, remember? Not quite in your league, but up there. You married me for my brains."

No, idiot, I married you because I loved you, because you were romantic and wonderful and caring—for exactly one year, six months and twenty-one days. Until she gave birth to her deformed child. Angry, she said, "Listen King Henry, there's more to this than imagined terrorist plots. Which we both know is nonsense."

"Do we?" He ignored her jab. King Henry. It was his nickname in the office, ever since her best friend Caff blabbed the whole story of how Dev sought a divorce right after she gave birth to her child. And the nickname had stuck, more because he was imperious and selfish than because of the nod to Henry the Eighth's penchant for dumping wives when they didn't give him suitable heirs. Behind his back, and sometimes to his face, nearly everyone called him King Henry.

"Dev, you know it's nonsense," she said, finally.

"Well, the president called."

"The president of what?"

"You know."

"No, I don't know."

"Of the United States. Of America."

"Speaking of low IQs," she quipped. She scanned the private jet compartment once more, remembered the flash and buzz of equipment as Nam had disappeared into the high-tech compartment of the plane. The machine guns and the men in black. It all seemed much more dire all of a sudden.

"Just cooperate, Ada." He sounded tired, almost pleading. "It's important."

It's important when Bane calls you, but not your ex-wife? She had been telling him for weeks how dangerous MADS could be if it turned out to be more than just a false trend. "Fine. I'll cooperate, your majesty. As long as some bozo cop doesn't try to tell me how to do my job."

"Ada—"

"I mean it, Dev. I'm a cowgirl, remember that."

"I know. Six shooters a-blazing. As long as you and Bane don't kill each other, you should make a hell of a team."

"I'll save the killing for you."

"Thank you." He must have covered the mouthpiece; she heard muffled voices. A moment later, "Ada, got to go. Homeland Security is at the door."

"Dev—"

"Just cooperate for once. Put that amazing gray matter to work for Bane. I'll see you when you get back to Atlanta—just a moment! I'll be right there." More muffled voices. "Got to go. You're not the only one being kidnapped." Then he was gone.

Homeland Security dragging the director of the CDC out of bed? Things were worse than even Ada could have imagined.

Ada used the screen and keyboard built into the chair to log in to the CDC database and spent an hour catching up on the responses to her Parameter Incident Watch. Another 413 reports. It was bad, very bad. She drank another coffee and continued her study of the reports, but her eyes burned with fatigue. For weeks she had been getting by on two hours of sleep a night as she tracked her emerging trend.

Trend? What trend? Pakistan, Australia, Hungary ... it was everywhere at once.

She needed sleep. Just a quick nap. She closed her eyes, and instantly fell into a deep sleep.

She dreamed, as she too often did these days. The dreams hadn't been this bad since the trauma of her baby Quentin's birth twelve years ago. In her dream, she saw Professor Gies, sitting in a pew in a church. Ada was seated somewhere behind him. Gies was praying, something she had never seen him do. She smelled incense, a musky, woodsy perfume, but it choked her and made her cough.

She found herself staring up at the front of the church. On a giant cross hung Jesus. Crying. With growing horror, she stared at the flowing tears. Except they weren't tears but blood.

She couldn't move in her dream. Then she realized it was a lucid dream. She concentrated on standing up. Her leg twitched in response, but she still couldn't stand.

Now every pew in the church was filled with people, all crying. Except, like Jesus, they cried bloody tears.

"God, no," she heard herself say.

Gies stood and turned, and she noticed two things right away. Her old professor wore a preacher's collar, and in his hand he carried a machine gun on a strap, just like Bane's soldiers. "I'm going to make a fizzing mess, Ada, believe you me," he said.

"Wake up, Ada!" she shouted to herself. In lucid dreams you were supposed to be able to do that, to wake up or move.

The gun lifted, and he grinned, but also cried tears of blood. She heard the clank of metal.

"Wake up, Ada!" she screamed it this time.

She willed herself to move or even fall to the floor. Gies stepped closer to her and fired, not at her, but at all the people in the pews.

"Just cleaning up," Gies said quietly yet somehow audible over the explosion of the gun. "Just cleaning up the fizzing mess."

People screamed and fell forward over the pew backs. Ada tried to scream too. She tried again to move. This time her whole body quivered. Her shoulder shook.

"Wake up!"

This time it was not her voice.

She woke from the dream instantly. Nam said, "Wake up, please," and she gently shook Ada's shoulder. She looked concerned. "You were shouting out, Doctor."

"Bad dream."

"We're landing now, Doctor."

"You can call me Ada if you like."

Nam sat opposite Ada. "I cannot, Doctor. Out of respect."

"Okay." Ada wiped sweat from her forehead. "Quite the dream."

"Coffee?"

"Aren't we landing?"

"Soon. About half an hour. I thought you might like a coffee is all. And you looked unhappy in your sleeping."

A male flight attendant in a black uniform brought her coffee.

"Thank you." Ada disliked cream in her coffee, but she nodded agreeably. Caffeine in any form was fine. She sipped cautiously. Cloying sweetness hung on her tongue, but she forced a smile. "Strong. Thank you." She drank more, recoiling from the sweetened condensed milk taste, but needing the underlying strong brew. "Will Director Bane be meeting us?"

Nam's smile faded for the first time. "There's a new incident, Doctor. But yes, he is at the airport already."

"An incident?" Ada was awake now. "From my Parameter Watch?"

"Maybe yes. Maybe." Ada hadn't known Nam for long, but her equanimity vanished with her smile and she looked desperately worried. "On Bane's plane. But they landed already. So is all okay."

"What happened exactly, Nam?"

"Exactly, I can't know that. But the pilot on Bane's plane, he acted strange, and sick too, then tried to crash the plane, but they stopped him. I don't know much yet. CDC and FBI planning to quarantine the plane and investigate, although I doubt they'll keep the Director in quarantine."

"What do you mean?" Ada stared at Nam, incredulous at the idea. "You mean he'd break quarantine?"

Nam nodded. "He does whatever he pleases."

"I see." No one broke quarantine on her watch. She picked up the phone in the armrest and dialed Doctor Cafferty Toy, her direct assistant at the CDC. He answered instantly. Caff Toy was eight years her junior at thirty-one, although he looked like a punk kid in his baggy jeans that hung low on his butt cheeks. He was a friend—as close to a buddy as she could manage with her twenty-hour workdays.

"Hugs and kisses, sweetie," Caff said. His voice was oddly masculine, deep and rich and sonorous, but he was deliberately flamboyant, an odd contrast that disconcerted everyone.

"Kisses back, love." She kept her voice serious so he'd know how important it was. "Are you still in LA?"

"Never fear, Caff's in LA-LA land, darlin'." She could almost see his impish grin. He was better looking than she was, and had more boyfriends, too. "I attended the autopsy—"

"It's not about that," she interrupted him. "Caff, bigger troubles. There's a plane landing at LAX." She covered the phone and mouthed, "What flight?" to Nam. Nam smiled and flashed fingers for four-one-one. "Flight 411, Caff. CDC and FBI already on scene, but there's a problem."

"Tell me, honey."

"Alban Bane is on that flight."

"Oh, he's a hunk. Did you see the movie—"

"Not now, Caff!"

Caff laughed. "Take a pill, girlfriend. This isn't like you."

"There's a possible emerging on 411. This hunk's going to break quarantine, Caff. I need you there to stop him."

"Those big FBI men can't handle the feisty Scot?" Caff sounded excited by the idea of meeting Bane.

"They'll be too star-struck by his badge to stop him. You find a way, Caff."

"I'll jump his bones, darlin'."

"He's not your type."

"They're all my type, girlfriend."

"He doesn't swing your way."

"We'll see about that."

"He might be contagious, boy Toy."

"I'll wear rubber."

In spite of herself, she laughed. She wished she could be there. Caff, young, hunky, pierced everything, bristly almost-shaven head, tattoo on his forearm—I'm a hunk, get over it—confronting baseball-capped Alban Bane. It would be too funny.

After Ada hung up, Nam shook her head. "No one stops Bane."

"We'll see."

"I wish I could be there to see your friend try."

Ada smiled. "Me too." She drank more coffee, but already her heart raced ahead of the caffeine rush. "What about—"

The seatbelt light chimed.

Nam shrugged. "We'll find out in minutes, Doctor. Both of us." She pursed her lips. "There's more you need to know. There's been an accident with Doctor Mister Begley." She punched a few buttons on the arm of her seat, her lips pressed together in an effort to hide her emotions. "Your screen, Doctor."

The screensaver dissolved to an aerial view of a highway, alive with flashing lights and emergency vehicles. An old muscle car sat sideways on the mountain highway, surrounded by a ring of emergency vehicles and busy with men in yellow hazmat suits. The camera rotated slowly around the scene, obviously in a helicopter.

"Doctor Begley, he's bloody dead," Nam said.

Ada found it difficult to swallow, as if an oversized vitamin pill had stuck in her throat. She tried to remain still under Nam's calm eyes, focusing on the scene on her monitor. She saw county health vehicles, and thankfully most of the emergency teams wore full protective gear, although the police on scene wore only masks. A long line of cars stretched up the highway, unable to move past the emergency vehicles.

He's bloody dead, Nam had said. It seemed like a premonition. Bloody dead was contagious.

7

Angeles Crest Highway

Shemar stared into the front seat of his blood-soaked GTO. He shivered. It looked no less creepy in the bright golden light of the rising sun. Could he ever drive his beloved muscle car without thinking of that pale lump of flesh—once the living, breathing, sneezing Doctor Begley, the hitchhiker? Would the smell ever go away?

The Kern County Forensic Sciences Division continued to photograph and measure the bloody carcass on the road. Even the Kern County deputies, all three of them, seemed distracted, focused on directing traffic on the highway.

Shemar drank coffee, brought to him by a nice lady deputy with the face mask—he forgot her name. His hands shook.

She smiled at him. "You'll need a ride. You live in LA?"

He nodded, still staring at Doctor Lump on the road beside his car.

"Your car will be impounded, sir. Do you understand?"

Shemar didn't care. At this moment, he never wanted to see it again. "Thank you. You've been—kind."

He heard the distant wail of klaxons. They didn't sound like Kern County

Sheriff cruiser sirens. Ambulance? Five bright yellow vans, more the size of fire department emergency vehicles, came around the corner, driving on the curb around honking cars.

"What are those?" Shemar stared at the vans. Then one streaked past them, the brightly painted sides displaying foot-high letters: HAZMAT and underneath in smaller type, Governor's Office of Emergency Preparedness. The lead vehicle parked in front of Shemar's GTO, lights flashing and klaxon still blaring.

Shemar dropped his cup of coffee to the asphalt. The virus. Hazmat. "Oh, crap."

The deputy seemed no less shocked. "Bogus," she said in a quieter voice.

Four men in yellow space suits jumped out of the lead van. The other vans took up positions front and back of the GTO. Another truck arrived, this one a tow truck.

One of the "space men" approached Ms. Deputy. This man was a scary big dude, and obviously his biohazard suit was specially made for him. He stood basketball-player tall, but he was immensely wide as well, like one of those old-time television pro-wrestlers. His face was round and fat, but there was nothing funny about his expression.

"Deputy, we're here on orders of the Governor," the Hazmat man said. He pointed at a badge. It said: Jon Schocken, Hazmat Field Operative.

"Deputy MacCauly, sir."

"Ma'am, you'll have to come with us."

"Pardon?"

"We must contain the scene."

"What's that mean?"

"Orders from the CDC, ma'am." We'll be taking you and your other deputies—and the victim, here—to a sterile facility for decontamination, observation and possible quarantine."

Shemar felt suddenly very hot. His nightmare seemed far from over. "Why? What kind of disease did this guy have?"

"I'm sorry, sir. That's classified information."

Three of the Hazmat men lifted the corpse from the road. The body of poor Doctor Begley was triple bagged. The Hazmat team then unwound a long hose from one of the vans. They sprayed the body bags with a foamy stream of liquid and the tang of disinfectant made him sneeze.

Oh God, no! The hose was turned on his car now. Sudsy purple fluid streamed onto his recently upholstered seats. "That's my car!" He knew it was a stupid thing to say. He wouldn't want his car back if it was infected.

But it just spilled out of him. They foamed his entire car, then continued spraying the asphalt. The liquid was an expanding foam spray, and puffed up like purple whipping cream. The tang stung his nostrils. Suddenly he felt very hot; his lungs felt scorched, as if he'd been smoking all night at a big banger; he felt dizzy.

"Sir, you must come with us. The sooner we disinfect, the better for you. And you, ma'am."

Shemar looked at Deputy MacCauly. At least he knew her name, now. She looked as afraid as he felt.

They followed the big man to one of the vans. He held out a thick rubber bag in his gloved hand. "Your gun, ma'am."

"Why?" MacCauly looked confused.

"Guns can't be sterilized."

Shemar shook his head. "That's not right."

The big man continued to hold out the bag. "I can't let you proceed into decontamination with a firearm, ma'am. Your radio and belt, too."

Shemar watched as the deputy removed her belt, handcuffs and sidearm. It didn't feel right to him, but he couldn't think of anything more to say.

They stepped up into the Hazmat van, a well lit, white interior with benches on either side. The other deputies were already there.

The door closed. Shemar heard the click of the lock.

The van immediately lurched forward, but it was turning, not heading down the mountain towards LA.

"Where are they taking us?"

Ms. Deputy shrugged. Her face was pale white, eerily unnatural. She looked as scared as Shemar.

One of the deputies coughed.

8

Los Angeles

Bane had little difficulty bullying the assigned Bureau special agent at the hatch—"I'll make myself available for your investigation, son, don't you worry"—but he found he was no match for this Doctor Cafferty Toy of the

CDC. Doctor Toy wore ultra baggy jeans that didn't hide an athletic body, and his bleached-white California smile was a startling contrast to a Filipino complexion. He wore nose rings, a tongue stud, multiple earrings, a virtual twin brother to Bane's own daughter Mags. Just a kid.

Bane tried to shove the Doctor aside, but in spite of his pretty-boy appearance, the doctor was no push-aside kind of guy.

"I could have you charged with assault, couldn't I?" He folded his tattooed arms across his body-builder chest.

"You enjoyed it," Bane quipped.

"Harder, honey. Do it again." Toy smiled, but didn't move aside. A row of LAPD uniforms with masks stood behind him.

"I wore a mask on the plane, Doctor Toy," Bane said again.

"Sweetie, I don't care if you wore a full body condom. Until Doctor Kenner clears you, you go nowhere." Toy's voice was oddly deep and musical.

Bane smiled, instinctively liking this kid. "Leave the jokes for me, okay?"

"You can do the straight jokes."

"Better be careful, Doc. My bladder's full, my gun's loaded, I'm not afraid to use either one."

"I'm so turned on," the young man said, his eyes crinkling as he laughed.

"Sorry, friend, I like something with more curves and a little softer."

"My boss is. Halle Barre look-alike. Really. Never wears panties or a bra."

"Yeah, I see that, kid" Bane smiled as Doctor Ada Kenner pushed through the line of cops like a Canadian icebreaker, followed by diminutive Nam Ling. Ada was more spectacular than her file picture and literally towered over Bane's number one agent Nam. She was at least as refreshingly stunning as Halle Barre. "So, now we're all here," Bane said. "Do we party or get to work?"

Ada Kenner stood beside her assistant, hands on her hips. "I thought Caff might be a match even for the infamous Alban Bane."

"More than a match," Caff said. "Although he's pretty hot for an old guy."

Bane did a Rodney Dangerfield impersonation. "Kids these days. No respect."

Ada shook her head. "Speaking of respect, the quarantine will be respected."

"You know, my doctor told me once that airplanes are flying sick wards. Like swimming in sick soup."

Ada nodded. "You are right, Director Bane. So you stay put."

"Really, Doctor. This has already been a below-par day." He smiled. "Gore joke. You'll understand later. Let's see, a bombing, and a mad pilot all in one day. That's just the beginning, unless I miss my guess."

"I'm trying to safeguard the public, Director Bane."

"Oh, Doctor Kenner, stop it. This is no way to win my affections."

"More bad jokes?"

"I leave those for your associate. Just prescribe me an antibiotic, and let's get going."

"You're going nowhere, Director. You've already breached protocol by making it this far on the gangway."

"I'm all about breaching." He lowered his voice. "Seriously, Doctor, we don't have time for this."

"You're saying you're the only man who can manage this investigation?" Her lip twitched, perhaps a sign she was annoyed.

Bane liked both Kenner and Toy, but he didn't really have the time. "This isn't going to be an investigation. It's going to be a chase. All out war. War and mayhem are my specialties, especially mayhem. Just ask anyone. So yes, that's more or less what I'm saying."

"Don't be melodramatic."

"I specialize in that too. Melodrama clings to me like an unwashed T shirt in summer."

"Eew."

"Five hundred and sixty-two responses to your watch notice, Doctor Kenner."

"That's an ugly argument, Director."

"Ugly ideas indicate a creative mind. Hey, I'm a jerk, Doctor, pure and simple. King of the Assholes according to an online test. I kill people, everyone knows that. I arrest people without due process. Ask anyone. I hate reporters, nearly as much as I despise politicians and lawyers. But people are afraid of me. So things get done fast."

"How?"

"Magic." He lifted his bare arms, hoping his ordeal on the plane didn't leave underarm stains. "See, nothing up my sleeves." He snapped his fingers. Almost magically, Bane's black-suited gun-toting enforcers appeared in a ring around the masked LAPD.

"You can't do that," Kenner said, her face revealing shock for the first time.

"I just did. I can do other tricks, too. You'd be more impressed if you weren't so angry."

"You're damn right I'm angry. You could be infected. This could be airborne."

"Ah, then you'll have to share my quarantine. That might not be so bad. Will we have to take a disinfectant bath together?" Bane winked. "I'm not infected, Doctor. Trust me. Men like me, we get a bullet in the head one day. But we don't get sick. No time. Besides I wore a mask."

"The whole time on that flight?"

"Well, yes. Ever since your watch, I've carried a pack of your recommended filters, right alongside a pack of jumbo condoms. You know, nothing personal, Doctor Kenner, but you're more stubborn than my daughters. The clock is ticking. Let's not kill a few million people just because you hate me."

Caff leaned close to Ada and whispered in her ear. She nodded. "Fine, Director. You can accompany us if you continue to wear a mask. And we do a full exam every twenty hours."

Bane smiled. "Ah. Now I'm turned on."

Kenner sighed. "Caff will be examining you."

Bane's smile faded. "Way to spoil a moment." His phone rang, a Star Spangled Banner ring tone. In that same moment Ada's phone rang—an old style 1950s telephone ring. And Caff's phone. Then Nam's.

Bane figured it would be more bad news. It was. He listened, frowning, and he was still frowning when he slid his satellite phone closed.

"More incidents," Ada said, before he could.

He nodded. "Pakistan."

"My report was on San Diego, honeys," said Caff.

"Kettle Cove, Massachusetts," Ada said.

"Orlando," Nam said.

"We're losing this race," Bane said.

9

Pakistan, Incident 542

Chris Andrews clung to the sheer rock face of Ujara Peak in northeastern Pakistan, his hand wedged in a fissure. He heard the shriek of a hawk circling below and the huffing of a rising wind, but nothing else disturbed his peace.

Though the monsoons were over for the year, the rock was slick with humidity. A drizzly October day made the climb treacherous. His own skills kept him alive, not a burly bodyguard or bulletproof limo. It was the best feeling in the world.

Here, at Ujara, eight thousand miles from America, there were no fans and no paparazzi. He was just Chris; he left his rapper name, Chaos, at the base camp thousands of feet below. His pest of an agent couldn't nag him about that damn reality show, *Superstar*. Today was just for the mountain and his brother Jerry.

"Anytime, bro," Jerr shouted.

Chris looked down between his dangling legs at his brother thirty feet below. Jerr's face flushed red with the strain and joy of the free climb. Jerr sneezed, but couldn't spare a hand to wipe away snot.

Chris continued to sway, enjoying the feeling of tension on his forearms. He knew he could hold for a few more seconds. Below his brother he saw the lap of the mountain as it swept out in jagged ripples to meet the Shaka Glacier. It made him giddy. He laughed now. What a charge! If he died in this moment, he would leave this chaotic world a happy man.

His arm muscles cramped. He could swing his other arm up, gain a better hold on the face or—drop.

He let the ecstasy of danger take him and released.

As he plunged past Jerr, his brother yelled, "Butthole!" Jerr pushed out from the rock and bent around, folding his arms and turning into a dive, in a futile attempt to close the distance. The ultimate BASE jump.

Chris let the rush take him. The blast of air stung his face, but it was a relief after the oppressive heat. He wore only a jump suit and chute. He angled his body down. There would only be a moment of free fall, then he had to pull. But he crammed a lot of living into those few seconds: the sensation of speed, the chill of high altitude atmosphere, the rush of near death and a momentary escape from the stress of his world. At the bottom of the mountain was their camp with the hired porters, the *Superstar* camera crew shooting out-takes of the climb, and his bodyguards.

He dove past a circling hawk, laughing as he realized he had free-fallen from heights to which only condors could aspire.

He pulled the cord, almost reluctant. After four hours of free climbing, the streak of speed was pure buzz. It didn't get better than that.

The glacier still rushed towards him and it took a few blinks of his dry eyes to realize: there was no hard jerk of updraft catching the parachute. He pulled again.

His canopy did not deploy.

He yanked on the cord now.

He was past the safe altitude.

Chris felt an odd combination of fear and thrill. Rocks blurred past him; craggy fingers seemed to reach out for him, so near he could almost imagine touching one. He fell toward a cluster of house-sized boulders.

He pulled his backup chute.

Nothing.

He jerked the cord again. This time he screamed his frustration.

Fear became terror, and in a lifetime of thrillseeking, it was the ultimate high.

He could see cracks and textures and shadows in the sweeping river of boulders. Too close now. Even if he deployed, he'd shatter both legs.

What a rush!

In seconds he would be a smear on the rocks below, and wouldn't the Real TV camera crews love action shots of that. He had no doubt *Superstar* producer Abbey Chase would use the footage.

Chris pulled again. No way his canopy and backup both failed. No frigging way. Jerr had packed it himself. His brother could pack a chute with his eyes closed, and Chris trusted Jerr with his life.

He laughed. *With his life.* Good one. Jerr could never make a mistake on both chutes. Which meant—Jerr had killed him.

He saw the terror on the faces of his bodyguards. He was so close he could see the cameras tilted up, as the *Superstar* crew taped his last moment. He spread his arms, smiled, and yelled, "Death—the final adventure!" The image of Chris Chaos Andrews laughing at death would make him a hero with his fans.

And in that last second of his life, it felt good: the blast of the updraft, the sensation of flying, and then the rush of adrenalin—the ultimate stimulant.

Fear, the highest of highs.

San Diego, Incident 544

Around the time rescue teams searched for the pancaked body of Chaos—eleven time zones away—Enrique Torres inline-skated along the Mission Beach boardwalk in San Diego with his mutt, Tito, panting behind him. It was sunny and Enrique's mahogany skin gleamed with sweat. The Strand was best at six in the morning: not too hot, only out-of-work locals on the beach, tourists still at breakfast, and you could hear the surf without the blare of traffic.

Tito, a mongrel in the truest sense, drew more admiring looks from the joggers than Enrique's muscles. Normally, he'd use Tito to chat up the shorts-and-bikini-top female joggers, but today he was not in the mood. He'd been suffering from a bad cold and was stoned on decongestants. The bug left a perpetual bad taste, as if Tito had crapped right in his mouth.

Friday the thirteenth would be his lucky day, even though nine days ago the judges on the touring reality talent show *Superstar* rejected him. The snub still stung; becoming a finalist on *Superstar* could have taken him away from a life that was killing him. Why hadn't they seen he was the next Enrique Iglesias? Even in his sexiest shirtless outfit he had earned only: "Dude, that was no good for me. Stick to body building."

The thumbs down from Chaos hurt most of all. Enrique was a monster Chaos fan. After months of practice and days in line with other hopefuls, all Enrique got from his *Superstar* audition was a cold.

But today would be different. Today he would make his mark on the world. He'd show the judges on *Superstar*. He'd be the lead story on the news.

Enrique carved a long arc left and onto his street, a row of World War II bungalows with browning lawns where he rented his basement room in old Lambert's house.

Tito barked at Mrs. Baker's collie, and Enrique yelled, "Leave it!" His own voice brought a stab of intense pain, as if someone had driven a four-inch nail right into his forehead. His mongrel obediently padded along beside his skates, breaking heel only long enough to pee on the old widow's sun-baked lawn.

Enrique sneezed. Really bad bug; he'd endured quite a few nosebleeds, constant headaches and restless nights since the *Superstar* auditions. And oh, the dreams. He couldn't remember much about them, but he woke up drenched in sweat; not a fever sweat, but a genuine fear soaking. He'd wake, shivering, screaming out, the monsters already fading and the sheets clinging to him.

Tito chose the cranky Irish veteran's lawn for his poop stop. Guint's manicured green lawn was a favorite of all the neighborhood dogs, probably because the old geezer's lawn was the only green patch on a street of brown grass. The veteran was a lawbreaker. He ignored the no-watering ordinance.

Enrique had his poop bag ready, but, as usual, Guint rushed out of the shade of his sagging porch and raised a fist. "Get that mutt off my lawn!" It was their ritual, a tired one, and it never failed to infuriate Enrique.

He wheeled to an expert stop on his skates, ready for Guint.

He felt a stab of pain of near-migraine intensity.

Hand shaking, Enrique reached into his fanny pack and pulled out his Browning .40 caliber, flipped off the safety with his thumb, and shot Guint in the head.

As bone and brain chunks flew in messy lumps to the immaculate lawn, Enrique bent to pat Tito.

"Old habits die hard." And he skated on.

Kettle Cove, Massachusetts, Incident 545

Massachusetts State Trooper Adam Allbright of Kettle Cove ate clam chowder by a long pier that thrust out into the Atlantic Ocean.

Allbright was a man of habit. He always ate chowder at this spot, always from Old Beatty's cart by the pier, and always at 11:45 in the morning. Old Beatty would ask him about his daughter and sons and give him free chowder and bad coffee, both in Styrofoam cups.

Today, a damn cold and the resulting fatigue had him running behind. The sneezes didn't bother him, but the headaches grew worse each day. The gulls circling the table and screaming for scraps usually didn't bother him. Today, their cries brought him agonizing pain.

Damn California bug. His daughter had brought it back from San Francisco after car-pooling with four friends to try out for that insipid reality TV show, *Superstar*. He could have told her she'd never make it—no daughter of his would be the next big superstar—but she was at that age she wouldn't listen. Now, served her right, she was sick in bed.

He needed the overtime, so he hadn't called in sick, but extra strength Tylenol no longer helped. The only high of his day was sneezing on the speeding tickets when he gave them out. A little extra fine for the tourists.

The nausea came on him fast. He barely ate half the chowder. Almost immediately he knew he'd never keep it down. After struggling with it for a moment, he tossed the chowder back up on the coarse sand. Bad clams.

The stabbing pain felt like someone drilling a hole right in his head. Bad. Very bad.

A bold gull flapped in, diving for the vomit on the sand. He kicked at it, but the sudden movement brought more queasiness. He threw up again, the cup held upside down between two fingers as he wretched and moaned.

Damn geezer. Beatty had given him bad clams.

He saw old Beatty staring at him from his wheeled cart, stirring the big black kettle of chowder. The old man looked scared as Allbright strode toward him.

"Trooper Adam, you all right?" Beatty's voice only brought more pain. The bitterness of bile cleared Allbright's sinuses and he wretched again.

"Bad clams," Allbright said, wiping his chin with the back of his hand.

"No, Trooper Adam. I never have bad clams!"

More pain, this time more like someone had a blowtorch on his skull pan. Damn Beatty. He was a menace to tourists and locals alike, serving his bad chowder. Allbright rubbed his temples with both hands, but the stabbing pain remained.

"I better call a doctor, Trooper Adam." Beatty put his ladle down and moved around his cart, his rotund body moving in nervous jerks.

"No! No, old Beat, forget it." His own voice brought searing thrusts of heat. "Jesus on a moped!"

He sneezed, and that made it worse. As the snot flew in red ropy filaments, he felt as if he had blown his own brains out.

When he opened his eyes, Beatty frowned at him, his salt-and-wind-worn skin furrowed into exaggerated wrinkles.

"I have to punish you, Old Beat."

Trooper Allbright pushed Beatty back against his cart. The old man struggled, but Allbright grabbed him around his shirt collar, pulled back on the stained apron, and shoved Beatty hard against the wheel. The kettle of chowder rocked. Withered hands came up, fingers raking at Allbright's face.

Allbright felt none of it. The rage bubbled up from a dark place.

Old Beat had done this too him. Poisoned him. He was the cause of Allbright's agony.

There was more stabbing pain, and for a moment he couldn't see.

"No! Trooper Adam!"

"I'm revoking your vendor's license," Allbright said. But instead of slipping on handcuffs, he pushed Beatty's face into the open kettle of steamy hot chowder.

10

Site F, California

Alban Bane waited for the big blades to spin down before he slid open the door for Ada Kenner.

Ada was a zesty breath of fresh air on an otherwise oh-crap sort of day. He put it down to his relief that she knew her business. In the face of the horrors revealed by her own watch notice, she was eerily calm. Even at the scene of the Begley incident, the sight of all that blood had barely made her blink.

They were too late. The body, the only witness, even the scene investigators had been whisked off in bright yellow Hazmat vans, on "authority of the CDC."

Bane smiled. "You working ahead of me, Ada?"

"I didn't give the order."

They had called their respective offices, and Bane called the Governor. No one had a record of the Hazmat containment.

Bane stared at the bloody GTO, now filled with foam. He said one word. "Braxis."

They had left Caff and Nam to contain the highway scene, and flown on to Braxis.

Now she waited for him on the Braxis heliport, looking elegant and wonderful, even in the harsh security lights.

Ada was a striking woman, tall, athletic, about his age, bright-bright eyes that almost seemed green in certain light. She clung to her bag as if it contained her whole life and kept a hand on her Fedora to keep it from blowing off. He knew a lot about her, long before he met her. Her Parameter Incident Watch caught Bane's attention, but his science advisor immediately dismissed it as nonsense. It was only after he researched Doctor Ada Kenner that Bane took her seriously. Her life framed a woman who had to be taken seriously.

She was the CDC's brightest rising star, held back from directorship only because she had a problem with authority and preferred seven days in the lab to the proven methods of advancing: golf club meetings, parties, socializing with the elite. He also knew she was divorced with a disabled child and the husband had custody, and that she blamed herself.

He found it distressing how much his own life mirrored Ada's—he spent his life in the field seven days a week, his wife had been murdered a decade ago, and he might as well have lost custody of his two girls. The danger of his work made him a target, and this kept his alienated daughters with their aunt Marilyn and in private schools. But what scared him more was that he already found Ada so simpatico. She put up a Teflon barrier, and all of his jokes bounced off her. She was eerily calm. And beyond smart.

On the way to the chopper, he had called his daughters, vaguely aware that Ada was close enough to eavesdrop as they walked quickly across the runway asphalt.

"Hi, Jen," Bane had said.

"Pops!"

"Jen, how's my little jewel?"

"What's wrong, Pops?" Ada wasn't the only smart one.

"Nothing, sweetie. How's first year university?"

"Cool."

"Only my sweet Jen would spend a fortune on university, just to become a low-paid social worker."

She laughed. "I'm not after money, Pops."

She was just like her dad. "Any new boyfriends?"

"No one steady," she said and laughed.

No one steady? How many boys was she dating, then? He resisted the urge to ask. She was too old for a protective father. "How's Mags?"

"Pissed at you. You missed her birthday again."

"I didn't. Fedex should have arrived."

"It arrived. Nice Iphone. But that's not what she wanted." *She wanted you.* Jen didn't have to say it.

"I know." He found himself blinking too fast. "Jen, I love you, sweetie. Mags too. Tell her."

"We know, Pops. But when do we see you?"

"Soon. I promise."

"After the next emergency?"

"Something like that, baby doll."

She sniffed. He heard it clearly on the phone. "You well, Jen? You have a cold?" He tried to keep the alarm out of his voice.

"No, Pops. No cold."

I was crying, idiot father. "Stay away from anyone who's sick."

"I'm in school. I can't stay away from anyone."

"I mean it, Jen!"

A long pause, maybe a sigh. "I promise."

"I love you."

"You said that already." A long pause. "I love you too, Pops." She hung up.

Ada didn't say anything as he pocketed his phone, but she gave him a peculiar, almost hostile look. She knew all. From that one phone call, Ada knew everything about his daughters.

They waited on the helipad, not speaking, surrounded on all sides by barbwire and high fences ominously labeled High Voltage. Almost in contradiction, an illuminated sign dominated the south side in cheerful warm colors: Braxis: A Better Life for Everyone.

Braxis. Bane's team had Braxis on their watch list ever since the hijacking of three Braxis trucks from one of their facilities in Spain, Site S they called it. It was the third attempt, but this one had succeeded, and the Spanish government blamed it on the Basques, as they always did. Braxis claimed the shipment was "flu vaccines" but who would steal trucks of flu vaccine? Braxis showed up more often than they should on the Intelligence Gists—*Reader's Digest* versions of important world events.

Bane watched a tall man, clearly ex-military, emerge from a concrete bunker. From Bane's own service as a captain in the Counter Terrorism Unit, he pegged this man as Special Forces, Delta, or some other elite unit, almost certainly an ex-officer. The man's expression revealed nothing, but Bane saw contempt in those flinty eyes. He was massive, too fat in the face and paunchy at his waist, like an American football defensive tackle. Something about the man put Bane on high alert.

Bane moved past Ada and thrust out his hand. "Alban Bane."

The man stared at him, as cold as a reptile, and like a snake, he didn't blink. "May I see your face, sir?"

Bane had forgotten the damn mask. He slipped it up, offered a crooked grin, flipped it back over his face. "Doctor's orders."

The security chief didn't speak for a long time. Finally, "Commander Markus Manheim—sir." After a moment's hesitation, he shook Bane's hand.

Bane struggled to retain his smile as crushing force cut off the circulation in his hand. Bane concentrated on returning an equal measure of pounds per inch force, ignoring the pain. "Let me guess. Your hobby is arm wrestling?" When Manheim released him, Bane stepped closer and whispered, "When you greet Doctor Kenner, pretend you care." Although Bane and Manheim were nearly the same height, Manheim was broader, thicker, billowing out in all directions. "This is Doctor Kenner, Coordinator at the Centers for Disease Control."

Manheim shook her hand lightly. "Doctor."

"Ada, please." She smiled, but it wasn't enough to thaw Manheim.

"If you'll follow me to the lounge?" Although Manheim's words were polite, his voice held a combination of husky monotone and menace.

Manheim took them into the concrete bunker and a sealed room between two metal doors, where their identifications were carefully checked, and only after verifying phone calls were they allowed to pass into the main compound, a sterile lot with dozens of windowless buildings, no trees and miles of electrified fencing. A car swept them through collections of buildings clad in the Braxis corporate colors, sunny oranges and yellows that seemed all wrong for the place. The designers of this facility had tried too hard to make a sterile environment welcoming, probably for potential visiting shareholders, board members and the press. Manheim stopped at a building simply labeled Forty-two and passed through several magnetically locked doors to an immense lounge with plush carpets and paneled walls that oddly contrasted the soulless concrete of the building. There were several mahogany tables with matching chairs and clusters of tall black-leather wingbacks by gas fireplaces.

"Make yourselves comfortable," Manheim said, and he started towards the door.

"Commander, a moment?"

Manheim stiffened and turned reluctantly.

"You know about the incident?" Bane asked.

"Sir?"

"Doctor Alistair Begley. Out on the highway?"

"No, sir."

Bane didn't believe him, though Manheim's face revealed nothing. Bane felt sure Manheim could beat a lie detector. Most people, when they lied, couldn't control their eyes. They'd either blink too rapidly or look sharply to the left. People who told the truth would look you in the eye or glance right as they recalled. Manheim did none of those things.

"He was hitchhiking on the highway."

Unblinking eyes continued to stare. "Doctor Begley drives a Porsche, sir."
"Yes, we found it. Flat tire."

"I see, sir. Is Doctor Begley all right, sir?"

"He's dead." Bane normally wouldn't reveal this much, but he wanted reactions from the man.

Nothing. Not even a shift in posture. Manheim said nothing.

"Aren't you going to ask how?"

"What happens outside this facility is not my business, sir."

Bane nodded. Icy cold. "Tell Gies we will see him now."

"He's in Paris, sir. We've linked you up with a two-way vid."

Bane stared at Manheim, the Commander. There was something distinctly unwholesome about the man. Manheim would be "a person of interest" in this investigation. He would have the man investigated, followed, and interrogated further.

Manheim left the room without a word.

Ada made her way to the bar and Bane followed. She ran her fingers along the highly polished wood. "No dust," she said. She slipped behind the bar. "Drink?"

Bane felt himself smile. Nothing perturbed this woman. "Coke?"

Ada passed him a canned Coke from the bar fridge and took a bottled water for herself. "You were a little edgy with the Commander."

"I suspect Manheim didn't notice." He set down his Coke in spite of a dry throat. "So, Ada. What are we dealing with here? Bad flu bug. Bird flu? A new venereal disease?"

"You're never serious, are you?"

"Evading my question?"

"Oh, that was a real question." Her smile wasn't exactly glamorous, but it was nearly impossible not to like Ada. She carried herself with a calm that made her attractive. "You read my Watch notice."

"No, I had someone with a much bigger brain read it and gist it for me. Do you know you write everything in sixteen-syllable words?"

"Do you want an answer?"

"Yes."

"I don't know."

"See, that's not so hard. Three one-syllable words."

She sighed. "Really, I don't know."

"I promise not to tell anyone, Doc. Your malpractice premiums won't go up."

She smiled. "As amusing as you are, Director, I have no other answer. I see emerging trends. I haven't identified anything other than some radical symptomology."

"That's five syllables, Ada. Couldn't you just say symptoms. That's two." He winked. "And can you call me Alban. Or Bane?"

"I can."

"Will you?"

"If you're a good boy."

"Go on, try it."

"Bane. It suits you. From what I hear, you ruin lives."

"Yup. And my street address is 666."

"I'm sorry, Bane, I didn't mean to insult you."

"Yes, you did. And it worked. I'm weeping inside. I'd cry if I could."

She smiled again. "They actually toned you down in the movie."

"Oh, you saw that? The actor was better looking than I am."

"Caff thinks you're hot."

"How about you, boss?"

"I think you're rude, smart, mean, a violent brute—"

"Actually, I'm only violent as a last resort. Usually I rely on extortion."

"A brute. And—" She stared at him.

He tried not to blush. "And?"

"And somewhat good-looking. The hat's stupid, though."

Bane clutched his Red Sox cap. "Sacrilege!" He couldn't return the insult. Her hat, a wide felt fedora, looked good on her.

They fell silent as Manheim re-entered the lounge. Without a word, he walked to the far wall and typed on a keyboard on a table. A large plasma screen lit up with a frowning image of Doctor Ernest Gies. Bane expected a white lab coat, but this man looked more like a European banker, dignified in a conservatively cut suit and designer glasses. He looked as if his best friend had passed away, his face drawn and lips pressed together, and his movements were jerky, like a puppet on taut strings.

"Ada. I'm sorry about this fizzing business."

Bane leaned close to Ada. "Fizzing?"

"He means f-ing. You know."

He continued leaning close to Ada, staring at her. "Oh God, you're braless."

Ada stepped away from him as if shocked. "Ernest, what's going on?"

"What we talked about in Firenze, kiddo, that still applies." He looked off-screen, nodded at someone not in the image, then said, "Commander Manheim told me what happened." His lip trembled; a "tell" as Bane called it. "Ali Begley was my good friend. I just don't know how I'll tell Jules, his wife." He spoke too fast, as if frightened. "What happened? Ali was on his way to Long Beach. His grandson's birthday. What on earth happened, do you know?"

Ada's voice was curt and cold. "Ali seemed quite sick. He may have infected others. And miraculously, a Hazmat team from nowhere appears and vanishes them all. You know about this, right Ernest?"

"I do?"

Bane watched Ada now, full of admiration. She was as cool as any law enforcement agent on Bane's team. He regretted the braless joke.

"You do. Remember your story about the lab break-in. The cleanup."

He frowned. "That was for your ears, Ada."

Bane covered his ears.

"Very funny," Gies said. "Ada, be plain. What are you saying?"

"I'm saying I think your Braxis people appeared out of nowhere in yellow Hazmat vans and scooped all the evidence right off the highway. They're in these buildings now, aren't they?"

Gies was not as guarded as Manheim. Bane saw the pupil reaction, and the dance of eyes as he looked from Ada to Bane, then back. Gies was panicky.

"I don't know anything about that, kiddo."

"Oh, that hardly seems likely, Ernest." Without hesitation, she launched into a new line of interrogation. "What viruses are you working with?"

"I assume this will be confidential. We have many competitors." Gies stared at Bane, waiting.

But it was Ada who answered. "When it comes to public health you can assume nothing."

Gies sighed. "Various viruses that attach to HN proteins, and strains of BDV."

"Why BDV?"

"Why not? No one is working with Borna disease, except one lab in Germany."

"And?"

"And current drugs are ineffective."

"What are you working on?" she said, her voice flat, almost angry.

"Vaccines, Ada."

"Vaccines? I doubt there's a marketplace large enough to support a vaccine. It hardly seems a commercially viable development protocol."

"Not all Braxis protocols are about revenue. We have a broad mandate under our CEO—"

"Professor Gies," Ada interrupted, and he stiffened at the use of his formal title. "I'm here in an official capacity."

"I see. Well, I guess I understood that—Doctor Kenner." Gies seemed to deflate at the harshness in her voice.

"The CDC must investigate your facility. Maybe several of your facilities."

"On what basis?"

"It is clear to me that Doctor Begley died of a mysterious illness not six miles from where we sit. I can only extrapolate that Site F is the reservoir."

Gies said nothing. He stared at Ada, still as a statue on the big screen. Bane also watched Ada now, surprised at her aggressive style.

"Since we don't know much about this virus, we would be forced to contain," she added.

Gies crossed his arms on the screen. "You can—should—investigate. Where corporate secrets are not revealed publicly, I will cooperate. There is no need to threaten."

"Let's talk transmission of this BDV you're working with."

"Fine. During the first stage of infection, the virus attaches to host cells by recognizing specific receptors on the cell surface. Productive virus-cell interactions result in membrane fusion between the viral envelope and the cell surface membrane—"

"I'll want your data," Ada interrupted

"Fine." Gies said it gently, but his eyes glittered, almost certainly with anger.

"Again, why BDV? What's special enough that a giant like Braxis spends hundreds of millions on this?"

"True, BDV is not widespread, but—" Gies leaned closer, sliding to the edge of his chair, his face excited, the anger disappearing. "Our research indicates that many violent psychiatric in-patients test positive for Borna Nabs." He glanced quickly at Bane. "That's antibodies, Director. We're at the human trials stage of a vaccine that promises to—well, we've already shown that our protocol inhibits violent tendencies. You see, we have proven BDV—never mind. The important thing is, in our trials, we have shown an eighty-two percent success rate in—"

Ada held up her hand. "You're telling me you are conducting trials. Human trials? You're approved for this?" She sounded furious. "On whom?"

"Dangerous offenders, schizophrenics and psychopaths who test positive for BDV Nabs."

"Right here? In this facility?"

"No, Ada. We're approved in France. Site F, where you are now, is a bio containment facility. We handle raw virus and bacteria there up to bio-hazard level 5."

"What other viruses are here?" Bane jumped in.

Both Ada and Gies glared at him for a moment. "We have everything at Site F. From Ebola to various trains of H1N1—"

"Translation please," Bane said.

"H1N1 was the 1918 Spanish Flu," Ada explained.

Bane shook his head. "The one that killed millions?"

"Over forty million," Ada said.

"And why would Braxis need such a dangerous virus?" To Bane it boggled the mind to allow private corporations to store mass-murdering diseases. If Braxis let loose one of these dangerous viruses, it could kill more people than Stalin in the Soviet Union.

"H1N1 is genetically similar to Bird Flu." Gies sounded pissed. "We're working on treatments and vaccines, Director."

"So what was Begley infected with?" Bane said.

"I told you. A strain of BDV." Gies voice rose in anger to match Bane's tone.

"Then, how did Doctor Begley become exposed? How is it transmitted?" Ada asked.

Gies bounced up and paced back and forth. Bane was fascinated. He found Ada to be a brilliant interrogator. She could have had a terrific career in law enforcement—always throwing the suspect off guard with a new direction.

"An accident in protocol 440," Gies admitted, much as a suspect might under intense cross-examination. "Begley handled raw virus. You see, the ganglioside GD1a and its more complex homologs GT1b and GQ1b are cell-surface receptors and—"

"Translation, please?" Bane interrupted.

Ada frowned. "It means Doctor Begley had to come into direct contact."

"That's right," Gies said, pausing suddenly. "BDV is not an airborne virus. There's no need to be severe. Cautious, yes, but you are over-reacting to—"

Ada's voice strengthened. "BDV does not cause cerebral hemorrhaging."

"A mutated strain, Doctor Kenner. We call it TZ-4."

"My God." She glared at the screen. "I spend my life trying to prevent emerging viruses. You create them."

"Doctor Frankenstein," Bane snapped, "if you have nothing to hide here, then you will have no problem with a search of your facility for the missing witnesses and the deputy."

"None at all, Director. Manheim will accompany you on a full tour."

Ada, still sounding angry, said, "Either way, I will err on the side of caution. This facility is locked down, Doctor Gies. I'm issuing a BioSecure

Notice."

"That's one step short of a quarantine!"

"A baby step." She scowled, and Bane found it wasn't attractive on her. "The only difference is you voluntarily agree. I'm sure Director Bane wouldn't hesitate to bring in his men. They have shiny new machine guns."

"Boys and their toys," Bane said, agreeably. Bane found his admiration for her growing. His best field agent couldn't have handled the situation better.

"Everything's under control in there, Doctor Kenner," Gies said.

"Doctor Gies, you don't understand. Full containment means I must shut down Site F. Precautions will have to be taken. A BioSecure on the other hand means no one can leave, but you can keep working. You choose."

"Is that not a little extreme, Doctor Kenner?"

"Until we know more about this virus—proof of what you're saying—no, it's not extreme."

Gies sighed. "Ada, Ada, I taught you better than this. You are jumping to all sorts of unsubstantiated conclusions."

"In the CDC we err on the side of extreme caution."

"You do not have the authority."

"Oh, but I do. BioSecure Notices I can issue on my own authority. Only containment orders require my director's signoff."

Gies stood up, the mask of calm falling away, and suddenly his face was cherry red with anger. "We shall see, Doctor Kenner. Expect a call from your director." The screen dissolved to black.

Bane stared at Ada Kenner, appraising her, admiring her. "Wow. You just blew my whole illusion of you as Shirley from the Partridge Family."

"The only thing I hate more than a liar is a dangerous liar," she said, ignoring his jibe.

Bane nodded. "Even doctors lie."

"Doctors always lie."

In that moment, Bane felt sure he was in love with this elegant, brilliant woman.

11
Site P, Paris

Subject 244-05 screamed and tore at his restraints.

Administrator Ernest Gies cleaned his bifocals then perched them on his slightly arched nose and studied the boy through the one-way observation glass. He didn't bother with notes for this group—the subjects of Permutation 244: subjects one through fourteen. Five cameras filmed every moment of the protocol as fourteen men and women, aged nineteen to thirty-six, thrashed and pulled at their armbands and leg straps. Seven were psychiatric in-patients, with a propensity to violence and psychopathic behavior, who tested positive to Borna antibodies. Five were early release dangerous offender volunteers from French Corrections, granted transfer to institutional supervision in exchange for participation. Two were violent runaways, also Borna antibodies positive.

He had met them one by one, eight days ago, in Braxis's cheerful paneled office on the Université campus along Boulevard Saint Germain, with his clipboard, armed security, and assistants. He had reassured them that the protocol was harmless—a highly promising and side effect–free vaccine that curbed violent tendencies. Not entirely true, but close enough that he managed to deliver with a smile in his immaculate accentless French: "Crazy world, isn't it? Here we are trying to find artificial ways to control our tempers." Then, with a "just a formality" he asked them to waive indemnity. The ones who signed were transported in a windowless van to Site P, their underground Paris facility. The ones who refused to sign were sent back to their hospital rooms and prison cells.

Gies yawned—not bored, exhausted. His reunion with Ada Kenner—his favorite protégée—had been anything but calming. She was too smart for her own good. Ada had no idea of the stakes, or her own danger, but she knew he was lying, that was clear, and she saw right through his PR façade. He doubted he could intervene with Domergue much longer. Gies' protective fatherly instincts wouldn't keep Ada safe forever.

Gies rubbed his eyes again. They had come too far. He could only hope she'd get distracted by some strain of the bird flu or something interesting, because an Ada Kenner in charge of Emerging Viral at the CDC was a very dangerous thing. She never slept, she was always pumped and bulldog stubborn, and she was at least as smart as Gies. But she had a conscience. A very dangerous equation.

He focused on the protocol to take his mind off Ada.

This group would not hit the statistical baseline. He assumed Permutation 244 was a failure already. The vaccine still proved highly antagonistic to the TZ virus that carried the genome, but this time—unlike Permutation 243—two subjects showed the early signs of expiration: 244-05, the subject nearest the glass, managed to tear free one arm restraint. Gies glanced at the data on the bank of plasma screens. Subject 244-05: Caucasian, nineteen, dropout at grade nine, runaway at fourteen years of age, long history of arrests for violence. Gies found himself clenching the clipboard until his knuckles whitened. He knew the probabilities, but it didn't change the horror he felt whenever they blew.

Regardless of the mortalities, there was no question of the necessity of the protocols. Not now. Ever since the break-in at Site F, there was really no choice but to accelerate the human trials without sanction. Rationally, he understood the critical need for the vaccine, before the inevitable mutation. But these subjects—psychiatric patients and prisoners or not—many of them were just kids.

Subject 244-05 was the worst for Gies. His blonde hair and piercing blue eyes were very like Francis's, his own son.

Francis, lost to violence all those years ago. Francis, the reason he allied himself with the Devil himself.

Gies focused. This was not Francis; this was subject 244-05.

Gies took a long breath of Hepa filtered air, taking a moment to restore his detached calm. He hated that metallic smell. The filtered mechanical air triggered a fear response in him, associated with bio-containment; he far preferred the clinical aroma of phenolic disinfectant.

The veins around 244-05's temples pulsed as he thrashed. Gies tapped the intercom switch and said, "Restraint."

Two large orderlies in biohazard level-four suits ran around the gurney and tried to restrain 244-05.

The boy was clearly in trouble. This was some parent's son, runaway or not. Designating him 244-05 couldn't change that. The boy clawed at his eyes, in spite of the orderlies' attempt to restrain him. He dug his fingers into his eye-sockets. His scream rose to a new pitch. He wrenched free of the orderlies and flailed at the air as if fighting off some unseen creature. What did he see in that far off place, a world where epinephrine spiked and generated explosive bursts of superhuman strength? The boy's EKG raced.

His EEG ran to steep cliffs.

"I see we are not making progress." Gies jumped at the voice. At one in the morning he hardly expected Gilbert Domergue to be touring the protocols.

He turned, trying to appear calm. "I didn't know you were in Paris, sir."

"I am everywhere, Ernest." Domergue didn't hold out his hand in greeting. He frowned, glanced briefly at the dying subject, then his glittering brown marble eyes focused on Gies. He was a dapper man, very tall in his black, tailored suit, crisp beneath a pressed, bleached-white lab coat, very athletic and imposing. His wide aristocratic face lacked warmth but was Richard Gere handsome under perfectly groomed silver hair. "How many more permutations do we have ready to test?"

"Six hundred and thirty-six, sir." Gies, as always, felt a little awe, a lot of fear and a little love in the presence of Braxis's infamous CEO, a man known for his reclusive behavior, arrogance and brilliance.

Who else but Domergue could have conceived of using a Braxis-patented gene—Gene A79377-2A, nicknamed A2A—to suppress violent urges. Braxis had scored a billion-dollar triumph with that patent, driving stocks into orbit, after a discreet press conference that proclaimed, "We've branded A79377-2A as the Peace Gene. The Peace Gene is the gene responsible for triggering the urge to non-violent behavior." Once the public was informed, it had been up to Gies to develop the virus-delivery method to ensure the genome was effectively target-delivered. Domergue drove the project with his ruthless genius, sanctioning human testing only last year in Colombia. Unfortunately, Gies's choice of a non-airborne Borna virus for delivery turned deadly when the virus mutated to an airborne strain in rhesus subjects and became antagonistic to the gene itself. This might not have been an issue, except for the ransacking of Site F by animal rights protestors. Some of the infected animals escaped.

Gies continued to stare at Subject 244-05 on the monitor. The boy was bleeding from self-inflicted wounds, and despite arm and leg restraints his body was arched in a paroxysm of pain. "I have only sixteen more volunteers from Corrections authorities."

"That's surprising. French Corrections is usually only too happy to offload violent offenders."

Gies pushed back his glasses and rubbed the bridge of his nose. "Actually, sir, they've been sending us terrorists lately. And a disproportionate number of non-Caucasians." Stabbing pain immobilized him for a moment. If Domergue was here, the situation had gone from terrible to tragic, because the Braxis CEO never appeared in public, and only a few dozen employees had ever seen him. It meant this wing of the complex would be sealed off by security to prevent "curious" employees from seeing The Man's face. Domergue ran a trillion dollar corporation employing hundreds of thousands, none of whom had every seen The Man, aside from Gies and a handful of others. He wouldn't have left his vineyards in the south of France if the situation was anything but deadly.

On the screen over Domergue's head, Gies saw that subject 244-05 still struggled. It was somehow easier to watch on video than through the glass, although Domergue didn't seem to feel the same way, his glittering eyes watching the tragedy unfold. The subject bucked on the gurney in a full frenzy. The orderlies could not control him. Subject 244-05's unblinking eyes, bloody from his earlier attempt to blind himself, grew impossibly wide. He shrieked.

Gies turned, forgetting Domergue for a moment. This had never happened before. The ones who blew usually flew into psychotic episodes, normally rage or murderous aggression. This boy seemed about to expire from terror. Gies watched, fascinated, horrified, seeing only his son's face through the glass.

Gies ground his teeth. He willed himself not to see Francis there.

He tried to keep his detached scientist persona intact. He tapped the red button beside the intercom. "STAT, Ward 24!"

The boy tore at the other restraint. One of the orderlies caught his waving hand but was knocked back. The subject managed to tear the second arm restraint. The boy bucked one last time and tumbled off the gurney. His leg restraints held him, like an upside down puppet. The EKG flatlined.

"Well, that was gruesome," Domergue said.

Gies said nothing. The respect Gies had for the genius of this man—literally The Man, as they called him in Braxis—was a hair away from hatred. Domergue was brilliant, but he had no compassion. Gies's three years with The Man had eroded his own sense of zeal and feeling.

Gies turned, ignoring the emergency teams as they swept away patient 244-05, the Francis look-alike. "I have nothing to report, sir, other than the BioSecure on Site F," Gies said, in a tone that really meant to convey, You came all the way from the Midi for nothing, sir.

"All our resources are on this project, as of now."

"I understand, sir."

"I doubt that, Ernest. All thirty-six of our facilities are at your disposal."

"I do understand."

Domergue stepped closer. The Man never allowed anyone in his space, kept a careful circle around him of at least five feet, never shook hands, nearly always towered over everyone in a room. The sudden towering proximity disconcerted Gies. "Especially Colombia, Ernest."

"Yes, sir." He knew what The Man meant: unsanctioned human trials by the thousands if need be. Fine. Gies would limit his trials to prisoners, with the blessing of the Colombian government. Violent men who might even be helped by the protocol. At least, that was how he rationalized it. He knew he was rationalizing, but it's what kept him borderline sane.

"Do you believe your student is right?" Domergue stepped close to the glass, staring at the other struggling subjects.

"Yes, sir. Ada saw trends before a computer could plot them."

"Well, then. It is well that I have shut her down."

Gies stared at Domergue's broad back, hating him, despising his cold rationality. One thing he hated about The Man was the way he spoke perfect, uncontracted English. He doubted The Man was French as his name implied, nor was he English, American, German, Italian or any other obvious nationality. The mystery of The Man bothered Gies to the point of obsession. "No one can shut down Doctor Ada Kenner, sir."

"It is done." Domergue turned.

Gies felt a flutter of anxiety. "What have you done?"

Domergue smiled tightly, his perfect white teeth gleaming. "No, not the twins."

Gies took a long breath. He couldn't bear the thought of the twins stalking Ada Kenner. "Thank you."

"Do not thank me." Domergue's voice never changed, but the hint of menace was obvious. "I have called the U.S. president. Doctor Ada Kenner is relieved of her role in this affair."

"Thank God, then." Still, he doubted anything would stop Ada Kenner.

Domergue smiled tightly. "Make no mistake, Doctor Gies. She may be prohibited from shutting down our plants, but if she is a sufficient nuisance, other solutions may be required."

"Mr. Domergue. I trust you'll remember my goodwill depends on Ada Kenner being safe and well."

"Do I look like a guardian angel, Doctor?" His voice was deep and flat. What Gies heard was, *Don't threaten me, Doctor.*

12

Atlanta, Georgia

The manager of Atlanta's most prestigious golf club stared down at Ada from a so-hip Segway. The man balanced on the two-wheeled gyroscopic pogo stick, a man of sharp contrasts: nut-brown, sun-kissed skin and a denture smile framed by white hair, bleached white dress shirt and cuffed white trousers.

"I'm sorry," the manager said, his tone a peculiar mix of civility and firmness. "You are not a member. Wives may only enter by invitation, Ms. Tomich—"

"Doctor Kenner," she said, her tone betraying lack of sleep. She hadn't rested since the nap on Bane's plane. Bane himself had disappeared as mysteriously as he had appeared in her life.

The manager of the golf club smiled, his teeth artificially perfect. "Doctor Tomich may not wish his ex-wife on the links, no?"

"It's important."

"Your ex-husband plays in a foursome. Very powerful people, Doctor Kenner."

Ada glanced at her watch. She had no time for the manager of the Green Lake Country Club to play his stiff role as gatekeeper. The prim man stepped down off his Segway, and she was astonished to realize he was two inches shorter than her own five-foot-nine. "Come with me, Doctor Kenner. You can wait in my office. How would that be?"

He walked past her, obviously expecting her to follow to the old stone mansion that served as a club house.

Ada stared at the Segway. The magnetic key lock was still in place, and she felt sure she remembered how to ride. "I'm very sorry," she said. She jumped up on the Segway.

"Doctor Kenner!"

She grabbed the handle and twisted the steering control. The gyros purred as the two-wheeler spun to the right, and then she leaned forward. The electric motors hummed as she flew across the rolling fairways of the Green Lake Country Club, pursued by the aging manager. The ride was rougher on the fairways than her last Segway tour, but she found it exhilarating and easy.

"Stop right now, Ms. Kenner!" She looked back, surprised the manager had kept up with her. His face was purple. She would never forgive herself if he had a coronary. Finally he stopped and bent over his knees. A faint voice called out, "I shall call the police!"

She leaned further forward, felt the burst of speed as she bounced down a long sweeping fairway, past a lake and groves of magnolias, then up a steep green hill.

You're too impulsive, Ada, her ex would tell her when he came to visit her in jail. Will you never learn?

She looked over her shoulder. Five golf carts and three Segways pursued her.

She sped along the shoreline of a small lake, focusing on the foursomes of golfers. They all had Segways or golf carts, probably necessary on such a challenging course. Ada saw no women on the greens or tees as she flew past, just silver-haired white men in dress slacks or cuffed shorts. Green after green, the immaculate course went on past lakes and stately oak trees, up steep hills and down plunging gullies—but no Devon. She nearly knocked over a groundskeeper—a black man in crisp green overalls; what must he have thought, she wondered, seeing the wild woman with her brown fedora, zooming by on a two-wheeler, pursued by scowling white security guards in golf carts?

Ahead was a perfectly manicured green, nestled between two groves of pyramidal oak. At last. Devon was about to sink his ball, looking particularly tanned and relaxed in Bermuda shorts.

She recognized Senator Stephens from his tours of the CDC. Ada surged up the slight rise onto the green, startling Devon and sending his putt wild. She tumbled off the Segway and fell near her ex's feet, somehow still clutching her bag.

"Well, that's some entrance," Devon said, looking mischievous and too handsome. It seemed unfair that he looked better now than when they were married more than a decade ago.

Devon glanced at his ball, now well off the green, and then back at Ada. His mouth trembled but revealed no other hint of annoyance. She rolled lightly to her feet and snatched up her crumpled hat.

Senator Stephens was silver-haired, his skin pasty white and scarred from a recent melanoma surgery. A wide Tilley hat and ample belly gave him a harmless, touristy look, contrasted by piercing predatory eyes. She knew him only from a hallway-hello at the CDC, and news clips. Riley Stephens was on several Senate Committees, including oversight on the CDC and the subcommittee on Homeland Security.

"Ada Tomich, isn't it?" The senator smiled, clearly amused, and held out his gloved hand.

She shook it lightly, forcing her best smile. "Kenner now, sir. Thank you for remembering."

Devon shot her a hard look.

Five of the security guards finally caught up.

Stephens laughed and waved at them. "It is all right. She's with us." His eyes lingered on her cleavage and she remembered news stories about Stephens, the philanderer.

The guards hovered, putting on fierce expressions, probably convinced Ada was an assassin or maniac. The Senator smiled and raised his voice: "Gentlemen, if you've dispatched the police or SWAT teams, please call them off. False alarm."

One security guard nodded and radioed in. No jail today, she hoped.

Ada stared at Devon. "You've been avoiding me."

Devon couldn't stop smiling. "Ada, I trust the end of the world is nigh."

Not so far from the truth. Ada snatched the golf club from his hand. "You canceled my BioSecure Notice at Site F."

Devon led her off the green to the shade of an ancient dogwood. He pulled off his gloves. "Ada, our teams determined no contamination. They voluntarily toured you through the facility. You and Bane. Did you find this missing witness, Begley's body or the deputies?"

"No."

"And I trust you're not planning a new career as a detective."

"And my investigation of the virus?" Her cool had returned, the famous Kenner veneer of utter serenity.

"There is no investigation. All the threads are wrapped up, so far as I can see."

"Who called you?"

"Pardon me?" His too-glittery eyes fixed on her, that flinty look that so annoyed her. It reminded her of their many fights after Quentin was born. "Tell me, Ada, what motivates you to disobey my orders, fly off to France, issue containment orders on your own without any lab work, then burst in here like some madwoman?"

Ada tensed; the muscle fibers in her neck twitched. This was too important for them not to work together, but did Devon always have to be an insufferable prick? "Devon, there's too much at stake here for you to play the 'I know better' position with me."

Senator Stephens leaned on his club watching them, although she doubted he could hear a word. "There's nothing at stake here at all, so far as I can see. Doctor Begley infected himself with a non-airborne Borna virus. He died."

She raised her voice for the first time. "And this mysterious cleanup by fraudulent hazmat teams?"

"Not your business. Not Bane's business, either. Leave it for the cops, okay?"

"No, it's not okay. What about my vectors? My models showing trajectories of violence?"

He snorted, an ugly habit she remembered only too well. "Ada, we work in conclusive, verifiable science. We're not psychiatrists hunting trends of violence. One minute you're a cop, the next you're Dr. Freud. Make up your mind."

"There's more to this than TV-provoked violence."

"So you say."

"You used to trust me."

"That was a long time ago." She could almost hear the subtext, *and you betrayed that trust.*

"I'm not wrong."

"You never think you're wrong. Ada, you have been wrong. You will be wrong again. And this is an amazing stretch even for your stunning brain."

"I can show you maps. Vectors. I trace it all back to LA. To Braxis."

He rubbed his neck with his gloved hand. "Yes, I see. It's unusual for people in the city of angels to be violent. And episodes in Islamabad and Hong Kong vector right back to our friends at Braxis, because they never have murders, right? I've seen nothing, Ada. Nothing. You've no evidence."

"The Director at WART believes me."

"That clown? Do you know how close he is to a jail cell himself? He's an outlaw with a badge, honey. And worse, a joker. Do you know how he got his job?"

Ada sighed. "No. I assumed because he's a celebrity. That reality TV killer thing."

"Oh, that's just the tip. From his stint in the military, to the FBI, to the Vermont State Police, he's been a troublemaker. He goes after officials, politicians, whoever. He lets his mouth run on with journalists. They made him head of WART because WART was supposed to be a joke, like anything sponsored by the UN."

"That's pretty harsh."

"Senator Stephens over there recommended him. Among others. They have history." He jerked his thumb at the senator on the green. "They thought they were getting Bane out of the way. As Chief of Detectives he was going after the state governor, senators, anyone in power. WART was almost created just for him. After all, what can a UN investigatory body do? They have no real authority."

"He seemed to have plenty of authority."

Devon laughed. "Yes, a thorn in every politician's side, right up to the president. It's worse now, because he takes it all seriously."

"Shouldn't he?"

"Chasing terrorists with a few men and machine guns? I'll admit he's sharp. Too sharp. But he's one step away from being a pirate himself. Breaks international laws everywhere he goes, then uses his badge and sense of humor to escape prosecution."

"What about Pakistan?"

Devon shook his head. "His work on Khan is the only reason he gets away with all of this nonsense. Take down one terror network, and the whole world worships the man. Craziness!"

Ada felt her own anger rising. Devon was the obstacle, not the jokester named Bane. "Bane is the only one doing anything about this!"

"And that should tell you how wrong you are. He's a rogue. A problem. Every world government complains about him and his thugs."

"You're saying Bane's never right?"

"No, he's a lucky one, that's true. But he's not accountable. No one knows where he is now."

"Not my business." Bane was a cowboy, that was certain. He had disappeared, following up on Ada's Incidents as he called them, and intensifying his investigation of Braxis, Gies and Manheim the security chief. But there was no reason to tell Devon any of this.

"Well, from what I've heard, he's probably kidnapping people off the street and torturing them for information. It's not his results, but his methods. He hurts as many people as he helps."

"And you're saying I'm doing that too? That I'm your Bane. Literally?"

"Financial liabilities for Braxis and stocks tumbling? Panic in the streets? Journalists following you around for a story. You tell me."

"You're paranoid. You read my report on Flight 411? And Manchester? We now have 632 incidents on my Parameter Watch."

His eyes betrayed rage, even if his voice didn't. "Another unauthorized abuse. I didn't approve your PIW." He stepped closer, hulking over her, trying his old intimidation routine. "Ordinary people go off the deep end all the time, Ada. All the time. I nearly did once when we were married."

"That was nice."

"Not so nice. I know. But Ada, you're emotionally involved here. It's distorting your sense of perspective. Where's your proof?"

"I ask you again, Dev. Who got to you?"

"I conferenced with World Health, USAMRIID, the Secretary of—"

"I know you're not happy that I applied for the position of coordinator of Emerging. But you should know why it's important for me."

"I know. That's why I didn't fight it."

What did he mean by that? 'Didn't fight it' wasn't quite the same as saying, 'I approved it.' She took a long breath. "You know what drives me."

"Yes." He sighed. "Ada, ten years is long enough for me to put aside bitterness. I'm not happy you applied, but you are the best virologist in the CDC. You and I both want the same thing. You're just obsessed with it. Which is why I shut your investigation down. Obsessive coordinators aren't good for the image of the CDC."

"This is about image?" Of course it was. She struggled not to scowl. Her entire life was dedicated to eradicating viruses. They killed without conscience. More people died each year from disease than from any other cause. A virus had destroyed her son's life. What was obsessive about that?

"Devon, I just need you to listen. Since my promotion, you've ignored every request for a meeting. You turned down my request to go to the Braxis conference—"

"You went anyway." His voice was clipped, terse. "Anyone else, I would have reprimanded officially."

"Anyone else, you probably would have commended, Devon, so cut the crap." She controlled her tone, kept it flat and low.

"Like I said, obsessed—"

"Just listen. This is hard enough, having you as my boss."

"I suppose I have no choice." He shaded his eyes and watched one of his foursome sink his ball. "Damn. So. What is so urgent that you come within minutes of unemployment?" He gave her a flash of straight white teeth. Of course she was a government employee, very difficult to fire, but theft of a Segway and trespassing meant Devon could make life very miserable for her at the CDC.

She wanted to slap his smug face. Instead, she pulled her laptop from her brown bag, cradled it in the crook of her elbow, and woke it from sleep mode. The screen lit up. "I've tracked several incident hotspots." She spoke quickly, but she knew Devon wouldn't be so fast to act; he would need all the facts. Even their divorce had taken years.

He leaned closer, peering at her screen. "Maps?"

"Hotspots."

"Violence hotspots? That's easy. Just pick any big urban center. Voila. Instant violence hotspot."

"Devon—just listen!"

"I'm trying."

She ignored his sarcasm, her voice calm and measured. "I've found hundreds of apparently unrelated incidents where suspects—with no history of violence—go on homicidal rampages. They later die—hemorrhaging from nostrils, eyes, ears. Elevated white counts and SED rates."

"How do you know this?"

"Some died in detention. I asked for autopsies."

"You what?" He scowled openly now, his authority challenged.

"I don't need your authority to requisition autopsies."

He pressed his lips together until they whitened. "Look, Ada, we're the CDC, not the FBI." He held up his hand. "And next time, I insist you go through me before issuing Parameter Incident Watches to the FBI, FEMA, USAMRIID, various metropolitan police forces and hospitals."

"I would have gone through you if you had replied to any of my requests."

Once they had shared a bed, now she was lucky if he read her emails. She stayed focused and clicked the *page down* button on her keyboard. Devon's face winced as he took in the autopsy photos, and she regretted her dramatics, but it was important he understand what was at stake. Devon loved children, one of his few endearing traits. "This is baby Joseph. What's left of him." She watched Devon's face, no longer stony but still not easy to read. "Sixteen-year-old single mother Sarah Levine, a month ago, just after the fourth of July, walking her baby, for no apparent reason pushed baby Joseph's stroller down Telegraph Hill in San Francisco, catapulting her baby down the slope. Witnesses reported Sarah laughed as her nine-month-old baby rear-ended a taxicab, fracturing his skull."

"Horrible. Did you come here just to gross me out? Spoil my day?"

"Police interviews of Sarah's family—she lived with her parents—indicated Sarah loved her baby. Well-adjusted kid for a single mom, just won a place in the semi-finals of the reality television show *Superstar*. On her way to Venice for the finals. Sarah was just getting over a flu."

"You're here because she had a flu?"

Ada realized she would have to slow it down and let him digest. The senator and the other two men in the foursome gathered around the screen, crowding Devon.

"Private business, gentlemen," she snapped.

"Ada, everyone here is involved with CDC oversight," Devon said.

Ada had no idea what "involved" meant. She changed the image on her computer screen, ignoring the fatigue in her arm. "This is the carnage caused by a seventeen-year-old boy. Shot nine students and one teacher in Vermont—Senator Stephen's home state I believe."

"Ada—"

She clicked the *down* key. "A real estate agent in Utah, now called the Crosswalk Killer in the media because he ran down sixteen pedestrians crossing at intersections."

"Enough, Ada," Devon said. "Violence is nothing new to America. Or the world." He pushed her laptop away with the shaft of his putter.

She clicked another key. "Two days ago, this slaughterhouse worker ground up his girlfriend in a processor at a sausage plant. We don't know yet if they recalled all the affected sausages."

"You have a flair for the grotesque," Senator Stephens said. His eyes still seemed fixated on Ada's low-cut top.

"And this is why you involved WART, the police and FBI? Quarantined an airplane?" Devon sounded furious. "I assume so, because clearly this has nothing to do with Emerging Viruses."

"But Devon, it does."

The corner of Devon's mouth twitched. "Is that so?"

"All of these vectors of—of violence—are perpetrated by people who have psychotic breaks."

"Jesus Lord, now you're a psychiatrist?"

She snapped her laptop closed. "Yesterday, a mild-mannered accountant blew up Toon Lagoon in Universal Studios. Thirty-six children died. Forty-two others maimed, lost limbs."

"Horrible," Stephens said. "I know about this. I believe Homeland Security suspects terrorists."

She shook her head. "Not terrorists. Police detained an accountant. A teenaged girl whose parents died in the explosion turned him in. He has no connections to terrorism."

"Then he's crazy." Devon stabbed the air with his putter. "Point is, Ada, you're coordinator of Emerging Viruses. *Viruses*."

"Exactly. Viruses. I've had blood samples, liver slice and brain section of the bomber sent bio-secure to our Level Four lab here."

"He died?"

"Explosive hemorrhaging six hours ago."

"Good Lord! Not Ebola?" Senator Stephens wiped his forehead with the back of his hand, and Ada noticed he was sweating.

"No, not Ebola, senator. Something new."

"Come on, Ada. Six months on the job and you discover an Emerging Virus? Your predecessor found three emerging viruses, all in the Congo area, in seven years at his post."

"Then I promise not to find any more this year. Okay? Can I continue?" She glared at Devon, noticing how they had slipped into the arguing-spouse zone. Was this how it would be, working with him? "Devon, we're dealing with something neurovirulent. And an immune system firestorm that is unprecedented."

"Contagious?" Senator Stephens continued to drip perspiration.

"All viruses are contagious, Senator. We don't know how this transmits, but that has to be our first mission. Of course, I can't be sure it's a virus. Could be bacterial. But it's spreading, so it's highly indicative."

Devon threw his putter to the grass. "Oh for Christ's sake, Ada, don't get ahead of yourself."

Ada turned a little to the side, partially shielding her bosom from the prying eyes of Senator Stephens. "I have information from Doctor Ernest Gies at Braxis. He referred me to a Doctor Begley in the Braxis LA facility. They are the leading experts in immunopathology in the central nervous system. The same Doctor Begley, now dead from explosive hemorrhaging."

"It's not enough," Devon said.

"No, I suppose not. Not when the CEO of Braxis is on the phone with you telling you how to run my department."

"Shut up, Ada."

"Shut up? That's all you can say?"

"I may have to shackle you to your lab. But I'm not going to have you running off on whims all around the world."

"I remember the shackles," Ada snapped, suddenly angry. She felt the heat boiling up.

He stared at her, lip trembling again.

Devon stepped closer to her, his face inches away. His breath smelled of brandy. "Ada, a moment alone?"

Stephens and the others slipped off, leaving them in the shade of the tree.

Devon sighed. "You never change. Always the drama."

She said nothing. Only drama worked with Devon. They both knew it.

"Are you going to let me pursue this?"

"It's either that or I have to fire you."

"You should know that won't work either."

"I know." He waved his hand. "Fine. Go. Do your thing. You always do."

"Then I'm returning to LA to examine the bodies." She turned to go.

"But I'll authorize no quarantines without evidence."

"I know."

She started to walk away. Walk faster, before he changes his mind.

"Aren't you going to ask about Quentin?"

Ada felt a flutter and the rise of heat. "Is Quentin all right?"

"Quentin's fine. He's in the special school now."

"Yes. I know." She had enrolled her son.

"He's learning to use prosthetics."

She knew Devon was trying to divert her, to manipulate her by appealing to the guilt that had once ripped her life to shreds, and still held her personal life paralyzed. She closed her eyes, fighting the tears. She saw Quentin there, in that dark place of her mind—in his wheelchair, or hobbling through life on prosthetics—because of her. Because of her carelessness with viruses. Because of her ambition.

He had dug up these memories with a purpose. "Go screw yourself, Devon."

"Can we stop this, Ada? Do we have to be so hateful?"

"I'm not the one who fought for custody." She found herself yelling. "I'm not the one who sued. Who took my only child from me." She hated how immature she sounded.

He didn't lower his head, didn't look ashamed. "Ada, you were emotionally unstable back then. No one could stand being near you. Then you lost yourself in your work. It wasn't hard to convince a judge.

Ada said nothing. There was nothing to say. He was right, but that didn't make it feel right.

"Ada, I want you back in Quentin's life. He needs you."

She stared at him. Tears pooled. "You pushed me out of his life."

"I've changed. The anger's gone. Mostly." He smiled. "Come see him?"

The tears flowed. "Yes."

"Stop blaming yourself," Devon said.

Devon being sweet infuriated her; Devon being right just made it worse. "How can I?"

"It was an accident."

"I was pregnant!" She shouted it. "I was pregnant and had no business playing with viruses. Don't you understand?"

"Yes. I understand. For years I believed that, too. That's why I fought to keep you away."

He rolled his top lip under his bottom lip, an old habit. Bittersweet memories took hold of her. Devon laughing as he pulled her out of the airplane on their first skydive and they fell for long moments, face to face. Devon making love to her on the beach in Spain. Devon crying at her mother's funeral.

"No, I was wrong not to try to understand your feelings," he said gently. He reached out his hand, as if to touch her, but then he dropped it to his side. "We were both angry. But it was an accident. And Quentin's our child."

She couldn't listen to this. Not without crying. Ada climbed on the Segway. "I'll call you from LA"

"Do that."

She sped off over the fairways of the Green Lake Country Club, the wind of her flight carrying away the tears.

13

Las Vegas, Nevada

The nine days in the *Superstar* audition line-up, under the animated dome of Freemont Street, had been a blast. But now that they approached the front of the queue, Joy Hensley, hope of Orovada, felt only anxiety. This was their big shot at fame, an audition for *Superstar*, but everyone in line had a cold, including her singing partner and fiancé Monty. He could barely talk.

Ten days ago, she had packed her best clothes in her Roots backpack and set out on a hot September morning to hitchhike to Las Vegas. She brought two pairs of jeans—plus one Veronique Branquinho outfit bought with a year of savings from part-time work at Mickey D's on Route 95—a tent and two-person sleeping bag, and fiancé Monty. He brought his too-charming smile and four hundred and sixty-three dollars.

Las Vegas was a sparkling wonder. Though they had no money for the casinos, they had wandered the strip, enjoying the press of people, the lights at night, the boozy casualness of the casino. To Joy, Vegas was the honey pot of the world. She might never visit the exotic cities of the world, but here in Vegas, in this adult playground, she recognized people from every country. Joy and Monty joined the thousands in line on Freemont Street for the *Superstar* audition. They slept and ate in line, watching the light show on the block-long domed roof that covered the old casino strip and enjoying the Mardi Gras–style parades. They partied with new friends, practiced songs on each other, laughed, buzzed much of the time, hammed it up for the camera crews. They saw their own faces on dozens of giant screens lit up with the *Superstar* microphone logo. The overhead dome lit up with giant images of *Superstar* hopefuls. They cheered as their fellow contestants sang, booed as the judges tore into and rejected contestants, many of them hoarse because of their colds.

Abbey Chase, the elegant producer of the show, seemed particularly vicious, crushing the hopes of many auditioners, sending most of them away in tears. Chaos's seat at the judges table remained empty, an eerier reminder of the tragedy.

The show's host, Kenji—the Ken Bomb the girls in line called him as they drooled over his giant movie star–handsome face on the big screens—intercepted the teary rejects on camera and tried to calm them as they left the audition room.

The people in line shuffled forward. After so long in line, nervousness transformed to jitters as the line entered the open doors of the Golden Nugget. The stench of cigarettes and the "jing, jing, jing" of slot machines assailed them as they stepped through the wide open doors. The line wound between banks of machines occupied by overweight tourists sipping on their endless flow of free drinks. Scattered throughout the busy casino floor were more flat-screen televisions and enormous speakers that somehow never overcame the loud electronic jingle of slot machines.

The line in front of them shrank to a dozen as Abbey Chase tore into every hopeful star. Monty was foggy now, almost delirious; he had gulped down an entire bottle of Benylin DM cough syrup.

Feeling nauseous, Joy slipped off to the casino washrooms and freshened, then changed into her low cut designer dress. When she returned, only eight remained in front of them. Now, after days of waiting and wishing the line would move, Joy found she wanted to be at the end of the line again.

"We'll make it," Monty said, hoarsely. He coughed, spraying her with spittle. Joy didn't answer. She felt suddenly hot. He was so dopey from the medicines that he seemed to be buzzing and high. It wasn't fair. After all the weeks of practice, the days in line, they would lose because of a damn cold.

They stepped into a chilly theatre, normally the sparkling home of old style can-can dancers. The stage was empty except for a small table in front of the three judges. Joy felt waves of panic. It was hard to move her feet forward.

She tried to look at the judges, and avoided the cameras. What was she supposed to do now? Unable to stare into Abbey's cold green eyes, Joy focused on Chaos's empty chair. Chaos had been the nicest of the judges in LA and Frisco.

"Joy," Monty whispered and he nudged her. Joy realized she had been standing there—for how long?

"Joy Hensley and Marty Bradley. A duet." Abbey Chase said the word *duet* as if it were a four-letter word.

"That's Monty," Monty said, his voice hoarse.

Abbey Chase interrupted him with, "Whenever you're ready, Marty."

He coughed. "Bad cold." Abbey stared at him. There'd be no sympathy for sickness in the audition. Monty took Joy's hand in his and she felt his sweat. "Now, Joy." Monty squeezed harder, hurting her, but it helped. Her voice burst out, lyrics too staccato and upbeat. She concentrated, slowed down, wavered a moment out of tune, then hit perfect pitch. The judges leaned forward and she opened up her vocals.

Now it was Monty's turn to fumble. He missed his cue and sang flat, then bent forward in a hacking cough.

Joy felt sure they had lost. Abbey Chase winced.

"That's enough," Abbey said, interrupting their song.

Monty's hand tightened on hers, almost painful.

"I liked them," judge Garraty said.

"No." Abbey's unblinking green eyes made Joy want to run from the room before the cameras could record her tears. How could someone so strikingly beautiful be so unspeakably ugly? Abbey was, perhaps, the most stylish and elegant woman Joy had ever seen. Even after ten hours of straight-through judging under the lights, she seemed cool and lovely, her big green eyes friendly and her smile charming, her waves of brown hair magnificent; but the words that came out of her perfect lips were pure poison. "That was painful to listen to."

"I have a cold," Monty repeated.

"It wouldn't make any difference, Marty," Abbey said, and she shook her head. "But Joy was wonderful."

"I'm down with that," Garraty said.

Abbey Chase smiled. "Joy, you're in." Life-changing words. No more small town Nevada for Joy Hensley. She was on her way to Venice, Italy for the semi-finals, courtesy of the Real TV network. First class airlines, luxury hotels and room service, making love in a queen size bed with the curtains drawn back to reveal a view of the Grand Canal. Joy screamed. For joy.

Monty swept her in his arms, smiled, kissed her, and wiped away her tears.

Abbey Chase held up her hand. "Marty—Monty—we can't take you. We don't take teams. Even if we did, frankly, you're terrible. Joy's lucky to be in after that duet."

Joy dropped her arms, but held on to one of Monty's hands. "We're a—we're a couple."

The nights of sleeping on the sidewalk, the weeks of practice, the endless high on adrenalin, the fear and the ecstasy, the sore throat, it all crashed in on Joy. She swayed against Monty, dizzy and fading. Monty propped her up, holding her arm and fanning her face at the same time. "Of course she'll go," his voice full of hurt and pride. He turned Joy and looked into her eyes, smiled, kissed her on the cheek. "She's going." Monty the martyr. Joy knew him well enough to know he didn't really want her to go, that he was angry. His words said "go," his eyes said "don't you dare."

Abbey shrugged and Garraty raised his eyebrows, then nodded, but neither said a word. Monty pulled Joy from the room, slammed the door, whooped his best Nevada "Eeooow!" and shouted, "She's in!" The crowd roared. They had seen it all on the screens, but they cheered.

Kenji, the oh-so-hot host of the show approached them, camera crews in tow. When Joy tried to weave past him, he gently intercepted. "I know how upset you are," Kenji said. He made a knife motion with his hand, slicing it in front of his throat. The red light on the camera went off. "Are you all right, Joy?"

Joy swayed. Kenji, the Japanese hottie. His eyes glittered behind overlong sheepdog bangs. She had a crush on Kenji when he won Abbey Chase's last reality show, *Haunted Survivor*. Now, here he was, talking to her. A big star, talking to her.

"It is best for both of you." Kenji stepped closer to Monty. "You understand that, do you not?" He tilted his head slightly. "You look angry, Monty."

Monty said nothing, but he nodded. Kenji hesitated one more moment, then walked through the crowd, pursued by autograph hounds.

Monty sneered. "Who does he think he is? You're going on the road with him? I don't think so." Monty seemed beyond angry. He continued to stare at Kenji as the TV host settled by the stage doors to capture the next contestant. It was hard to tell under all the hair, but Kenji seemed to be staring back. "There's no way you're going without me," Monty said, his voice a near growl. "Maybe I can get a job. Save for a ticket."

"Maybe."

"You don't think so."

"No. It's a lot of money."

"What about me?" Monty said.

Joy reached out and stroked Monty's hand. "I'll be back."

He pulled his hand away and his frown made him unattractive, his face full of ugly hostility. The last time she had seen him like this was two summers ago, and they broke up for three months, an entire season spoiled by his pouting and jealousy. Only this time he seemed worse.

"Go to Venice. Forget about me." He turned his back to her. "I don't need you." He sneezed. Then, without looking back, he disappeared around a bank of slot machines.

Joy knew he expected her to follow. He was waiting for her to run up to him and plead for forgiveness. "Oh, Monty, we'll find a way," she was supposed to say.

Instead, she turned quickly and left the casino, slipping out into the crowds on Freemont Street. On what should have been the happiest night of her life, Joy found herself hiding from Monty. Predictably, she heard him calling after her. She hesitated, but she wasn't ready to reconcile with him. She fled, consumed with guilt and anger.

Certain she had lost him, she went from casino to casino, until she tired of the crowds. At the end of Freemont, where the domed street ended and the glitter of casinos faded to darker night, she made the mistake of leaving the crowds. She wanted to be alone. She needed time to figure everything out.

Disoriented, she hesitated. The street was empty. Behind her she heard the crowd and the casinos.

She turned.

And there was Monty.

He looked wild, his eyes glazed and staring.

"You can't go," he said, sounding congested. He sneezed a long rope of reddish snot. "You can't go without me." He laughed.

In his hand was his pearl-handled knife, the blade folded open.

14

Wynn, Las Vegas

Bane felt oddly apprehensive as the elevator doors opened. There were only four suites in the private suites tower, top level. The halls were about as wide as his entire bungalow in Vermont. An armed guard frowned at Bane.

Bane flashed his badge. "I'm here to see Ms. Chase."

The man shook his head once, his gnarly forearms folded across a chest about as wide as the state of Texas.

"Tell her—tell her Beaver's here to see her." He smiled tightly. "An old friend." Old friend was a major exaggeration. She had been a suspect, obstacle, pain in the ass, later a lover, but never a friend. She had once called him the *Leave it to Beaver* detective. Go figure.

"You'll need an appointment. Sir."

Bane fingered his belt-holstered revolver, a chromed special engraved by the director of the FBI. "Here's my invite."

The guard's gun was bigger, but he looked as lumbering as he was gigantic. Probably Abbey chose him for his chiseled muscles and square-jawed good looks. Still, if the door hadn't opened in that minute, Bane felt sure he would have created another carpet stain.

"It's all right, Jimmy," said a soft, husky, almost breathless voice. Bane caught the familiar waft of Sandalwood, her favorite scent.

"Well, well. Abbey Chase in the luscious flesh." Still Armani-perfect. Time had been good to her, much kinder than she deserved with her nasty karma. Leggy, magnificent, lofty, perfect teeth and smile, her dress, as always, daringly low-cut and leaving nothing to the imagination.

"Alby." She studied him carefully with those magnificent blue eyes. "Your taste in clothes hasn't improved. Come in, my darling."

Reluctantly, and not without a solid glare at Bane, Jimmy stood aside. Bane winked at him and entered the black widow's web. She lightly kissed both his cheeks. "Still smell like vinegar and French Fries. I missed you, Alby."

"I missed you too, cutthroat movie-producer bitch."

She laughed and turned quickly, offering a visual treat as she sashayed into the expansive salon with floor-to-ceiling views of an illuminated Vegas strip. She sat with typical elegance on one of the two red sofas, crossing her enchantingly flawless legs; her hem slipped back to reveal perfect thigh. Bane almost sat on the opposite couch, but Abbey gave him a sharp look, and patted the cushion beside her. "Here, Beaver, here. Don't sit waaaaay over there."

She looked so warm and inviting in her daring scarlet dress, with her too-good-for-Alban-Bane smile, perfect hair, makeup-free face and those lips he remembered so well. He could still taste them. Bane wondered how he ever gave her up. Abbey was a hard habit to break, although she was no healthier a habit than street drugs.

A fifty-inch plasma television nestled in the drapes in the center of the skyline view. It was tuned, of course, to her own network, Real TV, a reminder of her "true" nature—conniving, twisted, rich, deadly, not to be trusted. She had spun a single, desperate reality television show into a mini-empire after the multiple murders on the set of *Haunted Survivor* drove record ratings.

"You're here about the murder, aren't you?" She leaned close enough for him to smell mint. "You're not a detective anymore, are you, Alby?"

"No, just a smart-mouth son of a bitch." He smiled.

"Did I call you that?"

"Among other things."

"How are your heart-breakers?"

"After Jen's braces came out, she couldn't keep the boys away. A father's nightmare. Mags isn't talking to me."

"Same old."

"Yes. Same old here with you, too, Abs? Greed, corruption, lies, cheating."

"Something like that." She ducked in for a quiet kiss, a light brush of intoxicating Abbey Chase.

"What was that for?"

"Old times?"

He sighed. "Old times imply fond memories."

"You don't have happy memories of us?"

"The sex was good," he said.

"The sex was okay."

"Ouch." He stared hard at her chiseled features. "Yes, I'm here about the murder of Joy Hensely. Once again, Real TV becomes Murder TV. And no, I'm not a detective anymore."

"Drink?"

He shook his head.

"I think I will." Again her poised movements were strictly for his benefit as she glided rather than walked over to the bar. He heard the tinkle of ice in a glass. She was perhaps the only person alive who could throw off his concentration. "Surely, you're not investigating her murder. Her boyfriend stabbed her, pretty much a simple case, isn't it?"

"Yes. And he's now isolated in the hospital."

"So?" She returned to the couch and sat so close their legs touched. "Sure about the drink?"

"Sure." He hesitated as she pressed her shoulder into his, then her hand was on his thigh. "Business, Abbey."

"Of course. You know this is how I conduct business."

"That's why your nickname is Manipulative Bitch."

"You should know by now I'm impervious to your barbs and jokes."

"That's what attracted me to you."

She leaned even closer, her breath hot and Scotch-flavored on his cheek. "I thought it was my ass—and other equipment."

"Those too. It was your balls that turned me off. Oh, they don't dangle, but they're bigger than mine."

"Why? Because I don't sweat in the presence of the great Alban Bane?"

"No. Because I've never seen you sweat." And it was true. Even when she nearly died at the hands of a psychopath, she never thawed, not for a moment. "I'm here to ask you a favor."

She set down her drink. Crossed her long, long legs the other way, brushing his calf with her shoeless foot. "Any time, Beaver."

"No. Not that."

"Hmmm? Sure?"

"Almost sure." He felt hot. She was always better than he was at this game. "Abs, this is serious."

"So was last time. People dying all around us. But we found time."

"Well, same old."

"People dying? A young girl. Killed by her boyfriend in a rage."

"More than that, Abs, and you're smart enough to know it."

"You mean the mini-riot in line?"

"Forty-three people injured is hardly minor. From my reports, all had a flu-bug."

"So?"

"So as always, wherever your reality shows go, death follows."

"Oh, come on. I don't control jealousy, riots or viruses. I'm a goddess, yes, but not that sort."

"An evil, cunning goddess. It's a big turn-on."

"I know."

"Abbey, I know you'll say no, but I'm asking you to temporarily suspend your mini-talent time."

She drew back for the first time. "Alban Bane. You should know better. You could never shut me down in Vermont. There's more at stake now."

"A lot more."

She laughed lightly. "If I had to stop to care about every person in America, I'd never get anything done." She picked up her glass and posed herself by the panoramic view at the windows. "This is Vegas, dear Alban. People get hurt all the time."

"My little Popsicle Queen." Bane joined her and looked down at the lights and flash of the strip.

"I'm never cold to you, Alban."

"I'm not the one in the hospital."

"So give me a reason. How is this anything other than bad tempers in a four-day lineup?'

"I can't tell you that. Just do it for me."

She finished her Scotch. "You cost me millions in Vermont."

"I made you many more millions than that, Cold-Hearted Ice Bitch. Spin it as a publicity thing again. Feds shut me down, again."

"It's not that easy. Our tour goes from city to city around the world."

"You know, Abs, they may not have found the gene for it yet, but I'm sure wickedness is hereditary. Like those perfect breasts."

"I'm sure. Bane, you come here with your stupid one-liners, your French fry smell and your sweaty baseball cap and hope to charm me into shutting down a hundred-million-dollar show? Stupidity must be hereditary, too."

"You obviously don't have the compassion gene."

She smiled. "You've known that for a long time."

"Let's look at the facts, then. Chaos dies in Packistan. He's one of your judges. Killed by his own brother it now seems. There's an incident in Maine where the father of one of your auditioners drowns a clam chowder vendor in soup."

"That's original."

"Isn't it? Wish you had your cameras there, don't you."

She caressed his shoulder. "You know me so well."

"There's this guy in San Diego who shoots his old neighbor over dog poop. Turns out he auditioned for *Superstar*, too."

She pointed to Freemont street with it's sparkling light show. "Bane, in

Vegas alone we auditioned tens of thousands. In every city the same. You mean to tell me, out of all that, a few would-be contestants killing neighbors and brothers is all that odd?"

"I deal in the odds, Abbey. Odds are, yes. You heard about the Orlando bombing?"

"Terrible." She didn't sound all broken up about it. "Let me guess. The bomber auditioned, too."

He nodded.

"That's a stretch, Bane, even for you. Maybe it's me. They can't stand being turned down by the evil ice queen." She smiled again, and she did look evil then. "You're not telling me something."

"That's right. Because if I told you, you'd put it on television."

"Probably."

"I'm just asking for a few weeks. Delay the tour."

"No."

"I forgot. Violence and death add ratings. Dying is no reason not to have fun, right?"

"True." She leaned in close and kissed him lightly. She smelled so good. Her lips were hot. "Sure about the sex? I don't like French fries, but I don't mind fast food."

"No time. Have to get a court order." He felt the old simmer of anger. She made him hot in more ways than one.

"Good luck with that, Bane. You've tried court orders with me many times. Ever succeeded? You should know by now, I'm better connected than you."

15

Security Council, United Nations

The UN Security Council Committee—formally known as the Security Council Committee Established Pursuant to Resolution 2178, or SCCEPR2178—was one of the smallest oversight groups in the United Nations. The five senior members, Bane's bosses, made reporting problematic. He couldn't ignore their summons to report, but he couldn't tell them much either. He had learned long ago that anything reported to the Committee would become tomorrow's headlines.

With one of his teams tailing the Braxis security chief Manheim, unexpectedly on his way to Asia, another team focused on the terrorist arms dealer Khan in Pakistan, and the rest of his organization investigating outbreaks of violence around the world that might be related to the virus, Bane couldn't afford the time to report to a long-winded committee.

But they were his bosses. Oh, he would have to speak, but he didn't have to say anything.

All five members rose to their feet as the US Vice President Ernie Samuels entered the committee room to address the Emergency Oversight Session.

Alban Bane rose with the rest, out of respect for the guest, joining the chorus, "Mr. Vice President," at the same time thinking, how ridiculous is this? Another committee meeting in the midst of a crisis. The idiocy of it made him feel like a two-legged twinkie at a diet farm—all these giants lumbering about trying to eat him up.

Around the shining metal and birch-wood table were his bosses, the senior members of The Five, so called by the press, permanent members of the NSC, and the chief reason WART never finished a job: Doctor Norman Cahill for the United States, plus the other permanent members from China, France, the Russian Federation and the United Kingdom.

"Welcome as an honored guest, Mr. Vice President," said President Hong from China, the current Madame President of the Security Council, and committee chair of the WART Security Council Committee. "The Chair recognizes the honored guest."

"Thank you, Madame President," said Samuels, standing in front of the UN charter on the wall: *We the people of the United Nations, united for a better world,* in raised titanium letters. The vice president stooped a little and he didn't look well. He rubbed his eyes constantly. His first term in office had aged him twenty years in as many weeks. Streaks of grey spidered out from his temples to join in a swath of white. Bane knew rapid aging went with the job.

Samuels spared Bane one of his "I'm disappointed in you" fatherly frowns.

"I have asked to act as *rapporteur* on behalf of the United States in the Braxis matter," Samuels said, staring hard at Bane. "Madame President, Committee Members, it is the position of the US administration that Director Bane be prohibited from prosecuting his investigation of Braxis Genetics, Braxis

Pharmaceuticals or any of its divisions. Further, that disciplinary action be administered."

Bane listened as Samuels elaborated, exaggerating all the events since Begley's grand "escape" from Site F and making it sound like Bane was personally responsible for nearly crashing Flight 411. "I yield the floor, Madame President."

"Thank you, Mr. President," Madame President Hong said. "Director Bane, please make a brief statement."

Bane stood up, his Red Sox cap tucked under one armpit. Regardless of his statement, the Inquisition would follow, likely with a jolly crucifixion of cheery old Bane. It had been a nice nineteen months while it lasted. "Actually, Madame President, I am rather too busy for a roasting. Maybe we can reconvene in a few weeks. Perhaps we can invite the press and have a good old-fashioned Bane-roast. They'd love it."

Hong was not amused; her lined face tightened with anger. She never did have a sense of humor. "Director Bane, these are serious charges." She patted a pile of files as high as a stack of all-you-can-eat pancakes. "These are indictments from various law enforcement agencies of countries signatory to the United Nations. Your cost overruns alone are in the hundreds of millions. The liabilities and damages run to much more."

"Is this a good time to talk about early retirement?"

"Director Bane!" Hong snapped, sounding a little like Bane's own mother.

"We could invite the press to my retirement announcement. I prefer a trial by journalists."

The implicit threat wasn't lost on Hong. She stared at him for a long time, her ears reddening. "Director Bane, your fitness for this dignified and important post is certainly in question."

"I work out daily, Ma'am. At least a one-hour run. Three days a week, weights. Some Tae Kwon Do."

"Director Bane. Your antics are front page stories in every country."

"I'm photogenic." His sarcasm was the only defense he could offer. He would either be fired and retire to a beach in Barbados with his girls, where they'd never find him, or they'd get pissed off and let him get back to work. Any facts, any real facts, would only protract the Inquisition.

"Director!" She hesitated, took a long breath, glared at him, then relaunched her attack. "While no one here can argue with your results, especially with Khan in Pakistan, Afghanistan and Somalia, your methods are an embarrassment."

"Embarrassment is a state of mind."

"WART was meant to be investigatory, not enforcement."

"Sounds very UN to me. Perhaps the name should have been Committee for the Organized Study of Threats, then the acronym could be COST. More appropriate."

Hong pointedly ignored him, but Bane saw the Russian member Sergey smile. "You were our last choice," Hong said. "No one else wanted the post."

Bane nodded. "No one likes a Committee for a boss. Too many rules. I thought of this too. And you know what? I remembered an old saying my Pappy used to tell me. 'The only way to be really sure if there's a shark in the water is to jump right in. If there is, swim like hell.' Smartest man I ever knew, my Paps."

"So you think it's all right to rewrite the rules just to get things done?"

"Don't you, Madam President? Would you rather I send you a report on why it can't be done? Then wait for the Committee's six-hundred-page response? Let's examine the name of my young organization. World Advance Response Taskforce. Advance implies we act before a disaster, not after. Response implies we actually act. If I kill the bad guy, you're mad. If I don't kill the bad guy, you're mad. Fickle."

Hong sighed. "You're also a dangerous man. International law doesn't allow for worldwide kidnapping or assassination."

"If you play with lions, it's a good idea to have teeth. Dentures don't quite cut it." Teeth—and eyes. Even now, his teams were following Abbey Chase in Vegas, Braxis security chief Manheim in China, watching the Braxis CEO's estate in France, and playing cat and mouse with Khan in Africa.

She picked up a file. "On your recent trip to France, an International arms dealer disappeared."

Bane shrugged. "They disappear all the time. A nuisance." He couldn't tell them, of course, that the dissapearance coincided with a visit from the Braxis security chief Manheim, and that Bane himself had no idea of the location of this arms dealer, a man notorious for dealing in Stinger missles.

"Last week you were in Neubrandenburg. That same week a food processing plant mysteriously exploded."

It was also the week Manheim visited the factory. The explosion had been a shock to Bane, and killed one of his best men, a man tailing the Braxis security chief. Again, he couldn't tell his bosses. He gritted his teeth and said, "There was a rumor that the factory was making chemical weapons. That stuff's flammable."

"A rumor?" Hong slapped down the file with so much force every head snapped around. "Intolerable!" Hong's red ears glowed redder. Bane watched with fascination. "Your methods are simply unacceptable."

"Just because I'm a jerk and universally hated doesn't mean I'm responsible for every break-in, fire, or disappearance in every city I visit." He smiled. "Has it occurred to you that I might have simply been investigating these incidents?"

The president glared at him. "You've taken us back to the dark ages of the Cold War."

"Of Spy vs Spy? No, 9-11 did that. I keep running into covert operatives out there from all of your respective countries, and they have all the neatest toys, real James Bond stuff. I just have a cool jet, some helicopters and this." He tapped his head.

Madame President Hong sank back into her chair. "I yield the floor to anyone more patient than I."

Sergey Lavrov stood. "Madame, I take the floor," the Russian representative said, speaking in halting English. He was a big, smiling man with wide red cheeks and a good sense of humor, one of Bane's few allies. "So far, Russia is luckiest, no? Bane has only wrecked a couple cars." The members around the table laughed.

"Oh sure, you laugh at Sergey's jokes," Bane grumbled.

Sergey circled the table and rested his hand on Bane's shoulder. "Director Bane, I like you, yes? You like me too, yes?" He squeezed Bane's shoulder. "But pretend we know none of what you know, yes? Now, tell us what's really going on, yes? I mean with Flight 411 and this most attractive doctor from the Control Disease people."

Bane nodded and Sergey dropped his hand. Unfortunately, although he had no choice but to come when summoned, he also knew the U.N. was a leaky boat, and he didn't dare come clean. So, again he fell back on diversionary humor.

"Anyone here got a cold? No one?" Blank stares.

"You referring to the Parameter Incident Watch, yes?"

"A gold star, Sergey. All joking aside, this is no time to fire me. No time for committees. This goes beyond just a potential epidemic."

"If you are involved, it means more than a virus threat, no? Terrorism?"

"If I say yeah, it's terrorists, you'll all let me go flying out that door, won't you? You'll probably give me a cheer on the way out."

Sergey smiled. "You could be right. So, are we thinking terrorism?"

"Top of my list is our old friend Chaudhry Shujaa Khan." And Braxis, and Manheim, but he couldn't tell them that. Bane's satellite phone vibrated in his pocket. He held up his hand. "Got to take this, boss."

"We're in closed session!"

"Won't be a moment, Sergey." Bane flipped open his phone. "Bane here." He listened for a moment, then said, "Fuel up Turtle One." He pocketed his phone. "Emergency," he said, curtly. "Gotta go, Dads and Moms."

Madame President Hong stood up. "I forbid it, Bane. We're here to talk about shutting you down."

"Urgent matters, Madame. Really." He smiled, rounded the table, saluted, then dashed out the door, pursued by an uproar of angry voices, hoping he wasn't out of a job. But he soon forgot his bosses. Manheim, the Braxis security chief, had slipped Bane's team in Hong Kong. Bane knew, for a certainty—even if he only had raw instinct—that Braxis and Manheim were at the center of the crisis. His teams had followed Manheim since Ada and Bane met the grim ex-soldier in California.

16

Cedars-Sinai Hospital, LA

Spooks. She studied the two men in their bland black suits with black ties: men in black, without the sunglasses. She almost laughed. God, she was tired. These two "spooks" were all she needed. Had Devon sent them to fetch her back to Atlanta? Or were they Bane's men?

Making a big show of calm detachment, she smiled at the two men and said, "This lab is a sterile environment."

Their stony faces indicated nothing. "Defense Security Service, ma'am. On urgent business. We'll just wait here, Ma'am, if it's all right with you."

DSS were here because of her Bio-Watch Notice, isolating anyone who came into contact with Doctor Begley and the mysterious virus. She had called a Bio-Watch alert under provisions of the Act, and found that it triggered an immense machine of resources. Devon didn't try to stop her this time. It wasn't a full-fledged quarantine, merely an isolation of suspected cases. She had already spoken to the Department of Defense and Homeland Security representatives. Devon had taken a strip off her smarting hide after she hung up on several journalists. She even took a call from the assistant secretary of health. All told her she was overreacting, but no one shut her down.

Ada rolled off the disposable gloves and tossed them in the dispenser, walked to the sterile sink and washed for three minutes, enjoying the warm water and the smell of disinfectant soap. She applied lotion to skin too dry from numerous washings, aware of the unwavering gaze of the men in black.

Ada shrugged. "You can wait if you don't mind being exposed to dangerous viruses."

Spooks. She almost laughed again, and that was a sure sign of exhaustion. She glanced at her best friend Caff, nodded, and said, "I'll be back in a while, Caff."

"You want me along, honey?" he asked, glaring at the two DSS agents.

"No, you continue with that viral stain." She realized her voice had an edge, and added, "I'll be fine. I'll bring you some coffee, Toyboy."

He smiled, but it was a halfhearted attempt. "I'll be waiting here. Gentlemen, you'll remember that we need Doctor Kenner right here." He winked at Ada. "I'll just call Nam. She's in the cafeteria."

Nam was a reassuring, if annoying presence. Ada liked Nam, but her presence was a reminder of Bane's overly protective nature. Nam went with Ada everywhere. It was beyond inconvenient.

The spooks said nothing as they waited for her. Ada stifled a yawn and then followed them towards the door. One of the DSS men brushed against the stainless steel counter, knocking a cage of lab mice. The mice chattered and squeaked, making Ada jump.

She stepped back, her hand covering her mouth, a momentary lapse in control, but enough.

"Is something wrong?" Spook number one asked.

"Scared of mice, Doctor?" Spook number two said.

Ada uncovered her mouth. She hated showing her weakness in front of these men. She worked with lab mice all the time, but sterile conditions and masks never entirely took away the fear. A lab mouse had infected her with Lymphocytic Choriomeningitis Virus in her final year at Harvard, ruining her life.

"What's wrong? They contagious?"

"Deadly contagious, honey," chirped in Caff from across the lab.

Now it was the Spooks who stepped back.

Ada tried hard not to scowl, but there was nothing she could do about the angry burn in her cheeks. Suddenly, she didn't care about DSS agents or emerging viruses or even the possibility of an epidemic. She could think only of Quentin. Her sweet son Quentin, born without legs, because of her. Born deformed because she had been careless with mice in her lab.

She leaned against the stainless steel counter top and stared at the mice, feeling nauseous as the memories choked her.

"Doctor?"

"Go to hell," she said, but her voice was quiet. And then she followed them out into the deserted hallway of the isolation ward.

"We are to take you to the field office, Ma'am," said Spook number one, as he led the way down the tiled hall.

She stopped following, finally making up her mind. Maybe it was the cage of mice and the memories of her viral run-in. Maybe it was anger at these nameless men. "I'm not leaving this hospital, gentlemen. So if you'd like a meeting, the surgeons' lounge is here." It sounded silly, really, talking tough to two men who outweighed her by three hundred and fifty collective pounds of beefy muscle and who had not-so-well-hidden firearms under their black jackets.

"Ma'am—"

She balled her hands into fists and planted them on her hips, probably looking comical, but still letting her anger take her. "That's Doctor to you—what was your name again?"

"Special Agent Ballantine, Doctor Kenner." Spook Number One's voice left no room for doubt that they were humorless. "This is Special Agent Delacroix."

"Fine. I'm in an emergency situation here, gentlemen."

"We're aware of that, Doctor. You invoked BioSecure provisions."

"That's right."

"Which makes our involvement mandatory at this stage, Doctor. We are investigating the propriety."

"The propriety?" She nearly wigged out this time. The propriety of her actions he meant. Instead, she simply said, "This isn't the time."

"This is the time."

"The CDC has full authority to invoke BioSecure. In fact, it's mandated."

"Yes, Ma'am—Doctor." The spook named Ballantine stepped closer. "We're prepared to detain you if that is what it takes, Doctor."

Ada felt the rise of her grandmother's temper, famous among the Kenner clan. "Then that's what you'll have to do. I have patients here!"

"That changes nothing, Doctor."

"What are you going to do about it?" She yelled, and the nurse at the isolation ward desk stared at them now. "Handcuff me?" Fatigue and anger were a dangerous combination for Ada.

Without emotion, he said, "If necessary."

"Nurse Hanson," Ada called out. "Nurse Hanson, please call the police. These men are abducting me."

The nurse picked up the phone.

The Spooks weren't spooked. One snatched out a pair of handcuffs.

"No one is handcuffing any persons," said a familiar accented voice behind Ada.

"And who are you?" asked Special Agent Delacroix, Spook Number Two, until now the silent agent.

"Assistant Special Agent in Charge Nam Ling, WART," said Nam, and when she spoke in her most officious tone, her accent slipped away.

Ada stepped back beside Bane's right hand, Nam Ling. Now that it was two to two, she felt better, even though Nam was an arm's length shorter than the smallest DSS agent. Nam almost certainly had the authority to challenge these two creeps, plus she had her nunchucky things and some martial training. No gun though. What kind of special agent didn't carry a gun?

"We have authority here ASAC Ling," said Delacroix. He studied her identification quickly and then showed his own.

"You have to take that to the boss, Director Alban Bane. You've heard of him?" Nam stepped closer to the two men. She looked less than diminutive as she looked up at them.

"We know of him, ASAC Ling," said Ballantine. For the first time Ada heard a touch of emotion in the flat tones of the man's voice, perhaps fear, definitely respect. "But our orders come from the assistant secretary of defense himself."

Nam shrugged. "I have no interest in your orders."

"Step aside, ASAC Ling."

Nam folded her arms on her bosomless chest. "Doctor Kenner, I worry about this now. You go back to work, Doctor Kenner."

Ada didn't want to move. What might happen to Nam Ling? She'd had no chance to get to know the tiny agent, not since Bane disappeared in his sleek black plane and left Nam behind to assist with the BioSecure containment order. What if these spooks kidnapped the little woman?

"We are taking the Doctor for debriefing." Ballantine scowled at her.

"Step back, please." Nam held out her tiny hand, yet it was an unwavering arm that conveyed a statuesque calm.

"I'll warn you only once, ASAC Ling. You can come with us to protect your interests, but we are taking the Doctor."

"You are taking nobody."

Ballantine reached for his sidearm.

That was as far as he got. Ada didn't quite see what happened. She felt almost a wind of motion and had an impression of tornado-like force. Then Ballantine lay on the tile floor, looking up at Nam, stunned, eyes registering shock.

Nam stepped back. "I have first jurisdiction. Understand?"

The man sprang lightly to his feet.

"You should leave now, I suggest." Nam said.

"We'll be back."

"Bring something in writing. Or bring more men." Nam stepped back beside Ada. "You go to work now, Doctor."

"Thank you. Yes, I will." But Ada stood and watched the two men retreat like battered cocks after a cockfight. She had no doubt she'd hear from them again. After they stepped into the elevator, glaring at Nam and Ada as the doors slid closed, Ada turned to Nam and said, "What happened?"

Nam shrugged. "Nothing much, right? Just bullies. Only one way to handle bullies."

"They'll come back."

Nam nodded, her face serene but flushed with energy. "Yes, I think so. But I'll be checking on them, yes? So you go back to work, right?"

"Right. Yes." She turned, then stopped. "Nam, thank you."

"No need, Doctor. It's my job."

"I know. But thanks anyway." Then she remembered. She bowed. "Namaste."

Nam smiled, a brilliant expression that made Ada feel at ease. "Namaste, Doctor."

Ada headed for the temporary lab, but didn't quite make it. Her satellite phone rang and she checked the call identification. Since she had called the BioSecure, she'd been screening the non-stop calls, but this one she would have to take. She slipped into the surgeons' lounge, deserted due to the containment order, and answered. "Yes, Devon?"

"Your report, A.K." said a tired voice. Devon's voice had an edge. He was official Director today, not ex-husband and friend.

"We have no new cases. It seems to be contained."

Devon sighed. "So you'll be returning soon?"

"When the crisis has passed, sir."

"Good. The lab has the last of the samples you sent."

"Great." There was a long silence and Ada thought the signal had been lost. The hospital scrambled cell signals to discourage cell phone use. "Devon, are you there?"

"Yes, I'm here." She heard him draw in a long breath. "Look, A.K. you've stirred up a real Pacific cyclone here."

She said nothing.

"Right. Well, I've fielded calls from the secretary of health. From the CEO of Braxis, currently in France. From the president's chief of staff. Even from the Department of Defense. All complaining about you."

Ada sat down on a waiting area bench. "And why is that, Devon? Why is the DOD involved?"

"I don't know."

"I had a visit from two DSS special agents," she said.

Devon said nothing.

"Why would Counter Intelligence be involved? Devon, did you send them?"

His breathing grew faster, but he said nothing.

"Devon, do you know something?"

"Nothing, A.K. Nothing I can say. But Homeland Security's involved too."

"This isn't right," she said.

"You're the one who called a BioSecure."

"Do you disagree with my decision—sir?" She tried to keep the anger out of her voice. Calling him sir would really piss him off.

"It's better if you return to Atlanta, A.K."

"Is that an order, sir?"

"If need be." Another long silence punctuated his displeasure, and this time it really annoyed her. "A.K. You can do your lab work here. You can leave standing orders on your patients to isolate for another—five days? The threat seems hardly to warrant an ongoing BioSecure."

"Sir, I—"

Devon shouted over her, "Doctor Kenner. A BioSecure comes to the immediate attention of the president. Which is why DOD is involved. You've created your own mess."

"But Devon—"

"Ada, for God's sake, listen! I gave you a lot of rope, but I don't want you to hang yourself with it. No one is happy about your actions."

"Yourself included, Devon?"

He sighed again. "Myself included."

"I'm sorry to hear that—sir."

"Just tone it down, A.K. I'm sure you're tired, but I'm not tolerating your bull. Tone it down, right now." He said it in a flat cold tone that immediately iced her fury. "Wrap it up, and get back here. I don't want you in the field." Even though sat-phones had no dial tone, she sensed he had ended the call.

She eyed the half drained coffee pot in the surgeons' lounge. She had promised Caff some caffeine. She needed some herself. As she poured two cups, her hands shook. One thing was certain. She had better head back to Atlanta now, or she'd be out of a job, or bounced back to lab rat in some obscure post in Alaska. As she walked back to the lab, her phone rang again. She thought about not answering. Perhaps it was Devon calling to apologize and the thought made her laugh. She set the coffees down and peered at the screen.

Call identification indicated Armin Buchler.

She smiled. Her old friend from WHO, a good man who rarely called except when he was in town.

She flipped open her phone. "Armin? How are you?"

He laughed. "Tired. But you sound worse."

"Thanks, chum."

"I have a problem here, A.K."

"Where's here?"

"Near James Bay in Canada."

"Well, a little colder than usual." Armin spent most of his career in developing countries in the tropics, where diseases flourished and many had no name.

He didn't laugh, and she knew he was in trouble. "What is it?"

"We may have an epidemic here, A.K. And it's a virus I can't identify."

17

Kinosewak Nation, Canada

Ada wasn't the only one on the trail of epidemics. The small Dehavilland Dash 8 aircraft brimmed with celebrities and journalists. Thankfully, the journalists were entirely focused on singing star Panji Maingan. Ada had tried to sleep, and must have nodded off because a loud rumble of voices woke her.

The journalists pressed their faces and cameras to the small round windows of the aircraft.

"Is that the child cemetery?" asked Shane Gerrold of *The Washington Post*. Cameras appeared over the headrests of seats, the videographers and photographers waiting for Panji Maingan to answer.

"Two hundred and sixty-two—babies." Panji said.

Ada considered herself lucky to share the flight with one of her favorite rock singers and found her chatty and fascinating. Panji had gone out of her way to introduce herself.

"I'm a fan," Ada said, a little awestruck. "I have three of your CDs.

"Thank you for coming, Doctor. Armin speaks highly of you."

All this time, the journalists snapped digital photos or videotaped. Ada tried to ignore them, and it was clear the diminutive rocker had completely zoned them out, as if they didn't exist.

Panji wore plain jeans and a button-up cotton shirt, disappointing material for their cameras, yet for all that, she was a dazzling bundle of energy, never for a moment winding down. Her eyes danced in lively circles, her skin and complexion were ageless, and in spite of one crooked tooth and a gap, she smiled nonstop. The only hint she was a celebrity was a practiced ease, and the only nod to First Nations heritage might be her trademark waist-length black hair and the trademark silver Coyote pendant given her by Dêde, her papa, when she was thirteen. Ada was a big enough fan to know the publicity bio, anyway.

"Why are you here, though, Panji?" said Ada.

Panji's smile vanished for just a moment. "Awareness. The one upside to celebrity is I can get headlines for people who need them."

"I'm not so sure headlines are what we need," Ada said.

"It's all I can do. That and moral support. Great Maker, it's all so idiotic."

She seemed vulnerable and younger than her thirty years. She smiled at Nam. "You don't speak much?"

"Strong, silent type," Ada said.

"Buddhist?" Panji pointed at the long string of beads Nam was fingering. "Cherry amber. Very soothing."

Nam smiled. "Tibetan Buddhist."

"Aren't you Chinese?"

Nam nodded.

"Cool."

"What's cool?" Nam wrapped her long string of beads back around her wrist.

"The Diamond Vehicle. Tantra. The Dalai Lama gave me the Kalachakra."

"Personally?" Nam sat straighter, her eyes alive with interest.

Panji nodded. "I did a benefit concert for the nuns at Dharamsala. Although I'm more a Zen Buddhist. My boyfriend is Zen."

Ada smiled. "I saw—in the tabloids. The infamous Kenji, host of *Superstar*. Mysterious ex-Buddhist monk who won *Haunted Survivor*. Hot body and puppy dog looks."

"That's the one," Panji said with a sudden frown.

"He's very sexy. But is he as mysterious as he seems on TV?" Ada, like half of American women, had a massive crush on the hunky host of *Superstar*, ever since he came across as a major hero in the cave scene on Real TV's *Haunted Survivor* show.

"More so." Panji's frown deepened.

"Sorry. I've upset you."

"No, no. I just miss him. We're always on different ends of the continent."

"So then you know Alban Bane?" Ada found herself thinking again of Bane. After she had cleared him of any virus, he almost immediately flew off in pursuit of some lead. The memory of their last dinner together was bittersweet. Bane was clearly either a secure or very insecure man. Even in the most private circumstances, the one-liners never stopped. It was annoying. But he was also very captivating. Attractive. Caff never stopped teasing her about Bane.

"Bane's a good friend of Kenji. I only met him once." Panji's eyes crinkled as she laughed. "A funny, funny man."

Then she was swept away by a thousand questions from the journalists, and Ada found herself sinking into a drowsy daze.

As they finally came in for a landing, everyone stared out windows. Ada leaned over Nam and peered down at the weedy, treeless grounds below, the children's cemetery, adorned with plastic flowers and the occasional wreath. These were children of Kinosewak, lost to diseases that were largely eradicated in most developed nations, or to suicide, violence, or hunger.

"What is the CDC doing about this, Doctor Kenner?" asked Jim Burness from CNN, turning around in his seat and thrusting his microphone at her.

Ada sat straighter. She hated journalists. "The Canadian government has not called us in. I'm here as an expert and an observer at the invitation of Doctor Buchler of WHO." And probably it was a "useless field trip" as Devon would say, but at least her team and Caff were still busily at work in their makeshift lab in Cedars-Sinai Hospital and her Emerging Lab at the CDC.

Panji smiled, a drop-dead gorgeous movie-star expression that brought the cameras to her like hummingbirds to nectar. Ada realized this was all engineered by Panji to humiliate the Feds into action. This was the type of media exposure that brought donations and awareness to First Nations causes. Ada didn't have to know Panji to know that was the game here. Panji even had a representative from Health Canada on the plane, although he was a low-ranking bureaucrat who had only come here under pressure from Armin Buchler of WHO.

Ada hated these games. Panji might use her celebrity card, but it was clear she cared. She spent ten months of the year traveling to developing nations, from Zaire to Ethiopia, and her weepy stories on talk shows brought chills and tears.

Panji fingered the beads on her shoulder bag.

Ada suppressed a sigh and pressed her face to the window. She could see the village on James Bay now, rows of dilapidated corrugated steel shacks along a treeless and muddy roadway. As the Dash flew over the dirt strip landing field, she could see that many of the windows of the "houses" were boarded up with plywood. They were low enough that she could see the large holes in the crumbling walls and the discarded, rusting fridges and ovens dating back to the fifties in the small backyards.

Ditches flowed into a river littered with garbage, discarded cars and empty bottles. On the west side of town was a metal junkyard piled with scrapped snowmobiles, dirt bikes and demolished shanties.

Ada saw people coming out of their homes now, disturbed from their sick beds and hangovers by the sound of the airplanes. The other airplane, a C-130 Hercules, had already landed and the rear hatch lowered. As the Dash lowered its landing gear with a thump, Panji caught a glimpse of the two-ton Reverse Osmosis Water Purification Unit. The Dash continued to loop the village giving the journalists a chance to film.

"I hear the water unit cost you all the royalties from your last album," Burness of CNN asked Panji.

Apparently reluctant, Panji faced the camera. "Jim, many people donated time and money to make this happen."

"Your agent, Mac Stayner, is on record saying you donated thirteen million."

"I wouldn't know, Jim. What matters is that these people are helped."

Gerrold of the *Post* squatted in the aisle, ignoring the seatbelt sign, his tape recorder thrust out. "My sources tell me you leased the unit from the army. Why wouldn't the government pay for this, Little Coyote?"

Panji took a long breath. "I don't know. You'd have to ask the Minister of Indian Affairs. He hasn't been returning my calls."

Ada smiled at Panji's PR cleverness. The headline had just become, "Minister of Indian Affairs turns back on Natives." Panji had learned how to turn a gesture into a circus.

Journalists crowded around her seat, ignoring the views below, and the strident calls of the flight attendant to return to their seats.

"Little Coyote, is it true you complained to the Human Rights Tribunal about Canada's conduct in this matter?"

Ada didn't even see who called out the question, but it sounded like the bubblehead from *Newsweekly*.

"It's a matter of record."

"Panji! Panji, what do you say to accusations that you are just trying to sell CDs?" asked McIntyre from MetroTalk.

"I can't say anything to that." She forced a smile and cameras whirred. "Other than to say again that every penny of my royalties goes to First Nations causes."

Elena from NWP shouted, "Little Coyote! Is your lawsuit another publicity stunt?"

Panji's smile flickered for a moment, but Ada doubted anyone noticed. "The suit I believe you're referring to is class action, on behalf of the First Nations Council and all the First Nations. We are suing the Quebec government in relation to the flooding of reserve lands to build hydro dams—a direct contributor to the poverty, starvation and disease you are seeing out your windows." She realized her delivery sounded canned, so she added, "Look, someone has to do something. You're doing your part by being here. Right?"

Some of the journalists laughed.

Panji prevented more questions by holding up her hand. "The flight attendant is already belted in. She's given up on us."

More laughter, and the journalists returned to their seats.

"Well played," Ada said, leaning across the aisle.

"I hate sensationalism," Panji said, and she rubbed her temples.

"Headache?"

"Big time migraine." She looked away.

Ada stared out the window again as they came in for their landing. Dogs scrapped in the street; a few people were passed out on the riverbank or in front of burned out shacks, with empty bottles in their hands.

Finally the Dash landed. Panji made for the hatch before they finished taxiing, pausing only to snatch her old beaded shoulder sling bag. No doubt, she wanted to deplane before the inevitable crowd gathered. When Ada and Nam made it to the hatch, Ada saw Panji was too late. Children ran across the airfield. Behind them, a steady stream of villagers marched, spreading out and surrounding the airplane.

"She is a hero to them," Nam said gently.

"I think so."

Panji waved as she crossed the field to cheers from the villagers. The children laughed, their gaunt faces lit up with delight. Panji kissed and hugged as many as she could.

A big man pushed through the children, both arms outstretched. He had a big toothless grin for her. "Panji Maingan, my Little Coyote, you are always welcome! Have you come to sing us more songs?"

"Chief Mathias, I bring reporters to tell our story," she said, in his language. "And a doctor from the CDC. Doctor Ada Kenner and her friend Nam Ling."

"More doctors?" Mathias nodded at Ada "That is well. We have many sick. Many many sick. Welcome."

Two young village girls hugged Ada and Nam.

"What do you mean more doctors?" Panji asked.

"Did you not send the doctors from Braxis?"

Ada, still stroking a little girl's heard, glanced sharply at Nam. Nam nodded, a sort of "aha" gesture.

Panji shook her head. "No, I've been trying to get private corporations to help, but without success."

"Then, they have heard of us through your work!" Mathias said, excited. "This is good! Very very very good!"

"Yes, yes it is good."

"Because since they came, many more have become sick. And the murders, too. All help is wonderful!"

"What murders?" Ada asked sharply.

"Three murders!" Mathias kept his voice low, probably conscious of the reporters. "The reserve police don't know what to do!"

Panji put her arm around Mathias and pulled him away from the journalists. When they tried to follow she held up her hand. "Private Nations business," she said crisply. She walked Mathias as quickly as his limp would allow towards the tail of the aircraft, away from the crowds. "Come, Doctor Kenner." Ada followed with Nam. "Tell me. What happened?"

Mathias pursed his lips, hesitating. "John Friday, he killed his brother Junior."

"*Nind anamietawa.*" Panji said, her voice low and husky.

"And Annie Franks. She drownded her baby!"

"Great Maker, but why?"

"And Grandmother Essie. She passed away, but it's mysterious. We have no coroner here, but the reserve police are holding her grandson."

Panji's eyes gleamed with unshed tears.

Ada leaned close to Nam. "I think you should call your Director Bane."

"I think so too," Nam said.

Las Vegas, Nevada

Hunter Gerrold sneezed as he stepped into the elevator.

Mrs. Foley from 910 winced, her smile fading, and she retreated to the back corner of the elevator. Hunter was grateful he couldn't smell her usual perfume through his congested sinuses.

On the sixth floor, June Law and her one-night stand entered the elevator. She smiled at Hunter. He smiled back. And sneezed.

On the third floor, the Gaines family crowded into the elevator.

At school, Hunter was hailed as a hero for his brave attempt to win a place in *Superstar,* the hot reality television show. No one seemed to care that he lost. He had become a legend already.

After class he attended basketball practice. In the showers, his friends asked him all about *Superstar.*

His best friend J.R. said, "That Abbey Chase is the bitchy bomb." Everyone in America loved to hate Abbey Chase, the brutal judge on the show and producer of *Superstar.*

Hunter thrust his pelvis, flapping his penis, and said, "I'd do her, the bitch." He laughed again. "But she's brutal. She told me I yelped like a dying puppy."

"She had the hots for you, Hunts," shouted J.R. over the noise of showers. "She called you a puppy."

"A dying puppy. But I'd screw her anyway."

And he sneezed again. Instinctively, his hand covered his nose. And came away with blood.

"Shit, dude, you're bleeding," J.R. said.

Not a little, either. Hunter pressed his nostril with his index finger, but the blood still poured. The steamy water from the showers diluted the stream, sheeting pink on Hunter's pasty white skin.

"Oh, man, a gusher."

Hunter shrugged, trying to soap and hold his nose at the same time.

Midi, France

Doctor Gilbert Domergue slipped out of bed, careful not to disturb Larraine, and trudged up the narrow stone stairs in his sheepskin slippers and terrycloth gown to see the first tendrils of dawn. He stepped out on the turret of his thirteenth century abbey, the Abbaye du Midi. Nothing would spoil this day, not even the news from Site F, or the various incidents. Minor annoyances.

Domergue breathed morning air fresh sweetened with the lavender that swept in purple carpets across the north slope. He scanned the vineyard. His vines were fertile and ripe, perfect rows of tangled green grapes. Some of his men already worked the fields. Below them was the winding path of the Canal du Midi, empty of barge traffic.

Larraine joined him with a café and steamed milk. He kissed her, reached over to squeeze her taut bottom, and inhaled the morning brew.

"Cool, this morning," she said, settling against him.

His wife was such a handsome woman, even with her cascade of silver hair, and she still had the face of his goddess, barely aged in thirty years. Since Boston, they had been together: she had first been a patient diagnosed as schizophrenic, later his wife and the mother of his splendid sons, the twins. Larraine remained, after decades of companionship, the perfect and loyal wife. She never wore makeup and he wouldn't allow her to dye her strands of grey. At nearly six foot one in flat shoes, she remained erect and imposing, with perfect breasts and nipples that remained pink and delicious. Her schizophrenia had been controlled over the years by his quiet treatments, but at a cost to him. He loved her through it all, but her schizoid behaviors sometimes led to psychotic breaks; it could be very hard on the help, and not so easy on him, but Domergue unfailingly cherished her.

"My sweet." He pulled her closer, drank more coffee. Larraine and his twin sons were everything. Many things mattered in life—the war on terrorism, the success of Braxis, and stability in a too-violent world—but if he chose only one focus in his busy world, it would be family. Life was good here in the hills of Corbieres.

"Have you heard from our angels?" Larraine asked.

"Yesterday, sweetness. Our boys are well."

That was enough for Larraine. She loved her tall, beautiful boys, even though they were now full grown men, and it was her sole mission in life to ensure her blonde, blue-eyed angels were well and successful.

After a breakfast of fresh loaves and cheese, Larraine left him to his business. She knew his work was of vital importance to a conflicted world. Domergue descended the stone steps to his Louis XIV desk in his study high in the north tower. Golden light suffused the room that once had housed the chief abbot of Midi, warming the patina of centuries-old plank floors. Three fifty-inch Nakamichi flat screen monitors on elegant metal stands surrounded his antique desk, each with a robotic camera.

Domergue typed in a lengthy and complicated password for mainframe access. A message appeared on one plasma screen: Welcome Doctor Domergue.

He went first to his blind encrypted email system: two emails from CIA Director Barry Lambert, three from Site M, fifteen from Site F, two from Site S, one from the secretary of health and one from U.S. Vice President Samuels.

Before he could open his emails, his phone flashed red.

He frowned at the screen. Encrypted line or not, Site P was not to call him here.

Domergue didn't answer it right away. He poured himself another steaming coffee, this time with heavy cream and honey from the vineyard hives. He held the cup under his nostrils and inhaled the heavenly roasted perfume, one of the three essentials of life: family, wine and coffee.

He leaned back in his chair and read the emails from Site S. The Spanish authorities had not recovered the stolen shipment of TZ-4 vaccine. That one worried Domergue, as much as anything could. Who would steal the vaccine? The only logical answer was a competitor. The vaccine was worth billions if it could be reverse engineered.

As he sipped, he studied his favorite painting, a little known Titian oil of the Virgin and the Holy Child. With all its imperfect cracks and faded color it still took his breath away.

A high chirp reminded him of the urgent call. Two lines were lit up. He smiled when he saw who was on line two. He sat straighter in the chair, fixed a smile on his face and hit the control on his desk. His face would be pixilated so that she couldn't see him.

"My dear, how are you?"

Abbey Chase wore a low-cut gown and looked marvelous even with an intense frown on her face. "Gilbert, there's a problem."

"Of course there is. Let me guess, my dear. Alban Bane?"

She smiled then, and it transformed her. "He threatened to shut me down again."

"You need not worry, dear. He cannot shut you down."

"I know. But I thought you might want to know."

"Very kind of you." Domergue kept his voice warm and civil, but he seethed inside. Only Bane could upset an otherwise perfect day. "I will worry about Alban Bane, Abbey. You leave him to me."

"I don't want him hurt." She sounded imperious.

"I will try." He frowned. Easy to say; hard to do. Bane's agents were a nuisance, following Manheim from city to city, sniffing around like bloodhounds. The easiest solution would be a permanent one.

"He has two daughters."

"Daughters who might be better off without him."

"You promised."

"I promised to try."

"I mean it, Gilbert. Bane is not to be harmed."

"Let us not forget, my dear, who finances your little empire."

She glared at him although he knew she saw only a pixilated profile. "I have other investors."

"Thank you for the call, dear. Just you keep your little show on tour."

"But—what if Bane is right?"

"Bane is never right, my dear."

"He's right too often!"

"There is a difference between being intuitively lucky and being right. I have another call, my dear. I love you. Goodbye, now." Without waiting for her response, he terminated her call and punched up line one.

Dr. Gies's worried, frowning face appeared on one monitor. "Doctor."

Domergue nodded. "Yes, Gies?" Domergue leaned forward until his face must have filled Gies's monitor. "Is this about Doctor Begley?"

"Yes, sir."

"Well, isn't he dead?" Of course Domergue knew he was dead. There was nothing he didn't know in the world of Braxis.

"Yes, sir."

"Well?"

"We have another problem."

"Yes, I am sure you do." Domergue sighed and poured a refill. Let the man get to it on his own.

"Sir, Begley infected two people."

"I see. Not entirely unexpected after your carelessness."

"Sir, we have reports of hot spots. Fires vectoring in California. Potentially hundreds infected."

Domergue tried not to sound annoyed. "What of it, Gies? The virus has been at large longer than a few days, thanks to the animal-rights break-in."

"But this vector is traceable to us."

"What are you doing about it, then?"

"Frankly, sir, I don't know what to do. We do have a vaccine that could save lives, but—"

Domergue waved his hand. For a brilliant man, Gies was quite stupid. "Yes, I see." He leaned forward, closer to the camera. "But of course you know that could ruin us. Investigations would trace patient zero back to Site F."

"Yes, yes." Gies's face was pale, drenched with sweat.

Domergue pursed his lips, trying not to reveal his emotions. That was a possibility that had also occurred to him: his enemies might have engineered the animal-rights incident to ruin Braxis and the theft of vaccine at Site S was a precaution against infection. Of course, he had foreseen this contingency. Only five months ago he had the "vision" to convert the plants in India to TZ-4 vaccine production. "Was there anything else, Gies?"

"We have to do something!" Gies looked frightened. He wanted to come forward; he wanted to save the world. It was what drove the man to work seven days a week; his life-long mission was to rid the world of violence, after the loss of his son Conner. With Begley's help, he had proven the connection between the "Peace Gene" and schizophrenia and some forms of psychosis. Delivering the gene with a modified killed BDV had proven remarkably effective in treating violent schizophrenics, bipolars, chronic depressives, even sociopaths. Of course, there was no profit in such limited treatments.

"Calm down, Gies. Remember the mission. TZ-4 can save many lives. Relieve the suffering of hundreds of thousands worldwide. You will almost certainly earn the Nobel prize."

Gies's shirt clung to his skin below his smock. The poor man was drenched. "At a cost."

"There are always costs. Keep the greater good in mind."

Gies's voice hardened. "Doctor Domergue, Begley carried a live Borna Mutate out of here—this strain has a mortality rate of over ten percent. Those that survive inevitably will develop other symptoms."

Other symptoms? Even for Gies that was understatement.

"Then you'd best get back to work."

Gies said nothing, but he began to blink, his eyelids tapping.

Domergue wagged his finger at the camera. "It was careless of you to let Begley steal the virus. We'll clean up this mess, don't worry."

"But sir—"

Domergue held up his hand. "Remember Conner."

The transformation was instantaneous. Gies looked angry at the mention of his son, then he looked away and took a long shuddering breath. "Yes. Yes. I understand, sir."

"Conner would want us to continue."

"Yes."

"We all have loved ones affected." He paused, glancing at an elegantly framed photo of Larraine on his desk, cradling their first baby, their angel.

Gies stepped closer to the camera. His hand reached out in a distorted wide angle. The camera shook and he tilted it up. "Doctor, there's more."

"I was sure there would be."

"Doctor Ada Kenner of the CDC has issued a BioSecure in LA. Limited, but likely to be picked up in the press."

"They can prove nothing. They will have cultured a mutated BDV. They will know, at worst, there was an accident." Domergue picked up a Mont Blanc pen, his favorite gold Alexander the Great fountain, a gift from Larraine, and he wrote the name Doctor Ada Kenner on a pad of paper.

"She threatened to shut us down."

"What did you do, Doctor Gies?" He exaggerated the title "Doctor" and watched Gies's face. The features seemed to sag, the tightness leaving them, as if someone had magically removed a plastic surgeon's pins that had held his skin taut. Gies looked suddenly old.

"I've ordered the protocols moved to site P."

"That is fine, then."

"Doctor, WART is involved."

Domergue drew in a long breath, held it. "Alban Bane."

"How did you know, sir?"

Domergue leaned back in his reclining chair, reasserting calm. "A past associate, Gies. Just remember Conner, do your part, and I'll take care of the rest."

"Innocent people will die."

Domergue clucked his tongue against the roof of his mouth. "No one is innocent, Gies. I will send the Twins to clean up your mess. How is that, dear boy? They will take care of it."

Gies visibly paled on the monitor. "Sir, I protest."

Domergue held up his hand. "Gies, your incompetence caused this. You alone must accept responsibility for your failure."

He was sure Gies was choking back tears. The man wiped the back of his hand under his eyes.

Relenting, Domergue said, "Just let the Twins deal with this. They know what to do."

Gies swayed, looked as if he was going to pass out.

Domergue punched the disconnect button.

He tapped the desk with his fountain pen, pondering the setback—the CDC involved too soon and Bane investigating and hot on the trail of Manheim. They would have to be dealt with.

Domergue pressed a speed dial button on his system and called the Twins—his beloved sons.

20

Kinosewak Nation, Canada

The prisoner sneezed. Ada could see he was very ill, his eyes red and the cot in the barren cell stained with vomit. The cell reeked of sweat, urine and stomach acids, an austere room with a cold, concrete floor, cracked porcelain toilet bowl and a single cold-water tap over a brown-stained sink.

Ada could imagine any prisoner getting sick in the dismal reserve jail, although it was clearly more than that. The prisoner wouldn't let her touch him, and would only let Panji, the chart-topping singer, into his cell. Ada watched, worried, as Panji sat facing the murdering fourteen-year-old.

At Ada's insistence, Panji wore a mask and gloves, her fine strands of waist-length hair drawn back into a quick tail, and she sat in the cell on a stool. Constable Dorsey stood behind her. Ada and Nam remained outside the cell, watchful, not allowed any nearer the prisoner.

Ada still didn't know what to make of Panji. She was probably the most sincerely caring person Ada had ever met, an enigmatic combination of celebrity and pizzazz.

"I hated her," prisoner Abdo said. "Hated her, hated her, hated her!" He sneezed again, and Panji flinched.

"When I was last here, Abdo, you kissed her and hugged your Gran," Panji said gently. "Do you remember that?" Panji had told Ada about her last visit, how proud Grandmother Essie had been when Abdo returned as a finalist from the *Superstar* auditions in Montreal. He came home and got sick.

"I hated her!" Abdo spat at Panji and she recoiled. She stared at the gob of blood red spit on the concrete floor of the jail cell.

"I'm here for you, Abdo, if you need me."

"Go away!"

"I can get you a doctor," Panji said, and she nodded in Ada's direction. "Doctor Kenner is one of the best."

"Screw off!" His hands were bundled into little fists, and he seemed about to lunge at her. He was only fourteen, and small for fourteen, but he looked dangerous, all wild-eyed and red-faced.

Panji stood up. Ada had never felt so helpless in her life. She was only an observer in Canada, especially on a self-governing First Nation, but she couldn't do much without examining this boy. He seemed irrational, bordering on psychotic. What could have driven the fourteen-year-old to kill his grandmother?

As Panji left his cell, she said to Constable Dorsey, "I know a psychiatrist in Winnipeg. I'd like him to see Abdo."

"Please," said Dorsey. "I don't know what to do."

"I don't either." Panji, Ada and Nam followed Dorsey to the only other room in the small police headquarters. Kinosewak employed three full time constables, all paid close to minimum wage.

"Coffee?"

Panji smiled and picked up her beaded coyote bag off his desk. "No, Dorsey. Thank you. Did you get him a lawyer?"

"He refused."

She reached out and touched Dorsey's arm. "I think he needs help."

"Yup. But the Justice of the Peace flies in only when needed—I've called and he'll be here next week—and we have no full-time doctors here."

"What about the Braxis doctors?"

"They came," Dorsey said, lowering his voice. "Yes, they came. But I don't think they should come back."

"Why?"

"Abdo became violent when they tried to enter his cell."

"Would you allow Doctor Kenner to see Abdo?"

"Of course, Little Coyote. Anything for you. But we might have to restrain him."

"Are these Braxis doctors in the infirmary?" Ada asked. She knew the village had no permanent hospital, only an infirmary with one full-time nurse. Doctors flew in as needed and once a month.

"Yes."

"I would like to speak with these so-called doctors." Ada couldn't keep the anger from her voice, and she led the way to the street followed by Panji and Nam.

Ada ignored the journalists at the door as they picked up her trail. Even though the wind blew hard into her face, picking up stinging dust, she yanked the tie off her hair and let it stream out behind her. It helped her feel clean after the stench in the jail cell.

They found Doctor Armin Buchler of WHO where they had left him, at Tansi, a squat clapboard restaurant that passed for the local hangout, morning coffee shop, afternoon diner and nighttime bar. Armin sat at an old fifties-style laminated counter sipping coffee. Armin was the only patron until the journalists crowded in behind Panji and filled all the booths.

He smiled as Ada approached, turning on a creaking stool. "Welcome to the five star dining of Kinosewak." He smiled at Panji and Nam. "Good day, my treasures. You sit, yes?"

"Just us and twenty friends," Ada said, giving thumbs up to the reporters.

He winked. "I think you say, they're doing background stories is it?"

Panji smiled at the owner-cook-waitress of Tansi. "Coffee, please."

The proprietor practically ran to pour her a cup. "I boiled the water, Little Coyote."

"Kinana'skomitin," Panji said, sipping the coffee. With the village on a "boil water" notice—for nearly two years—only hot beverages or drinks in a can or bottle were safe.

"It tastes like toilet water," Armin said, leaning close and patting Panji's hand on the counter. Ada smiled. Armin Buchler was in no way amorous and anything but a gentleman, but for some reason women loved him, Ada included.

Panji pulled back her arm, conscious of the cameras. "I'm involved, Armin."

Armin rocked back on his stool, nearly falling off, either startled she'd rebuff him in front of journalists, or disappointed she was seeing someone. "Unlucky me," Armin said, after a long moment. "Who is the—lucky—freund?"

Panji blushed. "Kenji Tenichi."

He surprised her by laughing. "The host of *Superstar*? I thought Panji Maingan, she hate Hollywood, yes?"

"Kenji's different," Panji said sharply.

"Ah, me." Armin sighed. "I suppose we must always just be friends."

"I like us as friends," she said it gently.

Armin cradled his chin in two hands, exaggerating his disappointment. "I guess we be friends." Then he brightened, swiveled on the stool, and played the whole refrain over again for Ada. "You be my friend, too, Ada my dear."

"Friends, yes." Ada pretended a scowl. "No more."

"You Americans. So cold. So cold."

"As my friend, can I ask you something?" Ada leaned closer so the journalists wouldn't hear.

"More somethings?" Armin's big smile was charming. "Friends do favors, of course."

She leaned forward suddenly and pecked his cheek. "Tell me what you suspect. Not what you know, just what you suspect."

"Nothing here is right. This is why I call you, yes?" He leaned close, whispering back.

"Yes."

"Many sick. Many violences. I remember your Watch Notice, you catch me?"

"Yes, but why call me? Surely sickness is rampant in these conditions? Bad water. Poverty."

"I'm not a foolish, *liebling*."

"I know. I know that, Armin."

"It's these Braxis doctors. They make me nervous, yes?"

"I do understand."

He wagged his finger. "Liebling, is time to visit these Braxis people."

Moments later, she found herself leading the way to the Infirmary, heading up a train of journalists who followed them up the dusty roadway that served as Main Street. Ada tried to dissuade them, but instead more reporters joined in, then some villagers. They were Panji's hangers-on, not here in pursuit of Ada, thank God, but that didn't make them any less dangerous. Again she felt helpless. Her authority in Canada was non-existent.

By the time they reached the large cinder-block building, a crowd had gathered.

Ada turned. "No one may enter," she said as authoritatively as she could.

"On whose authority?" shouted a CNN correspondent.

"On mine!" shouted Constable Dorsey. Ada hadn't realized he had quietly followed them from the jail.

What they found inside shocked even her. Rows of beds lined each wall, every one of them occupied. An IV drip ran to the arm of each patient. Many of them seemed sick, sneezing and coughing, and some were asleep, in the throws of violent dreams.

An Asian doctor in a white smock and face mask ran to greet them at the door, his finger coming to his masked face in a shush gesture. He pointed back at a rack by the door lined with masks and gloves. Armin led by example and snatched up a mask for her and him.

"I am Doctor Cheung." When he saw the journalists filming from the door, he waved his arms. "This is an infirmary. My patients are resting. You must leave, please." Constable Dorsey slammed the door shut.

"This fine woman, she is Doctor Adalia Kenner of the Centers for Disease

Control. And this is Panji, the Little coyote, understand? Very famous. And the really dangerous one on the end, she is Nam Ling, a cop."

Ada saw the alarm in Doctor Cheung's eyes only momentarily. "Please, we are contagious here, you understand?"

"Yes, I understand," Ada said. "Do you have a diagnosis?"

"No," said Cheung a little harshly.

"An opinion?"

"No." Even with the mask on his face, Cheung appeared startled by the news of the CDC's arrival.

"Doctor Cheung, I am Panji Maingan. Please, tell me what's wrong here."

Six white-coated doctors and nurses worked on the patients, ignoring the visitors' arrival, busy taking blood and adjusting IV drips.

Cheung put his gloved hands on his hip. "Ms. Maingan, we came at your request. Do you remember?"

"Yes, I remember asking various corporations for help." Panji's hands matched Cheung's, firmly planted on hips. "But your vice president brushed me off."

Cheung shrugged. "I guess he changed his mind. We came to help. It seems at the right time."

"You seem to be offering treatment. Based on what?" Ada asked.

"Seems to be influenza. I have no way to test up here. Symptomology is very similar to type A flu"

"These people are very sick."

"Oh, they are, Doctor," said Cheung. "Dehydrated. Vomiting in some cases. Headaches. Fever."

"When did all this start?" Ada bent over one of the patients. She leaned close and peered into the patient's eyes. "There's hemorrhaging here, some burst capillaries."

"Yes," Doctor Cheung said. "I've drawn blood and sent off by private plane."

"I would like blood samples for my lab," Ada said. She shone a light into the patient's ears. She saw evidence of hemorrhaging there as well, although it had been recently swabbed clean.

"You'll have to draw your own blood, Doctor Kenner," Cheung said, and without another word he strode across the infirmary and left through the back door. The other gowned doctors and nurses followed.

"What was that about?" Ada asked, shocked at the reaction.

"Very mysterious," Armin Buchler said, as he examined another patient.

"It seems the Braxis doctors have left," Panji said.

Even as she spoke, one of the patients convulsed and vomited blood.

21

Yau Ma Tei, Kowloon

Bane felt unusual exhilaration. His excitement had little to do with his return to Hong Kong, or the crowds and noise, or the sumptuous smells from street vendors hawking food on Temple Street, or the clang-cling-clang of the Peking Opera performers. After losing Manheim on the busy streets of Hong Kong, Bane had ordered his teams to watch all the known arms dealers in Hong Kong, hoping Manheim would re-appear. Over the last few days, Manheim had visited arms dealers in five countries. At last, they got lucky. This time, Bane was determined not to lose him, and flew straight from New York to Hong Kong to supervise the teams himself. He'd stay on the Braxis security chief personally. His other key team followed Chaudhry Shujaa Khan, currently in Islamabad, Pakistan.

Adrenalin pumped a natural high as he followed Manheim. The conspicuously tall ex-Seal cleaved through the river of people, rushing past food carts, fortune-tellers and professional chess players huddled under kerosene lamps.

Old buddy Armitage Saulnier walked silently beside Bane, although he stood out from the crowd more than was desirable—a towering black man with his red-dyed dreads and big smiling face. By rights, neither of them should be here as field operatives, the Director and Assistant Director, yet it seemed like a good excuse to relive old times, and between them, Manheim would be easy to manage. He justified the high-level field work because his hunch about Manheim, the security chief at Site F, had proven correct—ex-elite military, dangerous, on three terrorist watch lists, including Homeland Security, but somehow impervious to arrest and prosecution due to the influence of his boss, Domergue. Since the surveillance, he had visited several arms dealers.

Six of Bane's best stood by in nearby cars, another ten in the crowd and he had a tracking sensor in his pant cuff.

Manheim surprised Bane by stopping at a noodle booth. The Braxis security chief sat on a stool stained with years of noodle-slurping, ankle deep in leftovers from the hundreds who came before, and sat beside an Asian man with dozens of face, nose, tongue and ear piercings. They didn't speak. Mr. Piercing sucked up long ropes of rice noodle from a bowl, while Manheim grabbed a pot of tea. The noodle cart seated only five, and every stool was occupied.

They circled back around and sat at a rice cart with a view of Manheim.

Arm ordered "assorted" rice—steamed rice with eggs, dichon, sausage and preserved vegetables—and they watched Manheim push an envelop on to Mr. Piercing's leg.

"Well, I'll be," Arm said, in his pleasant Creole drawl. "Another arms dealer, bro. He be called Gui."

"Ghost," Bane nodded. "Heard of him. He's like the discount supermarket for terrorists."

Arm smiled, as always, and lifted his bowl, scooping rice into his mouth with chopsticks. They had followed Manheim all day, losing him five times, but it was clear Manheim was on a mission, and not a legal one. He had visited three arms dealers and a mercenary.

Manheim—or Braxis—was going to war.

Bane felt alive, surrounded by the sounds and sights of Hong Kong and the thrill of the chase. "I missed Hong Kong."

Arm laughed. "Nostalgia's not you, bro."

"You realize this is our first job in the field since Vermont?" Normally Bane was flying somewhere and Arm was back in their UN offices in New York. They worked together in theory, but saw each other only at Christmas and at high-level meetings with the UN Committee.

"For true, bro. I'm lovin' it." He ordered another bowl of rice. "So what be really happenin' here?"

Bane poured more Jasmine tea.

"I don't have a big picture yet, bud. The threads are there—Braxis and Abbey Chase's new show. Manheim's moving."

Bane slammed down a hundred Hong Kong dollars and pursued. Manheim bolted suddenly into the crowd. He stood out from both tourists and locals alike, but the crowds were shoulder to shoulder. Manheim cut through them like a snowblower through drifts, pushing roughly. Arm and Bane got separated by the press of people, but Bane stayed focused on Manheim and turned his own shoulders into the unyielding flow of pedestrians.

Manheim knew they were following him, of course. The ex-Seal had noticed them on the ferry, but instead of confronting them he had smiled and waved.

Manheim clearly meant to lose them now. There were a million hiding places and slow-moving crowds on Temple Street. Bane caught sight of Manheim ducking around a cart of pirate DVDs. Instead of following, Bane darted between two sweatshirt vendors and jumped over a tangle of power cables through a rack of T shirts. He nearly knocked over an elderly woman, managed to avoid her by swinging right, then pressed through a cluster of laughing teenage girls. He turned in time to see Manheim duck between two competing watch carts near the temple of Tin Hau. Bane weaved among chess tables wreathed in swirls of cigarette smoke and swung around a blind fortune-teller tracing the lines on a young woman's hand.

Arm was long gone, invisible in the crowd even with his height and red dreads. Bane wondered again if he alone was a match for Manheim. The big ex-Seal was younger and taller and wouldn't hesitate to kill; Bane's research on Manheim turned up a stunning service record with dozens of service medals, but also links to violence, mercenary activity and possible assassinations in seven different countries, so he had no illusions about his chances in a straight-on confrontation. But he hadn't come this far to lose Manheim.

"Where are you, bro?" he heard Arm's comforting voice in his wireless earbud.

"Just passed the temple, going west."

"I see him!"

Bane found it harder and harder to make headway in the crowd without pushing people aside. There were too many tourists and locals. Manheim would not hesitate to knock down elderly shoppers.

Finally he saw Arm, and almost a block ahead, Manheim crossing Bute. They were going to lose him.

"Unit sixteen, close on Bute," Bane said into the transmitter. "But not too close. Do not apprehend."

Bane plunged into a younger crowd. He didn't hear the reply on his two-way as he passed a street band with a young lead singer who made a passable imitation of Anita Mau. He couldn't see Manheim.

"Anyone. Who's got Manheim?"

Silence.

"I'm right here," said a loud voice.

Bane swung around hard, instinctively crouching. He reached for his small chromed revolver. Manheim smiled at him. His hand already held a semiautomatic pistol.

22

Kinosewak Nation, Canada

Ada flinched when Jim Burness of CNN intercepted her and Panji at the coffee-shop door, camera crews in tow. A press of journalists soon closed on them.

Ada, edgy from caffeine, barely had the strength to stand after twenty-two more hours with no sleep.

In the last two days, she had taken blood samples from all the patients and rush-couriered them to Caff's temporary lab at Cedars-Sinai and also to her main team back in Atlanta. She did what she could with inadequate drugs to make the patients comfortable, but it was already clear they were losing. They had no idea about treatment. All she could do was go broad-spectrum on everything that was safe to give.

Nam pushed aside the CNN correspondent, but the man yelled out his questions, pursuing them across the gravel parking lot. "Doctor Kenner, does the CDC involvement indicate an epidemic?"

Ada darted around him but Burness caught up, comical as he jogged, circled around, then realized his cameras weren't ready. By the time they caught up, Ada had reached the infirmary door.

"Does this have something to do with the BioSecure you called, Doctor?" Burness yelled.

She turned, held up her hand to silence the shouted questions, and said, "I'm sorry. I have no comment yet. I haven't any answers. I just got here."

"But why are you here, Doctor. Aren't you coordinator of Emerging Viruses?"

Panji rescued her this time. "I asked my friend to come," she said blandly. "Now you'll all have to wait here."

Ada and Panji slipped inside, but tiny Nam Ling took up position in front of the door. Though she was a slip of a girl, she folded her arms and stared down the journalists. When they tried to squeeze past, Nam's voice stopped them. "I have a gun!"

Cameras filmed, journalists shouted questions, but no one tried to get past her again.

Ada found Armin still busy at work, masked and gloved as he went from cot to cot, assisted by the village's full-time nurse. They had been taking turns, as the only two doctors with any viral experience. Ada carried a digital recorder and recorded all her impressions, symptoms, temperatures, reactions to drugs, everything.

Armin didn't look up at her as he drew blood from an unconscious patient. "I have hemorrhaging here!"

One of the villagers screamed, a shrill sound like a train whistle, then thrashed on the cot. As Ada ran to the opposite side of the cot, she saw blood oozing from an elderly villager's eye sockets.

Even with Armin trying to restrain him, the old man convulsed, snapped free, and fell off the bed to the wooden floor, thrashing like a fish out of water.

"Can we risk a sedative?" shouted Armin.

"We have no choice," Ada said, hunting through the sparse medicine cabinets. "There's not much here."

"In my bag," snapped Armin, still holding the patient. "By that table!"

Ada remained calm, opened his flip-top metal case, carefully drew out a hypo, read labels and then measured a dose. As she finished, she glanced at Panji. "Did you find out if the Braxis doctors have flown out?"

Panji nodded. "Long gone. Like ghosts." She ran forward and helped restrain the villager.

23

Temple Street, Hong Kong

The crowds on Temple Street flowed around Bane and Manheim. No one seemed to notice that the Braxis security chief had an automatic pistol discreetly pointed at the WART Director. Bane used his peripheral vision to scan for buddy Arm or his other men, but it seemed rescue was not nearby.

Manheim lunged closer, his automatic pistol now pressed hard against

Bane's Kevlar vest. "This will hurt like hell."

Bane nodded, not moving. With a muzzle velocity of over eight hundred feet per second, a forty-five caliber would likely kill, and if he survived it'd tear up his guts. Very painful. He saw that Manheim's weapon was a standard Marine issue semi-automatic, which meant no hammer, recoil-operated and dangerous if a round was chambered. So he didn't move and used the only weapon he had.

"So what turns your crankshaft, Manheim? Obviously guns. Guess you're into the rough stuff, too. Like to tie up your girlfriend and play with candles? Or is it a boyfriend?"

Manheim said nothing.

"You freelancing, or is someone pulling your strings?" Bane saw Arm's red dreads bobbing towards him. Bane shook his head once and Arm stopped.

"That's fine," Manheim said, his voice soft, almost friendly. "We'll just have a quiet talk, shall we, without your buddy. He looks like he could take me in a fair fight. Not that I fight fair." He reached out with a quick snap of his arm, and pulled the earbud receiver/transmitter from Bane's ear. He dropped it and stepped on it with his heavy healed boot. "Well, sir. A small world, isn't it?"

Bane waited. There would be an opportunity, a moment when Manheim concentrated too hard on the crowd, or was distracted by a little girl running, the call of a hawker, or the laugh of a tourist. He watched for the betraying quick dart of eyes. Then Bane would take the initiative. But for now, Manheim was all tension, like a cat tensed to pounce on a mouse. Although they were nearly the same height and close in body weight, Bane was at least ten years older. "Commander Manheim, what are you planning?"

"Nothing you need to worry about."

"Somehow I have trouble imagining you as a guy I don't have to worry about. The image of you going to PTA meetings doesn't click, you know?"

They were so close, Bane could smell Manheim's breath, a mix of garlic and tea. "Smart mouth, Bane."

"I go to smart-mouths anonymous meetings. Nothing helps."

Manheim winked. "I'm just recovering our property, that's all. That's all I'll say. Nothing to do with you or WART."

"This is off the record, Manheim. Okay?"

"If you say so, sir."

"I'm good for my word."

"Yes, I've heard that."

"You checked on me?"

"Not hard to do, Colonel Bane. Google Bane, you're everywhere."

Bane frowned, suddenly in no mood for jokes. "What happened to you, Commander?"

"I retired, sir. I have a new career."

"Your service record was most impressive."

"Mutual admiration done?"

Bane pursed his lips. This might be a mistake, but he had to take the chance. "You lost your wife in 9-11. She worked for a small insurance company on the thirty-second floor. I've done research, too, Commander Manheim."

Manheim's hand reflexively gripped his gun.

Neither of them paid any attention to the crowds around them, the noise of chattering families and tourists, the nearby street band performing a horrible imitation of Chaos's number one hit. There was just ex-Marine Colonel Bane and ex-Navy Seal Commander Manheim. Both trained to kill.

"Standing orders, Manheim. If I'm out of radio contact, my teams move in." Bane pointed at the crushed radio. "Okay, I'll play. You're recovering property." Manheim nodded. "Who's the thief?"

"Let's just say he's dangerous."

"You're dangerous."

"More dangerous."

"Dangerous like your wife found out you had an affair, or dangerous like Bin Laden on a bad day?"

"More dangerous."

"The only man more dangerous than your boss, and Bin Laden, is Chaudhry Shujaa Khan."

"Yes."

"You're buying guns and men to go after Khan?" Bane stared at Manheim's expressionless face, unsure whether he should respect the man or consider him a madman. Obviously, Manheim knew Khan had stolen vaccine from Braxis in India. "Isn't that a little like shooting a rabid grizzly bear with a BB gun?"

Manheim grinned. "You could say that, Colonel."

"I go by Bane. Or Director. Now let's put this together." Bane stepped closer, until the muzzle of Manheim's gun touched his vest. "You lost your wife in 9-11. Believe me, I know about revenge, obsession, all that."

"I know. I saw the whole thing on TV."

Bane sighed. "Like half the world. So let's suppose you're out for revenge against terrorists. It'd have to be against any terrorist, since I don't think Khan was involved in 9-11. But you want a symbol, right?"

"An interesting guess, sir."

Bane felt the man's anger. "What I want to know is: are you using Braxis or are they using you?"

Manheim said nothing.

"Tell me something, Captain Manheim. Still off the record. Off the record because lives hang in the balance here."

Manheim's eyebrows lifted, but he remained silent.

"Was Doctor Begley an accident?"

Manheim studied Bane, as if deciding what to tell him, mouth slightly puckered in thought. Finally, he said, "Doubtful sir."

"So Braxis didn't engineer the release of a virus? Say, a virus they have a cure for?"

Manheim continued to stare at Bane. "That would make Seigneur Domergue a monster. I don't believe that, sir."

"You admire the man."

"Yes."

"Why?"

"Because he gets things done." He scowled.

"But you don't think he's capable of ruthlessly releasing the virus? To make a profit? Or prove a point."

"Capable, sir? He's certainly capable. What you need to understand, sir, is that Seigneur Domergue, he'll protect Braxis. He would never create this situation, sir." He frowned. "But whatever the reason for release—accident, Begley's incompetence, Khan, corporate greed, act of God—the important thing to know is that Khan is stealing both virus and vaccine. It has already been sold, but not delivered. I know the North Koreans and others have made purchases. I am sure, once delivered, these weapons will be ..."

Manheim glanced to the right, as if concentrating on not disclosing too much.

Bane took the opportunity. He moved in with a hard elbow thrust, pressing close to the gun and rolling to the side. The barrel slid down and off the vest as Bane spun around, and his other elbow snapped back and connected with Manheim's ear.

Bane's hand slipped under his jacket and came out with his small chromed revolver, woefully inadequate against a semi-automatic.

A woman screamed as Bane took aim, but Manheim had shouldered his way into the crowd of tourists and sprinted towards the sounds of traffic.

Bane ran after him. He saw Arm trying to intercept, too late.

Bane fell behind further as he weaved around a frail woman with a cane. He shoved his revolver back in its holster as he ran, trying to keep Manheim in view. Two of Bane's men closed from the south, but Manheim was faster.

The big ex-Seal ran out on the busy street where the market ended, waving his arms in front of a taxi. The taxi screeched to a halt, blaring its horn. Bane wouldn't be fast enough. Manheim opened the taxi door, yanked the passenger out, threw him to the sidewalk, and then jumped inside. The gun went to the driver's head. As Bane ran up behind the cab, it lurched ahead with a spin of tires.

He pounded on the trunk as the cab raced up Nathan Road.

24

Islamabad, Pakistan

Chaudhry Shujaa Khan barely broke a sweat, in spite of the one-hundred-eleven-degree temperature in the shade, at just before eleven in the morning.

C. S. Khan fed the monkeys against the backdrop of the Shah Faisal Mosque with its four white minarets, as he did every day, aware of, but ignoring, the eleven bodyguards who kept him safe. He was a national hero, even in these times of political façade, the "apparent" crackdown on radicals for the benefit of the mad Americans, but the crowds in the park always gave him space. It gave him some satisfaction as people peeled off the paths, deferring to him. His people. It pleased him that they thought of Khan as a national icon; he had spent millions on the last earthquake relief, he was famous for his vintage car collection, and though there were rumors that he bought and sold nuclear weapons and other WMDs—weapons of mass destruction—he was still the most powerful man in Pakistan. And all of this pleased him. But the simple pleasures of his daily walk among chattering monkeys bonded him to the ghost of his Mahiah, his wife. She walked with him.

At noon, in time for tea, he returned to his pink and white marble home with its fourteen car garage, surrounded by worn stone walls covered in vines that hid a razor-sharp barbed wire crown and the famous water gardens scented with jasmine. His guests waited impatiently in the gardens, knowing his habits but never daring to violate them. He had five guests, all with their bodyguards and three with translators.

"Tea, gentlemen," he said in English and waited for their translators.

His manservant, dressed in white, poured tea for the five guests in their dark suits. The buyers sat and sipped tea, and waited, simmering. Khan felt their hatred, but also their fear, even though these were five of the most dangerous men in the world. He also sensed their unease, meeting together in an open garden. They hated each other, but they hated the Americans more, which kept them from each other's throats. There could be no doubt that American agents had watched their arrival, although Khan's magnetic pulse generators and white noise screeners would ensure nothing was recorded or heard.

Finally, after he had sipped half of his tea in ritual silence, he said, "We have a supply of the vaccine."

The representative from Iran showed his arrogance by not waiting. "How big a supply?"

Khan didn't need a translator, and his gleaming black eyes turned on the Iranian bidder. He despised rudeness.

"A thousand pardons," Abu Reza Masefi said, bowing his head.

Khan, even at seventy-one, frightened these men of terror. And that was good. "I have enough for thirty-six million doses." He spoke slowly, to ensure they all understood. "I can get more."

"How?" demanded Ayatollah Ruhollah Jannati.

Only because Junnati was a holy man, Khan allowed him a little rudeness. "Braxis began full production in Mumbai months ago."

"That was fortunate." The Ayatollah's bearded face was hot with doubt. "But how did you get the vaccine?"

"I have thirty-three employees in the factory," Khan explained, this time glaring at the Holy Man. They waited, and he knew they needed details. "Many were arrested, but I have more that they did not discover. I have men in all of the Braxis factories and research facilities. In all of their competitors as well."

"And how much do we pay?" the representative from North Korea asked.

"One billion each." He waited until they were quiet. "For this, you will each have ten million doses. No negotiating."

The silence was long, broken only by the squawk of Khan's parrots.

Khan steepled two fingers in front of his lips. "Even as we speak, Satan's plague spreads across America." He laughed. "Spread by this Whore of Babylon. Abbey Chase and her touring *Superstar* television show will be the instrument of destruction."

They could believe whatever made them happy. God, fate, Allah, Kali—he didn't care. As long as they were frightened enough to buy. Allah-God-or-Kali had done nothing to save his sons from enemies. Millions of dollars donated to mosques, thousands of hours of prayer, crusading against the enemies of God—none of it had saved his sons from the Americans. God hadn't saved Mahiah, his beloved wife, or his sons—Kahlil, Sharif and Yahya—from Alban Bane and his assassin, Nam Ling. It didn't matter that his wife and sons had been collateral damage in a bigger operation, or that Bane's teams had been after Khan, not his family.

Now, the only god Khan knew, the only real Allah, was the almighty power of money. And the only cause that mattered was revenge: against America, Alban Bane and Nam Ling. He would send them all to oblivion.

25

Cedars-Sinai Hospital, LA

Doctor Caff Toy rubbed his eyes, took a gulp of cold coffee, and then stared through the Zeiss eyepieces once again. The slide bothered him, but he wasn't sure why. The antibody response seemed to indicate a killed virus—as in a vaccine—rather than a full-blown viral response, but how could that be? He yawned, gagging a bit on the sterile lab scent of phenol disinfectant.

He wanted to call Ada and discuss the findings with her, but it was two in the morning. He doubted she slept, but the last call from Ada indicated she was in full-blown epidemic. He wished he was with her up in Canada, instead of left behind in LA. There had been no new reported cases after the initial vector in California, and no fatalities, although he had assigned a team to the hospitals.

His satellite phone played the theme from *Star Wars*, and he answered it without looking. "Ada, honey?"

"No, honey, but I'm looking for her."

Fatigue dropped away, replaced by fear, and he found himself snapping to attention, his voice hardening into his crispest, most professional best. "Sir, how are you, Director Tomich?"

"Not getting much sleep, son, what with calls from the secretary of health, complaints from the Canadian government and a call from the special medical advisor to POTUS. Do you know who that is, son?"

"No, sir."

"POTUS—President of the United States. Doctor Domergue."

"Isn't that a conflict, sir? Domergue is the CEO of Braxis."

"Don't get smart with me. Where the hell is Doctor Kenner?"

Fear would not overcome loyalty. He felt as if someone had rammed a hockey stick up his butt. He stood up and paced the lab. "Sir, I don't know." He had no choice but to lie. Ada made it clear Tomich wouldn't support her inquiry, certainly not into Canada. He had no idea why everyone seemed bent on obstructing their investigation. He assumed it had something to do with Braxis and Domergue, and his influence with powerful people.

"Don't bullshit me, son," Tomich said. "You're not a good liar, and I'm not in the mood."

Caff paced faster and faster. The lab was empty, and his footsteps were loud on the tile floor. "Sir, I really don't know. She had a call. She left. That's all I know."

"I doubt that's all you know. By any chance is she in Kinosewak, Canada?" Tomich's voice rose like a stern father, not hysterical or emotional, just loud.

"She didn't tell me, sir." That he didn't know was sort of the truth, but only technically. He knew she was in Canada, but he'd never heard of Kinosewak.

"Damn both of you. She doesn't answer her phone and you give me crap."

Feeling woozy from lack of food and sleep, too much coffee and the tongue-lashing, Caff leaned against the door and focused on calming himself. "If it helps, sir, she was called by the World Health Organization."

"I know that, damn it. You think I'm not on top of you two?" Tomich sounded eerily calm, now. "I'm shutting you down, Doctor Toy. You are to return to Atlanta for new assignment."

"But the outbreak, sir?" Caff found he was clutching his phone. How could Tomich not understand the seriousness of the situation?

"What outbreak, Toy? There's no bloody outbreak. There's a flu bug, according to a Doctor Cheung from Braxis."

"But sir—"

"Be quiet. Just listen. I'm angry at Kenner, not you." Caff heard an audible yawn on the phone. "Look, you've contained in LA. Bring your research home—son."

"Yes, sir."

"I mean, now. There's a red-eye. Take it."

"Yes, sir." Then he remembered the slide on the microscope. "Sir, I did find something—"

"Bring it home, Toy. You don't want me angry."

"No, sir, I don't."

"I've already lifted the containment order. I'll meet you in the morning. I mean later this morning. You can tell me then."

"Yes, sir."

The hard edge returned. "And Toy. I want you to reach Doctor Kenner. Tell her I want to talk to her. Now."

"I understand, sir."

He tried calling Ada, but there was no answer.

The wooziness continued and he found he had to sit down. Had he been fired? And what about the disease? Tired, he started shutting down the equipment, the hum in the room gradually fading as he circled the lab tables. He packed the samples in a wheeled case, turned off the fluorescents, and then stood by the door. He felt wrong leaving. He had been on the verge of a discovery. But he didn't have Ada's balls, that was sure; he needed his job and would not stand up to Tomich.

The phone rang again, and this time he checked the caller ID: unknown. He ignored it and rolled the case up the main hallway toward the elevators.

The isolation ward was eerily silent. The hall lights were in energy-save mode, half the tubes turned off, and the nurses' station was empty. He was probably on rounds. A shame. Hot Buns Robbie was cute, and they had a "maybe" date for tomorrow night. Perhaps he should wait to say goodbye. Robbie wouldn't be long, since there were now only seven patients in isolation.

He listened. Somewhere he heard a humming, probably a bad light tube, but nothing else. This wing was far from active due to containment issues, but strangely the blower fans were silent as well. Tomich must have already ordered the shutdown of the facility, including the negative pressure fans.

He jumped when his phone rang again. It echoed off sterile tile and laminated walls, but he was grateful for the company.

"Yes?"

"Doctor Cafferty Toy?"

He hesitated. The voice was deep, low pitched yet forceful. "Yes."

"I'm Doctor Franklin Castle."

"Yes doctor?"

"I work at Site F Braxis."

Caff stopped wheeling his case. "Yes, Doctor Castle, how can I help you?"

"I think I can help you. You're assisting Doctor Kenner, correct?"

"Yes, that's right."

"I'd like to meet with both of you. I have something you should see."

Caff hesitated and then said, "Doctor Kenner's out of town."

"Oh. But Doctor Toy, it's urgent."

"I can meet with you."

"Yes—but it is—I really should meet you both."

Caff felt his own excitement rise. This could be important; it almost certainly was critical if it involved Braxis. Once he flew back to Atlanta, Tomich would never let him continue on the case. "Doctor Kenner's in Canada."

"Could I have her private number?"

Suddenly Caff felt apprehensive. The voice was too friendly, too insistent, or something else. "I think we should meet first. Her satellite phone is private."

"Doctor, this is critical. It has to be soon."

"I'm Doctor Kenner's assistant."

A long silence emphasized the man's disappointment. "Fine. Fine. I'm at the Four Seasons. Can you meet me right away?"

"I can get a taxi."

"Fine. It must be now."

Caff grabbed the handle of his bag. "What room?"

"Just ask the concierge. They know me."

He left a note for Robbie: Hot Buns, got called away. Take you up on that drink next time. Kisses, Caff. He jotted his satellite phone number and made his way quickly to the main entrance of the hospital. By great good fortune, a cab was waiting at the entrance, engine idling. He climbed in the back, threw his bag on the seat and snapped, "Four Seasons." The CDC couldn't budget for the Four Seasons, but Caff had studied the tour maps and knew it wasn't far, just over on Doherty, not far from his own hotel.

The cab driver said nothing, answering with quick acceleration and a merge on to San Vincente, then Santa Monica. The cab seemed very new on the inside, the seats immaculately clean and springy, but it must have been a high mileage car because Caff noticed a loud humming from behind him. He knew nothing about cars, but burned out bearings popped to mind.

He dialed Ada's number, excited, wanting to share the latest. If he could find out something from Castle, he might be able to save the investigation, and his own butt. Ada didn't answer, but he left her a message: "Ada, honey, it's Caff. I just had a call from a Doctor Franklin Castle at Site F." He grabbed the door handle as the cab took a corner too fast. The tires squealed and the buzz became louder. The noise reminded him of something, a childhood memory, disquieting but distant. "Sorry, Ada. Wacky cab driver. I'm meeting Doctor Castle at the Four Seasons. He said it's important. Oh …" He giggled. "Honey, I think we're fired. You ex is pissed and he wants you, babe. He wants you bad. Ciao for now."

Caff pounded on the security divider between him and the driver. "Honey, slow it down, willya? I want to get there alive." If anything, the cabbie drove faster. Caff didn't know LA all that well, but he was pretty sure they passed Doherty. "Hey, don't bother running the meter. I'm not a tourist. There's a twenty in it if you get me there fast—but in once piece." The cabbie accelerated and raced past Beverly Hills. "You passed it long ago, sweetie. Just turn left and go back."

The cab jumped ahead, faster and faster, suspension clanking, wheels buzzing louder.

Caff felt a tickle of unease. Did the cab driver not understand English? Or was he just being stubborn and running the meter for all it was worth? Worse, was he some kind of gay basher?

The buzzing was louder now, as if the wheel bearings would burn out at any moment. Scared, Caff surveyed the cab. He couldn't find a cab license. The only ornament was a pendant, hanging from the mirror in the front seat, an ivory carving of an angel.

Caff pounded on the glass. "Slow it down. Damnit, I mean it!" The cab sped along and the cab driver did not turn his head. To Caff he was nothing but an anonymous silhouette. Caff tried to lean over, to see the man's face, but he saw nothing, only a general impression the man was some kind of freakish giant. The bench seat seemed too small for this massive man with his bodybuilder shoulders, and his blonde head pressed against the headliner.

"Am I being kidnapped here?" Caff said it with a laugh, but his voice cracked with nervousness. Still the cabbie said nothing. "Look, butch, I'm calling the cops!" He started dialing his cell phone.

The cab tires screamed this time and the drone became unbearably loud.

Something batted against Caff. He swatted at it. In the dim light of streetlamps, Caff had a quick impression of movement in the backseat. *What the hell?* The buzzing was all around him now, but it was more organic than mechanical. He glanced down at the armrest in the middle of the seat. It had popped open and—

Caff screamed.

The bulbous ball of insects flew out of the hole in the armrest, buzzing and angry.

"Stop!" Caff screamed. "There are bees back here! Stop the cab!" Caff pulled at the lock pegs on the doors, but they wouldn't unlock. He pressed the down button on the window, but nothing happened.

The bees swarmed around him, not stinging him, but swirling around. Terror paralyzed him. Suddenly, he was the six-year-old boy, stung by a single bee, rushed gasping to the hospital, overdosed on Benadryl and surviving only because of emergency treatment.

"Please! I'm allergic to bees!"

A soft voice laughed. "I know."

Caff recognized it.

The voice of Doctor Franklin Castle.

Caff screamed. He tried dialing 9-1-1 again, but the bees were all over his hands, angry now from their bouncing journey in the trunk of the cab.

The first sting was enough. Searing pain shot up his wrist, as if someone had shoved a six-inch spike under his skin. A bee flew into his face and stabbed him on the nose. He screamed, batting at it even as it attacked, and then his entire face was aflame. His sinuses closed. Desperate, Caff smashed his elbow into the window but it just shook and didn't break. Pain and fury drove him and this time the window flew out of the frame. He heard his own forearm snap, but the pain was nothing next to the knife stabs of the bees. Every sting felt like acid pumped into his flesh. The bees flowed out of the broken window as they sped along Santa Monica, but Caff knew he was already dead.

He couldn't breathe. His heart raced. He opened his mouth, gasping, and a bee flew into it. He spit, but too late. His tongue instantly swelled.

Caff lost his focus. His vision blurred. He tried to dial his phone again. He heard a voice on the phone. "9-1-1. What is the emergency?"

But he could only mumble, "Eeeellpp eeeee". His tongue filled his mouth, a great slab of meat that choked him.

"Sir? Sir? I can't hear you sir?"

In the front seat the cabbie laughed. Caff struggled with blackness. He wanted to know why? Why had this man attacked him? His thoughts were chaotic. Through the pain, through the haze, he realized that this man had planned it. The bees in the trunk and the hole in the armrest. The call to the hospital, luring him out.

The giant in the front seat turned for the first time, and through the fog Caff realized the cab had stopped. The dome light came on, bringing stabbing pain to his swollen eyes, and a new dizziness. In the euphoria of immunoglobulin E responses, he was both delirious from lack of air and in anaphylactic shock, and he recoiled from the bee demon—but the giant had the face of an angel. Long blonde hair framed a Hollywood handsome face and bright blue eyes. But the face glowed, golden and magical. He wore a mask of gold.

Caff wondered if this was the angel of death.

26

Karachi, Pakistan

Markus Manheim, Braxis's chief of security, watched from the unmarked Braxis helicopter as Khan's Millennium super yacht powered out of Karachi, her two-hundred-and-seventeen-foot hull cleaving through the harbor traffic. In the last two weeks he had discovered that the *Hanu* was a familiar sight steaming in and out of Karachi. Most of the fifteen million people who lived in the port city knew that this was Khan's second home, that he refused to travel by air, that she was protected by the name on her hull, that she was custom-built by Millennium to be the fastest and safest ocean-going yacht anywhere.

Hanu meant *scabbard* and anyone who saw the *Hanu* sailing towards them would yield, except the naval ships; not to yield meant the sword might not stay in its scabbard. The few pirates who were not on Khan's payroll would never touch her, not since five years ago, when Somali pirates were massacred in the attempt.

Markus's helicopter swept past the sleek hull. He hoped his information was correct. If Khan was not on board, many men would die for no purpose. His boats could never catch the *Hanu,* with her top speed of 75 knots; she was propelled by water jets courtesy of twin Paxman engines generating nearly 18,000 horsepower, supplemented by a Lycoming turbine pushing out another 12,000. Even if a boat could catch her, the *Hanu*'s double aluminum hull was sheathed with Kevlar, and triple reinforced.

As they flew over, he saw the gun placements, bow and stern, but those, he knew, were only the obvious armaments. Khan was paranoid, and he traveled with more protection than many heads of state.

Markus knew everything there was to know about Khan. His investigation in the last few months had revealed that Khan had infiltrated several Braxis facilities. Khan had stolen vaccine and virus. Already, the most ruthless men in the world had bid. Markus and his team were expendable. Stopping Khan was all that mattered.

Markus knew the exact layout and equipment of the *Hanu,* thanks to his boss's efforts. Domergue's yacht also came from Millennium and he had "asked" politely for the *Hanu*'s plans: "I'll want something better than the best you've ever built," he had told the designers. Of course the best they'd ever built to date was the *Hanu.*

"Don't fly by" Markus warned his old friend, pilot Alf Blegen.

Alf nodded but didn't speak into the headset. They had flown missions in the Gulf and he knew better than to question his commander. Another fly-by would be suspicious.

He surveyed the six men, belted in to the spacious belly of the Sikorsky S-55, one of three massive helicopters—a seventy-five-million-dollar investment—run by Braxis in the Arabian sea theatre, supposedly for cargo runs, but currently retrofitted with Avenger 30mm cannons firing API rounds that could pierce tank armor. His men were his own elite team, ex-Seals he had commanded in the past, men who would kill without question.

And today, it would be kill or die. Bane was too close to wait. The encounter in Hong Kong had made it necessary to move up the attack on Khan. But Khan would not be easy, at least as ruthless as the Somali pirates that lay in wait for him off Cape Madrak. The Somalis were promised the ship and the vast fortune they would find on board—and revenge for their defeat in '04. All that mattered to Markus was that Khan must die. The future of Braxis, and perhaps a million or more lives, hung in the balance.

"Commander," Alf's voice crackled in his headset. "She's cruising at thirty-eight knots."

"Stay below the horizon, Alf," Markus answered. There was no need to tell his six soldiers to check loads and equipment. To do less meant death out here.

"You know what's at stake," Markus said, because he had to say something to his men. A commander always spoke to his men before battle, even when they knew what they were doing. "We're here for control. Hopefully the Somalis will take care of Khan. But we'll engage if need be. Khan must not live past today."

All of the men nodded, their helmets bobbing, their eyes hard and cold. They had all fought terrorists as Seals, as his men. Now they were the Braxis A team. They would not hesitate to gun down a known terrorist like Khan. To them, what was at stake was their fifty thousand dollar danger pay, high stakes for two weeks of work, but they were also motivated by their target. Markus and his team had let down Braxis, allowed Khan to create an international incident for which Braxis was liable. Many people had died and would die.

They were about to engage in piracy and murder, albeit attacking men of terror, but at risk to Domergue and Braxis was their international reputation and, perhaps, billions of dollars. To Markus personally, this was a mission about recovering lost face. Nothing mattered more than that. Khan had infiltrated Site F, caused a terrorist incident, released a virus, and stolen the priceless vaccine—all on Commander Markus Manheim's watch. Only Domergue knew Markus's shame, but that didn't matter. A man had nothing if he had no self-respect. And the stakes for the world at large—well, the world would be rid of a mass murderer who bought and sold WMDs.

"Our job is to stop that ship if the trap doesn't work. Let the Somalis do the rest."

The smell of sweat was strong, mingled with the oily fragrance of the three turboshaft engines. But there was no smell of fear. He had flown many missions with these men, had commanded them once as Seals, used them whenever he needed expert mercenaries. With him he had two snipers, and the best hand-to-hand killers money could buy. The snipers carried M25 sniper rifles. Three of the team handled MK19 40 mm Model 3 guns that fired grenades able to pierce two inches of armor, set up on tripods at the doors. The rest manned 240B Machine guns. All carried automatic weapons and grenades.

They expected the worst. No one hoped for the best. Their target was Khan; he hadn't survived for all those decades as the world's most notorious terrorist without being the best.

One of the men tapped his helmet. "Getting static, Commander," he said.

"Now's the time to fix it, Dave." Markus began the ritual check of his loads. He carried his favorite pair of .45 caliber semiautomatic M1911A pistols, one holstered on each hip, and even though they were recoil-operated, he kept them chambered. One day, he'd lose a kneecap over it, but not today.

Markus found the ritual check kept him steady. He had seen too much to feel fear, but Khan was, perhaps, the scariest dude he had ever gone up against. Still, he felt no heat, his heart rate was steady—he had long ago trained himself to sense and manage heart rate and sweat—and he felt a smile creep on to his features. Being security chief of Braxis had its rewards—authority, prestige, stock options, excitement—and today's mission was one of them.

"Sir, it has begun," said Dave.

Markus moved forward, balancing himself against the sway of the big helicopter, and peered through the giant scope on the tripod. It was set to the widest field, but even so it took a moment for Markus to see anything. The helicopter wailed along, just two hundred feet above the Arabian Sea, throwing back a wide channel of froth and wake. The image settled and Markus saw the smoke.

"Ready, team!" he snapped automatically.

Part of him hoped the Somalis would fail. He wanted action this day. But the amount of black smoke indicated the attack was well under way.

"Close range," Markus said to Alf, the pilot.

"Yes, sir."

Markus moved up beside his friend and leaned close. He gave Alf a thumbs-up. Alf smiled in return, his blue eyes lighting with excitement. No words were needed. They communicated silently. *Fly well, my friend. They may have anti-aircraft missiles.* Alf nodded.

Markus feared they had Stingers. The heat seekers at short range would be nearly impossible to avoid, even with countermeasures.

Markus watched as they swept up on the battle. Because of their low altitude, they burst onto the scene rather than revealed slowly. At first all he saw was black smoke. He heard no gunfire over the howl of the compressors. He glanced back. His men were ready, alert, watching him.

As they blasted into the smoke, the big Sikorsky's blades swept away the black fog, revealing the *Hanu*, surrounded by six Top Gun F2 Cigarette Boats. The Top Guns had been the under-the-table fee to the Somali pirates—Markus had felt a tug of conscience over the fee, knowing the performance boats would be used to attack innocent victims if the Somali pirates survived—but Khan was an overwhelmingly important target. After all, the risk to the pirates was far greater than their normal hit and run on defenseless cargo ships and pleasure craft. And perhaps Braxis could do something about the boats after the battle.

As the Sikorsky screamed in to the theatre, the *Hanu* was in full flight mode. The six Top Guns fell behind, unable to match the seventy-two knots, even with all four engines churning long spear-like wakes.

"Dave, bear with the cannons!" Manheim said into his microphone.

Dave was already targeting.

The thirty-millimeter cannons spatted, rocking the helicopter. Dave, to his credit, only missed on his first burst. Small explosions erupted along the *Hanu*'s starboard hull. All of the Braxis "security men" fired now, armor-piercing rounds, machine gun blasts.

The *Hanu*'s bow leapt up, her stern dipping below the surface as her captain engaged the turbines. The extra 12,000 horsepower left the Cigarette boats—and even the helicopter for a moment—well behind. No wonder Khan felt safe on his armored boat. She had to be clipping eighty knots! The wake speared backwards in a knife-like thrust.

But Alf adjusted speed and the Sikorsky easily caught her. Dave fired the twin cannons again. A car-sized hole appeared in the side of the *Hanu*, but she didn't slow down. Her captain was good, moving into an evasive pattern.

The first Stinger missile came so suddenly Alf barely had time for countermeasures. The only sign of it was a puff of smoke from the deck. Instantly, Alf hit the counters, and took them so hard to port that the six men in the back hung from their safety straps. Markus's chin smacked against the glass.

How many Stingers would they have? Each was a single-shot disposable launcher and cost a fortune. But of course, Khan bought and sold Stingers.

His answer came as the second missile fired.

Alf deployed and evaded, but the third missile fired simultaneously.

"It's going to hit!" Alf shouted. But it didn't. He managed a third evade.

"Give us distance!" Markus shouted, even as Dave gave cover fire with the cannons.

Two more Stingers flew from the deck of the *Hanu*.

"Bail!" shouted Alf into their headphones.

Three of the men threw themselves out of the open doors, taking their chances with pirates and the sea.

Markus felt the Stinger hit, a loud concussion that deafened him and he sensed the scream of metal. He hurled himself out the door. But already it was too late.

27

Arabian Sea

Bane saw the Sikorsky erupt in a ball of flame. The big blades flew in three directions like giant swords.

The *Hanu* sped on, still pursued by the long Cigarette Boats, but pulling well ahead of them.

"There's men in the water," Bane said into this headset. "That's our priority."

"We may never have another chance to get Khan," said Ridpath, the pilot.

"I know, Rid. I know."

The black chopper swung around in a long arc, heading for the men in the ocean.

By the time they recovered the four survivors, the *Hanu* had vanished.

Markus Manheim was badly burned but conscious, and he took the headset one of Bane's men handed him. His face was blistered, the skin peeled back like a layer of dry onion flakes, but he glared at Bane. The cabin was pungent with the stench of burned flesh, like some mad barbeque gone wrong, even with the sliding hatch wide open.

"Piracy is a serious offence," Bane said mildly.

"Go to hell."

"You look like you've been and back."

"You followed us?" Manheim said.

"Of course."

"You were going to watch us? Not interfere?" Manheim's lip trembled, the only sign he was in agony.

"That's right."

"Isn't that illegal?"

Bane shrugged. "International waters. I'm not police, you know that."

"It would be convenient if we killed Khan."

"A happy day for the world," Bane agreed.

"So what now?"

"Now you tell me everything you know."

"Or what? What can you do?"

Bane smiled. "I can throw you back in the sea."

"I don't believe you."

"As far as anyone knows, you're dead. I'm just feeding the fish."

Manheim brushed away flakes of his own skin as if to show he didn't care about something as insignificant as severe burns. "Do it then."

Bane nodded. Arm and Jeff grabbed Manheim, one by each elbow and dragged him kicking towards the open door. They half shoved him out of the hatch.

Bane held up his hand, but Arm and Jeff left Manheim dangling at the door, his body tussled by the turbulence of their flight.

Still dangling from the chopper, Manheim shouted, "What do you want to know?"

"First, tell me all you know about the virus."

Manheim bucked and pulled at Arm and Jeff, as if he wanted to be thrown back in the sea.

28

Kinosewak, Canada

Ada sat on a stackable plastic garden chair between Chief Mathias Hughie and Armin Buchler, exhausted, sad, and elated. Nam stood behind them, arms folded, a silent statue. Ada felt a little guilty, sitting here with her phone off for one more night, but she wanted just a little time with these lovely people, then one night of sleep—her first in how many days?—and then back to Atlanta to face her ex-hubby's wrath.

They had contained the mini-epidemic, losing only three patients, and they had collected a lot of data; there were no new cases. After the stifling, bitter disinfectant smells of the Infirmary—that universal stench of phenol, fever sweat and shed blood—the mossy fragrance of the hillside was uplifting, almost spiritual.

The size of the crowd astonished her. At least a thousand of the Kinosewak nation sat on the uncut grass overlooking the muddy river and the village. Only Ada, Armin and the chief sat in the five-dollar chairs.

The audience sat silent, enraptured by Panji Maingan's—the Little Coyote's—haunting song. Panji sang to the occasional chord on her acoustic guitar, in a language Ada found both lovely and impossible to understand. Yet, as she closed tired eyes and listened, she was taken to a land of myth and tricksters, a time when the earth was pristine forest and the people talked with the animals. At least, that's what Ada got from the sweet sound of Panji's voice. Ada had heard Panji's English songs on the radio, especially the number one hit "Coyote Blues," but to hear Panji in her own language went beyond lovely.

The Kinosewak nation had gathered together to honor them now that the immediate crisis was over, and though three people had died of the mysterious virus, the rest were recovering and many of the patients had been carried to the hill to hear Panji's performance. Ada had focused only on saving lives, on working alongside Armin, but soon she'd have to face her ex-hubby boss and the consequences. For tonight, though, there was just the people and the music.

Panji's impromptu concert drew everyone from the village and surrounding lands. Unlike concerts Ada typically attended, the audience fell entirely silent when she sang: no hoots, shouts, claps, cheers or whistles. But between each melody, the cheering and screaming lasted for long minutes. Panji was beyond a hero to these people.

Panji sang by moon- and firelight, and somewhere, to more cheers from the village, a coyote howled in the forest.

Later they roasted corn on the fires and Ada found herself swept up in the biggest party imaginable. Nam stayed with her, watchful and silent, but Ada took the chance to unwind and enjoy. Everyone wanted to thank her and talk to her.

Munching on corn, Ada found herself wondering about Nam. What was her story? She never spoke, rarely sat; she was always the watchful guardian. She stood now at the edge of a ring of firelight, her head turning slowly, eyes darting everywhere. Ada brought Nam a bottle of water and a bottle of good Canadian beer for herself. Nam nodded but didn't smile.

"You're not eating?"

"I'm on duty," Nam said, her arms folded. She wore her strange nunchucky weapon on a tiny belted waist, carried no purse but slung a plain messenger bag across her slight chest. Even as Ada tried to engage her, the always-active eyes scanned the crowd.

"Let me guess. You were Secret Service once?"

Ada meant it as a joke, but Nam didn't even look at her as she replied, "No, I was in D.E.A. when Bane found me. Before that, Hong Kong Police."

Ada sighed. Oh, well. Still, she tried again. "There're no assassins here, Nam."

"Never know that."

"But you have to relax sometime."

"Bane says you are important. I see you are important too. So there."

So there? Ada felt her own smile. "Well, thanks anyway, Nam."

"No thanks needed, please."

Ada shrugged. Nam was a creature of duty. "So tell me about yourself."

In the long silence that followed, Ada heard the laughter of villagers, the mournful howl of a coyote, night birds and crickets. She almost gave up on an answer, then Nam said, "I told you. D.E.A. And Hong Kong Police."

"Yes, you told me." She took a long chug of beer. God, there was nothing like Canadian beer. "So boyfriends? Girlfriends?"

Nam stared at her, unblinking. "What do you mean?"

"Small talk."

"How can talk be small?"

Ada didn't know whether to like or resent Nam. The agent was somewhat charming in her absolute focus and dedication, but mostly frustrating. But she couldn't forget Nam's quick action in the hospital with the DSS agents, and her work in controlling the journalists in Kinosewak, and it was clear she was a good person to have around in troubled times. "Sorry. I like to talk."

"Not me."

"I gathered." Ada frowned. "Fine. I'll leave you be. But eat something."

"Doctor?"

Ada hesitated. "Please. Call me Ada. I don't like Doctor from my friends. Makes me feel old."

"I give you something, Doctor ... Ada?"

"What's that?" Ada stared down at Nam. She seemed so earnest, in some ways childlike, at the same time too serious and too all-business, but there was something about the wisp of a woman that Ada liked, and she smiled a lot for someone so grim.

"I give you this?" She slid her canvas messenger bag around to the front and pulled out a little black box.

"What is that, Nam?"

"Is called a stun gun."

"I don't need a stun gun. They're illegal aren't they?"

"In six states, yes. Yes, in six states."

"So, I … well, thanks, but I don't need it."

"I'm thinking you do."

"No, I don't." She said it firmly, hoping not to offend Nam, but then she realized there was probably nothing she could say that would upset the girl.

"Doctor Ada. I'm recalled to Washington. But I'm thinking you need protection. Just recharge every three weeks."

Ada slid into a mock karate pose. "I know karate. Brown belt."

Nam smiled. "Ikkyu grade not good enough, Doctor Ada. Not good enough, no."

Ada laughed. "I'm not in danger. Stun guns are no good against viruses, trust me."

"I trust you, Doctor Ada." Nam said it so earnestly, Ada found herself reaching out her hand. Nam dropped the stun gun into her palm.

"You touch attacker, and push button."

"Fine. Okay. Thanks, Nam, I appreciate your concern." She slipped it into her big Fendi purse and hoped stun guns weren't illegal in Canada. She had a feeling they were.

"Don't thank me—Ada."

"Well, I'll miss you, Nam."

"We meet again, I'm sure."

Ada nodded, held out her hand to shake. Nam hesitated and then shook. Her hand was crusty and calloused, like a farmer's hand, which startled Ada for a moment, and her grip was almost painful.

Well past midnight, as the angry red eye of Mars swept up into a starry sky, Ada found Panji sitting on a log by the embers of a bonfire, chatting with Chief Mathias, Armin, and some of the elders. She smiled as Ada approached and waved for her to sit on the log beside them. Nam stood behind them until Panji insistently patted the log beside her. Reluctant, little Nam sat beside Panji.

"Ada, have you even slept since you got here?" Panji asked, her smile fading.

"Not much."

Panji put her hand on Ada's shoulder. "There are no words for what you've done here."

"I did my job."

Panji laughed. "You have my eternal friendship."

Ada didn't know what to say. Panji's offer of friendship meant more than any other reward ever could. Before she could answer, a phone rang. She started. She hadn't turned her satellite phone back on. Then she realized it was Armin's. He smiled at them, stood up and answered, scowled for a moment, covered the mouthpiece and held out the phone to her. "Actually, it's for you."

Ada looked at the phone as if it were a venomous snake. Her boss had thought to phone WHO to track her down. She sighed. Well, no avoiding this, then.

"Hello, this is Doctor Kenner."

"Ada, I've been trying to reach you," said Devon.

"My battery died." A white lie, better than the brutal truth—*I don't want to talk to you.*

"Ada, you need to come back."

"Yes. Yes, I know." She let her gaze wander the cheerful hillside, glowing with embers of a dozen bonfires. She didn't want to leave these wonderful people. But she had no more reason to stay. The immediate danger was over, and Health Canada had taken jurisdiction.

"No, you don't understand," Devon sounded strangely subdued. "Ada, it's Doctor Toy."

"What about him, sir? I know he's—"

Devon interrupted. "No, babe, it's not what you think. They found him in the South Coast Botanical Gardens."

Ada gripped the phone, not understanding, but on edge because of Devon's tone. Why was he at the Botanical Gardens? Devon never called her babe, not since Quentin was born. Something was very wrong.

"Devon?"

"Caff's dead, Ada. I'm sorry."

29

Dish, Atlanta

Ada stood at the door of Dish, Atlanta's current number one gay club, kissing each of Caff's hundreds of friends as they arrived. By the door, a sign on an easel proclaimed Sunday: Caff—eteria Day. Wake the Dead Wake. Beside it was a poster-sized blow up of Caff dressed in a sexy Saturday-night outfit, and underneath in bold pink lettering: Dish closed to the public in honor of our dear sausage junkie Caff—eteria. Invited Guests Only. Costume optional. Clothing optional.

It seemed Caff's Wake the Dead Wake drew everyone from the community and they took the sign literally: some wore elaborate costumes, drag, masks, makeup; others were as near to naked as respect for the family would allow.

Caff's casket sat on an elevated platform in the middle of a smoky dance floor and already his friends danced and flowed around him to the beat of Chaos's music. The rap of Chaos seemed right, too, considering all the headline news about the suicide-murder. The big dance club glowed with flashing lights and smelled of pot, tobacco, dry ice and spilled beer.

It made Ada happy to know he had so many friends. They all seemed to know her, too, although she could only put names to a few dozen of the "regular crowd"—the ones not in costume or drag—since she had stopped clubbing four years ago after her second promotion at the CDC. Obviously, Caff talked about her at the clubs, because everyone who entered kissed her cheek and called her "A.K. honey."

The party was Barbarino Fosco's idea. The gay community knew him as Barbie and he owned Dish; he was also Caff's best friend outside of work. Barbie had met her at the airport on her return from Canada and helped her with the arrangements, staying at her house for the entire week. He seemed to sense her dark despair and wouldn't let her out of his sight. He talked non-stop: "Caff would have liked red … Sweetie, Caff-eteria loved you to death, you know that, don't you … Let's make it a costume wake … We have to do posters of bees and flowers, it'll make Caffie laugh …"

Now he stood beside her, greeting everyone in line with a variation on "Oh, baby butch, who have you done?" Barbie was resplendent in drag tonight, a huge surprise for Ada who had only ever seen him as a simmering hunk, brooding and masculine most of the time, macho in skin-tight leathers that revealed everything. He was a four-hour-a-day bodybuilding junkie. "It's my fix, honey, so get over it!" he'd scream when friends teased him about his habit. She laughed at the sight: Barbie's muscles revealed through a diaphanous low cut gown under a tanned face crazy with makeup and a wild red I-Love-Lucy wig. Barbarino Fosco was a macho-macho man, even in drag, and it didn't help that he wore a see-through thong that revealed "above average prime" as Caff would have said.

Ada could almost hear Caff laugh. In fact, Dish was full of Caff's laughter. Every partier in the club laughed for Caff, danced for him, one by one hovered over his open casket and kissed his cold cheek.

Also standing in the reception line was Caff's mother Marakit, all four foot, five inches of her. She seemed bewildered, but she giggled as each boy kissed her. The joy of the wake had wiped away the woman's grief, and came close to helping mend Ada's wretched despair as well. Caff's straight brother and sister looked less comfortable, but they smiled a lot.

"Here comes Scrapbook girl," Barbie yelled, over the music. Jersey was another close friend of Caff's, heavy into "scare drag" with harsh makeup that exaggerated his huge nose. He carried an easel with a massive scrapbook, knocking into dancers as he ploughed through the crowd. Ada, Jersey and Barbie had worked on the "Story of a Sausage Junky," a scrapbook tribute to Caff and all his friends. The pages showed his entire life, from diapers to death, but most of the photos were party pictures.

Ada was as happy as she could be at the wake of her best friend. She knew, somewhere, Caff was having a ball, ogling all the hot men who danced nearly naked on the club floor.

"Babe, who invited the crows?" Barbie asked, laughing in her ear. "Crows" was Barbie-speak for "straight"—straight as the crow flies. He preferred it to "breeder."

Ada turned to see a scowling ex-husband Devon and his latest fling, Julie MacKenzie. He wore his best suit and a silk tie and his consort was timid but smiling in a Prada dress. Behind him was a long line of CDCers. She never thought for a moment so many would come from the office, let alone Devon. His girl Julie had obviously never been in a gay club before. Her wide eyes roamed everywhere, but her smile revealed both amusement and excitement.

Devon was nearly knocked over by a pair of sweating, half-naked male dancers. Finally, he made the reception line and held out a stiff hand to Ada. "I'm so sorry, Ada," he said.

She didn't hear his words over the too-loud Chaos rap, but she read his lips easily.

He stunned her by leaning over and air-kissing both her cheeks.

"Thank you for coming, Dev," she yelled back.

He nodded stiffly and took his girl-toy in tow, using her as a shield as they moved towards the open bar. Ada couldn't help laughing when one dancer goosed her ex's butt.

Over the next half hour, they greeted at least two hundred of Caff's friends from work. Most were more Caff's age, far more comfortable at the "Wake the Dead Wake" than Devon. It would give them all something to talk about for weeks at work.

Some of them she didn't know. One man arrived around nine-thirty, an overly tall man who stood out in any crowd, but Ada only caught a fleeting glimpse of him. Like some of the others in the crowd, he was in costume, but what made him stand out was a golden mask. The men in the club swarmed the butch newcomer, hanging off his six foot six muscular frame. He wore a clingy spandex shirt and a thick gold chain hanging with some kind of white ornament around his massive neck. Over the next hour, as she finished the greetings, she occasionally spotted the golden mask turned her way, piercing blue eyes staring at her from behind it.

Devon circled back through the crowd around eleven, without Julie. "Didn't recognize Barbie under that wig," Devon said with a smile.

"I love it," Ada said.

"I'll miss Caff buzzing around the labs," Devon said.

Ada laughed. Devon knew better than to offer phony "sympathies."

By midnight, most of the people had arrived. Laughter chased away the tears that had been threatening to spill all week, although seeing Devon brought a morbid sense of doom with it. Not since Quentin's birth, not since that terrible day when she saw her baby boy, legless and crying—not once in the twelve years since—had she cried. But tonight, even more than when she heard the news of Caff's "accident," she wanted to cry. Caff had all these friends, so much life ahead of him.

His death felt like her fault.

Later, Ada and Barbie joined the dancers and gyrated beside Caff's open coffin. As they danced, she stared at Caff's too-pale face. Ada hated that the funeral director she'd hired hadn't got the makeup right. Caff's lovely dark complexion was all wrong. "We did our best, with the bee-sting marks," the director apologized; they made him look pasty white, although he seemed to be smiling. The bee stings were slightly visible through the makeup.

Again Ada almost cried, but no tears flowed.

The music went into a new high, and the dancers came alive to a wilder beat. Barbie and Ada escaped the dance floor and found a table by the stage, empty because of the *Reserved* tag.

Barbie brought drinks. For a long time they sat, listening to the music, in their own worlds.

"You're in some other universe, baby-cheeks," Barbie said after a while.

Ada shrugged. "Thinking about Caff."

"Me too." He smiled.

At Ada's request, the DJ played a mix of Panji's work. It soothed her, and the quieter music gave them a chance to talk.

"Babe, I know you. Give it up." He kissed her cheek. "Give."

"He was murdered," she said suddenly.

He slid closer to her, his muscular leg pressing against hers. "Come, baby-cheeks. Leave it outside for one night."

"I'm serious."

"But the cops ruled accident."

"Impossible. Caff was terrified of bees. He avoided gardens."

"Homicide by bee sting?"

"Yes. That's exactly what it is."

He pressed his head to her shoulder. "Darling, I love you to death, you know that. But even I don't believe this. If someone wanted to kill Caff, why go to so much trouble?"

"To make it look like an accident."

"A car accident would be simpler."

"A message, then."

"Message? You're stretching, baby, stretching all the way to outer space."

"I don't know. I just know it's not right."

"Leave it to the cops."

"Since when do you love the cops?"

"Since never."

"I checked with the Agricultural Research Service." Ada leaned close so that he could hear her. "Bees die after stinging. I had some of the bees sent to the Carl Hayden Bee Research Center in Tucson."

"Bee autopsy?"

"The bees had virroa mites carrying malaria. Long story short, these are African bees."

"You mean African Killer Bees? Like in the movies?" Barbie sat up. He pulled off his Lucy wig, revealing long strands of black shoulder-length hair.

Ada nodded. "Africanized bees are all over California, but they're interbred with local bees. Their mites wouldn't carry malaria. But these bees did."

"Meaning?"

"Meaning, someone imported real African bees."

"How is that possible?"

"That's what Agriculture wants to know."

Barbie leaned closer to Ada, pressing harder against her, his voice hardening and angry. "You're telling me Caff was killed?"

Ada scowled. "What the hell do you think I've been telling you? Caff was afraid of bees, more than anything else in the world. Someone had to really hate him to go to the trouble of importing African bees to kill him in the most horrible way possible. I've insisted they re-open the homicide case in LA. Did Caff have any enemies?"

"Plenty of one-nighters, but he never let them get close. He was hot stuff, and maybe there was some jealousy, but no one hated him."

Ada scanned the dance floor. One of Panji's rougher rock ballads played but the floor remained jammed with people celebrating, people who loved Cafferty Toy. Why would anyone go to such horrible lengths to kill him? Only one possibility made any sense. His homicide had to be related to Braxis and the virus. She felt certain of it now. Which made Caff's murder her fault: she had dragged him to LA; she had left him behind, alone, while she went off to pursue the epidemic into Canada.

Ada felt a little woozy. She closed her eyes, feeling sick to her stomach. She opened her eyes, saw Barbie's worried face, and said, "Going to the little girls' room."

She made her way through the crowd. The heat in the room made her feel sicker. African bees. It was the most horrible, frightful way that Caff could have died. It was sociopathic. There was nothing normal in it. Homicide in any form was terrible, but why would someone focus on Caff's worst fears unless they were sadistic? It meant research. It took time. It made no sense.

But worse, she suddenly found herself visualizing Caff fighting off the bees, unable to kill them all, swatting at them as they stung him, screaming as they flew into his mouth.

She almost made it to the little girls' room.

There he was again, the towering man in the golden mask, over by the hallway to the bathrooms, watching her approach.

She hesitated. Who was this man? There was something threatening and scary about him.

But that just made her more determined. She pushed on through the dancers, heading at full clip for the man in the mask.

He waited for her, arms folded across his body-builder chest. It was a strange sensation for Ada. In a room of hundreds, full of smoke and sweat and partying people, her world shrank away to just this giant stranger and her. His costume was odd, without flair. Cowboy boots with an angel mask?

He loomed over her, more than a foot taller, so broad and imposing.

"Are you a friend of Caff's?" she shouted over the music.

He leaned closer, as if he couldn't hear her, and his pendant swung toward her, an ivory carving of an angel.

"Intimate," the man bellowed back, his voice rich with good humor.

Ada relaxed a little. Caff was intimate with many men, and particularly liked the body builder type. "Thank you for coming."

"Wouldn't have missed it, A.K." He knew her name, but many of the men in the room did, even the ones she had never met. His unblinking blue eyes captured her, hypnotic and disturbing. Was he on drugs? His pupils seemed dilated, almost glassy.

"How long have you known Caff?"

People flowed around them, a steady stream of Caff's friends making for the toilets, but she saw only this giant man in his spandex muscle shirt and golden mask.

"Oh, not long, dear. Not long."

Dear? She couldn't imagine any of Caff's friends using such a quaint word.

Something hit her, then, hard and certain. Not long. Perhaps only since LA?

"Terrible how he died, wasn't it?" She watched for his reaction. For days running up to the wake, Caff's friends had been abuzz with bees: "Just like Caff to go with such flair!" "Bees, how drama queen!" "Caff was so sweet, honey, he drew all the bees."

It seemed morbid, reminding one of Caff's friends about his horrible death, but she wanted his reaction.

The giant masked man stepped closer. Just a small step for his big legs, but it felt bullying. Ada didn't back away, but she felt herself tense.

Those unblinking eyes.

Something was terribly wrong here. He didn't seem like someone Caff would befriend or bed. Caff liked body builders, but not the scary ones.

"At least he was surrounded by flowers," the man said.

Ada stepped back, bumping into one of the dancers. "What did you say?"

"Didn't he die in the botanical gardens?"

Ada couldn't take her eyes of the golden mask and the blue glazed eyes. "How did you know that? It was never reported."

He lunged in with speed that startled her, until his golden face was inches from her face. She felt his breath through the mouth hole, and it was naturally sweet, without the staleness of a smoker or the sourness of a beer drinker or the chemical freshness of a gargler.

"I would like to get to know you as well."

Ada bounced back, moving instinctively into a defensive stance, turning to the side, lifting her right hand into a loose-balled fist in front of her face.

"Ah. You know karate." He laughed, a booming sound that sounded artificial. "Another time, my dear." And he turned and strode off, swallowed quickly by the crowd.

Startled, Ada looked around for Barbie or anyone who might intercept him. She saw no one but dancers intent in his or her world.

She plunged into the crowd to chase the phantom angel, but he was faster than her. By the time she reached the door, she saw no one.

She glanced around one more time for help but saw only Caff's mother.

Ada knew she had to follow this man. Safely, at a distance, with or without help. For a moment fear paralyzed her. Then she focused, calmed herself. She faced the world's deadliest viruses every day in her lab, where a simple tear in her isolation suit could be deadly. Every single day. This was no different. She just had to be careful.

She stepped outside.

30

Euclid Street, Atlanta

Barbie Fosco straightened his low-cut Prada gown as he ran after Ada onto Euclid.

He slipped from high and dizzy mode to bouncer in an instant, an easy transition for him. He often had to burn through the alcoholic haze and get down to business if patrons of his dance club got rowdy or if gay-bashers tried to barge the entrance. Tonight he drank more than usual, in honor of Caff.

He saw Ada running up Euclid, chasing the hunk in the mask. Barbie had noticed the side of beef in his club with the admiration of a fellow body builder, but he was confused when Ada pursued the man out of Dish.

"Stop!" she shouted.

The Sunday night crowd on the street noticed her running and yelling at Mr. Giganticus: Dish patrons, smoking on the street, and clusters of the crow crowd—straight dudes and dudettes who hung around Dish to laugh up the antics of "queens and queers" or to shout insults or compliments at the patrons in drag. But Barbie ran past them in the see-through gown, running hard in heels to catch up to Ada.

Giganticus turned a corner by Starbucks, but Ada was right on his heels. At least the street was crowded, because it was clear Ada was angry and the monster she chased didn't mean well.

He heard a scream from one of the patrons at Starbucks sidewalk tables.

Barbie tossed his heels and ran barefoot on the concrete. He stepped on gum, stones and spit, but he ran faster now.

The Starbucks patrons were on their feet as he turned the corner. He heard the squeal of tires and the roar of a big block engine, and saw a vintage sixties black Mustang with tinted windows scream off, the back end breaking loose in a dramatic slide.

Ada lay on the road between two parked cars. Barbie found he couldn't breathe, in spite of the hard run. He couldn't lose two friends in one month!

Giganticus was gone.

Barbie dove to his knees beside Ada, his dress flying up. "Baby-cheeks, you all right?"

Ada's eyes fluttered open, and she looked dazed as she stared at him for a moment. He felt her shiver, and he pulled her closer.

"I think ..." Ada panted for breath now. "I think that was ..." She didn't finish.

She settled against him, took a few steadying breaths.

"How about a coffee? At Starbucks?"

"Good idea," she said.

They settled at a table, all eyes on them and the buzz in the place was unmistakably about them.

"I saw it all," said one woman at a table beside them. "Are you all right?"

Ada nodded.

"That beast knocked you down!" The woman said, "You should call the police!"

Ada shrugged. "Ex husband. Behind on his alimony."

"I hear that!" The woman laughed, so did other Starbuckers, but Barbie felt his face heavy with an unaccustomed frown. Ada obviously didn't want to get into it. She would, eventually. He'd stick with her like overcooked pasta until she spilled the sauce.

Barbie brought them double espressos—none of these Cinnamon Dolce Lattes for them—and sat at their tiny table, staring at Ada's sweaty face.

He watched her chug her espresso in one manly gulp.

"Time to spill, baby-cheeks."

Ada stared at him. "I had words with Mr. Mask. I think he had something to do with Caff's death."

Barbie leaned across the table and grabbed both her hands, full of admiration and fury. "And you chased that beast alone? Are you mad?"

"You've always told me I am." She sighed. "I know. It was stupid. But I saw him getting away. And he's wearing a mask. What could I do?" She dug into her bag and pulled out a plastic device.

"What's that? A vibrator?"

"Not unless you want a shock."

"You were going to stun the guy?"

She nodded.

"And if he was just some innocent friend of Caff's?"

"He was no friend." She said it with a certainty that made Barbie believe. "I got his plates. Texas plates."

"I mean it, Ada."

"What?"

"I'm sticking to you while you're in Atlanta." He patted her hand. "You're staying at my love shack."

Ada shook her head. "Don't want to cramp your style, Barbie. I'll be all right."

Barbie laughed. "Baby-cheeks, don't believe my reputation. I'm not into one-nighters."

"No, but you have three hunky boyfriends."

Barbie waved his hand. "Oh, they're nothing, dahling. Won't leave me alone, that's all. I need a break. We can play Scrabble."

She laughed. "Right."

"Really. I'm good."

"Right." She stared at her empty cup. "Okay, Barbie, I could use the company."

But first they returned to Dish and gave Caff a genuine Atlanta-style party. It wasn't until six in the morning that the last of Caff's "guests" left the wake. The last to leave were falling-down drunk, and Barbie took the time to call them cabs. Barbie and Ada finally made their way upstairs to his love nest over the Dish nightclub. The first thing he did was run up the open stairs to his suspended bedroom loft, strip out of the dress, and slip on track pants. Ada curled up on his sectional couch by the surprisingly real electric fireplace. He stared down at her from his open platform. His loft, and the club, were built in an old wax factory, so he had twenty-five-foot ceilings and the two bedrooms were perched over the expansive open concept living area with views over Euclid. Eclectic was how Ada had always described the loft, although Barbie thought it was cozy with his dozens of antique Buddhas, the fifties soda fountain counter and stools that served as a dining room, and the restaurant-equipped stainless steel kitchen. His private parties were the stuff of legend in the gay community. Barbie loved people.

"I'm setting the security system, honey, so no sneaking out on me," he said as he trotted back down the open stairs.

In his genuine fifties milkshake blenders he made them both his "hangover special" fruit mix, then he crashed onto his king-sized sleigh bed and fell into a deep sleep. He dreamed of Mr. Mask Giganticus, but it was not an erotic dream. Giganticus chased him, surrounded by a cloud of angry bees.

He woke to the smell of coffee and found Ada in his kitchen scrambling eggs, even though it was mid afternoon. Thankfully, his hangover was minimal and he was able to eat her special fluffy cheese eggs at the thirty-foot long soda-fountain counter. It was the pride and joy of his loft, a genuine fifties fountain counter, bought from an estate, complete with floor-bolted seats, period deco art and complete ice-cream parlor equipment.

"I'm going out for a while," Ada said as she sipped her coffee.

"I'll come with."

"No. No, it's all right."

"I meant what I said last night."

"I thought you were drunk."

"Nope, Giganticus took the drunk out of me. And while you're in Atlanta, I'm stuck to you like peanut butter." He spread peanut butter on his rye toast, smiling at her.

"This is lonely-time stuff."

"I see." He smiled. "Well, Caff was alone when he was attacked. You don't get out of my sight. Not in my town."

"It's my town too"

"I love you, baby-cheeks. And I'm not losing another friend."

"I was probably wrong about that big guy."

"You're never wrong, Ada. That, I know about you."

"I need to be alone." She looked sad beyond hope. "You have work to do."

"That's what staff are for."

"Must be nice to be rich," Ada said. She shook her head. "No, Barbie, I need to be alone."

"You're going to see your son." Barbie didn't ask. He knew.

She nodded.

He stood up, sidestepped to her stool and massaged her shoulders. "Babe, I respect that, but I don't think it's a good idea. I'll just sit in the car."

"Fine."

"Good."

Later, dressed in his favorite soft lambskin pants and shirt, he drove her in his '59 candy-red Corvette to the little wartime bungalow near the East Lake Country Club with its Cape Cod yellow and blue paint. They parked under an oak tree across the road.

He scowled. "Whose idea was that awful color?"

"Mine."

The sun was hot on the car, even with the top down. After a few moments, he said, "Aren't you going in?"

She cupped her chin in two hands and leaned on the window sill. "No."

"Don't tell me. You never go in."

"I never go in."

"So we just sit here?"

"Yes."

"Baby-cheeks, this isn't healthy. Go talk to your son."

Ada said nothing. For five minutes more they sat and Ada said nothing.

"This isn't a cemetery, babe."

Her head snapped around. "What the hell's that mean?"

"It means your son is a living, breathing boy who wants his mother. Don't mourn him. Visit him, experience him, love him."

"You don't know anything about it!"

"I do. All boys want their mother. I wish I had one."

"Shut up, Barbie."

"No, you shut up. And think. This is your son."

She resumed her staring.

"You want to."

"You told me to shut up."

"You can speak now."

"Fine. I don't want Doctor Jung-Freud, whatever. You insisted on coming. But don't pretend you can understand my relationship with my son in ten minutes of sitting in a car."

"Ten minutes that told me a lot."

"You know nothing."

"I know what Caff told me. What you've told me. You blame yourself because Quentin's disabled. So? Life's never fair, babe. We all have disabilities, don't we, honey? I blame myself for being a sleaze bag into man-flesh who never has time to finish my screenplay for Hollywood. So? What good is that? I went from being a sleazy man-cruiser into a bar owner. It made me successful."

Ada said nothing.

"Honey, are you listening? I'm saying our weaknesses define us. Make us who we are."

"Spare me your soap opera psychiatry, Barbie. It's not so simple."

"Of course it's never simple. But we all have our miseries. I grew up without a mother. Like your boy, there. Trust me, even if he hates you, he wants you."

"I told you to shut up!"

"Honey, I never shut up. It's my nature. See? And you've got to stop blaming yourself for an accident. You're ruining your life. You're ruining his life. He wants you. Go talk to him."

She opened the door of the Corvette, but instead of crossing the street, she walked up the sidewalk, away from the house.

Barbie sighed. He turned the key and the old engine rumbled to life. He loved that manly sound. He shifted into gear and eased up the road, cruising along beside her. "Honey, grow up," he called out to her.

She gave him the finger.

"Oh, very mature!"

She stopped. He braked. She leaned on the door frame of his car, glaring down at him. "It's not that easy."

"Yes, it is. It's as easy as ringing the doorbell."

She circled the car, opened the door and jumped in. "Not yet," she said, after a long moment of silence. "I'm not ready. Too much on my mind."

"There'll always be too much on your mind."

She stared at him, an ominous stare full of strength and contempt that made him wince. "Barbie, you can be such a frigging nag. Caff just died. He was murdered. I think I chased his killer up Euclid last night. I'm trying to stop a virus from becoming an epidemic. Do you really think this is a good time?"

He leaned close, touched her shoulder, felt her quiver. Then he swept in and kissed her cheek. "Don't you, baby-cheeks? Why else are we here? What if … well, honey, we never thought Caff would join the angels so soon, did we? What if there isn't another time?"

Ada flinched. "Then it wasn't meant to be." She stared back at her old house. "Get me the hell out of here, Barbie."

31

Near Moon Lake First Nation, Canada

Panji Maingan clutched at her horse's mane and leaned back to regain her balance as Agawase wound down the steep slope, north of her farm. Her cell phone continued to blare the Canadian anthem, making her horse nervous.

"Agesse." Relax, she said in her native Anishinabe tongue. "Easy, Aga. Easy." Panji ducked a pine branch.

Agawase responded to her voice and bounced to a stop.

She stroked her mare's neck. "That's my girl." The horse tossed her head.

Panji pulled out her phone, hoping it was Ada. Panji's new friend had flown off almost immediately after news of her friend's suspicious accident, but she had kept in touch with Panji every day, trading news. Their friendship was no mystery, considering Panji's debt to Ada, but it amazed her how much she already cared for Doctor Ada Kenner.

Panji glanced at the caller identification, but it was ex-husband Mac. She flipped her cell open. "Mac?"

No answer. Often she lost the signal up here, although Windigokwe village had a tower. She thought about turning off the phone while she had a chance. Instead she waited for the inevitable call back and tilted her head to enjoy the warming rays of the sun on her face. She felt the restless energy of Agawase. Today, they would ride for hours. Even Mac couldn't spoil a perfect day on her little farm in northern Ontario. This fall there would be no Mac, no tour and no stinking cities. This autumn would be her first break in six years: a few weeks at various reserves, bringing supplies and much needed help; a few trips to Ottawa as a lobbyist for the First Nations; most of the summer on her farm enjoying days of horse training; the cool, clean air of her windy farm; stories by the fires with her favorite elders; and the big event, the summer inter-tribal powwow, with all the color and extravagance of costumed dancing, chanting and camaraderie.

The phone played Oh Canada! She snapped it open. "Mac, you could have killed me."

"Funny you say that, Nono," Mac Stayner said. Her ex-husband and current agent never tired of calling her Nono, a crude abbreviation of the word nonokasse, honey-bird, one of the twenty or so words he knew in her language. He always abbreviated Anishinabe words because he was unable to pronounce the complexities. He was just lazy that way.

"Who died?" She meant it as a joke.

"Chris Andrews."

"I know. Chaos was all over the news long ago." There was more to the call than news. Panji slid from her mare's back, landing lightly on her feet.

"Are you there, Nono?" A moment of silence. "Damn all cell phones."

"I'm here, Mac. What's this really about?"

"A strange thing. The investigation indicates his brother killed him. Sabotaged Chris's parachute. Then killed himself."

"Why call me? I didn't know the man. I knew his music."

"You don't remember?" Mac's voice dropped to a near whisper. "Our agreement?"

"No," she said it sharply, letting him guess if she meant, "no, go away" or "no, I don't remember." When Mac didn't answer right away, she leaned on a maple tree and scanned her farm: three hundred acres of blessed forest on the Moon Lake First Nation—one of the more prosperous Nations because of the casino. Below her, her little yellow house on the lake seemed so lovely. The wind gusted, pushing clouds across a pastel blue sky. "Mac, what agreement?"

"You contracted to be Chaos's alternate on *Superstar*."

"That's what this is about? I told you, Mac. No way."

"You said you'd sign on as a backup judge. The signing fee went to the

First Nations Water Fund. Paid for that distiller you sent up to Labrador."

"James Bay. Mac, you told me I'd never have to—"

"Who knew the primary judge would be murdered?"

Panji pressed harder against the trunk of the tree, needing the support. She didn't speak for a long time. What had Mac gotten her into? Murder and reality television. She allowed her body to slide down the trunk of the tree until she sat in a patch of thistles. She hardly noticed. "Mac, I'm not going to be a judge on junk television. Get me out of this. Return the money."

He sighed. "Panji, I checked. There's no escape clause. And the producer—you remember Abbey Chase?"

"I'll never forget." Chase: equal measures of beautiful and blizzard cold and perhaps the least likeable person Panji had ever met.

"She insisted."

"Why? I came within seconds of breaking her perfect nose." They had met six times over the four-day negotiation in Los Angeles, and each time Abbey and Panji verbally sparred.

After a long silence, Mac finally said, "Panji, I know. But she wants you."

"She's on the judging panel. We'd fight nonstop."

"They want that. They want the bitch and the sweetheart on camera." Before she could ask, he added, "You're the sweetheart. America's sweetheart."

"Mac, I'm First Nations Canadian." Panji took a long breath and enjoyed the freshness of early summer, pine, wildflowers and horse dung. "No, Mac. I can't go on the road this year."

"Venice, Paris, Moscow, Beijing, Hong Kong, Tokyo. It's not so bad, Nono."

"It'll be pure torture."

"C'mon. Panji. It's your chance for a soapbox. You'll be in front of eighty million every week, more towards the finals. It's broadcast in forty-nine countries. Here's your chance to say whatever you want to a huge audience—on live television. Think of the causes you can plug. And the records you'll sell."

"I sell enough records." Even without a publicist, something Mac never let her forget, she had gone triple platinum with Little Coyote. The title was Mac's idea. He dressed her up like some stereotypical Native, complete with buckskins and beads and they used the corrupted English translation of her name Panji Maingan as the CD label: Little Coyote. And she looked so small on the cover of the CD, all five foot one, and ninety-six pounds of her, standing next to a panting coyote.

"No, Mac."

"C'mon, Nono. You can spend time with Kenny."

Panji closed her eyes, annoyed. "You mean Kenji?" The show's host. She squirmed against the tree. The June wind felt suddenly hot. She loosened her lumberjack shirt, flapping it to catch the breeze.

"You know who I mean. It's like someone stuck you two together with Crazy Glue."

She felt her own smile. "He's the only likeable person I met in LA"

"I'm hurt. I was there the entire four days and I don't remember having dinner with you once."

"I said likeable."

"Ouch." Then he laughed. "I'm not being a critic, Nono. It's time you dated again. Three years is long enough."

"Mac, he's just a friend!"

"More than friends, I think. Because we're friends now, right? That's what you keep telling me. I didn't even get lunch."

She exhaled slowly, focusing. "Mac, stop this."

"Hey, I don't blame you. He's hot."

"Mac!"

"If I dug men, I'd be all over him."

"Mac, shut up!"

"I'm just saying—"

"Shut up!"

"Oh. I struck a nerve."

Change the subject before we fight for real, she thought. "Mac, is there no way out of this contract?"

"No. But you can send me a postcard from Paris."

She couldn't help it. She laughed. Mac had always been able to make her laugh. He had just never been able to make her happy, or give her children, or keep his mind off the next tour. She wanted to sing for the pleasure of singing, and to settle down with a family, her horses and her people; he wanted a superstar for a wife.

Panji scanned her farm again. The birds filled the wood with cheerful song. A flock of wild turkeys flew up from one of the hayfields. A herd of horses grazed the summer pasture, nicely greened up. "I haven't had a summer off since I met you. You owe me."

"No, you owe me. Ten percent, remember?"

"I only have two local kids helping out with the horses." She tried to imagine her two farm hands handling all the foaling and training.

"Your mom can watch over them. How is the old cow, anyway?"

Mac had always called Ninge "the old cow" even to her face. They had sparred daily, but Mac and Ninge liked each other. Mac used to say, "The old bat'll live to one hundred and thirty."

"Ninge's fine. She'll blame you for all this." Panji knew her Ninge could manage the farm, as always. Was Panji just being selfish? Wanting to spend time on the farm with the foals, close to Mom and Mother Earth, instead of touring or promoting? Her music, after all, remained a key source of funds for sixteen charities. It was her whole reason for being.

"Who knows? Maybe Kenny is Mr. Right this time."

Panji closed her eyes. Mac was supposed to be Mr. Right. Until he turned out to be Mr. Wrong. She wasn't ready. "On this tour, there'll only be prima donnas and fans."

Mac laughed. "Well, for your dating pleasure let's hope prima Dons." A sigh. "And I have it on good authority that Kenji's a genuine nice guy. Not a Hollywood phony."

"Are you an agent or a matchmaker?" She tried to sound angry. "Because I don't think you're good at either."

Television. She felt nauseous. Still, Mac had a point. She could drop a few names on live television, a few of her favorite charities.

The turkeys flew again. Then the horses abruptly broke into a full run across the fifty-acre pasture. They were beautiful in full gallop, manes streaming and tails flying. But something was wrong. Panji saw a pair of coyotes in the pasture, but knew they weren't the cause. They were a bonded pair and permanent residents of the farm and never bothered the horses. Sometimes Panji saw them moving through her herd, munching on horse chips, and the herd ignored them. Two or three times a week, she came across the coyotes on her morning walks.

Something else spooked her herd.

Then she heard it. Thrumming. A vibration.

The sound swelled, disturbing the peace of Bidânimad Farms. The thrumming became a howl, and now a flock of geese rose up from the lake. It sounded like a mechanical wind. The wind is coming, Panji thought, just like the translation of Bidânimad: 'the wind is coming.'

"What's wrong? Panji?"

"Did you send someone?" She tried to keep the anger out of her voice. Mac sent someone before he even asked. "You sent a helicopter, didn't you?"

Even as she said it, the chopper swept into view, rounding a high hill to the south of her land. And she saw this was no ordinary chopper, it was military. This machine was sleek and fast and black with tinted glass. Panji was sure she even saw rocket launchers.

"Panji, What's going on?"

Panji stared at the helicopter as it tilted its sharp nose down. The chopper hovered, turning slowly as if searching. Yes, those were weapons. It circled her small farmhouse like a bird of prey.

"Ninge!" Panji felt the rise of sweat. She reached for her mare's reins and vaulted on to her horse's back. "Mother!"

Panji leaned forward and dug her heels into her untrained mare. The mare snorted, reared, then bolted down the steep hill, chasing the black helicopter.

32

Oak Lane Cemetery, Atlanta

Ada sat on the stone bench under the ancient oak tree until her buttocks were numb. The magnolias were in bloom, the grass lush green, and all was at peace. Except Ada. She stared at the fresh mound of soil on the side of the hill overlooking the swan pond, unmarked except for dead and shriveled brown flowers. The irony of a blanket of dead flowers was not lost on Ada; in life Caff loved flowers but avoided them because of bees.

For almost a week since the wake she had come here every day, on leave of absence, unable to face Devon and his syrupy sympathy, and deferring their inevitable confrontation. She had to figure things out by herself, since the only person who would listen was with her in spirit only. Alban Bane was in Canada somewhere.

The Atlanta police didn't take her seriously when she called in the bizarre encounter with the masked giant in Dish, putting it down to a campy drunken exchange. She had chased the man out on to Euclid, but he had vanished. The police took a report, but never called her back.

Devon had already referred the emerging portfolio to Containment. "It's a matter of containment right now, A.K. You understand that, don't you?" In other words, she was off the case file, the internal equivalent of being vertically fired; in the CDC, horizontal discharge meant you left the CDC for good, vertically fired meant you were bounced off a case.

Even the LAPD stopped returning her calls about Caff's "suspicious death." Probably the detective thought of her as "that nut from Atlanta."

Caff had been the only one who would listen to her. And Barbie, but he was cloying, sticking to her too close, always talking so she couldn't think.

Since the wake, she had come each day for five days, bringing a bouquet of camellias and a stack of newspapers. Each day she sat on the same bench, talking to him as if Caff were on the bench beside her. At first she felt asinine, later self-conscious if someone "caught her" babbling, and finally she came to feel that he was really there—or that she was cracking up. On this Friday afternoon, she read newspapers out loud to Caff's ghost as if he could hear the stories.

Her only company was a groundskeeper with clippers who trimmed tightly formed yews: clip, clip, clip.

It was already sunset, a wonderful time in the old cemetery, even in the newer annex, and the air was fragrant with the sweetness of camellia. Ada was glad for the peace. The wind was strong and the sun still hot, but the oak and a stand of old dogwood sheltered her.

With a sigh, she picked up the last newspaper. She normally didn't buy this one, but the headline screamed "buy me" as she scanned the news rack that morning.

The headline under the banner *Crime Times* shouted: Rage Plague Rocks LA and Las Vegas with Violence. And under the headline the subhead, Rabies-Like Virus Spread by Superstar Cast? and the byline Hugh King beside the picture of a ferret-like, white-haired man.

Rag or not, Ada speed-read the article. King made some interesting, if unsupported, claims. What struck her was the parallel to rabies. Rabies virus was of the BDV family. King reported on dozens of incidents of spouses killing spouses, friends killing friends, brothers killing brothers. An inset article screamed: Chaos Killed by Brother! Linked to Virus! It even mentioned the car accident near Site F.

"What do you think of that, Caff?" she asked, looking up at his mound of earth. "The only one who believes me is a supermarket tabloid reporter. You used to read these conspiracy newspapers, right?" She waited for Caff to answer, sighed, and then said, "Well, Toyboy, no need to be rude." Somewhere, she could hear Caff laughing. "Imagine what Devon would say if I came to him with a copy of the *Crime Times* and demanded a new investigation?"

When he didn't answer her, she thought, I am going crazy, then she read bits of the *Crime Times* article out loud to him: "Sixteen patricide cases, twenty-one sibling attacks and nine spousal beatings in the LA area within the last eighteen days indicate a new type of plague, a Rage Plague. He capitalized Rage, Caff." She smiled. Sensationalism. Still, it bothered her. This all seemed to correspond to the timing of the incident on the highway near Site F—two weeks or so after the death of Doctor Begley. "The incidents appear to be unprovoked occurrences of psychotic violence between friends, brothers and lovers, statistically six times above normal before the outbreak." She winked at Caff's grave. "He has the words *outbreak* italicized."

She could almost hear Caff's reply: "Maybe he's right, honey."

God, she missed Caff. She felt an ache deep in her abdomen, a familiar feeling, and a sensation she endured every time she thought of her boy Quentin. Her exposure to LCMV had permanently changed her, not just delivering to her a handicapped child, but also leaving her own body changed in some chronically achy way.

The sun was setting now, glittering on the pond at the foot of the hill. Time to go. She had been here all day, but she didn't want to be in a cemetery at night. Her car was a good five-minute walk.

She picked up the newspapers. There were no runners or walkers and the groundskeeper no longer clipped and cut. The only sound was the soft breeze rustling leaves.

"See you tomorrow, Toyboy," she said, and she blew him a kiss.

"Ciao for now, honey." She could hear his voice. Nuts.

As she started up the path, she heard a distinctive click.

She looked toward the formal yew garden. The gardener, the man with the clippers, still stood there, but he held a camera, not hedge trimmers. He was tall, slightly stooped. A reporter?

She glared at him. Was there a more intimate place to intrude than a cemetery? She could see the story headline: Crazy Doctor Babbles to Dead Friend in Cemetery.

Caught, he nodded, then walked towards her, bouncing along with jerky motions. His hair was shockingly white, but she felt sure he was no older than late forties. There was something sleazy and distinctly unwholesome about the man.

Ada glanced around quickly. No one was nearby.

She stared at the creepy man as he approached, putting on her fiercest frown. She fumbled in her bag and touched Nam's stun gun but did not pull it out, still hanging on to the bundle of papers with her other hand.

"Doctor Ada Kenner?" the man asked.

Ada said nothing.

"I'm Hugh King. Of *The Crime Times*."

Ada stepped back, startled. The newspapers dropped from her hand and tumbled away in the light breeze. He surprised her by stooping to pick them up. He snatched at pages as they tumbled past him. One of them was his own front page, the article carrying his byline.

"I see you have good taste," he said, but his tone sounded frightened and edgy, not proud.

"What do you want?" Ada could guess, though. She had read his insightful but unsubstantiated article. He had made connections, some of them true, but he had no evidence, all anonymous sources and speculation.

"Yes, I want to interview you," he said, breathless. "But there's no time, now. Come with me."

She tried to sound casual and shrugged. "Why?"

"Because I just saw him park his car. You don't want to be here right now." He spoke quickly, too fast almost to understand.

"What are you talking about?" Obviously the man was paranoid, like his newspaper.

"The man with the Mustang."

Ada found herself glancing around the cemetery at that. How did King know about the masked man? It meant he had been following her since last Sunday.

"Too late. Now it's too late." He dropped the newspapers. "Better run."

Ada saw genuine fear on the crime reporter's face. She glanced behind her. Standing by a mature dogwood was the giant man from Caff's wake, no longer wearing a golden mask, although now he wore an isolation filtration mask.

Long blond hair tumbled out and sharp blue eyes glared at her, unblinking as before.

"Run if you want to live!" And Hugh King turned and ran.

33

Oak Lane Cemetery, Atlanta

Hugh King had trouble keeping up with Ada. His long legs were no match for Ada's athleticism—but neither of them managed to out pace their stalker: this man with his filtration mask and his massive Schwarzenegger body and long-striding legs seemed to lope, keeping up, always just behind them, not needing to sprint. Her Fendi bag bounced against her hips as she ran, and she knew she should grab the phone and the stun gun and toss the bag with its precious pictures of Quentin and her laptop of critical data—but she clutched it instead and ran faster.

Run if you want to live, King had said.

Ada found herself running faster. "Move, King!" she snapped. "He's right behind you!"

She tried to punch 9-1-1 on her satellite phone, but it was difficult in full gallop. Her fingers kept missing the send button.

Twilight was deepening and the cemetery was empty, except for the ghosts of the dearly departed, less scary than the monster behind them. She doubted her brown-belt karate would have any impact on this giant.

She pressed the phone to her ear and heard, "9-1-1. What is your emergency?"

She heard a shriek behind her.

"We're being attacked at Oak Lane Cemetery!" she shouted. "Send police. Please! In the new annex. Please, he's going to kill him!"

When she heard another scream she stopped and turned. She didn't know King and she was no match for this monster—and she knew she would probably do more good fetching the police but—she couldn't leave King.

The reporter dangled from the ground, his legs kicking above the gravel path. The attacker, this blond body-building giant, held him easily with one hand, in spite of skin tight gloves. King's face was purple, his eyes bright with terror.

"I've called the police!" She waved her phone at the attacker.

The man laughed. "Well, good for you, Doctor Kenner." His voice was pleasant, not threatening at all, a hint of Texas. He shook King like a child's doll. "You know, he will not last long, Doctor."

"What do you want?"

"Nothing from him."

King's legs spun in place as if he was trying to run. Ada saw that he had wet himself, a wide stain spreading out in his blue pants.

"Please. Put him down before you kill him." Ada was surprised how calm she sounded.

"Yes, I will. I will because I like you Doctor Ada Kenner." The man spoke quietly, with just a hint of an accent.

King's feet touched the ground and for a moment his toes kicked up gravel, but the attacker still held him by the neck.

"What do you want from us?"

"He is a nuisance, nothing more. No one believes him. He could write this whole incident up, and only the Supermarket moms will believe him."

"Let him go, then!"

"In a moment." The attacker pinched King's neck one more time and the reporter collapsed at the assassin's feet. The big man shoved him to one side with one of his cowboy boots. What size shoes did he wear? They had to be size twenty.

Ada didn't run, yet. She tried to calculate the time it would take for her to reach her car. Perhaps a minute? Then, she would have to fumble with the locks and the doors. She had a feeling it would be forty-five seconds too long. Her hand remained in her bag, clutching the stun gun. Would thousands of volts of stun power be enough to immobilize this man? Somehow she doubted it. This massive creature would take a lot of zapping. She focused on calming herself. This man—a man, not a creature, not a fearful beast, just a man—whoever he was, had a mission. It was important to her to understand more. He held the key to something important. He had probably killed Caff. No, she wouldn't run. Not yet.

She studied him with a researcher's eye to detail: his skin tight suit stretched taut over well-defined muscle was not spandex but thin rubber. He wore gloves and a mask. Was this to prevent the inevitable seeding of sloughed skin, DNA evidence and hair? No, his golden hair tumbled out from the mask, and hair carried DNA coding. Why else would he wear all this protection? She decided she didn't like the possibilities.

King lay still on the ground, perhaps already dead.

"What do you want?" she said, calmer now, sinking herself into the reassuring researcher mode.

"Very little." He bent quickly. His massive hand held a pneumatic hypo gun, the kind she used in her own lab. It could dispense multiple doses.

"No! Don't!"

She heard the light hiss of air as the man pressed the hypo to the journalist's still purple neck. She instantly smelled the disinfectant, the smell of phenol, pungent and sterile.

Now she understood the rubberized jump suit and the muffled sound of the man's voice behind the mask and the gloves. This was exactly the type of hypo she used, the kind she used for injecting test subjects, mostly animals, with live viruses; it would dispense a phenol spray as it broke the skin and injected virus, to help protect the person administering direct injections of viruses, especially when used with a filter mask and gloves.

"What have you done?"

The laugh was low and warm. "I have given him a dose of fear."

"The police will be here any minute."

"Yes. Yes, I am sure they will come, Doctor Kenner." He stepped closer, one giant stride that seemed to cover half the distance between them. She fumbled back, and swung her bag like a weapon. He stepped in again and she swung again. She felt the blow as her designer bag bounced off the giant bicep. She heard the muffled clang of her laptop computer crumpling. The giant grabbed the straps, laughing, pulling her closer. She released the bag, but held the stun gun defensively in her hand. Ada pressed the trigger and blue sparks arced between the contact points. "I don't want to hurt you."

She smelled him now, the strange mingling of something metallic and—almonds?

She heard his muffled laugh. "Oh, I like it. Hurt me, Doctor Kenner."

She tried to gauge his body language.

"So, tell me, Doctor Kenner. What do you fear?" He wore a large fanny pack, like the kind the cool kids wore, except on him it looked tiny. He slid it around on his hip and reached into the bag. "I call this my bag of fears." More laughter, and it chilled her.

Ada said nothing. What was he waiting for? The police couldn't be far away.

He dropped the pneumatic hypo into the fanny pack. "Let me tell you about your worst fear, Doctor Kenner. You are afraid of very little. You work with the most dangerous viruses on earth. You successfully fought off a mugger in Chicago, two years ago—"

"How do you know that?"

"The angel of fear knows all the things that make you afraid."

"You searched the Internet and found the story on the mugging in Chicago." The giant nodded.

Ada used her peripheral vision to plan her escape path, noting the tree to her right. She felt confident that she could outrun this powerful creature. He was big. She was fast. She would just have to stay out of reach of his ape-length arms.

"So, shall we talk more about your great fear, Doctor?"

Ada tensed, readying her sprint.

"You see, I know you have one big phobia. It goes back to a newlywed Ada Kenner, working busily in her lab on her doctoral thesis."

Ada didn't move. "Your mask, the research you've done on me. Obviously, all designed to incapacitate me with fear. Why? Is it because you're too big and lumbering to catch me?"

"Perhaps." His hand moved in the bag. "However, I do believe you have a disabling terror, Doctor Kenner." His hand emerged abruptly from the bag. "Yes, I believe it is—mice?"

He held a tiny mouse, dangling by the tail from two sausage-sized fingers. The mouse chattered and struggled.

Ada backed away, holding her stun gun lower.

He thrust the mouse in her direction, stepping closer, one long stride that brought him so close she felt sure his big arms could reach her. "Your doctoral thesis in LCVM, isn't that right? Such a shame you were pregnant."

She tumbled back, nearly tripping on a tree root.

"You should face your fears. That is what I believe, Doctor Kenner." He swung the mouse at her.

She countered with a zap of her stun gun, missing him.

"The lowly mouse. How humble. How dangerous."

She stepped back.

"I guess you know this, Doctor. I mean, you are the doctor. But fleas from this little creature carried the black plague that devastated Europe."

Ada felt icy cold. Where were the police?

"And mice, they carry LCVM. I believe your son Quentin is a living testament to the mighty mouse?" And he lunged forward, terrifying in his abrupt burst of speed. Her legs couldn't move fast enough. He wrapped his arm around her, a big tree-trunk of a limb, and pressed the mouse to her nostrils. "Unfortunately, this little fellow has a mutated LCVM."

Ada pushed away, with her one free hand. She pressed the stun gun to his forearm and squeezed the trigger. Enough current transmitted through his body that she felt it too, part of the circuit. He jerked, but didn't release her.

He pressed the mouse to her mouth, muffling her shouts. She had to close her mouth.

Ada felt the light fur against her nostrils. She inhaled the light musky stench of mouse, unable to hold her breath any longer. The stench was vile, more disgusting than her grandma's old outhouse on Lake Oshanawak. She gave up struggling, limp in the arms of the angel of fear, breathing in the memories of twelve years ago, of the accident, of the lab, soaring ahead to the terrible moment in the hospital when she saw Quentin's enormous deformity for the first time, her baby born legless, the weight of guilt, the terrible knowledge she had done this.

Sudden fury took her. She drove her heel into the arch of the angel's massive foot. She pressed the trigger of the stun gun until the battery gave no more. And still he held the mouse to her face, the little creature crushed now and no longer alive.

She focused her mind. Focused all her strength, concentrating all on one single back thrust with her free arm to his chin. She closed her eyes, and then drove her elbow back with a snap.

She heard the crack of her bone and felt the scream of pain as her ulna fractured. She didn't shout out, unwilling to draw in more fur and droppings through an open mouth, but the pain sent a tremor through her. She felt her radius fly out of her elbow socket. She had seen it many times as an intern, especially in children, treating them with clinical detachment and a smile, and the words, "There, be a brave boy." Now she realized the horrible pain those children felt. How could they be brave boys and girls through this terrible agony? No wonder they screamed.

But Ada didn't scream. She was more conscious of the big hand holding the mouse to her mouth and nostrils.

The sirens were closer now. But she knew they would be too late.

34

Bidânimad Farms, Ontario

Agawase galloped through a row of early roses and wheeled to a dusty stop. Panji jumped off.

The shadow-black helicopter dominated an empty paddock, foreboding and angry. The engine ticked but the rotors were fully wound down. A man stood by the chopper with a slung rifle. He stared at her now, nearly as terrifying as the machine he guarded. She could clearly see rocket launchers and strafing guns, cannon-like protrusions of the fierce machine, aimed at her small stucco farmhouse.

She slid behind the barn, out of his sightline, and paused to tie up her waist-length hair. She shot a look around the corner. The sentry stared at the barn, but had not moved.

Panji tried not to panic. Military helicopter. High caliber guns. Rocket launchers. Guards with automatic guns.

She refused to let fear paralyze her. She focused on her mother, alone in the house. Or perhaps not alone. She sprinted from the south wall of the barn near the rear porch of the house. This time she didn't pause to see if the sentry followed her. She charged across the small patch of sunlit grass and burst through the kitchen door. The screen door whacked the wall, nearly coming off the hinges.

"Ninge!"

No answer. In the living room, the radio blared, set at FNB, First Nations Broadcasting.

She didn't repeat the call for her mother.

The kitchen smelled of fresh baking and cinnamon. Mother had been at work here only moments ago; she would never leave her kitchen without wiping up the scattered flour and turning off the oven.

Panji slipped through the sunny breakfast area. Dust motes swirled, catching the sunlight from the wide-paned windows that faced out on the hummingbird garden.

Panji ran to her study, concentrating on abolishing fear. Her father had taught her that, early on, sending her out to camp in the hills as a child, all by herself. "You face your fears, Nonokasse," he would say as she clung to him. "Face them, and you'll never let fear control you."

She pressed open the door and scanned quickly. Then she ran to the rifle cabinet, fumbling with her keys. None of them fit. Why couldn't she make them fit? Finally the key slipped in. She ground her teeth in frustration as she turned too hard and broke the tiny key. Why was she so out of control? Last year when the bear got in among the dogs, she had calmly unlocked the cabinet. What was different this time?

She swung around and broke the glass with a reverse elbow thrust. The glass scattered, fragments glittering in the high pile carpet. She didn't think about what it could all mean. An armed helicopter, clearly not Canadian military, armed sentries, her mother missing.

Aware that she had made a lot of noise, she fumbled with another key and unlocked the secure gate. This time she managed to get it open.

She pulled out her Dad's old pump action Winchester Ranger and found herself expertly chambering shot. She pressed her back to the paneled study wall and lowered the barrel, her fingers on the guard. Without hesitation, she sprinted up the short hall, through the Ninge-tidy living room, unable to hear anything but the radio—a call-in show with her mother's favorite host. She didn't turn off the radio, not wanting to warn any invaders of her presence. From the front door, she scanned the yard and its rows of manicured cedar.

Where was Ninge?

She opened the door a crack.

The back of another soldier.

She thought only of her mother and focused. She slid out onto the wide veranda that spanned the front of the house.

The soldier in black was broad but not tall, a storm trooper–looking guard like the one by the chopper. His machine gun was at the ready.

Ninge sat in her rocker, facing a man with his back turned.

Before the door swung closed, Panji pressed the barrel of her shotgun to the soldier's back. "Don't," was all she said.

Through the barrel, she felt him stiffen. "Lower the weapon," she said softly.

The soldier didn't move. She felt his tension. Felt the coiling of muscles.

"If you do, I'll shoot."

He started to make his move anyway.

Panji swung hard and high, turning the barrel of her shotgun in and up as she spun her hips. The mahogany gunstock struck the guards chin as she swung around and he fell backward against the rail. In the same motion, Panji's shotgun swung back around, now aimed directly at the men opposite Ninge. They were on their feet now, eyes alarmed. One reached for a revolver.

"Don't try!" she snapped. "I'm fast."

Only her mother remained seated.

Ninge shook her head, her mouth hardening. "Panji Maingan!" She frowned, glancing at the shotgun, then at the groaning guard in her garden. The man lay sprawled in Ninge's roses. "Put that gun down!"

Panji lowered the shotgun only slightly, reacting instinctively to her mother's sharp voice. But the barrel remained on the man, and then she realized who he was. "Alban Bane?"

"In the sagging flesh." Alban Bane smiled and put up both his hands. His jacket flipped open. Panji saw a small gun, a chromed revolver, and the pistol he had reached for a moment ago. She stiffened and reflexively the shotgun inched up.

"Ninge, are you all right?"

"Panji!" Mom frowned. There was something about crankiness that youthened her mother's face. The lines lifted and the eyes came alive, and even surrounded by long waves of white hair, she seemed so strong. "This man is from the authorities."

Panji stared at her mother for a long time, then at Bane, then at the man she had knocked off the porch—who was now on his feet and rubbing his jaw—but the shotgun did not waver. She noticed that Mom's best teapot was on the small table.

"Panji. I'd hate to be a burglar." He gave her one of his famous smiles. "I guess I'd be dead."

"You might still be. I'm allowed to shoot trespassers."

"Panji Maingan! That shotgun had better not be loaded." Her mother shook her head. "Director Bane, I apologize for my Panji. She gets her impulsiveness from her father."

"And her right cross from Mom?" Bane chuckled lightly, probably to diffuse the tension.

Panji winced. "I'm sorry, Ninge." She lowered the gun. "I saw guns."

"Threw me a bit, too." Now her Mom smiled, revealing her two missing teeth. She vaulted from her rocker and grabbed Panji's arm in a painful grip and pulled her towards the visitor. "Come, meet our guest."

Panji relaxed only slightly. "Well, I know Alban Bane." She'd always thought of him as a funny man, the two times they met over dinner with Kenji. But black helicopters and black storm troopers made him a little more sinister.

Again Bane smiled. "Sorry we alarmed you, Panji. How about that shotgun?" She lowered the shotgun. "Perhaps back in the rack?"

Panji glanced at the other invader. "What do you want, Bane?"

Bane laughed now, a low rumble. "I feel like I'm at home, not in gun-free Canada."

Panji de-chambered the Winchester and set it against the rail. She glanced at the bruised soldier. He glared back at her. "Sorry."

The soldier nodded, eyes hard and angry, but he resumed his position by the door.

"You're handy with hand-to-hand." Bane nodded at the gun. "I think I'm all hot."

"Christ, Bane." She frowned. "You could have picked up a phone."

Bane snapped his fingers. "I never thought of that!" He stepped closer. "Really, Panji, I couldn't. It was important I see you."

"What's going on? This is First Nation territory. My land."

"Yes, yes, Panji. In case you haven't heard, the A in WART stands for Assholes." Bane grinned.

Her mother nodded. "Well, I'm going to bake us all some nice corn bread and leave you to your chat." She snatched the shotgun from Panji and disappeared into the house. Mother turned off the radio on the way, probably to allow her some freedom to eavesdrop.

Bane sat facing her. He sighed, breathed deep. "Would it help if I said, lovely place you have here? Bit of a hurry, sorry."

Panji sat in her mother's rocker. She stared at Bane.

"You've heard of Chaos, I assume?"

Panji nodded. She said nothing about her conversation with Mac.

Bane frowned, perhaps puzzled by her silence. "Well, Chaos—a.k.a. Chris Andrews—was murdered. By his brother Jerry. Hell of a way to go. Flat as a pancake."

"That's not funny."

Bane nodded. "Not meant to be. You might ask, why would his brother kill him?"

She didn't ask, but she found she wanted to know.

"Some of this I can't disclose. Let's just say that we have followed a bizarre trail of sibling murders. Not just siblings, but spouses killing spouses, and in one case patricide." Bane paused, apparently waiting for her reaction.

"I'm no expert. Aren't the majority of murderers found to be family members?" She shot a glance at the kitchen window, thinking suddenly of her mother. She heard Ninge humming a native ballad and the clatter of a whisk in a bowl. Mother was never happier than when she was baking.

Bane nodded. "There's a reason I had to see you in person."

"Why?"

"My daughters demanded your autograph. Can we talk a moment? Just you and I?"

Panji sighed. "You're a cliché, Bane." She nodded. "Fine. Come with me. I have to groom my mare."

He followed her to the back lawn where Agawase stood grazing dandelions. Panji scooped up the reins and led her Icelandic horse to the immaculate barn. Her mare nickered softly, anticipating sweet feed.

"See, Aga. We haven't forgotten you." She ran the rubber curry over the horse's sweaty hair. "Now, what's this all about?"

Bane stood on the other side of Agawase, brushing her neck. "Nam spoke highly of you."

Panji worked Aga's mane and said nothing.

"These incidents, the deaths, they're not ordinary."

"I assumed so." She thought of Ada and Kinosewak, of little Abdo who killed his beloved grandmother and two other sudden murders on the reserve.

"Ada found a—we'll just call it a viral antibody—in blood taken from the attackers. You see?"

Panji felt the intrigue, and she paused her grooming to stare at Bane over Aga's neck. "You're linking this violence to a virus. Like rabies?" She remembered a run-in with a rabid skunk. The little creature had almost killed her Newfoundland dog and she had just managed to shoot it. Even with half it's head blown away, it continued charging her big happy galoof of a dog.

Bane continued to groom, silent a moment. "You figured that out quicker than a teenager falls out of love." He contemplated her. "These other homicides I mentioned?"

"Yes? Let me guess. UFO conspiracy."

"Half right, maybe. I won't tell you which half. All the attackers had the exact same antibody, in their systems."

She took a long breath, taking in the musky scent of sweat and horsehair, and she thought of the outbreak on James Bay. The patients in the infirmary had been so violent during treatment that many had to be restrained. "You think this virus triggered the homicidal behavior?" And, remembering the psychiatrist, she made a final leap: "Something fear-induced?"

Bane stepped around her horse. "Why do you jump to that conclusion?"

She shrugged. "I didn't make a conclusion. A wild guess. Most psychosis is somewhat fear-induced."

Bane stroked Aga's neck but his eyes stayed on Panji. "I better watch what I say around you, Panji. You're too quick."

Panji wasn't really in the mood for flattery, but Bane seemed nice enough. "Nam and I were with Ada—Doctor Kenner—in Kinosewak."

"Yes, I know. That's part of why I'm here."

"Go on."

"Doctor Kenner has reported the Kinosewak epidemic is the same virus."

Panji stopped grooming and stared at Bane. "I think I like you better as the jokester."

"You're probably the only one."

A hundred questions occurred to her. Where did the virus come from? What is it? Is there a cure? But she waited. Her father taught her the power of patience.

"The thing is—many of the victims have been linked to this *Superstar* show in my background work."

"Does Ada know this?"

"Ada's still on leave at the insistence of her ex-husband. Maybe ex-director now too." He sighed. "Right now, this *Superstar* reality show is doing the preliminary judging for the American contestants, moving from city to city. Wherever they travel, there are multiple victims. We've been unsuccessful, so far, in convincing the CDC to shut down the tour."

"Why is that?" She couldn't imagine Ada taking chances with people's lives. Not the Ada she had come to know.

"Ada's been removed from the case. Her director's less inclined to act."

"Sounds like Canadian politics."

Bane laughed, but it was a sad sound. "We need more evidence to convince them. We're working on that, of course." He stared at her now. "Abbey Chase is a very powerful woman. So is … Well, I can't talk about that, Panji. Let's just say money talks."

Panji closed her eyes. What had Mac gotten her into? "Why are you involved, then?"

"If you can get past my vices, I have lots of merits." He smiled. "Actually, no one wants me involved, but I'm involved because I can't be influenced by any one government. People like Ada and me can't be stopped once we're on the blood trail." He stepped around Aga. "Unfortunately, no one's really supporting me either. It's like being adopted by a Hollywood actor. All show, no substance."

She put down her brush and settled for simply hugging her mare. "I still don't get the link to me."

"Well, one of the victims was the man you are replacing."

Panji said nothing, but she was sure she wore her surprise naked on her face.

"WART knows all," Bane said, in answer to the unasked question. "Abbey Chase informed us."

"I'm a very reluctant judge. That doesn't explain why a busy man like you would fly up here to see me?"

"Two reasons."

"Yes. I'm listening."

"One—Ada Kenner. She said you are passionate, smart, and tough. Two—to ask you to be my eyes and ears. Okay, three—I'm a fan."

"And why should I?"

"Because neither the CDC nor WART can act without more information."

"And?"

"And—Nam speaks very highly of you."

"I see." You must be grabbing at wisps of smoke, Panji thought.

"This will be dangerous."

"I gathered."

"But you seem able to handle yourself."

Before she could ask one of the dozen questions that occurred to her, Bane's phone rang. He snatched it out of his pocket and glanced at the screen. "Oh. I have to take this." He flipped his phone open. "Bane."

Panji rubbed down Agawase with a terry towel, pretending not to listen, but what she heard put her back on high alert: "Tell me! Who's on the scene? Fine. Get Nam down there. Have Turtle One fueled and crewed."

Bane closed his phone with a too-loud snap.

"What happened?" Something told her she needed to know. Bane looked shaken, and Panji doubted he was easily disturbed.

"It's Ada. She's been attacked."

35

Northside Hospital, Atlanta

Ada felt new pain as Devon entered her room. He wore such an intense frown it almost made him unattractive. He carried a bouquet of her favorite flowers.

"There you are." His voice sounded dry, as if he was dehydrated, but Ada realized, even through the fog of pain, that he was probably just nervous.

"Here I am," she said, trying to sound light.

"And here I am, honey," Barbie re-entered her room from her bathroom. Ada was glad for his daily, long visits, and was also secretly happy the drag costume from Caff's wake was a one-time adventure. Now he wore tight fitting leathers that showed off his over-the-top impressive physique and masculine endowment. He smelled of leather and something like cinnamon. Ada thanked God for Barbie, who kept her spirits up through the doctors, the police inquisition, and the latest briefings on the virus.

"Hello, Barbarino," said Devon stiffly.

"Oh, baby, don't call me that." Barbie spoke quickly, his voice low and breezy. He bent to kiss Ada's cheek. "I'll be outside."

Barbie slipped out of the room, making sure to show off his ass as he slowly opened the door.

After an uncomfortable silence, Devon said, "Funny dude."

Ada closed her eyes, took a breath. Finally she opened her eyes again. "He's a good friend." It was all she could say.

"I see they gave you a private room." He laughed and circled her bed to the windows. She noticed how scrupulously distant he remained as he looked out the window instead of at her. He put the vase of flowers on the table by the window.

"Room's courtesy of the CDC, I'm told," she said, trying to sound calm.

"That's right." Was he taking credit for the room? "Broken arm, huh?" He said it with so little emotion she didn't bother answering. "Have the police learned anything?"

"Nothing they've told me." Ada felt angry now. Why had he come? Just to annoy her.

"That reporter, Hugh King, I've isolated him."

"He's infected?"

"High fever. Although the guy's pretty tough." His tone sounded official now. He was here as Director of Containment at the CDC, not as her ex-husband who cared about her injuries. "You're clear, though. Negative for Nabs."

"Fine."

"Fine? I was worried to death."

"Were you?" And she realized he was. It showed on his tired features as he stepped closer to her bed.

"What happened?" he asked suddenly.

"I was attacked. He pushed a mouse into my face. I know it sounds stupid, but that was what he did. A mouse! I stomped his cuboid bone. Nothing. I elbowed his chin ..." She pointed at the cast on her elbow. "And I'm the only one hurt. Then the sirens came closer and he said, 'You're infected Doctor Kenner. You're infected with LCVM. Just like before.' And he laughed then ran off."

"I didn't mean that."

"Be clearer then!"

He sighed. "You never change, Ada. Always the tough Doctor Kenner. Where's my sweet Adalia?"

"That Ada doesn't exist anymore, Devon. You should know that."

"I guess I never gave up hope."

"You should," she snapped. She didn't want him here. She didn't want to be reminded of her guilt, of her past. But it was too late. In a quieter voice, she said, "Is Quentin all right?"

"Quentin's fine."

Ada said nothing. She closed her eyes, fighting the tears. She saw Quentin there, in the darkness of her mind—in his wheelchair, or hobbling through life on prosthetics—because of her. Because of her carelessness. Because of her ambition.

"Do you know why someone might attack you?"

Ada opened her eyes, blinked back the tears. Thank God. He was changing the subject. Oh, thank God. Now, if only he would leave her room and never come back.

"I think it has something to do with the emerging. With Braxis."

Devon folded his arms across his nicely defined chest. "Why would you say that?"

"It's no coincidence. This guy, basically a psycho assassin, he attacks us, first Caff, now me. He knows all about our pasts. Bees. Mouse. Why attack us? Because we were investigating Braxis."

"That's a big leap."

"No, it's not." She scowled at him. "They killed Caff."

Devon's face betrayed his shock, but he didn't move. "I don't believe that. The police said he was stung by bees."

She stared at him. "No, it's murder. African Killer Bees?" When Devon said nothing, she added, "Think about it. The bastard held a mouse to my face, infected with LCVM. Caff's most afraid of bees. I'm most afraid of LCVM. I guess King was afraid of this 'rage plague' of his. That's no coincidence."

"Maybe you should leave the detective work to the police."

"Devon, why are you here?"

"I'm worried about you."

"Screw off. I don't need your phony sympathy. Or your sarcastic flowers." Hell, she sounded so bitter. She didn't like this side of her. She didn't like what Devon did to her, the memories he stirred, the smugness he conveyed. There had been too much bitterness for them to now be friends.

"Do you want me to leave?"

"That would be nice, thank you."

He stood, arms folded, staring at her. "You might as well here this from me."

"You're firing me."

He shook his head. "You're on semi-permanent leave. With pay."

"You here to rub it in?" With her left hand she found herself rubbing her nose. Rub it in, ha, ha, her mouse-attacker would get a yuk out of that. She could still smell the mouse on her, even though she knew the hospital had sterilized her thoroughly.

Devon sounded desperate, his tone pleading: "No. No I'm not."

"Then why are you here?"

"To offer support. There's talk about letting you go. Permanently."

Ada felt as if Devon had elbowed her in the stomach. Fired by the CDC? The lab was her life. She had come to the CDC as the star recruit, worked her way through nearly every department except the Center for Health Promotion. She had buried herself in work in her lab at the expense of marriage and child.

"You can't do that."

"Not me. They. Pressure from Washington."

"Washington. From whom in Washington?"

"The vice president himself."

"And that doesn't make you wonder?"

"About what?"

"Why a politician interferes with a medical emergency? How a vice president becomes so interested in my affairs he has me fired."

"Not fired."

"Devon!"

"Fine. I wondered. What can I do? Ignore the vice president of the United States?"

"Why not? He's not your boss."

"He's my boss's boss."

"Up yours, Devon." Ada saw him flinch, hurt by her words. She didn't care. He was a spineless moron. She didn't care about her job. But what could she do as an unemployed virologist? She'd have no resources, no lab, no staff, and no authority.

"Get out, Devon."

He looked hurt. She couldn't bear the look of pain on his handsome features. But he left.

36

Room 323, Atlanta

Panji waved at Ada as she entered the room with an armful of gladiolus and magazines. "You're looking better."

Ada smiled. "More flowers. People will think we're dating."

"Flowers make you feel better."

"Actually, statistics indicate the pollen and dust on a bouquet of flowers can inhibit—"

Panji smacked the flowers down on the bed. "Spare me. I brought your favorite magazines. *Science*. *Nature*. Had trouble finding *Virologist*. Don't you read anything fun?"

Ada laughed and Panji joined her. It was strange how they had slipped instinctively into the zone of friendship. Panji had only met Ada at Kinosewak, had hardly talked to the tireless doctor as she treated the villagers, but for the last two days they had done nothing but talk. Sometimes you just knew people. Ada was more or less an open book: compassionate, brilliant, but troubled somewhere in her past. And Panji knew they would be good friends.

"Where's Barbie?" Panji liked Ada's friend Barbarino Fosco. He teased her that she was a Cher wannabee, "but that's not a bad thing, honey," and was very protective of Ada.

"Said something about Chinese food when I complained about hospital diets."

Panji sat on the edge of the bed. "When are you getting out?"

"Today."

"That's good."

"Is Bane's watchdog still out there?"

Panji laughed. "Nam? Give her a break, Ada. She has demons of her own, but she's a nice kid."

"Demons of her own? Meaning I have demons?"

"We all do." Panji put on her best smile.

"So, what are mine?" Ada looked mischievous, and Panji knew she wasn't trying to be serious.

"Oh, probably you have five husbands in five different cities, something like that."

Ada laughed, clutching the bouquet of gladiolus with her good hand.

"Oh, that's good. I couldn't stand my one ex-husband."

"Ah. So there's your demon, eh?"

Ada's smile disappeared, but she said, "So Canadians really talk like that, eh?"

Panji put her hand on Ada's forearm. "Never in my life. I just know you Americans expect it."

They laughed together, and it felt good. "I wanted to thank you again for what you did in Kinosewak."

Ada shook her head. "Don't ever thank me for things like that."

"Why not?"

"It's my job."

"No, it's not. Your director was here earlier, you know."

"No, I didn't know." Ada sounded angry.

"The gladiolus are from him."

"You're joking, I assume."

"Yes, I am."

"What did he say?"

"He said you were in big trouble because you helped my people."

"Actually, I'm told I'm on leave."

Leave. Panji knew this was code for "fired." She knew Ada well enough to know that leave meant she was out of the life she loved, the lab she built. She knew the bitterness and sarcasm came from her director taking away the one thing that mattered in Ada's life. How could Ada fulfill her life's mission to stop a virus that destroyed people's lives—viruses like LCVM, that destroyed her life and Quentin's, or this mysterious emerging virus that threatened to become an epidemic. She knew all this because Ada had told her, and it made Panji want to cry.

"Medical leave." Panji bent forward impulsively and kissed Ada's cheek.

"You're not gay, right?" Ada asked, lightly.

"No, I'm not. Nam maybe, but not me."

"Just checking." Ada tossed the flowers to the side table. Panji stood up, fished a dying bouquet of roses out of a vase and pushed the long gladiolus into the water.

"I told Devon that you were a hero. That you saved people. That I asked you to come on behalf of the First Nations."

Ada laughed. "You're on a first-name basis with my boss?"

"He's a fan of my music, believe it or not."

"Fan or not, I doubt he believed any of that hero bull."

Panji winked at Ada and sat back on the bed. "No. He used more colorful language. But I said I'm going on record as having asked. So's Doctor Buchler, your friend from WHO."

"He's here?"

"Not anymore. He's on his way to South America." She leaned closer and whispered. "But he said you always have a job at WHO."

"Does everyone know I'm fired except me?" Ada stared hard at Panji, then blinked rapidly. Holding back tears? The detached power persona of the scientist seemed to crumble, just for a moment. "I'm sorry, Panji. I'm bitchy today."

Panji saw real pain on Ada's face. It was time to change the subject. She leaned closer and whispered, "Nam has good ears. So why do you care about her guarding the door?"

"Because I want out of here."

"They're going to discharge you."

"I mean, I want to get away from all of this. The doctors, the police, WART, all of it."

"Well, ask her. She's a cool chick, you know."

"Chick? Please tell me you don't really talk like that."

"You seem hung up on the way I talk, eh?"

Again, Ada laughed and Panji was glad. Laughter was the best healing power in the Maker's Universe, and once Ada left the hospital, Panji doubted there'd be much laughter. Panji had read the headlines, talked to Bane's people, knew that things were getting bad out there, with flare-ups of the "Rage Plague" in five cities already. It wouldn't help that Ada's boss had relieved her.

"So I'm really out of a job?"

"Not really, no," said a new voice, answering for Panji. Alban Bane stood at the door with yet another bouquet of flowers, this one a sweeping arrangement of tropicals: stunning birds of paradise arching out of a bed of ginger flowers.

"Hello, Alban. Eavesdropping?" Panji slid off the bed and scooped the bouquet out of his arms.

"I'm a peeper, too."

"He's a spook," Ada said. She smiled. "But thanks for the flowers, Director Spook."

Bane smiled and it made him attractive. He was a man's man in the true sense, but right now he looked weary, clearly weighed down with pressures and lack of sleep. But when he smiled, the boyish charm emerged. Panji knew people. Deep down, Bane was a good man.

"I've asked the UN secretary general to ask the US secretary of health to ask for your temporary reassignment." Bane stood at the door, the smile gone and the weight of the world back.

"That's a whole pile of secretaries," Panji said.

"Sounds like a pile of horseshit," Ada said. "You're telling me that without asking me, you've gone through channels to re-assign me?" She sounded angry.

"He did something like this on me, too," Panji said. "Flew up to my farm with guns and storm troopers, scared my mother half to death—"

Bane laughed. "I doubt anything scares your mother."

"Okay, scared me half to death."

"Actually Ada, she scared me," Bane said. "Came out of the house with a big gun, like Dirty Harry. Make my day, all that. I nearly pooped my depends."

Forceful now, Panji snapped, "He drafted me, Ada. Just like he's trying to do with you."

"Something like that." Bane paced the room. "You've heard the rumors, read the rags? One thousand nine hundred and seventy-three incidents reported on your watch notice. For this virus you're chasing. Growing exponentially."

Ada squirmed on the bed, trying to sit straighter, and Panji helped her by tilting the back of the bed up. "The mutated BDV?"

"That's right. The same one you identified in James Bay." Bane finally stopped pacing.

"Are they moving to quarantine?" Ada asked. "Has FEMA become involved?"

"No one has," Bane said. "There's been no containment order. There's not enough evidence of risk of epidemic, so says your director Tomich."

"Bullshit! That man's so full of bullshit it's just pouring out the anal fissure he calls a mouth!"

Ada struggled to get out of her bed.

"What are you doing?" Panji asked, moving to her side.

"Getting out of here."

"You're not discharged," Panji snapped.

"It's just a frigging Monteggia fracture!" Ada waved her cast.

"I'm told that if it doesn't set properly, you'll never regain elbow movement," Bane said.

"That's why it's in a cast, Bane." She shook her head. "Leave the doctoring to doctors."

"I intend to." Bane moved to the other side of Ada. "That's why I want you to help me."

"Is this the secretary to secretary thing? Moving me around like some chess piece without asking the pawn?"

"I think of you more as a queen than a pawn."

"Spare me, Bane."

"You're on permanent leave, thanks to Tomich," Panji reminded Ada.

"So? You don't think I can appeal?" Ada was angry with them both now, Panji could see. She had a temper, that was certain.

"It will take time, perhaps weeks. Weeks we don't have to spare. This virus isn't going to wait for you to appeal to a committee to be re-assigned." Bane spoke in a soft voice. "And WART has a lot of resources."

"So you're making me a job offer?"

"Yes. Think how cool it will be when you turn out to be right."

"I don't want to be right."

"Just think. You can stick it to Devon Tomich."

Ada smiled. Then, "I don't like spooks!" There seemed to be no stopping her fury. She moved across the room to the closet then stood there, staring. "Who brought these clothes?"

"I did," Panji admitted. She had gone shopping yesterday, mostly for herself since she had flown off with Bane without a suitcase, but also for her friend, because the clothes she had been admitted with were torn by the attack.

"Good taste," Ada said, her voice quieter.

"Listen to the man, Ada," Panji said it quietly, but forcefully.

"I'm intuitive about people. He's a good man, this Bane."

Ada scowled, and it wasn't attractive. "If you're so smart with men, why are you divorced?"

Panji stiffened. Ada was striking out, angry because of her attack in the cemetery, because of her frustration, because she had been all but fired. "No one's perfect," Panji said, with a smile. "And I'm still friends with my ex. He's my agent."

"I'm not sure that shows good judgment." But Ada's tirade was finished and Panji saw that she was relaxing slightly. She reached out with her single good arm and tried to snatch down the designer jeans from the hanger.

"What's the news with my attacker?" Ada asked abruptly.

Bane sat on the edge of her bed. "You didn't give us a whole lot to go on. We're busily rounding up all the six-foot-six blonds with size twenty cowboy boots."

Panji noticed the tension in Ada's shoulders. "Why would someone go to such great lengths to kill Caff and scare me?"

"Trying to impose rational behavior on irrational events works about as well as a scientist going to Church to pray for her next breakthrough."

"Your metaphors suck, Bane."

"I'm running out. My Bartlett's Guide to Metaphors is pretty much falling apart."

"The attacks seemed pretty well planned to me."

"Planned by a psychotic, yes." Bane patted the bed. "Sit. Take a load off. I have more questions about the attack."

"I've told you all I know." She sat anyway. "You're the famous detective. What do you think's going on? Is he just someone infected with this virus, going around targeting specifically the people trying to stop it because he read about us in the papers?"

Bane's smile faded. "Same old, really. You're close to an answer, and it's got someone worried. The only thing I hate more than a psycho is a psycho with a mission."

"So you have ideas?"

"I always have ideas. Bad ideas are the currency of an open mind. Good ideas are the currency of persistence. It's like when you were in high school, turned down by every girl in class—"

Panji saw the annoyance in Ada's expression, the tightness of her lips, and it erupted suddenly in a loud tirade: "No more dumb-ass metaphors, please!"

Bane shrugged and waited. Finally Ada shook her head. "So, what are you? A bad ideas guy or a good ideas guy?"

"At least nine parts bad ideas. But that one good idea, it's like your first sex in high school, after all those rejections. What a thrill. Scary, but thrilling. There, I had to finish it."

"And you want me to work with you?"

"Only if you can take my relentless metaphors."

Ada sighed. "But you have an idea of who this attacker was?"

Bane smiled. "I know exactly who it was. Finding him, that's another matter. I have a warrant out for him and his brother. But my standing warrant's been out for four years. They're as slippery as a water slide."

"They?"

"Twins. Twin brothers. Ran into them a few times. To call them sociopaths is to be generous. Their nickname is the Fallen Angels, probably because they're pretty handsome if you like that sort. Charming."

"Why bees? A mouse?"

"They enjoy their work. The fun is in the small things, as they say."

Ada stared at Bane, but the tears welled. "That definitely was not funny, Bane," Panji said. "Maybe, give us some privacy?"

Bane smiled. "Okay. But think about my offer. Just think. A shiny badge. Half the pay you got at the CDC."

"You make it sound so appetizing," Ada said, and in spite of herself she smiled this time.

Bane left with a wave.

Panji said, "He's like you. Driven, workaholic, compassionate. He didn't like being called a spook."

"What is he then?"

"I've done a little research. Ex-FBI profiler. After years of pursuit he caught the serial killer Tyler Hayden when no one else could even figure out a profile. But it cost him his wife. She was raped and killed by a man sent by Hayden. His daughter was even kidnapped. He rescued her, but she's never forgiven him."

"You know a lot."

"Everything's on the Internet. Who needs detectives anymore?"

Ada smiled. "So Bane's obsessed."

"Remind you of someone?"

Ada stared at Panji. "You're trying to say I'm obsessed now?"

"Aren't you?"

Ada's scowl deepened. "More online research?"

"I talked to your ex when he visited."

"Go to hell, Panji."

Panji said nothing.

Finally, Ada said, "Someone's trying to kill me. They killed my best friend. Bane knows who did it, but he seems to be some kind of ghost. A virus is on the loose and for some reason the CDC is doing nothing. And you think I'm obsessed?"

"Fine, it's serious."

"And—I've been fired," Ada said, her voice calm, but her rigid body posture revealing her true feelings, "which means I have no resources."

"Maybe. But I've been researching WART. At least the things I can find out publicly. They're like FEMA, but on an international scale. It's a good group."

"Is good the only adjective you know?"

"It's all good, sister."

"They have military personnel."

"The world's a dangerous place."

They stared at each other for a long time, Ada frowning and unconvinced. "Well, I guess the important thing is stopping this virus."

Panji nodded. The "Rage Plague" was more widespread than Ada knew, sheltered in her hospital room. Thousands of incidents of violence had now been attributed to the virus. And Panji had a feeling Ada and Bane would be the only two with a chance to stop it.

37

Fort Detrick, Maryland

Lieutenant Colonel Bailey Beckett aged like fine wine, and that was damned unfair. He hadn't aged in six years, his hair still solidly black at fifty, and he was as fit as any regular army soldier. They called him Boomer in the lab, but his friends called him BB.

"Hello, old friend," Ada said, waving with her cast.

BB came around his tiny metal desk and kissed her lightly on the cheek, careful to avoid her cast. "Don't give me friend, A.K. In a fair world, we'd be married."

She smiled; she knew his wife Janine and knew he meant it as a joke.

"Who's your—companion?" He held out his hand to Barbie Fosco.

"Barbarino Fosco. Colonel Bailey Beckett." She watched as they shook, neither looking enthusiastic: Barbie hated authority and uniforms on principle, and BB didn't know what to make of the muscular man in skin-tight leather.

After the encounter with the assassin in the cemetery, Barbie had taken it upon himself to become her "body guard," but he was hardly inconspicuous. Bane had asked her to take Nam, but Ada had refused. "If that thug had wanted me dead, I'd be dead. And you need Nam."

"We need you safe." Bane had said, staring at Barbie. "He's a strong guy, but no gun, no training."

Back and forth they argued until Ada made it abundantly clear that she wouldn't work with Bane with a shadow.

In the end Barbie was the compromise Bane could barely live with.

He had surprised her on the flight to Fort Detrick. "I want Caff's killer, too," and that probably tore to the naked truth of his motivation. She was glad of his company.

"I'll wait outside, baby-cheeks," Barbie said, and he left BB's tiny office.

"My bodyguard," she said with a smile.

BB laughed then saw she was serious. "Funny damned bodyguard."

"I guess you were surprised I called?"

"Understatement. Big understatement." He gestured for her to sit in one of his functional but uncomfortable chairs, then sat on the edge of his desk. "Job hunting? Or here to have me sign your cast?"

"Oh, you heard." Ada felt a burn of anger but controlled it.

"Where else can a specialist in Emerging Virology go?"

She smiled. "Special Pathogens Branch of WHO. University of Anvers. Bernard Nocht. Even Pasteur. Anywhere but here, BB."

He gave her a scowl of mock anger. "And what's wrong with USAMRIID? We hire civilians, you know."

"I have a job," she said, and she explained about WART, even showing her temporary badge.

"So, this is business." He sounded disappointed.

"I need you."

"Ah. I've waited twenty years to hear you say that, love."

She shook her head. They had to get out of old friends mode. "Sorry, BB. Serious shit."

"Must be. Don't hear the word shit from your lovely lips often." Reluctant, he circled back around his desk and sat down. "What can an old army doctor do for you, the great Ada Kenner?"

She sighed. "I came in person, so you'd know it's important."

"I get that." He chewed his mustache, an old nervous habit. "Is this about your emerging virus? The BDV mutate?"

"How much do you know?"

"I'm keeping up. I think all the Level Four installations are. General Stouffville's very concerned."

"I'm glad to hear it. Someone has to take this more seriously." And aside from the CDC, in the United States that left only the army's infectious diseases research center at Fort Detrick.

She told him everything she could: about the initial vector, the "supposed" accident, the spreading infection rates in six cities, Braxis, Domergue's evasiveness, the pending Congressional Committee—a ten-minute update.

"Some of this I knew about. But Braxis mutated the BDV? Why?"

"Why? Why does everyone find it so hard to accept Braxis would pursue the almighty dollar instead of nobility."

"That's not my concern. But Braxis is a major contract supplier to the armed forces."

"I know."

He rubbed his eyes, looking as tired as she felt. "I've been working on the virus you sent."

"Find anything?"

"Unusually aggressive. Scary."

"That's your scientific appraisal?"

He laughed, a mirthless sound. "What is it you want from me?"

"You're not going to like this."

"I never thought I would."

She slipped her shiny new laptop out of her bag with her good hand. She missed her old one, but all the files were here. She booted up from sleep mode and turned the screen to face him. "These are the projected infection vectors, taking into account virulence, transmission, migration patterns, assuming ten-day incubation for safety."

He whistled. "At this rate, we'll have a pandemic."

She nodded. "Unless USAMRIID imposes quarantine on cities."

He closed the lid of her laptop. "Old friend, you said." He paced his tiny windowless office. It was eerier how much he mirrored her previous life at the CDC: Emerging Virus Specialist, closet-sized office, middle level supervisor, top secret clearance. "Well, we were more rivals than friends weren't we? You come to me, why? Because the CDC won't act."

She watched him but remained sitting. "Someone has to act, BB."

"Right. Someone. Well, city-wide quarantine requires higher authority than a Lieutenant Colonel. Even my General doesn't have that authority."

"Well then, we have work to do."

"We? I don't think so. You're tarnished goods right now, A.K."

"Am I?" That hurt more than she thought it might.

"Alban Bane's influence has saved your reputation somewhat. But you're still riding his balloon."

"I see." So he knew about everything, more than he let on. She clenched her teeth and tried to remain calm.

"I don't think I can sell this, A.K."

"You can." She stood up, angry now, and stepped in the path of his pacing. "You will. You will because millions of lives could be the price tag of inaction. You will because it's the right thing to do. We may have been rivals, we may have fought, we may have often disagreed, but I always thought you would do the right thing, Doctor Colonel Beckett. That's what I always thought."

He didn't show his surprise at her outburst. "Do you know what you're asking?"

"I know. You could be reprimanded."

He snorted. "Reprimanded? I might be discharged, but that's not what I mean!"

"Why? For doing the right thing?"

He took a long breath. "For disobeying orders. General Stouffville memoed me that you would come. The Pentagon's concerned about your involvement with WART. The Secretary of Defence has instructed us not to engage with you."

"Not engage? What the hell is that supposed to mean?" Her voice rose to a growl, and it scared even her. A dozen questions flew through her mind: Why were people so hesitant to do the right thing? Who was covering up? Was Braxis producing bio weapons for the armed forces? A stab of pain shot through her left temple. She bent over, rubbing her head.

"Are you all right, A.K.?" BB guided her back to her chair and poured her a glass of water.

"I'm sorry, BB. Not your fault." Oh God, that hurts. "Hell of a migraine."

His worried voice dropped to a low hush. "Do you get migraines?"

"No." She bent lower now, propping her elbows on her knees.

He refilled her glass and brought her two buffered aspirin.

Ada closed her eyes, popped the pills and said, "Sorry."

He massaged her neck gently. "A.K. you're coming to my house tonight. Janine's doing pot roast." He knelt in front of her, looking up at her. "No arguing. Let me see your eyes."

She opened her eyes. The fluorescent lights in the room gave her more pain.

"You're bloody there, babe." He shook his head. "You're coming to the homestead, and no arguing."

"Thank you. I like Janine's pot roast."

"Liar."

"But you don't get off that easily," she said. She took a long breath, feeling better. The pain was still there, but the invisible rod of hot metal was gone.

"Oh, the quarantine."

"Yes."

He sprang up and stood in front of her. "Quarantine under army control is only possible if emergency powers are initiated—either a state of war, or under the auspices of FEMA. Why not try law enforcement first."

"Police authorities cannot usually enforce quarantine."

"It's a long road from here to FEMA. We'll have to present to Senate Committees."

"Then we'd best get started."

"But it may dead end, A.K. Why? Because what you're asking will cause widespread public panic. Economic disaster for the cities involved. Bankruptcies. The FAA will have to ground flights. It's big, A.K. Too big for us."

"Like I said, let's get started."

He looked about to throttle her. Then, impulsively, he leaned forward and kissed her cheek again. "I hope you know what you're doing."

"I hope so too."

"Because if you don't, it's disaster, and nothing less."

38

Las Vegas, Nevada

Bane's special operations plane Turtle One touched down in Vegas, the current stop in the *Superstar* tour. After Bane zinged Panji through security, she felt a little deserted as Ada, Bane, Colonel Bailey Becket of USAMRIID and Nam flew on to Washington to meet with the Senate Committee.

Her spirits improved when she saw Kenji Tenichi, standing alone at the arrivals gate, hands clasped behind his back. The on-camera host of the *Superstar* show looked as tasty as she remembered, dressed in baggy jeans that hung down too low on his butt cheeks and tight T shirt that revealed defined pectoral muscles. There was an ageless, childlike quality about the Japanese man that captivated her: a round face softened by puppy dog eyes, barely visible behind sheepdog bangs, and pouting kissable lips that parted to a shining smile. Normally, Panji wouldn't go for Hollywood handsome, but he wasn't aware of his own looks and that appealed to her. He was as sexy as all get out with his serene demeanor and easy grace.

"Hello, Panji Maingan," he said, and his hand appeared, holding a single long stemmed white rose. "I have missed you." He spoke impeccable English, slightly accented.

"I didn't expect you." She took the flower, feeling the light brush of his long fingers on her palm. But he made no attempt to hug her or kiss her.

"I have rented a car," Kenji said, and he surprised her by holding out his hand.

The rented car was an unpretentious Toyota Prius hybrid. He opened the door for her, and she slid into the passenger seat.

"I am not a very good driver." He gave another of his dazzling smiles.

He drove in the right lane and well below the limit as people honked at him, even when a pickup truck tailgated him, filling the rearview mirror and flashing high beams.

"You're right about the driving," she joked.

"You are at Bellagio?" he asked, apparently ignorant of the honking horns and one-finger salutes around him. She loved his equanimity above all, the way he spoke quietly and with respect, and even how he spoke perfect English without contracted words.

"Are you hungry?"

"Starving."

"There is a good noodle place in the Bellagio."

"Is that where you are staying?"

"We are staying at Wynn. Abbey picked it."

"Pretty hoity toity."

"What is hoity?"

"Never mind. Noodles sound wonderful." She found herself glancing frequently at Kenji as they drove. He utterly thrilled her, and that shocked her. He was so quiet, so charming, totally unthreatening. He was childlike in the way he looked at the world, an innocence that was nearly impossible to find in America, but intelligent and well educated in other ways. And he was the most moral and compassionate man she had ever met. The contrasts made him exotic.

They ate superb noodles in the clinical cheeriness of Noodles against the muffled cling-cling-cling of slot machines. The nice thing about Vegas was that autograph-hounds rarely pursued you and celebrity was not a major handicap.

She found herself watching his lips as he slurped up long ropes of rice noodles. The way she felt right now, he could pick his nose and she'd find him sexy. She'd been divorced too long, or hadn't dated enough. Whatever it was, she felt giddy.

Until Abbey Chase and entourage barged into Noodles. The producer and judge of *Superstar* waved at Panji, smiling coldly.

"Oh, Great Maker." Panji stared at Abbey Chase, tall, chic and coldly beautiful.

Kenji didn't look over his shoulder. "Is it Abbey?"

"You must be psychic."

"No. I read your body language."

Panji was as stiff as an arthritic joint, and probably her face betrayed the sudden rise of anger and anxiety.

Abbey Chase nodded curtly then swept with regal grace to their reserved table near the front of the restaurant. After her team sat down, she made a none-too-subtle beeline straight for Panji and Kenji.

Kenji, always polite, stood and gave a slight bow. Panji reluctantly stood up.

"Well, Panji Maingan. Vegas is the city of miracles after all." Abbey's voice conveyed cold detachment, but her eyes revealed a hotness that could only be rage. "May I sit for a moment?"

Do we have a choice? Panji almost said it. Kenji pulled out a chair for the elegant television producer and Panji poured her a cup of tea.

"I was just discussing you with our lawyer. You remember Sam Stein?"

Panji saw that Stein was at the reserved table. "The inevitable lawsuit?"

Abbey smiled, a fleeting expression, and Panji decided Abbey's beauty was contingent on sternness. The smile destroyed the illusion of dark exquisiteness and, in fact, made her look ordinary. "A demand letter more likely, my dear."

Oh, Panji hated "my dears" almost as much as she despised Abbey Chase. In all of Panji's life, it would be fair to say that she only ever hated one other person, a bully in high school who destroyed the egos of many a student. "Well, here I am."

"Yes. There you are. And I assume we'll see you on set tomorrow?"

Panji didn't answer right away. She studied Abbey, putting on her best power stance: eyes steady and calm, body relaxed but upright.

"Because that was the deadline set for you by Sam Stein."

"Are you sure it was Sam's date?"

"Contractual, my dear."

Panji couldn't take it. "I'll thank you to refrain from calling me 'my dear' or anything except Ms. Maingan. Panji, if you must."

Abbey's lip twitched, the only betrayal of anger. "Fine, Ms. Maingan. I'll expect you at eight tomorrow morning." She started to rise.

"If this virus doesn't stop the show."

Abbey glared at Panji now. "What do you mean?"

"Well, as I understand it, your crew, cast and many contestants are quite sick."

"Who told you that?"

"Doctor Ada Kenner if you must know."

Abbey said nothing. She folded her arms across her ample chest and smiled her unattractive smile. "The meddlesome Doctor Kenner. Well, she won't be a problem for much longer. I understand she's out of a job."

"Actually, no. She's now part of Alban Bane's team." Panji couldn't help feeling a little gloat.

"Another annoying person." She scowled. "Just you show up, Panji Maingan. Alban Bane and Ada Kenner and all the powers-that-be will not stop *Superstar*. You can count on that."

Then she turned and, instead of returning to her table, she strode out of the restaurant onto the casino floor. Her startled crew chased after her.

"Well, that was fun," Panji said.

Kenji smiled his oh-so-tempting best. They hadn't even progressed past the hand-holding and light-kiss stage, yet he felt so right, so skin-tight perfect for her. She supposed she had Bane to thank for getting them together again.

"Shall we walk the strip, Panji?"

"No tables?"

"I do not gamble."

"No, you wouldn't, would you?"

He held out his hand and long warm fingers wrapped hers. Happy, Panji snugged up close to him as they wound through the busy casino, past full tables, through clouds of smoke and the ringing turmoil of slot machines. The crowds on the strip were almost serene after the excitement of the casino floor.

They talked very little, content to hold hands as they watched the musical fountains and the sinking pirate ship and the laughing tourists.

"You've known Bane a long time, haven't you," Panji said as they both signed autographs outside MGM. Kenji seemed to draw all the girls, and Panji the boys, and both had a lineup.

Kenji's grin revealed his affection for Bane. "Yes. Four years, five months and a few days."

"You nearly lost your life thanks to him." She lifted her hands to the fans. "No more, please. Writer's cramp!"

Kenji laughed and this time they ran down the strip, pursued for a while by young fans. Finally, the fans gave up around the Pyramid, and he said, "Yes, Panji Maingan, I nearly lost my life. Bane saved us all, though. I doubt I would be here if Alban Bane had not arrived on Abbey Chase's set."

They had almost left the strip by the time they finished chatting about Bane, and the crowds were thinning. He told her all about their adventures, of the rescue in the Vermont caves, of how Bane had once held him as the chief suspect. Finally he said, "We should go back."

"We should."

She leaned in suddenly and brushed his warm cheek with her lips.

He didn't blush, flinch, or respond. He just stared at her with his puppy dog eyes. "What was that for?"

"For being Kenji."

Then he kissed her properly, shy at first, leaning in slowly, his lips parting gently as they touched. His lips were warm, even against the desert heat, and she found herself flushing even hotter. God, he was so sexy. His hand was on the small of her back, pulling her gently against him. She hoped he would never stop.

"May I have your autograph?" said a husky, pleasant male voice.

Startled, Panji and Kenji pulled away from each other immediately. Panji saw the autograph-hunter over Kenji's shoulder. He was a big, big man, not a typical "fan," with golden hair—and a face filter mask?

She tensed.

Kenji smiled, started to turn.

Panji wasn't exactly sure what happened in that moment. She smelled it first, a pungent tang reminiscent of antiseptic. Kenji's hand flew up to his neck.

Panji screamed, an involuntary reaction, as Kenji collapsed, an untidy heap on the pavement. She fell to her knees and cradled his head, brushing back his long tangle of hair, feeling for a pulse. She was only barely aware that she was shouting, "Why? Why?"

And then the golden-haired attacker was gone, clopping along the sidewalk on gigantic cowboy boots.

Panji continued to scream for help, digging in her bag for her cell phone.

Kenji moaned.

39

Washington, DC

Ada Kenner's elbow cast was unwieldy and wide as she sat in the Senate committee gallery between Alban Bane and Colonel Bailey Becket, two nice manly bookends. Nam Ling stood at the door, arms folded and watchful. On this trip, Barbie had stayed home in Atlanta.

Ada stared at her ex-husband, Director Devon Tomich of the CDC. He couldn't see her, and that felt strange. He was also oddly subdued as he testified before the Senate Select Committee on Homeland Security, Subcommittee on Prevention of Biological Weapons of Mass Destruction, Closed Session.

She noticed how he fidgeted in his chair, shifting from side to side under the combined eyes of twelve representatives of the House. She was glad it wasn't her, but then she realized that it soon would be. Bane had insisted she come, to present their combined findings, as expert on behalf of WART to support Colonel Becket's testimony on behalf of USAMRIID.

Devon sounded rested and sure of himself as he finished, "We are confident the situation is contained, Mr. Chairman."

"I thank the gentleman," Chairman Nathan Dobbs, representative for NYC said. "We now turn to the next member on our panel of experts."

Devon rose from his chair and stepped down, and as he turned he saw Ada sitting two rows back. If he was startled, he didn't show it, but he immediately moved to their row. He excused himself as he slid past various witnesses and then stood over Ada. Colonel Becket stared at Devon coolly, then slid aside. Devon sat beside Ada on her cast side.

He glanced at Alban Bane, who nodded. "This isn't what I had in mind by leave of absence. Rest, A.K., that's what you need, not a new job."

"You know very well, Director Tomich, that the situation is not contained." They might be in D.C., but she was not a games player. Especially when the stakes were death.

The committee chairman rapped the long raised table. "Order, please," he said, staring directly at Ada. "The Committee welcomes Doctor Ernest Gies, VP of Research and Development of Braxis Genetics, Ph.D., magna cum lauda in chemistry and biology, past surgeon at various prestigious hospitals, Chief Medical Resident and later Chief of Staff at Manhattan

General, fellowship in Clinical Pharmacology and Infectious Diseases at UCSF, Ph.D in Virology, Harvard—"

The representative from Vermont, Senator Riley Stephens, raised his hand. "Mr. Chairman, we have heard testimony from the esteemed gentleman on numerous occasions. We acknowledge his vast credentials."

The chairman looked annoyed. "Doctor Gies, are you satisfied?"

"I am well satisfied," said Gies, his English nearly accent-free but laced with a rich French warmth.

Gies was no longer a hero to Ada. In fact he had refused all her phone calls, but now seeing him, stooped under the weight of obvious stress and worry, she felt some of the old warmth return.

From the way Senator Stephens scowled at Gies, she understood there was history there. Bane leaned close to her and whispered, "Stephens was a Congressman a few years back. I had a few run-ins with the man. Not an appetizing character."

Ada smiled at the analogy. She found very few politicians "appetizing." She focused her attention on Gies, wondering what her old professor would say, if anything, about the accident at Site F.

"Good morning, Chairman Dobbs, Ranking Member Stephens and distinguished members of the subcommittee. I thank you for the opportunity to appear before you today to discuss the risks posed by the accidental release of the virus we have designated TZ-4."

Ada was on full alert now. He had as much as admitted culpability. For the VP of a major public corporation to do so was unprecedented. She sensed a ploy.

"As I indicated in yesterday's session, TZ-4 vaccine is part of an FDA approved trial. Braxis is currently at human trials protocol for vaccine development with positive third-stage results. Our eminent Doctor Begley developed the practical medical protocol. As you know, violent in-patients at various institutions have tested positive for various mutations of Borna Virus."

"Perhaps the gentleman could review?"

"Certainly, Mr. Chairman. The etiological agent of Borna disease is a persistent virus infection of the central nervous system with differently expressed symptomatology and phenotypic architecture. The biological parameters of Begley's original abstract postulate an unsegmented single-stranded RNA ..."

Bane whispered, "Do you follow any of this?"

Ada nodded, listening attentively for a few moments.

"… single-stranded negative strand RNA virus of the order mononegavirales. This order contains the family of lyssaviruses which includes the viruses responsible for rabies …"

She listened for five minutes then slipped her Palm LifeDrive out of her bag. She wrote a few notes on her screen for Bane using the screen pen. She passed it to her new boss: In a nutshell, they mutated the BDV virus to ensure the highest possible virulence, then created a vaccine against it. The idea is to "cure" neuropsychiatric disorders in violent patients …

Bane nodded, understanding her laymen's explanation as Gies continued his full disclosure to the rapt committee. Beside her, her ex-husband Devon sniffed, and she saw that he had been peering at her tiny screen.

"Doctor Gies, the committee is grateful for the explanation," Chairman Dobbs said when Gies finished fifteen minutes later. "We also have your written statements. Perhaps the gentleman could explain the incident at Site F?"

"I can only speculate at this point, of course," Gies said. "Our security chief has investigated. Of interest is an abrupt improvement in Doctor Begley's financial status. Two new homes, a villa in Italy, a Porsche, Land Rover and several suspect accounts …"

Ada wrote on her Palm Pilot screen and tapped it in Bane's direction: Did you know this?

Bane nodded. He took her pen and wrote: Didn't want to distract your investigation or influence you.

What have you found? she wrote.

Before Bane could write an answer, Gies said, "Basically, through forensic accounting we followed the money to a terrorist cell in Pakistan headed by Chaudhry Shujaa Khan."

Even the congressmen were swept into a roar of voices. This information was new. Of course Ada knew of Khan, a man famous for selling aging Soviet-era nuclear bombs and as ruthless as they came. She looked at Bane, who nodded. How much was he holding back?

Finally, when the uproar would not quiet, the chairman resorted to pounding the table. "Come to order!"

Ada wished she could see Gies' face better, but the witness chair faced the Senators, not the audience. Gies remained statue-still through the excitement, betraying no nervous gestures.

"The gentleman is invited to continue."

Gies' voice carried deep concern and warmth. "It is important to understand that Doctor Begley acted alone. We did not realize Doctor

Begley had become infected with TZ-4."

Ada wrote on her Palm Pilot: He's hiding something.

Bane nodded and took the pen: I think so too.

"We can only make assumptions after analysis of security recordings. It seems he stole fourteen samples of the vaccine. However, he carried with him, on that night, the live virus. Since he has passed away, we continue to support authorities in their investigation."

Ada wrote: Has Braxis volunteered information to us?

Bane shook his head. Ada swung her Palm over to Devon and stabbed at the screen. He shook his head as well.

The chairman leaned forward. "We certainly appreciate the gentleman's efforts. Perhaps you could give your analysis of the threat?"

"TZ-4 has a 64.5713 percent probability of infection on exposure," Gies said, infuriatingly calm. "It has only a fatality projection, statistically, of 12.3415 percent. I do not mean to belittle these horrifying numbers, Mr. Chairman, but I find it somewhat reassuring that the incubation averages eleven days. In some cases, sadly, symptoms come on faster, occasionally within twenty-four hours. We do have a working vaccine."

The chairman seemed speechless.

"I have contacted the White House directly, with an offer to increase production of the vaccine as quickly as possible."

The session became very tense, with Gies and the chairman shooting back and forth in a lightning round of raised voices that seemed more akin to cross-examination than testimony.

Bane held out his hand and Ada passed him the PDA. He wrote: Braxis seems to stand to gain billions in revenue.

Ada nodded, appalled. She herself had called the BioWatch Alert, which had provisions for seven billion dollars in discretionary funds for emergency acquisition of vaccines and drugs.

Bane held the screen up for her again: He hasn't mentioned the hijacking of Braxis trucks.

Ada nodded. Bane had told her on the flight from Atlanta that his team had discovered several armed robberies of Braxis shipments, focused mostly in Asia and India.

Bane wrote: Trucks with vaccine??? You think?

She nodded.

Bane was the next to be called and Ada watched as he passed Gies. There was a moment of tension.

After introductions, Bane began his testimony: "My expert on these matters, Doctor Ada Kenner, formerly Coordinator of Emerging Viral at the CDC, will speak to some of the direct implications of this epidemic. I can report that we have, to date, four thousand, six hundred and thirty-two incidents of violent attacks in six cities directly attributable to this virus. Although I dislike sensationalism, it is not entirely inaccurate to portray this outbreak as a "rage plague," a term picked by many journalists." He went on to list the most horrifying scenarios: the mother who drowned her twin babies, a radical group in Texas who blew up a shopping mall, a thirteen-year-old boy who shot fellow students in a rampage that took thirty-three children—all fairly "normal" incidents of violence, except that the assailants invariably committed suicide and autopsy indicated TZ antibodies. "We believe that our numbers represent less than ten percent of the violence perpetrated by victims of TZ infection."

The silence was complete in the room. No one moved. The chairman and all the other congressmen stared at Bane. Devon seemed frozen.

"As you know, from my written submissions, we believe the outbreak was caused by Chandry Khan." He waited for the chairman to restore order. "In a deliberate terrorist act."

The silence was replaced by a roar of angry voices. Everyone spoke at once. This time, when the chairman pounded the table, no one responded to order.

"It is important that air travel be suspended," Bane shouted.

Finally, when there was silence, the chairman said, "What is the gentleman suggesting?"

"That we cannot afford to spread this virus around the world."

The chairman pounded the table for several moments. "Order! I will have order!"

"This is a crisis, gentlemen of the committee," Bane said sternly. "If we don't act now, it will be too late. I recommend a full quarantine of Las Vegas, Los Angeles and the three other hot spots we indicated in yesterday's presentation." Ada was quite surprised at how controlled Bane appeared when he didn't crack wise.

The chairman stood up, and this time the people in the room stilled. "Director Bane, thank you. Without objection, we acknowledge your recommendation, sir."

Bane and the chairman stood, staring at each other. "Does this mean, Mr. Chairman, you will act on my recommendation?"

The chairman hesitated then said. "I can only promise we will consider it."

"But the time, Mr. Chairman! Eleven days incubation. Millions could be exposed!"

"Your submission is on the record, Director Bane. I can offer no more."

"This is why I don't bother with Senate Committees," Bane said, loud enough for everyone to hear.

"I wasn't clear on that, Director Bane?" The Chairman held the gavel aloft like a defensive weapon.

"If you want action, you go to the movies. If you want fairness, you go to your parents. If you want medicine, go to a doctor. But for MADicine, testify at a Senate Committee."

More shouting. Thankfully, journalists weren't allowed in the closed sessions, or there'd be utter chaos, Ada thought. She shook her head. Bane didn't help in these scenarios.

"The gentleman will limit his statements to facts."

"I was, Mr. Chairman. MADicine. What else would you call this? Medicine points to a quarantine. Lobbyists point to 'let's delay as long as we can.' Let's call it MADicine."

Looking weary, the Chairman pounded the gavel some more. "We thank the gentleman for his—clever as always—testimony."

Bane didn't stand up. "How many lives have been lost because of geriatric committees."

"That's enough!" The Chairman for the first time lost his cool.

Bane set down the microphone. He said something that Ada couldn't hear.

"What was that, Director? Did I hear correctly?" The Chairman glared at him now, his face red.

"You heard me correctly, Mr. Chairman. I believe you are a shareholder of Braxis? A substantial one? Perhaps you're not unbiased in this matter?" Bane's voice was loud enough that everyone in the room heard him.

"I will not tolerate this, sir!" The chairman's face was as red as a ripe apple.

"Then I assume my comments will not be on the record," Bane said. Bane ignored the chairman, stepped off the podium, and walked up the aisle.

Ada caught up to Bane as he slammed open the door. "Well, that went well," she said.

He laughed, but it was not a happy sound. "They'll do nothing."

"Then many will die."

"Not if we can help it."

Ada ran after him, barely able to keep up with his furious pace. Alban

Bane was a man of action, a man who mattered. For the first time, she was glad the CDC put her on "leave."

40

Mountain View Hospital, Las Vegas

Panji worked her way through various doctors and nurses, increasingly more insistent as the hours wore on. Finally she engaged a young intern, the most receptive to her demands so far, simply because he was a fan of her music. With a straight face, he asked her for her autograph—for his niece.

"I'm sorry, Ms Maingan," said the young doctor, plucking at his goatee. How young was this guy, anyway? The goatee and connecting sideburns seemed designed to age the man's face, but he still appeared younger than Panji's twenty-one-year-old brother. He kept stroking his goatee.

"What are you sorry about?"

"Isolation admits only family."

Isolation? Didn't he mean intensive care? "Doctor—" She peered at his badge.

"Bronson Riley."

"Why is Kenji in isolation?" She remembered suddenly the horrors of Kinosewak, of the disease that swept through the nation by James Bay. Only there, a kindly and brilliant woman cared for the patients. Here, Kenji had a child-doctor.

"You're not family, Ms. Maingan. I'm sorry."

"Yes, Yes. You've told me that." She took a long shuddering breath. She hardly knew Kenji, but those words plunged her into an abyss of pain. She tried to rationalize: we've only had five lunches, three dinners, a bowl of noodles and a hell of a kiss; he's nice, but he's a stranger; he's a work associate; we're just friends. So many contradictions. So what was Kenji to her, anyway? She blinked her eyes.

And now she had to deal with this boy-doctor. "Doctor?"

Doctor Bronson Riley plucked his goatee again. "You're not immediate family. I just can't help you."

She wanted to reach out and slap away his hand, to stop his rhythmic stroking of his beard; it seemed vaguely sexual. At best it was an annoying habit, like a child picking his nose, or chronic nail biting. "Can I call you Bronson?"

He hesitated. "Fine."

"I'll sign your niece's autograph, okay?"

"She'll be so happy." More stroking, faster now. "But I still can't admit visitors."

"Kenji's direct family are gone. Passed away. His distant relatives are in Japan." She was surprised she knew this about the reserved Kenji Tenichi. Five lunches, three dinners, a bowl of noodles and miles of walking had pried surprisingly little from the quiet man. "I'm the closest thing to family he has here." She fought hard to control her temper. She just wanted to be with Kenji. To show him he wasn't alone. It was the least she could do for him, especially after what she had seen on the news.

"It's just not a good idea, Ms. Maingan. He's isolated due to risk of contagion."

"But why is he contagious?" She almost shouted it. "He was injected with a narcotic, wasn't he?"

"Partially." Suddenly, he realized he had said too much, and his face sagged, making him finally look older. "I'm so sorry, Ms ..."

"Panji, please. Look, Bronson, I'm not some fan after Kenji's autograph."

He flinched and flushed red. "Yes, well, already there've been dozens of reporters, five so-called agents, and a steady stream of crying fans. We've actually had to post a guard for the first time in my memory."

Which can't be that long, she thought. This man was probably a first-year resident. She almost said it. "Just let me see him. It'll help."

"All right. Fine." He dropped his hand from his goatee. "Come, I'll show you."

Panji followed the athletic young doctor down a gleaming white-tile floor, past gurneys with patients on IVs. She breathed through her mouth, vaguely queasy at the blend of smells; the smell of fear hung in the air, and no amount of antiseptic could neutralize the subtle blend of sweat, urine, blood and chemicals. Ever since her father died of a lingering cancer in a Toronto hospital, she had been barely able to walk into even a small clinic; hospitals terrified her. And this hospital was busy, full of unattended injuries. She should have been grateful he was taking the time to help her.

They halted as a team rushed by with a patient. The man screamed, his face a mask of terror and blood.

Doctor Riley glanced at her. "We're busy tonight." He smiled. "I can spare you a couple more moments, then I'm back on call." He held out his prescription pad.

Panji sighed. He meant, I might get called any minute, so give me my autograph. "Your niece's name?" She always felt awkward signing autographs. It was such an American thing.

"Lucy."

Panji scrawled a quick note, added a smiley face, and signed her first name in her traditional flourish with the coyote symbol. "One for you, too?"

He laughed. "I would like that."

She spoke the words as she wrote them, to make sure he knew she appreciated his help. "To my favorite doctor, Bronson. With much love, the Little Coyote." And she signed her name again.

He took the pad almost reverently. "This way, Ms—Panji."

They rounded a corner to pandemonium. A waiting area was crowded with reporters. Kenji's female fans filled most of the room. One girl screamed, "It's Little Coyote!" and the crowd surged towards her.

Bronson grabbed Panji's forearm, a little roughly. "This way." And he led her through a red door to one side. "Short cut."

Panji looked back. A security guard blocked the fans at the door.

Bronson touched her arm again. She pulled away.

"Sorry." He stopped abruptly. "So, is Kenji your boyfriend?" There was something unsavory in the way he said "boyfriend" and Panji couldn't help wincing.

"No. A friend."

"I can justify this visit if you tell me he's your fiancé." He winked.

Great Maker. She took a long breath. "Fine. He's my fiancé." And oddly, the alien thought didn't turn her stomach. Why was that? Yet it didn't amuse her either. "Can I see him now?"

He contemplated her for a long moment. "He's a lucky man."

"Right. Right." Panji knew she was blinking too rapidly and her heartbeat was accelerating. She sweated too. "Which way?" Her voice sounded panicky.

He led her to isolation critical care, a wide hall illuminated by banks of fluorescents. Each of the critical care rooms was fitted with observation glass and curtains, individual ventilation, evident by the stove-like vents over the doorways, and sealed doors with tented beds.

They passed three rooms before she saw Kenji, alone in a room to the right. She pressed her hand to the cold glass. "His breathing's so shallow." Several tubes ran into his veiny arms.

"Yes, well, his attacker injected him with an overdose of narcotics. But now he's running a major fever. With the BioSecure alert, we had no choice but to isolate."

Panji placed both her hands on the glass. "Oh, Great Maker."

"Prayers can't hurt." He touched her shoulder lightly. Normally she would have pulled away. He was using her grief as an excuse to touch her, she knew that. But she stood, eyes fixed on Kenji's bandaged face. "We've keeping his fluids up, and we've run a full spectrum. But without more information, there's little else we can do."

Her voice sounded like a whimper. "Do you have any ideas?"

"No. Nothing. When the tests come back."

Panji stared at a monitor, rapidly spiking and erratic. "What's that? An EKG?"

He pulled his hand away. "EEG. That's what's going on in his head, Ms. Maingain."

"Is it supposed to do that?"

"No. It's definitely not supposed to do that."

"He's unconscious?"

"Yes. But that EEG indicates that he's not only conscious but in fear flight mode. As if he was physically fighting for his life." He pointed. "That's his EKG."

It was erratic as well.

"Yes. Heart rate elevated. Hormone production abnormal, especially active adrenal gland. Whatever's going on, he must be in a terrible place. He's tripping."

"Can't you do something?" She didn't want to sound hysterical. Part of her was in the critical care with Kenji and this young boy-doctor, but the other part of her was a child, in intensive care, watching her father die, screaming at the doctor, "Can't you do something?"

"I can't do anything unless we know what's going on."

Panji remembered Bane's words at her farm. Could this be related? She grabbed the doctor's arm, perhaps a little too fiercely. "Bronson. I have a friend. In the World Advance Response Taskforce. He's had several homicides related to a … well, he said something about elevated antibody titers. Does that make sense? And radical white-cell somethings."

"Differentials?"

"Yes!" She caught her breath, trying not to sound hysterical. "And it's all related to this show—the one on which he is the host."

He peeled away her hand, one finger at a time. "I'll need all the information your friend can give me on this virus. And now."

Panji flipped open her phone. She punched speed dial 91, Bane's satellite number.

41

Washington, DC

Ada Kenner followed Bane off the private elevator of The Pinnacle, a prestigious condominium that catered mostly to the wealthy and elite who lobbied in Washington. They stepped directly into the foyer of Domergue's Washington residence. The foyer was probably the size of Ada's entire house, and reminded her more of a museum than a residence. The floor was old tumbled marble, surrounded by a circle of stone columns set on either side of alcoves in the cherry-wood paneling. Asian antiquities were displayed in the alcoves.

A security guard greeted them politely and guided them through a security system. Bane set off alarms, but no one asked him to remove his weapons. "This way, please," the guard said, smiling. He led them to a salon off the main foyer, a room no less impressive but somewhat more intimate.

"They're not taking your gun?" Ada whispered, leaning close to Bane until her cast pressed his shoulder. It was strange how she enjoyed spending time with the enigmatic director. She found excuses to lean close to him, sometimes to touch him. It worried her.

"The scan was for recording devices and microphones," Bane said.

"That would be correct," said a voice behind them. Ada turned, recognizing the hard, toneless voice. Markus Manheim, the Braxis security commander seemed less imposing, somehow, here in Domergue's retreat, especially with the left side of his face covered in pressure bandages, but he still towered over them, unsmiling and cold. Manheim winced from pain. Her nose told her the rest. She had been in burn wards many times, never a pleasant experience, and it was clear to her that Manheim had been badly burned. "Director, sir. Madame Doctor."

Bane didn't offer to shake hands this time. He folded his arms across his rumpled jacket. "At your convenience, Commander Manheim."

"Seigneur Domergue will be a few moments, sir."

Ada's eyebrows must have notched up. Domergue was a lord?

"Fine. I wanted to discuss something with you as well, Commander," Bane said. "You know, the bandages are an improvement. Not quite so ugly."

Ada waited as they went through their male dominance ritual. Manheim glared at Bane and the director stared back. They remained cool but tense. Neither moved for a long time. Men are so dorky, she found herself thinking.

"My contacts have good information about theft of vaccine from your facilities," Bane said, finally.

"Is that so, sir?"

"Some indications Mr. Khan sold your vaccines to Al Qaeda."

Manheim's only reaction was a subtle shift of weight from one foot to the other.

"Can I assume you are doing something more about the Khan situation?" Bane stepped closer, dropping his arms to his side.

"You can assume whatever you like." But he nodded, very discreetly.

"That's enough, Commander," said Domergue, stepping into the room. The golden mask on his face shocked Ada. Her attacker in the cemetery, the giant at Caff's funeral—it couldn't be a coincidence. She stared at it, horrified. The workmanship was exquisite, angelic, almost certainly 24 carat gold. Domergue appeared distinguished and unflustered, dressed immaculately but plainly, perfectly tailored, but not ornate.

"Forgive my little disguise, Doctor Kenner, Director Bane. I am a famous recluse, as you know. For security reasons, no one may ever see my stunningly handsome features." He laughed, a deep and pleasant sound.

"So I've heard," Bane said.

Ada leaned close to Bane and whispered, "The man who attacked me wore a mask."

"I know," he whispered back.

Manheim stepped back and Domergue glided across the salon with an elegance that was quite improbable.

Domergue held out his hand to Ada. Of course he wore white gloves. When she reached out to shake, he took her hand, turned it, and kissed it lightly, although it was the touch of the golden mask's lips that she felt. Ada felt her own flush. What century did this man live in? "I am delighted to meet you, Doctor Ada Kenner. I have followed your career."

"I have no doubt," she snapped. Followed my career, you bastard. Followed me into a graveyard, too? But no, as large as Domergue was, her attacker had been much burlier.

"Is something wrong, my dear?"

"No," she lied. "Nothing."

His voice was soft yet strangely forceful, tinged with a hint of an accent. "I was impressed by your quick actions in Los Angeles."

"I am honored to meet you, Doctor Domergue," Ada said, recovering from her shock at last. "A rare privilege, I understand. Your reputation—"

"I can just imagine," Domergue laughed, finally releasing her hand.

"I mean ..." Ada's voice failed. Domergue was the elite of intellects in the viral world and she felt suddenly inadequate. Bane had brought her along as his expert, but what could she offer to challenge this man, a genius?

Domergue turned to Bane. "Director Bane. As always, a mix of pleasure and apprehension." He shook Bane's hand, a long drawn out affair, stiff with formality.

"Well, shall we sit?" Domergue led them to a cluster of Louis XIV furniture. He waited until they sat before folding his perfectly postured body into a chair. "How can I help today?"

"We were impressed by Doctor Gies's testimony on your behalf," said Bane. "Too shy to show your own mask in public?"

"You would like to hear it from the equine's mouth, so to speak." He nodded his head. Instantly, a servant appeared with a three-tiered tray. "One thing the British certainly do well is afternoon tea. A lovely tradition." He gestured at the tray of dainty, finger-sized sandwiches with the crusts neatly trimmed off, not quite what she expected of a French Lord.

"Please. Cucumber and mayonnaise. This may sound peculiar, but this is one of my favorites."

The servant brought a sterling silver tea service. Ada was very conscious of Domergue's piercing stare, unblinking grey-blue eyes focused a little uncomfortably on her cleavage. She felt naked.

"Well, this is all very lovely," Bane said, but his voice was hard. "Perhaps I can ask you a few questions while you stare at Doctor Kenner's love pillows?" Domergue's head snapped around, the hard glare fixing now on Bane.

"I was quite impressed by your company's bravery," Bane said. "You exposed yourself to liability in the committee, didn't you?"

Domergue passed a cup of tea to Ada, then to Bane, before answering. "Yes, well, we must accept responsibility for our actions. The greater good is all that matters, oui?" He sipped no tea himself.

"Are you certain you didn't accept responsibility because Doctor Kenner's investigation left you no choice?" Bane set down his teacup without sipping from the cup.

Ada felt her own heat. Bane had used her as his weapon against a man who was world respected.

Domergue smiled. "Aha. Am I to be cross examined?" He laughed gently. "Well then, I will admit to the possibility. After all, Director Bane, we are a business. I must analyze the variables, assets and liabilities."

Ada set her own cup down. "That's rather slippery, Doctor Domergue."

He stared at her again, this time focused on her face. "I do not mean to seem so."

"Would you be able to provide me with all the data on TZ-4?" She tried to sound crisp and authoritative, but something about Domergue made her feel like a student in front of her professor.

"Yes, I anticipated that, Doctor. Oh, dear, that is so formal. May I call you Ada?"

"Most people call me A.K."

"No, no. That will not do. Not at all. Ada is such a lovely, lovely name."

"Ada's fine," she said, hoping she was not blushing.

"On your way out, you will find a package. This contains all the data on TZ-4 I am able to disclose. I ask only that you not publicly disclose our proprietary data."

"No promises," Bane said. He waved his hand in front of Domergue's face. "Would you like souvenir pictures of Ada? Or do you already have them?"

"Bane!"

Domergue laughed. "I do appreciate beauty." He gestured vaguely, indicating the artwork in the room. "My sincerest apologies, Ada. Most impolite." He topped their tea.

Ada decided she had to heat things up a little. "Doctor—"

He held up his hands, long fingers stretched out. "Ada, you must call me Gilbert."

Ada refused to be thrown off guard because she knew Bane wanted her to challenge him, to throw *him* off guard, to cut through the evasive maneuvering. "Gilbert. I do wonder about something."

"Yes, Ada?"

"I wonder how it is that you are able to provide nearly two hundred million doses of your miraculous vaccine. That's what Doctor Gies indicated in cross examination. Isn't that a little improbable?"

He stared at her for a long time with his cool, cool eyes. "Well, now. I am not at all sure Bane's a good influence on you, Ada." He paused. "I know, I know. I am being—how did you put it?—slick?"

"Slippery."

"Ah, oui. I see. Very humorous."

"Doctor?" She deliberately put an edge to her voice.

"Yes. Well, not that I am compelled to disclose our business affairs. But let us just say, it is a big world, my dear." He sighed. "I am sorry. 'My dear' was not meant to sound patronizing. I apologize. You see, your country may very well have a population of hundreds of millions, but Braxis is internationally concerned. We cater to billions."

"Yes? It seems to me that every single one of your facilities would have to produce vaccine full-time for several months to stockpile such a supply."

For the first time, Domergue smoldered. His eyes revealed anger, even if his posture did not. "Well, let me just say, long before we started development, eleven point two percent of the world's population had been exposed to, and carries antibodies to, a form of BDV. That represents hundreds of millions."

"A convenient slice of data," Ada said. She was very conscious now of Bane and Manheim, staring at her. Was she being too forceful? She realized she must indeed have sounded like a prosecutor.

After a long silence, Domergue stood up. He paced the silk rug in front of them. "You are a lucky man, Director Bane. Ada is a find. A true find."

"I believe so," Bane said. "But I don't believe we have an adequate answer, Doctor."

Domergue continued to pace. "How do I put this delicately? Braxis has invested a lot in TZ-4 vaccine. We could, in normal circumstances, make many billions of dollars."

"Especially now that there is a bit of an epidemic," Ada said.

He stopped, clasped his hands behind him, and stared at her again. "I would not call this an epidemic yet."

"What would you call it?"

"Unfortunate."

"How so? You stand to make billions. Remember?"

He wagged his finger at her. "Ada, Ada. You must slow down your mental gymnastics, here. There is no conspiracy. We became worried when three of our sites were robbed at gunpoint. You see?"

"Yes, I know about this," Bane said.

"Our Indian facility, Taiwan facility and Spain."

"So you stepped up production?" Ada pressed her lips hard together, trying not to scowl.

"I had information that a terrorist was—"

"Sir!" Manheim interrupted.

Domergue gave Manheim a quick glance, and the man stepped back. "Forgive the Commander. He is protecting our interests." He sighed. "After 9-11, we must all be concerned about these things. In addition to our TZ-4 vaccine, and also other vaccines. We're part of BioShield, as I am sure you are aware, Ada."

"Yes, sir, I am. And that concerns me." BioShield suppliers stockpiled approved vaccines in the event of a biological emergency or epidemic.

"How so?"

"The convenience with which you profit from your vaccine."

Domergue sat back down. His breathing was normal. His eyes were steady and unblinking. She thought he could beat a lie detector. "First of all, Ada, understand our vaccine's market value is nine hundred dollars per dose. With this emergency, Congress has approved acquisition of two hundred million doses at just under ninety dollars. That is very close to our cost."

"Can you verify that?" Ada didn't quite understand why she was so relentless.

"We were compelled to provide evidence to the very committee you attended yesterday."

"It's still close to two billion dollars."

Domergue waved his hand as if batting away a fly. "At a ten percent margin, this news won't move our stock by a penny."

And Ada knew, with absolute certainty, he was lying.

42

Las Vegas, Nevada

Within ninety minutes of her call to Alban Bane a team of four specialists descended on Kenji's room, outfitted in bright yellow isolation suits and masks. They were crisp and attentive, and a bewildered young Doctor Bronson Riley became a spectator outside the glass wall, standing beside Panji.

Nearly four in the morning, and these specialists magically appeared.

Their faces were expressionless but they worked fast, drawing blood, examining printouts, arguing back and forth. When Riley tried to inquire on the intercom, they ignored him.

"Your Alban Bane is a connected man," Riley said.

"He's important," said Panji, nevertheless as surprised as her young doctor friend.

Panji felt more on edge now. Instead of calming her, the masked specialists highlighted the seriousness of Kenji's condition.

"The chief of staff is here," Riley jerked his head in the direction of a balding man who stood outside the room, talking on his cell phone. "That's like God himself around here," mumbled young Riley, his voice conveying awe.

The balding chief of staff beckoned Riley. Riley left Panji by the glass, and the two men whispered back and forth. Then Riley just listened. At first, Riley's expression seemed reserved, then his eyes began to blink too rapidly, and his cheeks burned red. When he rejoined her, he seemed stiff, as if someone had stuck chopsticks up his butt. A nurse ran to the observation windows and drew the curtains.

Panji looked up at young Doctor Riley. "Well? What's happening?"

"We're told it's classified top secret."

"Who said so?"

"The secretary of homeland security. That's who called my chief."

Panji stepped closer, until their bodies were inches apart, invading his personal space. She rarely used her "power stance," not since her divorce, but she found it intimidated men, even with her diminutive stature. The first reaction was often a smile or a laugh, until she refused to back down. Perhaps it was a mother-complex thing, but after a minute of Panji's power stance, men always gave in.

In a low voice she said, "I want to know Kenji's true condition." When he didn't answer, she snapped, "Tell me!"

"I can't," whispered Doctor Riley. "I have no idea. That room is off limits to me now."

Panji leaned hard against the glass. She felt it, hard and cold. What had she done?

That was when the alarm sounded, and a page echoed through the halls: "Stat, Isolation 5."

Riley ran across the hall. He disappeared into a room with a blue door, labeled Authorized Personnel Only. Panji tried to follow, but the door was locked.

Nurses ran up the hall with a cart, dressed in breathing masks, gowns and gloves.

Riley emerged from the room, wearing an isolation suit.

"Bronson! What is it?"

But he ignored her again. Thankfully, he didn't run into Kenji's room.

Instead, he veered left into a room opposite.

Panji stared through the glass wall. A young man thrashed on the bed, pulling at his restraints. Blood poured from his nostrils, even his eye sockets.

Panji pressed back against the wall and watched in horror.

Doctor Bronson Riley snapped at the nurses and they handed him a hypo. He injected the patient. Though Panji couldn't hear Riley's voice, she heard the scream of his patient. Where Riley had injected the man, blood poured, a surging pulse, like water breaking through a dam.

The man bent his head back and howled.

Panji heard a commotion behind her. She turned and saw through the glass door that the specialists from Kenji's room had exited to the small alcove. There was a puff of steam, then a hiss, and the men in yellow suits disappeared in a thick fog. The air filters pumped and pulled the mist from the alcove. Dripping, the men opened the outer door and ran across the hall. They entered the distressed man's room in their yellow spacesuits and clustered around the patient, restraining him, yelling back and forth.

Even the doctors seemed afraid.

Great Maker. Great Maker. This will happen to Kenji too.

Panji turned away from the gore, crossed the hall and pressed her face against the glass of Kenji's curtained room. She started to realize the depth of her feelings for him.

Panji found herself swallowing bile.

She moved closer to the cart, left outside Kenji's room.

A mask. And gloves.

Without thinking, she slipped on the breather mask with plexi goggles, and the glass fogged, but cleared quickly. She could breathe. Then she slipped on a pair of gloves. She tried the door, but found it locked. She turned the lever handle down hard, pushing against the door. She saw a green button beside the door. She pushed it, and the door hissed open.

Without hesitation, she entered the airlock. The door closed with a snap. Her ears popped in the lower pressure. Panji felt a rush of cold air. Then she pushed open the inner door and entered Kenji's isolation room.

43

Washington, D.C.

Vermont senator Riley Stephens vomited into the Italian designer toilet. He straightened, fought the urge, then retched again. He flushed and ignored the pounding on the door.

"What's wrong, Riley?" His wife's strident voice only made him feel sicker. More pounding. "Riley, damn it!"

Stephens dabbed his chin with tissue and levered to his feet. "I'm fine, Lara."

"We'll be late."

"For Chrissakes, Lara, I'm sick. Leave me alone!"

"You can't be sick. Riley, the speaker, vice president and CIA director will be at the dinner."

Leave me alone, woman! He damn well knew who was at the dinner. He clamped his mouth shut, hating the taste of vomit and bile. Don't say anything you'll regret. We'll fight for days. Don't say it. "Just let me clean up, dear."

"Don't you call me dear," she snapped, and he heard the bedroom door slam. She was already dressed in her Orcimar Versolato evening gown and emerald pendant, waiting for him to clean, change his shirt and Armani-up.

Christ. His stomach gurgled, and he fought the urge to throw up yet again.

His shirt clung to a cold film of sweat. He shivered. This was worse than just a cold, and it went beyond overwork and stress. The worst thing was the stabbing pain behind his eyes. It felt like his head would explode. Damn flu bug. He popped Tylenol Flu. It had to be the flu, because if it wasn't—he couldn't think about that. He wouldn't. But he couldn't help it. The committee testimony made it clear there was an epidemic, nearly thirteen percent fatal. Bane's involvement sickened him further. Bane was always nearby, fluttering around Stephens' affairs like a hummingbird on a flower. Bane knew too much. He was dangerous. And he was too often right.

He stripped off his shirt. Where did that pot belly come from? And he was so pale. His white skin matched a shock of stark white hair. And the wrinkles around his eyes, tight nests of worry lines.

He put on a fresh shirt, wrapped a cummerbund around his bulging waist, and slipped on his tux.

It didn't help. He still looked like a creature from a fifties horror movie. A Patek Phillippe watch and diamond pin did nothing to improve his appearance—the haunted look of a man who didn't sleep.

Lara sat in the Astoria suite's lounge, her elegant shoe tapping the air. "Well, you look awful."

"You too," he said, pressing his lips together to prevent either a smile or frown, he wasn't sure which. And when he sneezed, he didn't bother to cover his nose; let her suffer too, it was only right. Truth was, she was elegant, beautiful, hadn't changed in ten years, still the dark and elegant queen, to be admired but not touched.

They didn't speak in the limo. Her scowling face was reflected in the glass. She transformed forty minutes later, as they entered the Manifesto Club. A stunning smile lit up her face. By the time they entered the marbled foyer, the overdose of flu drugs had kicked in, leaving him with just a headache. Vice President Ernie Samuels bent to kiss her gloved hand. His handshake to Stephens was somewhat enthusiastic. "Good evening, sir," Stephens said.

The vice president smiled. "My friend, welcome."

Stephens sat near the head of the table. Lara sat beside the vice president and his wife Marie. Vice President Ernie and Marie Samuels were the perfect American couple known to be gracious and scandal free. Even their children were perfect political child clones. Top five percent in high school for both of them, one boy, one girl, both into sports and all the wholesome things American teens should do. No drugs, no sex, no booze, thank you very much.

He scanned the overwrought room and all its trappings of wealth and power. The urge to retch came again. He gagged, swallowed bile. He slurped wine and nearly choked.

He said very little through dinner. It was a strange, dignified affair, not an official state dinner, just a meeting of the elites.

Stephens' wife Lara was in her glory, laughing and holding her own with world leaders, scrupulously avoiding the lesser known senators, focused only on the power players in the Game. That's what she called it, and she was right: the Game, with a capital G.

Beside her, Stephens sipped a fine Domergue Bordeaux and pretended to smile, dabbing the stubborn sweat on his forehead. He nodded at all the wise things people said around him, but the headache punctuated every sound:

"The terrorist attack at Universal Studios was terrible ..."

"What about the suicide bombing in London ...?"

"I heard Senator Platt lost a sister in the mall explosion ..."

Stephens wanted to massage his throbbing temples. An old song. The Game. Except, in this Game, no one won. People were pawns. The big stakes were fortunes to be made, reputations and country security. The lesser stakes were people's lives. People died in this Game.

"What do you think, Riley?" said CIA director Lambert.

Stephens straightened his shoulders. "I think we're boring our significant others with this talk."

"Cheers to that," said Shannon Kaplan, wife of the FBI deputy director.

Stephens raised his glass. There was a moment of awkward silence. Then deputy director Kaplan raised his glass and clinked his wife's. "Cheers to boring our significant others." Laughter rumbled around the table. "Well, I suggest we prevent unnecessary boredom. Perhaps some of you would care to continue our discussion over cognac in Mensa Hall?"

Here we go, Stephens thought. Here we fucking go.

They waited in Mensa Hall, sipping cognac, as secret service men swept the room for listening devices. When they got the nod, the men of power sat in ridiculously overlarge wing chairs by the fireplace, lit in spite of the summer heat. The doors snapped closed, three inches of solid ironwood. He heard the click of the lock.

He tried not to scan the room. It wasn't wise to seek eye contact with these men of power. He almost smiled. Men of power. Not a woman, visible minority or person under fifty in the room. Old world influence. Money.

"I'll bring you up to date," said Franklin Farrier, a man with more power, both tangible and intangible, than all the other men in the room together, including the vice president. "Universal Studios was the worst, so far. Eleven hundred people killed by a chemical engineer. No history of violence. He just decided to build a bomb and planted it in Toon Lagoon." No one spoke. Six degrees of separation meant that they all knew someone who knew someone lost in the Universal Studios bombing.

"So we're sure it wasn't terrorism?" Samuels said.

"The perpetrator was turned in by a young girl, a Barabara Anne Kelly, who lost her family in the bombing. The bomber turned out to have no ties to terrorism. He had borderline manic depressive tendencies. And he was sick with TZ-4."

"This is bad," said Samuels.

"Yes," Farrier said. "LA remains the hotspot. Even now, the riots have lasted seven days, although no one attributes it to the virus yet. Looting is widespread, but fatalities are limited, so far, to a few hundred. There was another shopping mall bombing. The worst thing is there are so many children victims."

Samuels held up his hand. "Are you saying these are all directly attributed to the virus?"

"Yes, Ernie. We have used the Nab test kits provided by Braxis. This guy who bombed Universal tested positive for TZ-4. So did the mall bomber. And we've sampled the rioters."

"What's the body count, so far?" Samuels sounded unusually emotional.

"If you count collateral damage from rage attacks, thirty-six thousand, nine hundred and sixty-two."

Stephens felt the queasiness return. He wanted to vomit. Even his information had not put the numbers so high.

"And WART is a problem," Farrier continued.

"Surely their authority here in the homeland is limited," said Jerry Staughan.

"We are signatories of Resolution 2178," said Farrier. "Let's move on, gentlemen. No one feels safe, even in their own homes. There's widespread panic."

"That's not such a bad thing," said CIA director Lambert. Every elevation in alert status allowed the CIA, FBI and various other agencies extra measures of power, letting them do their jobs more efficiently.

Vice President Samuels held out his glass for a refill. "Thanks to this Ada Kenner, we also have a BioSecure Alert. The president has approved seven billion for vaccine delivery. More to come."

"What are we talking about here?" Samuels perched himself on the edge of the wingback chair.

Stephens, who was on the Preparedness Committee, answered, "Doctor Gies testified that there is approximately a thirteen-percent risk of fatality for anyone exposed to the virus, who develops symptoms." He felt his own heat, the urge to sneeze.

Farrier said, "And with the vaccine?"

Stephens sniffed. "The latest numbers from Braxis, based on the final version of the vaccine, put risk of immune firestorm at just under three percent. If the patient is vaccinated within forty-eight hours of exposure, there's a ninety-seven percent chance of survival."

"That's manageable," Farrier said. "Damned terrifying, but manageable."

Manageable? Stephens stared at Farrier, as always astonished by the man's coldness. With an airborn virus, especially in absence of a quarantine, three percent could be close to ten million people.

Samuels nodded. "So we stockpile, distribute to all major hospitals, and hope we don't have to use it."

"Oh, we'll have to use it, gentlemen," said Lambert of the CIA. "Our operatives tell us five key terror groups have supplies of the vaccine."

"Christ, Barry, did they release the virus?" Samuels swirled his cognac, working hard at sounding calm.

Barry Lambert studied the vice president, perhaps deciding what to disclose. "Yes, sir," said Lambert. "Bane discovered Khan's group had infiltrated six Braxis facilities over the last eleven years. Once they secured a supply of vaccine, they triggered this crisis with an apparent lab accident in one of Braxis's bio containment labs in California. The Begley incident."

"A point of order, sir?" Stephens felt his own resolve cracking. He was on the very outside circumference of the circle of power, and normally he avoided speaking in the company of any of The Ten. They stared at him, waiting. "I think we have to consider Bane's suggestion."

"Did he make a suggestion?" Samuels asked.

"Yes, at the congressional committee. Dobbs shot him down." There, he had committed. His main contribution to this meeting.

"Go on." Vice President Samuels stared at him now. Dobbs and Samuels were golfing buddies going back to prehistoric times.

"Bane was concerned about the international spread," Stephens said, trying to sound confident. "He proposed curtailing international and even domestic flights with the FAA."

The vice president stood up and paced. "I thought you hated this Bane character."

Stephens frowned. "It's not a matter of like or dislike, sir. He has a point."

"Yes, well, the president will not sanction such a move," said Farrier. "It could cripple our economy."

Vice President Samuels jumped in. "Well, perhaps not cripple. But it would be devastating. Airlines bankrupt. Trade hampered."

Stephens tried not to purse his lips. "We closed the border for mad cow."

"That's different!" snapped Samuels. "Limited to one industry, import only!"

Stephens couldn't believe he was helping out Alban Bane; Stephens' personal mission, since the Vermont incident, was the utter destruction of Bane. "Then, we must at least consider limited containment." Stephens felt ill again, woozy.

"Something, yes. We'll have enough for our domestic population." Farrier said, coldly.

"And what of Britain, France, Canada—all our allies?" Lambert asked.

"They can source vaccine from Braxis, of course," Samuels said.

Stephens felt a chill. Was he getting a fever now? "Is there enough?"

Farrier shrugged. "Domergue said they are at full production in India, Taiwan, and Germany."

"At a cost," said Stephens, angry now.

"Yes, Senator. At a cost. They are a business," Farrier shot back.

Stephens wasn't ready to concede. Political career suicide, perhaps, but millions of lives hung in the balance. "But the vaccine still means millions can die if this vectors around the world."

Farrier nodded, looking sad. He leaned closer. "You don't seem so well yourself, Senator?"

"I just don't believe this!" Stephens stood up. Was it lack of sleep, his headache, or just his wife's nagging? Whatever it was, he was close to self-destruction. "We can stop the spread of this virus, but won't because of the economy!" Heads nodded.

"And cause an international scandal?" Farrier's voice was loud. "Think this through, Stephens."

"I have!" But he knew this was all pointless. These men of power had made their decision, and if he moved against them openly, by going to the press, they would destroy him.

He realized his only hope to stop this, to save perhaps millions of lives, was to go directly to the man he hated most in the entire world. Alban Bane.

This time, he couldn't stop himself. He stomach churned. It wouldn't do to vomit on the silk carpets. "Touch of the flu," he mumbled, and he nearly ran from the impeccable paneled suite, startling a Secret Service Agent on the door. He barely had time to close the toilet door. He knelt, landing hard on the tiles, and threw up one last time, bringing up five course of fine European cuisine.

44

Mountain View Hospital, Las Vegas

Golden streamers of dawn light poured into Kenji's room. Panji held his hand, surprisingly hot through the gloves. Exhaustion had a way of tuning her mind, filtering her senses, and now she noticed odd things about the room. No dust motes swirled in the filtered air and it was too cold; the room was sterile, mostly glass, gleaming white laminates and plastics; the gurney-style bed was covered with a secondary tent with its own positive displacement ventilation. Cold air moved around the room, sluggish but forceful, chilling Panji until she shivered.

No one had found her yet. Something else was happening; the hospital was in an uproar, and no one had checked in on Kenji in hours.

Kenji's EEG and EKG, while erratic, hadn't triggered any alarms, the curtains were drawn, and she could hear the muffled cries from outside the hermetically sealed room. She held Kenji's hand, stroking it, shocked at the depth of her feelings for the enigmatic man. She loved his long fingers and the veins that protruded so prominently under his soft brown flesh. She remembered their meals together, his easy smile, his warmth, but also that he was the gentlest, politest man she had ever met.

She studied Kenji's too-handsome face. His wide features were alive with activity, eyes fluttering, cheeks twitching, mouth muttering. Was he about to hemorrhage, like the poor man across the hall? She couldn't get the picture out of her mind. He suffered, that was clear. His long black hair was plastered back with sweat, revealing a tall forehead she had never noticed before behind the bangs.

Her Ninge, her mother, had always said, "If you want to know a man, watch him while he sleeps." Elder wisdom. Well, she watched now, as he twitched and pulled at the restraints. And what she found was that he was a man she wanted to know better. For all the sweat and furrowed brows and trembling lips, she saw a man who fought back. And that was a man she could admire.

He battled demons, and at times seemed to be losing. The tribal elders would have said he was on a Vision Quest, battling monsters in the other world, the place beyond day seeing.

She felt guilty for admiring him in this way as he battled for his life. But even drenched in sweat, shivering and moaning, he was every inch the image of an ancient noble warrior from her people's legends.

With a start she realized his eyes were wide open. He stared at her! He pulled at the restraints, grunted in alarm, but then he seemed to recognize her. He sagged back into the pillow, exhausted from his long nightmare.

His lip trembled, but this time into a feeble smile. Feeble, but warm.

"What …?" But his voice trailed off and he faded again.

She squeezed his hand and felt him squeeze back weakly, his grip like a child's.

He was coming around.

His alert midnight-black eyes stared at her. The famous Kenji equanimity had returned. It was what she found most appealing about him. In her short time getting to know him, he had always impressed her with his deep serenity. He explained it away as Zen Buddhist meditation, but she didn't care about the reason; she felt deeply attracted to his tranquility. She had endured enough relationships with unstable, emotional men.

"Panji," he said, his voice hoarse. "Panji Maingan."

She smiled. "That's me, Kenji Tenichi."

"What are … what are you doing here, Panji?"

"Just here for a visit." She laughed lightly, so delighted that he appeared an entire magnitude of better. It was as if a fever had broken.

"I felt you here," he said.

"Yes?"

"Yes. I was in a very bad place. Full of terrible things, dark creatures who preyed on children, serial killers who …" He shivered. "Then I saw a glow, a glowing Bodhisattva."

She laughed lightly. A Bodhisattva was a savior, a perfected being. "I'm pretty far from a savior."

"You're my savior." The smile strengthened, revealing straight white teeth. "You brought me back from a terrible place." His voice now seemed to settle into the low dulcet tones she loved.

She felt her own blush, a heat in her cheeks. How could she love such simple things? Was she so shallow? White teeth, a calm demeanor, perfect English, athletic body. Was that all it took to attract her? Yet there was nothing shallow about Kenji. It was his depth that pulled her in.

"I was …" But then he retched and flew into a fit of coughing. He heaved with dry spasms. But thank the Maker, no blood came.

She released his hand and reached for a sealed bottle of water on the side table. He drank greedily, choking on the water, but wanting more. She watched his Adam's apple bob and she realized that, even sick, he was a gorgeous man.

"The water tastes like straight bleach."

But he was better. She could see it. Thank the Great Maker, he looked better.

He smiled, and it was brighter than the Vegas sun. And that was when she knew her feelings for him were out of control. She hated that. She hardly knew him. She was thinking like some infatuated high school kid. She had to get over that.

"More water?"

"Please." He sagged back on the pillow, still exhausted, but his breathing was better now. The EEGs and EKGs were settled and normal—well, they didn't look as mad and erratic as when he was sleeping. "How long?"

"Not long."

"I mean how long have you been here, Panji Maingan?"

"A few hours."

"Thank you."

He tugged at the plastic tenting around him. "Am I contagious?"

"They say so."

"Then, why are you here?"

"Because I say so."

He frowned. "I do not want you here, Little Coyote."

"Yes, very unwise," said a booming new voice. They both looked up.

Panji tensed. The airlock door was open and a man stood there, very striking, imposing in his weight and height. He bent his head as he entered the room—and she noticed giant hands that stretched the latex gloves. Bright green eyes, the most luminous eyes Panji had ever seen in a man, stared back at her through the face mask.

Panji stood up, stepping between Kenji and the stranger.

45

The Strip, Las Vegas

Vegas was no longer a noisy, bustling adult playground. The casinos felt ghostly, the tables immaculately clean, the rows of slot machines grim and silent as gravestones. The air in the casinos was smoke free and cold, the air conditioning units still pumping. Tourists remained trapped in their rooms, watching the latest news of the quarantine on television, terrified, studying their companions and spouses for the first sign of a sniffle, unable to leave their suites for a bucket of ice. Scary soldiers in masks marched the halls of the hotels.

Bane drove the Hummer past the burning casino and watched the chaos of smoke, shadowy rioters, determined National Guard looking very Darth Vadar in their masks, and police in riot gear. There weren't enough soldiers to entirely secure the city from looting, not with American armed forces involved in so many theatres around the world, but they made a good show of control.

Already the MGM casino had been looted, and only continuous pelting with rubber bullets and gas by riot-equipped police drove the rioters back. Even now, the fire trucks battled a blaze at the New York, New York resort. The façade of the New York City skyline was ablaze, a miniature city enveloped in black smoke, in a way an eerie precursor perhaps of what might soon come to the city that never slept if the virus reached Manhattan. Overhead, armed helicopters buzzed like angry hornets, keeping the TV helicopters at bay.

"We're not winning, are we?" Doctor Gies asked.

Bane didn't bother turning. "We? We are trying to clean up your mess. And no, we're not winning."

"I renew my protest," Gies said. "I can do more good in my own labs."

Bane smiled. He would always treasure the moment when the handcuffs went on Gies chubby wrists. It was the little joys that kept Bane going on these hopeless days. "You've done enough good work, Gies."

"I don't appreciate your sarcasm, Bane."

"No one ever does." He stabbed a finger in the direction of the burning New York skyline. "Your Frankenstein legacy, Gies."

"You'll keep me in protective custody?"

"Who said you're in protective? I'm not stupid. I want to live past *my* next birthday."

Gies fell silent and Bane glanced at him in the passenger seat, his face pressed stupidly against the window, staring at running looters, screaming rioters, the fires. Gies's face reflected back, pale, frightened, framed in a wreath of flames. Bane could smell the fear on him, the sour tang of panic sweat. "Then why am I here?"

"This is you, under arrest. Facing life in prison or worse, hopefully somewhere nice where you'll find a protective Daddy. And this is me giving you a chance to impress the judge with your miraculous solution to this Armageddon you created."

"Armageddon?"

"What would you call it?" Bane nearly shouted it, as he shifted gears and accelerated past a knot of soldiers crossing the strip. He honked as he raced past them, saw their fingers fly up in one-fingered salutes.

"I was trying to ..." Gies took a long shuddering breath.

"Yeah, well we all try. It's not the trying that matters. Your mamma was wrong. Only results matter." For some reason, Bane found himself thinking of Tyler Hayden. For four years Bane had tried to stop the serial killer as the madman took one child after another. Bane barely slept in that whole time. He became alienated from his own family in faraway Vermont. He put his all into stopping the monster. But in the end, many died. And he learned the first lesson of law enforcement. To save lives, break every damn rule you can get away with. All that matters is getting the bastards off the street. It was back then he learned to use intimidation and his smart mouth.

"What do you want from me?"

"I want you to help fix this. It might make the difference between me pushing you to a jurisdiction with the death penalty, versus one with boyfriends in the shower. You'll help Ada, and you'll make her believe it's your idea."

"And what about you. You're not staying?"

Bane smiled. "Places to go. Terrorists to kill."

"Khan?"

Bane nodded and mashed the accelerator to the floor. He'd faced many monsters in his time: Hayden, Bartlett, the Twins, a dozen or so terrorists, sundry serial killers. But Khan was the only one who frightened Bane. He found himself thinking of Ada. Would he ever see her again? Or his daughters? Or Arm or Nam? He was flying half way around the world to take out Khan, breaking every international law and guideline he lived by. If he survived, he would no doubt be charged.

But chances were good he wouldn't survive.

46

Mountain View Hospital, Las Vegas

The towering man in the containment suit and mask stood at the door, big forearms folded across his orange space suit. Panji bolted around Kenji's bed, standing between the giant and her friend. He didn't look like a doctor, although she supposed some doctors could be six foot six. Inside the bio suit she saw kinky hair that stood straight up, bright green eyes set in strange contrast to his dark skin.

The man was fast, feinted left then right, and reached the opposite side of Kenji's bed in two long strides.

Panji tried to intercept, but already the man dove through the tent material and locked forearms with Kenji.

"Stop!" she shouted, pulling hard on the tall man's suit. He hardly seemed to notice.

It took her a moment to realize the man was not attacking Kenji, in fact he was laughing.

Kenji's face was lit up in one of his trademark smiles.

"I'll be," said the bio-suited man, his voice deep and edged with humor. "Ain't this a pot of gumbo." Panji recognized the Creole warmth of someone from Louisiana.

Kenji struggled to sit up. "It is good to see you, Arm."

"Wouldn't miss it, and that be true, my bro," he said, the Cajun accent fading gradually into a soft, low voice.

"This is my good friend, Armitage Saulnier," Kenji said. "And my dearest Panji Maingan."

Arm thrust out his gloved hand. Her hand disappeared into his, and somehow through two layers of gloves she could feel his heat. "You just call me Arm, there Miss. Anybody who is dearest of Kenji, well that be special."

He spoke with no accent now. She could see that he was tall and athletic and muscular, and she wondered where he found a suit to fit him.

"Arm is Bane's assistant director," Kenji explained.

"And I'm here to make sure you two behave, now." Arm's smile was pure magic and lifted Panji's fatigue and stress. His warmth was infectious, and she knew instinctively they'd be good friends.

"Bane sent you?" Panji asked, finally letting go of his hand.

"He did that, Miss."

"Please call me Panji."

"Well, I'll do that Miss Panji, I will." He shook his head. "Now here's me, in this big old space suit, and this thing's hot, Miss Panji, you trust me on that. And there's you, in a simple mask and gloves. Now, who do you think them doctors is mad at?"

"Do I have three guesses?" Panji sighed, and returned to her chair beside Kenji's bed.

"I'm thinking you don't need more than one."

"Now what?" Panji hadn't thought that far ahead.

"The doctors, they tell me you'll be staying here, Panji. Until you're cleared of infection." His voice sounded grave.

"Fine. Better than judging that stupid reality show."

"Oh, Lord, Panji Maingan, and doesn't Abbey Chase carry on!" Arm laughed. "She's short a host and a judge. But I don't think there's any kind of show right about now with the quarantine and all."

"Quarantine? You mean the hospital?"

"No Miss Panji, the entire city. And LA, too, Miss."

Panji found she couldn't breathe through the filter mask. "Oh, Great Maker."

"A big ol' mess, and that's true." But the smile didn't fade behind the plexi mask. "But Bane'll put it right, you'll see. He always does, Miss Panji. Abbey Chase is having fits, though, and that's the truth."

Panji smiled in spite of herself. "She'll play all this for ratings, you wait and see."

Arm laughed, a bottomless well of mirth that somehow made her feel better and better.

"How do you know Kenji?" she asked him.

Kenji answered for him, his voice full of sudden energy, a good sign for his recovery. "Bane and Arm suspected me of murder."

Arm shrugged. "A long story. And not for today, my bro. I'm going to shoot out of here, and guard that there door. That's what I'm here for, oh yes.

Bane tells me some bad guys are after both of you." But instead of sounding serious, he laughed again. "Well, no one gets past Arm."

"I believe that," Panji said, somewhat in awe of his size, and equally of his good humor.

After he left, they waited for the whoosh of disinfectant sprays in the alcove. Finally Panji said, "A nice man."

"Arm is the best friend a man could have."

Kenji looked drowsy. He faded, closed his eyes, and suddenly Panji felt tired too. She wondered if they'd bring her a cot.

"What is that?" Kenji was abruptly alert, half sitting in the bed.

Panji listened. She heard it too. An indistinct rumbling, some distant muffled shouting, the sound of diesel engines? She went to the triple-pane window and levered the California shutters open.

Coming up the hill to the hospital was a long row of army troop trucks. She watched, horrified, as soldiers in bio-warfare masks jumped out of the trucks and began to assemble barricades.

47

USAMRIID Mobile Lab, Las Vegas

Ada tipped her head back and dropped Red Out into her eyes, arching her back in a stretch.

"Why don't you get some sleep?" Lieutenant Colonel Doctor Bailey Beckett asked.

"You first, BB," Ada said, then stifled a yawn.

"Really, A.K." He stood up from his circular workstation, a recessed curved nook of monitors. He leaned over her stainless steel desktop and flipped the switch off her scope. "Enough."

"I'm on to something!" she said, but her voice was too sharp, a sign of her fatigue. "The TZ-4 recombinant progeny viruses have a distinct competitive advantage compared to the parental inoculum." Ada yawned again. "Oh, maybe you're right. Do these damn trailers have bunks?"

BB nodded his head and smiled. "Four tiny bunks over the galley."

In better times, she would have admired BB's mobile lab. She knew it was his pet project: the Mobile Army Infectious Disease Lab—in Army speak, MAID. Double trailers crammed with equipment from stainless steel ceiling to polymer floor, connected by an accordion tunnel that doubled as an airlock to the forward trailer. The forward section served as an emergency bio-hazmat lab, with an at-a-pinch level three suited environment—level four in an emergency with proper suits and four-stage airlocks; the second trailer was jammed with terawatts of power-hungry equipment, a tiny galley and four bunks. It reeked of metal, plastic and disinfectant. Lighting was blue-dimmed to allow the eighty-two monitors a glare-free home in the mobile pride and joy of USAMRIID. It had been BB's concept, a post–9-11 initiative that cost six billion, mobile trailer labs connected by satellite to a lab in Fort Detrick. Currently USAMRIID had one MAID in Vegas, one in LA, and a third overseas in Iraq.

When she didn't move to the bunks, he said, "I don't think I'll ever understand you."

"Don't try."

He sighed. "Braxis gave us a viable vaccine, already somewhat tested in human trials. So what are we trying to achieve here? We should be managing the quarantine."

"The vaccine has a three percent fatality rate."

"I know. But anything we discover here won't be viable for months. If we find anything at all. Could even be years."

She nodded. "I'm not looking to cure, BB."

He sat on the edge of her stainless steel workstation, peering at her screen. "Ah. I see. You're the detective."

"Something like that."

"Something like, you can't stand the idea of the creators of this mess profiting in the billions from it."

"Fair to say."

"Don't we have bigger worries?"

"Those too. There has to be a way to improve the survival rate on the vaccine. What if you're a mother of four children. They're healthy right now. Do you vaccinate, knowing there's a good chance one of your children might die, but the vaccine will save the rest?"

"Of course you do," he said.

"I don't know of many mothers who would."

"So this is a woman thing." He smiled, and she knew he was baiting her, taking her mind off the research.

"Sure. The sisterhood."

He laughed. "My wife taught me the secret handshake."

She laughed too.

"But that's not the point, A.K."

"Then what is? Christ, BB, spit it out. I'm tired."

"That's my point. You're going to kill yourself. You're obsessed."

She patted his hand, not rising to his jab. "No. When people's lives are at stake, it's necessity not obsession."

"A fine line."

"A good line." She smiled. "If we just treat the patients but don't track down the reservoir of the disease, we've done nothing but slow it down. If Bane's quarantine stops this here, and we can find the reservoir, we don't have to give mothers that choice of vaccinating even though there's a chance their children may die."

"Tell me what you really think." He smiled in return.

"What I really think is that we're all busy chasing the obvious. Why did Domergue so quickly accept responsibility? Isn't there a legal liability there?"

He nodded. "Yes. But also billions to be gained from the vaccine."

"That bothers me too. He testified to the Congressional Committee that he had over two hundred million doses. How could he? How's that even remotely possible, if this wasn't all planned?"

"Aren't we just glad he does?"

"No. We're not."

"So you're saying he released this virus to profit from it?" He looked more alert now.

"Maybe I am. But I'm not jumping to conclusions yet."

"Crap in a sink, A.K., no one's that cold."

"Yes. Many people are arctic cold."

"What about this Khan link?"

"Another too-easy solution. Terrorists. Since 9-11 we assume everything's terrorism. We're so frightened of weapons of mass destruction, especially bio weapons, we'll believe this without proof. Just the name Khan is enough to send Congressmen scurrying. Bane used Khan's name like a magic spell to get them to approve these quarantines."

"Terrorism's real, A.K."

"I know. But Braxis started out telling us it was Begley, a man acting alone. Insane, they supposed."

"So, three theories."

"Oh, I have more than three."

A knock on the door interrupted them.

Ada glanced at the security monitor near the door. She stood up, attempting to disguise her surprise. "Well, well. Here comes one of my other theories. That's Gies, Administrator of Site F Braxis. And my mentor-professor at Harvard." On the monitor she watched as the nervous man walked a tight little circle in front of the door, his face conveying annoyance, his glasses sliding down almost to the tip of his curved nose. "He looks pissed." Soldiers with guns stood behind him.

BB pressed a button and the door slid open with a hiss of air. Gies stepped up into the high tech trailer, looking a little surprised as he took in the equipment in the room. Then he offered a tired smile.

Wary, Ada said, "Doctor Gies."

"Doctor Kenner," he said, his voice edged with tension. He seemed more stooped, as if he carried a lot of weight, and his bifocals could not hide deep pouched bags. He held out his withered hand in greeting. She stared at his hand as if it were a venomous snake. He dropped his hand with a sigh.

"You're the only two here?"

"The quarantine's keeping everyone in the field," Ada said. "This is Colonel Beckett."

"Colonel." A little of cranky old Professor Gies slipped into his crisp voice.

"How can we help you, Professor?" Ada asked. "Isn't it a little late for a visit?"

When Gies didn't answer, BB jumped in with his own questions. "I'd like to know how you got through the quarantine barricades. And the guards around this trailer."

"Your Alban Bane arranged it." Then, as if he remembered something, he added, "On my personal request."

"Request to do what?" Ada forgot her fatigue. Here was the man who, with Begley, engineered the virus that was infecting and killing people by the thousands. If not contained here, soon that number would be millions.

"To help, of course." Gies's eyes batted a little too fast, a sign he was nervous or lying.

"I find that hard to believe," Ada said, trying to keep her tone neutral.

"Why?"

"Because this is your damned mess!" Ada stepped closer and Gies snapped his head back.

"That's a little unfair," he said, in his professorial voice. She could almost hear him say, I'm disappointed in you, Ms. Kenner.

Ada stared at him. Gies had been her most brilliant professor, at the time a taciturn man who showed interest only in above-average students, scolded her in subtle ways that did not destroy her ambition. But she would never forget that he was one of the few on the faculty who visited her in the hospital after the lab accident involving the virus and the mouse. He had been like a grumpy, stern but loving father to her. But when she last met him, he had become a stranger.

"I'm—I'm sincere, Ada. I am," and now she thought maybe she had imagined his earlier curtness, because he suddenly looked vulnerable and his voice trembled with some pent-up emotion.

"Fine. But call me Doctor Kenner."

"You don't give an inch, do you?" Tears flowed down his cheeks and he trembled. He looked frail and ancient all of a sudden.

She didn't know what to say. Was this all an act? Could the old reptile fake tears? At Harvard, Ada had been the only postgraduate student who had any affection for the professor, more known for ruthless critiques that inevitably started with, "No, no, no, Miss Kenner. Are you sure you belong in this program?" Yet he had shown his tender side when he was the only professor who took the time to help her analyze her options after the accident in the lab.

That was why she had been so stunned and disappointed when she discovered he had lied to her when they last met: "BDV is not an airborne virus," he had told her. A lie. He had blamed the outbreak on an accident, on Begley's incompetence. A probable lie. She was not about to trust her old professor again.

"Sit down." It was all she could think of. "We have coffee on. It's an hour old, tastes like brown sewer water, but ..." She shrugged.

"Please." Gies sat in her chair and carefully wiped away the tears. The composure had returned by the time Ada handed him a cup of bitter brew.

He put it down without sipping. "I lied to you, Doctor."

"Did you?" She sat down, crossed her legs, and waited. She noticed BB standing behind Gies, arms folded, watchful.

"You knew that. About the airborne virus. The accident."

"Yes, I knew that."

"I lied because—oh hell." His voice rose to a new level, and he sounded nearly hysterical. "I lied because I was told to lie. I lied because I'm responsible for TZ-4. I lied because of my stock options. I lied because—I guess I lied because that's what we do at Braxis. It's corporate culture."

"I see."

"Damn it, I'm trying to come clean."

"Don't let me stop you."

He glared at her, eyes glassy with more tears. "Do you want to know why I created TZ-4?"

She frowned. "I think I would like to know that."

"It was for Conner."

She stared at him, searching what few memories she had of his personal life. Finally she said, "Your son."

He smiled. "You remember."

"I met him at that party. At your house."

He nodded, and the tears flowed again. "Conner was taken from me by violence. He was always an unpredictable child. He was diagnosed bipolar."

She unfolded her arms and forced a smile. "Go on."

"He—well, he ran away at fourteen. Joined a gang. Killed a kid."

Ada didn't know how to reply to that. She didn't try. She leaned forward and waited. It took several long moments before Gies spoke again. "You don't know what it's like."

Actually, she did know. Conner was bipolar. Her son was disabled in a different way. "So you thought you could cure violence?" It was naïve, but who was she to criticize? Her own accident in the lab had led to Quentin's deformity, and years of guilt. She could have prevented Quentin's suffering if she had agreed to a radical abortion. He didn't have to be born. She could have ended his—and her—suffering in the womb. Instead, she made a decision that ruined many lives, broke up her marriage, led to Quentin's suffering existence. If she could turn back time, do it again ... She felt her own tears threaten. If she could turn back time, she doubted she would do it differently. All life was special.

"I was wrong to try," Gies continued, his voice fast now. "But it worked, don't you see? We tested it. Not just a cure for neurological disorders, but it actually reduced aggressive tendencies in violent inmates who didn't test positive for BDV antibodies."

"There's no such thing as a miracle cure, Professor. There are always consequences. You told me that." He told her that at her hospital room, after her doctors informed her Quentin would be deformed. She had cried on his shoulder, asked him what to do: should she abort, against her beliefs, or could she hope Quentin could somehow be happy. Life was life. What right did she have to take away Quentin's life, especially when it was her fault? By then, she had stopped talking to Devon. Her Professor, Doctor Ernest Gies, replaced her husband as the wise counsel in her life. He had said, "There's no such thing as a miracle cure, Ada. You have to decide. Do you want Quentin, handicapped, born without limbs? Because we can see that's the way your fetus is developing. You can stop it. Or not. But don't expect a miracle." At the time it had seemed so harsh. Now she understood how right he had been.

He smiled, but his lip trembled. "I was beyond wrong. I can't live with what I've done."

Ada stared at him. Was this the kindly professor who had been her only regular visitor at the hospital, helping her deal with her tragedy? Or was this the cold, calculating, lying Doctor Gies who owned stock options in Braxis?

"What do you want, Professor?"

"I brought you my personal notes." He handed her a DVD in a case. "All my journals, observations, what I did, how I did it, all the logs."

"Unedited?"

"No. I'm not a fool, Ada. I left in what you need. Took out anything that could …"

"That could implicate you or Braxis."

He nodded.

She didn't thank him, but she placed the disc carefully in her Fendi bag.

"You understand I'm a consultant for WART?"

"Yes."

"It's not inconceivable you'll be compelled to testify based on what I find here."

"Yes."

"Why risk it?"

"Because. Because this has gone too far."

"What aren't you telling me?" Suddenly it felt wrong. He wasn't here because he felt guilty. She remembered the armed soldiers outside.

"I'm not telling you many things."

"You want to tell me something."

He nodded, but said nothing.

Ada glanced at BB. "Could you give us a moment, Colonel?"

BB nodded, frowned and left the trailer.

"Okay," she said.

"Okay." He didn't speak for a long while. She tried not to coach him. She waited. He sipped his bitter coffee. Then finally, "Ada, Domergue's out of control."

"I know."

"But you can't stop him. Your Colonel can't either. Neither can Alban Bane."

"Why?"

"Why?" He laughed. "Because with a phone call, Domergue could have both Bane and the Colonel in jail on trumped up charges. Or worse."

"He's that powerful?"

"Beyond that. I could be dead tomorrow for talking to you."

"Then he needs to be in jail."

"That's naïve."

"No. No, it's not. It's no more naïve than your advice to me all those years ago in the hospital."

"This is different. Oh, grow up, Adalia Kenner. The real world isn't about right and wrong."

"Yes, it is. That's what the real world is."

"A fool's dream. Domergue owns half of congress and all of the current administration."

"Did Domergue have anything to do with Doctor Toy's murder?"

Gies didn't speak. But he nodded. Once.

Midi, France

Gilbert Domergue stared at his sixty-inch monitor. He touched a few illuminated keys on his flush desktop keyboard. Ada Kenner's face stared back at him. It was a static file picture, her private CDC dossier, but even the harsh glare of a frontal strobe could not burn away the intelligence and life in those luminous eyes.

"Shall I put him through, sir?" Della asked again on the intercom. "He's most insistent."

Domergue smiled. Six minutes' waiting should be enough. "In exactly one minute, Della, thank you." He finished reading Ada's Doctoral thesis summary. It was brilliant, and that alarmed him. That, and the arrest of Ernest Gies.

A quick flash on his elaborate vidphone told him Alban Bane was queued. He punched the flashing button. Alban Bane appeared on the screen, looking bulldoggish, but smiling. He appeared to be in a private jet. "Alban. How delightful to hear from you so soon."

Bane's image jumped out of synch with his voice, probably because he relayed through satellite. "Just wanted you to know, Doc, that we've arrested Ernest Gies. Right now, my team are pulling out his finger nails."

Domergue took a long breath. Alban Bane was perhaps the only man who could unnerve and surprise him. He went beyond being an irritation. He realized he had paused too long and forced a laugh. "Ah, very amusing, Director Bane. From what I hear, you are quite the busy one. In high pursuit, from city to city. Rescuing my security chief. Thank you, by the way, although I am not quite so delighted by your arrest of my senior researcher, Gies. Busy, busy. You took a day to testify to the Congressional Committee. You talked to every official short of the president. You jumped on USAMRIID and FEMA, got them to quarantine Vegas and LA. That took some convincing with General Stouffville, I would think, but a brilliant move after the CDC refused to engage. And you recruited the redoubtable Doctor Kenner. Bravo, Director."

"It's all part of the game, isn't it?"

Again, Domergue fought a surge of anxiety. Did he know? "Whatever do you mean, Director?"

"Running here, running there, chasing our tails."

"Thank goodness we have you to do the chasing."

"You know, Domergue—it is Domergue, isn't it?" Bane waited, then plunged on. "I don't have to visit a barnyard to know it smells."

Domergue saw activity behind Bane, a steady flow of scientists in lab coats and black troopers with machine guns. "Your flight seems crowded. You seem very busy. Now, tell me, what can I do for you, Alban Bane?"

"You know you sound awfully familiar to me."

"And you do as well, Alban. We have talked many times, have we not?"

"Have we not? You see, that sounds disturbingly familiar."

"We French all sound the same?"

"I need you to explain to me about Protocol 440."

"I am not sure what you mean?"

"Something Gies mentioned as I pulled one of his nails."

"I see. Well, I have heard you can be quite convincing." Domergue shifted in his chair. "That was actually Doctor Ali Begley's protocol. We did create vaccines for BDV. It was relatively ineffectual on our B group."

"Yes? What is your B group?"

Domergue studied Bane's inscrutable face. It would be impossible to mislead Bane for long. "Our protocol, as you know, was funded by many partners."

"Yes. It's in the file you gave me."

"Fine. Each group had different requirements. Homeland Security funded defense against possible bio terrorism."

"Against a virus that doesn't exist? How cliché."

"Yes, well, government coverts can be cliché."

"Yes, just as corporate CEOs and politicians lie."

"We pick at the truth, Director. Let me just say that our vaccine has proven broadly applicable to any mutate of BDV. Meaning, it can be used defensively."

"Go on."

"My goodness, Director, you do not—how is it said—'let up for a moment?' Well, let me see, then there was the Department of Corrections. They wanted treatment for dangerous offenders. To accomplish this, we needed a more virulent virus, one that caused the desired neuropathy in nearly every instance, not just some. In other words, we expected our vaccine might mitigate these tendencies" He trailed off, thinking of Larraine and her schizophrenia, and Gies and his son Conner.

"You expected to be able to cure violence?" Bane laughed.

"Nothing so grand," he said, angry that the conversation was taking an unexpected path, and that Bane was in charge. "Curb tendencies, perhaps."

"Lobotomies might be simpler. And less deadly. Viral lobotomies. How delightfully mad scientist."

"Director, the truth is we have all been impacted by violence in this world, yes? Whether it be the abusive husband, the son who turns to crime, the rape of a colleague, increasingly deadly terrorism, or just the mayhem in our streets. Does that not make the improbable desirable, Alban?"

"Tell that to the widows and widowers. Your legacy is death, Domergue. Although I really must remember to buy shares in Braxis. Sounds like you're about to make people rich."

Domergue smiled, in control again. "This is not about profit."

"How convenient for you that this virus 'escaped' your labs."

"That's a grotesque thing to say, Director. Talk to the animal rights protestors who ransacked our labs."

"Oh, I'm sure they're among the first casualties of either the virus, or your twins," Bane said.

Domergue couldn't help smiling. "Fine, Bane, let me have a little fun, will you?"

Bane waved his hand, impatient. "I'm not in a joking mood. This is a serious situation."

"Of course I understand. I have been nothing but accommodating."

"Yes, you have. And I wonder about that."

"Pardon?"

"Well, Domergue, in my experience, the most accommodating people use their cooperation to control situations. Like the politician or the lobbyist or the …"

"Corporate CEO?" he finished for him.

"I was going to say scum-sucking greedy capitalist. You were telling me about your partners."

"Our other partners are classified."

"The armed forces?"

"I cannot say."

"CIA?"

"I do not want to tell any lies."

"Terrorists? Khan, perhaps?"

"Of course not! We were trying to recover our property."

"Yes, yes. Manheim tells me so. Do you know a Doctor Franklin Castle?"

"No." Domergue's fingers drummed a nervous tattoo on his desk.

"Franklin Castle of Site F."

"I know all my doctors at Site F."

"There is no Doctor Castle at Site F?"

"No. You do not seem to trust me, Bane."

"Trust is only of value if you can manipulate it." Bane was uncharacteristically scowling now. "Ada Kenner's assistant, young man by the name of Doctor Toy who was recently murdered, left a message on Doctor Kenner's cell phone. Something about a Doctor Castle."

"Well, I do not know a Franklin Castle." He said it too quickly, but now he was annoyed by Bane's persistence. "Why do you say murder? I believe the police report indicates an accident of nature."

"You shouldn't believe everything the police tell you."

"What are you implying?"

"I'm implying that since Franklin Castle is from Site F, you might be able to shed light on my friend's 'accident of nature.' I owe it to the bees to get to the truth. Wouldn't want an innocent hive accused."

"There is no Franklin Castle."

"Anywhere in Braxis?"

"Director, we have tens of thousands of employees."

"Is that a no?"

"A probable no. Speaking of employees, when can I expect the release of my Doctor Gies?"

"Ah, yes, well quarantines and emergency powers legislation do get in the way of your high-priced lawyers, don't they? Gies is detained indefinitely."

"I see. Well, enjoy your martial law while you can, Director."

"You know, it's odd, Domergue, that your accent has slipped in the last few moments. You're sounding more and more American all the time. A bit east coast, if I say so."

"Really?" Domergue took a long breath. "I could fence with you all day, Alban, but I have a video conference with Taiwan in three minutes. Is there more?"

"How much is this vaccine worth to Braxis?"

"I will not discuss that." He thought, a trillion dollars.

"Billions, certainly."

"Fair to say." Much more.

"What would you do to protect Braxis's interests?"

"Oh dear, there is my other call." Too smart, this Bane. "But I will not leave you hanging, Director. There is nothing I would not do to protect Braxis. Do you understand? You give my best to your girls, Mags and Jen. The Queen's is a wonderful college. Good bye, Bane. I will miss you." He terminated the call as he saw the flash of understanding in Bane's face. He doubted the implied threat would slow Bane down much, but it all helped.

He pressed the intercom. "Della. Get me the twins." Domergue sighed. Gies had become a handicap as well.

49

Over the Atlantic

Bane didn't like it: "You give my best to your girls, Mags and Jen. The Queen's is a wonderful college. Good bye Bane. I will miss you." Domergue didn't make idle threats. He had proven that.

Bane pressed a button on the seat panel. "Captain? Do we have enough fuel to divert to London?"

"Yes, sir," came the instant reply.

"Divert."

"Yes, sir. It will take five hours or so."

"Step on it. Let's see what this hot rod can do."

Oxford University, where his two daughters hid out in plain sight, was the least secure place on earth, but also the least likely place for someone like Domergue to find two Vermont girls. They were both enrolled under pseudonyms in The Queen's College, watched over by a few trusted old friends in MI-5. No journalist had ever found their "hiding place." But it was clear Domergue knew.

Bane punched up McGregor in MI-5.

"Laddie, it's Bane."

A moment of silence. "Don't laddie me, McBane. You still owe me on the Manchester United win."

Bane, for once, played dead serious. "Remember the scenario we talked about, Gregor?"

"I remember. And since you're not cracking with the jokes, I assume you're serious."

"Very."

"I'm on my way."

"Make it fast, Gregor. Call in anyone you can trust. I have a bad feeling."

"For once, may your feelings be wrong."

"Aye."

For the first time in four years, Bane felt true fear. No doubt that was Domergue's goal. To delay and distract.

Khan would have to wait. Nothing mattered more than Bane's daughters. Not even the whole damned world.

50

Mountain View Hospital, Las Vegas

As Ada followed Doctor Ernest Gies and BB off the elevator into the isolation ward, she noticed at once the absence of guards and the dimmed lights.

On high alert, she inserted her access card and opened the sealed doors for the isolation ward. "Something's wrong, BB."

BB followed her. "Maybe you should go back to the elevator."

Ada didn't move. "Don't be ridiculous. I have patients here."

BB stepped in front of her. "Then move to the doctors' lounge."

Ada followed BB. Doctor Ernest Gies pressed close behind her, clearly alarmed, his head snapping back and forth. The ward was eerily quiet. Where was the nurse? At this time in the morning, the rooms and hall were slightly dimmed to allow patients to sleep, but someone should be at the ward station.

Finally Ada saw someone on duty. A very tall man stepped out from the sterile room, wearing a full isolation suit. "Is that Arm?" Bane's lieutenant was the only man Ada knew who would stretch an isolation suit to such proportions. The man had his back to them, and moved to one of the labs. Without looking back, he stepped inside.

"Where's Nurse Hemmingway?" Ada called out to the big man. She walked quickly towards the ward station.

Then Ada saw Hemmingway at the desk, slouched over a keyboard, sleeping.

"Nurse?" Ada said. They were all tired, but Hemmingway was the only duty nurse at two in the morning in isolation. "Nurse Hemmingway?"

When Hemmingway didn't move, Ada reached over the counter and touched her shoulder lightly.

Hemmingway's head lolled to one side, flopping off the keyboard with a plopping sound.

Dead eyes stared up at Ada.

Ada held her breath for a moment. Then she ran around the desk and pressed her fingers to Hemmingway's bruised neck. No pulse. Burst capillaries were plainly visible in the open eyes. Strangled.

"BB! The man who went into the lab!"

BB nodded. He had his sidearm in his hand. He ran lightly up the hall, his army training asserting itself.

Ada picked up the phone on the workstation. There was no dial tone.

"Doctor Gies! Back the way you came! Get help."

Gies didn't move. She saw panic in his pale features and trembling lips and eyes that blinked too quickly.

BB yelled, "Don't move!"

Ada heard a crash.

Forgetting Gies, Ada ran up the hall, moving too fast and sliding on the slick tile as she tried to stop. She slammed open the door to the lab.

The man in the isolation suit stood at the far end of the room, by a spinning centrifuge. BB was on the floor, unconscious or dead, his eyes closed. A lab technician, Lacey Barnes, sat in a swivel chair, her face pale, her blue eyes wide with fear.

Ada knelt by BB and pressed her fingers to his neck. He was alive. She found she could breathe again. She picked up his fallen pistol.

Even as she did, the giant in the yellow isolation suit turned, swung behind Lacey Barnes, slid her chair in front of him, and faced Ada.

She froze.

Behind the plexi of the isolation hood, she saw another mask. She couldn't make out features.

She lifted the pistol in her one good arm, the wrong arm for shooting, and aimed as carefully as she could at the killer's chest. Here was the man who attacked her in the cemetery. The man who killed Caff.

Without thinking, her finger put pressure on the trigger.

The giant in the suit grabbed Lacey Barnes' blond hair and lifted her from the chair.

"We meet again, Ada Kenner," the man's voice was muffled behind the plexi face plate.

Ada steadied her arms, trying to aim the gun.

"Your gun doesn't matter," Gies said, his voice a whimper of fear behind her.

"Take my phone," she shouted at Gies. "It's in my bag!"

Gies didn't move. His breathing was rapid, but he made no attempt to retrieve her fallen bag or her phone.

"I'll shoot," Ada said.

"Do no harm?" said the giant, his voice betraying amusement. "Isn't that the Hippocratic oath?"

For a moment Ada allowed BB's gun to drop, an involuntary reaction, but then she steadied her grip, centered her index finger, and aimed as best she could.

"My phone!" she shouted again.

Still Gies didn't move.

"Ernest! Professor!"

Gies backed away, across the hall. She heard his shuffling steps.

"Then go get help!"

Gies let out a whimper.

The man in the isolation suit laughed.

"Just back away from Lacey," Ada said, sounding surprisingly calm. She had dealt with this beast before. She would not give in to terror this time.

"I like Lacey," said the killer, and he stroked her straw blonde hair.

"I am a good shot!"

"Yes. Yes, I'm sure you are, Ada Kenner."

BB groaned, stirring beside her, then slipped back into unconsciousness. At least he was alive.

"Who are you?" It was a damned stupid thing to say in the circumstances, but she needed to focus, to say something, to keep him occupied until someone came to help.

"Ask him. Ask the professor."

Ada heard a sniff behind her. She could just see him, in her peripheral vision, pressed up against the far wall of the hallway.

"Tell her," the killer said.

"An ex-patient," Gies said, his voice edged with terror. "Once a serial killer, offered as a patient in our early protocols."

The man laughed again, obviously insane. His mask tilted, eyes fixed on the gun.

"Do you think you're immune to bullets?" Ada asked, her voice panicky as the killer stepped even closer, holding Tech Barnes in front of him like a puppet. Ada backed away a step.

"You can't stop him," Gies said, his voice shaky.

Another step forward.

Ada steadied the big pistol, hoping it didn't have some complicated safety switch. She knew guns. Her ex-husband, in their happier days, had collected pistols, and had taught her to shoot at his gun club. She wasn't the best target-shooter, but good enough.

"Just stop. Put down Barnes, and I'll step aside."

The killer shook his head, once. "Put down the gun, I'll let you and your friend here leave."

"Then stalemate."

The giant said, "No." With a barely perceptible movement, his large gloved hand squeezed Barnes's neck.

She screamed, a shrill sound full of a craving for life.

Ada found it impossible to steady her hand with her heart racing. She saw Barnes's face, the shock, the burst of red in her eyes, the rigid clench of her mouth in mid-scream, then the relaxing of muscles as she died.

Ada fired. The bullet went wide as the giant killer weaved to one side, still holding on to the limp body of Barnes, like a useless puppet. "Fire away. Go on!" She was his shield.

Ada fired again, this time aiming for his face mask. He ducked to one side, and pulled Barnes in front of him, simultaneously stepping closer. The killer pushed a center island workstation with one leg, toppling the equipment and sending microscopes and a centrifuge rack of vials to the floor.

Then the giant tossed Barnes, an effortless throw it seemed, and the dead technician crashed on top of Ada, pushing her back into a counter of equipment. Ada fell to the floor. BB's gun discharged. A colposcope fell on top of her, bounced off her arm cast and cracked the plaster. Sharp pain telegraphed through nerve endings. Suddenly it was hard to breathe.

The killer bent over her, his big foot on top of the handgun, pressing hard on her fingers, not enough to break bones, but enough to bring pain. He held out a hypo gun, the same type he had used on Hugh King in the cemetery. "A dose of fear, Ada?"

Ada stared up at the masked, space-suited man, terrified. She crouched, waiting, trying to burn away the fear with anger. This man had killed Caff and Hemingway and now Lacy—a sad and still warm pile of broken flesh—and others. He was unstoppable. He didn't care that the police were on the way or the army was outside the building.

The giant lowered the hypo gun. "Time to die, Doctor."

"Leave her be!" Ernest Gies shouted.

The killer hesitated, looking again at Ada.

In that moment, Gies ran at him, charging from across the room. The giant turned, easily blocked Gies, and grabbed him by the collar. "Then we'll make it your time to die, Doctor."

The attacker drove the hypo gun into Gies's neck. Ada shouted. She heard the hiss of the injection, smelled the sharp tang of carbolic acid.

Instantly Gies collapsed. "Oh," was all he said, and his eyes closed.

He sank first to his knees, then fell hard on to his elbows.

The world shrank to just two people. Ada and the killer. The angel of fear.

Her anger grew hot. The killer loomed over her, icy eyes unblinking and gleaming like marbles.

51

Mountain View Hospital, Las Vegas

Kenji sat in full lotus in the middle of his bed, eyes half closed in *zazen*. He had no doubt that the serenity of meditation and his unshakable belief in the power of his own mind were the primary reasons he survived the virus, especially since he was one of the unfortunates who received the vaccine two days after exposure.

Now he was in a neutral space, empty, a good place to be, given the horrible events of the last few days. An epidemic, deaths, violence, friends in trouble—the turmoil could only be tamed with one-point mediation.

But not even the serenity of *zazen* could filter out the sharp discharge of a gun.

Kenji sprang from his hospital bed, catlike. Even through the hermetically sealed glass he could hear the screams. Without hesitation he yanked the IVs from his arm.

The curtains to his isolation room were drawn but he pulled one back and peered outside.

A shadow passed his room, running.

Kenji yanked the door open, disoriented for a moment in the dark airlock portico. Waves of nausea swept over him, and he fought the urge to vomit. He still felt so weak.

He tensed as a hard, wet burst of disinfectant hit him, plastering his hospital gown to his skin. Without thinking, he tore off the gown and then opened the door a crack. Air whooshed in from the hall. It was late in the ward. He stepped out. He felt cold, wet from the spray and chilled now as he stood naked in the air-conditioned hall. He slid against the wall, using it to remain steady. He heard voices.

He jogged up the hall, still wobbly.

He found the duty nurse slumped over her station. He reached over with two fingers and felt for her pulse. He felt no life. He said a quiet Buddhist blessing and then moved up the hall. No longer dizzy, he followed the sound of voices. Outside, he heard police sirens.

Kenji didn't stop to analyze or register shock. He could smell the danger. His skin tingled and his fists were balled into fists, all his martial instincts tensing for action. He half resisted the natural transition to killer, but then he heard a female voice. Doctor Kenner!

He rounded the corner and saw three men, two on the floor, the third, a giant in an isolation suit, bending over Ada Kenner.

Kenji had no time to analyze the situation. Instinctive killer controlled his carefully conditioned muscles.

The big man in the yellow containment suit turned and ran towards him at full charge. Kenji zoned out, allowing instinct to fully take over, assuming a versatile defensive stance. Kenji saw clearly that he was no match for this attacker. This man was easily six foot six and nearly three hundred pounds of solid muscle, like one of the big American football players.

"He killed Hemmingway!" Doctor Kenner shouted.

Kenji was in no condition for a major confrontation. Whatever he did, it had to be fast and decisive. At the last moment, he spun to one side, so that the giant only clipped him. Even the light graze was enough to toss Kenji into the wall. He heard the crack of drywall, then a splash of fiery pain.

He propelled himself off the wall, using the pain as a booster, his leg snapping out striking the back of the giant's knees. The man stumbled, nearly fell, then recovered.

Kenji continued his full three-sixty spin and brought his elbow snapping around to the back of the attacker's neck. The helmet cracked from the inpact, and again the man stumbled, but he was running again.

Kenji collapsed to the tiles. "I am sorry," he said.

Kenner was instantly at his side, holding his head. "You were wonderful." She pushed the bangs out of his eyes. "Are you hurt?"

"No, just feel sick in my stomach."

Kenji heard Nam's distant shout. "Freeze! I'll fire!"

Kenji fought for air and clear vision. He saw the hulking shadow, nothing but a blur now, already at the far end of the hall. Nam stood by the fire escape, gun aimed at the charging bull of a man. She fired twice. The big attacker staggered back, his yellow bio suit tearing away. But he was quickly back up.

"He has Kevlar!" Nam shouted, and then he was on her. He batted Panji aside like she was a hummingbird, and Nam fell below big pumping feet.

Kenji roared back to his feet, ignoring bruises and cuts on his naked body. He staggered to Panji and slid to his knees beside her. She had a bruised cheek and held her shoulder, but she said, "I am fine!" She laughed. "Are you naked?"

"I think I am."

"It looks good on you."

Nam lay on the tiles, gasping for air, looking as if she had been struck by a car. She nodded and pointed at the fire escape.

"Stay here!" Kenji shouted then plunged through the fire escape door, focusing all his adrenal energy on not collapsing.

He peered over the stair rail, down the staircase. Four floors of nothing.

He heard another door. One flight up.

Kenji sprinted, taking three steps with each bound. The attack on Panji had given him miraculous energy.

He hesitated only a moment at the top of the stairs, then slammed his shoulder into the fire escape release bar. The door opened hard and bounced back.

He scanned the roof of the hospital, saw no one, and stepped quickly outside.

He listened but heard only the thrum of the air-conditioning units on the roof.

He concentrated, focused on breathing normally. The dizziness returned. He drew in hot desert air, sampling the smells on the roof: kitchen exhaust, smoky and full of garlic, car exhaust, and a distinct sweet tangerine smell. Cologne.

He took two steps forward, his sharp eyes taking in every shadow, every nuance of movement.

Nothing.

Three more steps.

Then he heard a clang to his left. The giant stepped out from behind an air-conditioning unit.

Kenji saw a golden mask behind the plexi face shield of the bio suit.

"Who are you?" Kenji blinked as his own sweat stung his eyes.

The man said nothing.

Kenji swept his leg around and crouched into a defensive stance.

He readied himself. He doubted all his years of martial practice would be enough to overcome this giant, not in his current weakened condition. Why didn't he just turn around and get police? Because it would have been too late. The killer would be gone.

The man feinted with a fist half the size of Kenji's head. "Are you afraid?"

Kenji nodded. "I am."

The smile faded. "But you don't run."

"I am afraid. I do not let fear control me."

Kenji's Eheiji training had taught him to preempt the strike. He knew from the shift in the man's body stance, that the killer was tensed to attack.

Kenji didn't wait. He dove forward, flipped lightly to one side, out of reach of the big gorilla arms, and spun off the air-conditioner plating, pushing off with his bare heel. The added momentum wound him into an elegant spin that was so fast the man barely had time to react. The fist swung hard at him, but Kenji's hand caught the man's wrist and snapped it back with all the force of his flying spin.

They both slammed back and crashed into a second air-conditioning unit. Kenji deflected off the stalker's expansive chest. For all of Kenji's years of training and muscle-building, he felt like a child next to Goliath.

Kenji's shoulder struck the corner of a railing. He lost all wind. A stab of pain shot down his left side. His shoulder slid out of its socket.

Kenji knew he must die. He had no more strength.

52

Queen's College, Oxford

Bane found Macgregor smoking in his trademark Mini, not one of the new ones from BMW, but a good old-fashioned, restored and hot-rodded cherry-red Aston Mini Cooper. Gregor jumped when Bane rapped on the glass.

"Give a bloke a heart attack, why don't you?" Gregor said good-naturedly. He jumped out, they embraced briefly, the hug of old friends who had saved each other's lives a few times. The smile faded as quickly as it came. "No action, Bane. I've got Stew on Mags. She's out on a date with some biker dude."

Bane sighed. He probably didn't want to know about the biker, especially since she should have been studying. It was barely six o'clock. Mags liked the dangerous dudes, almost certainly a reaction to her kidnapping ordeal four years ago. Eighteen months of therapy had only dented the hardened veneer of her shock, then she had dropped out and found her escape in "thugs and slugs" as Bane called them. She retreated into an emotionless fog, punctuated by bright bursts of dangerous dating and drugs. "Stew's still got Mags?"

"Aye, MacBane. They're in a smoky off-campus club, eating bangers and mash."

"Jen's on campus?"

"In the library. I have Winston in there. She's a bright lass. I think she's spotted him."

"She'll know he's a bobby," Bane said with some pride. His girls were cop-kids. They knew their own.

Gregor lit up another fag. "I've got three bobbies on campus. All the men I can discreetly trust not to blab."

"You blab enough for ten men."

"Did you just insult the man who raced over here on his night off? You know I was in the middle of a pint."

"Who's going to have a pint with you, Gregor? You scowl like an orangutan and you're just about as ugly."

"Bonnie Prince Bane. Always with the jokes."

"You sure I'm joking? The good news is ugly people are usually smart. I'm going in. Can you call your man on Mags? Make sure everything's hubbly bubbly?" He couldn't even think about Mags in danger. He had nearly died the night his then-sixteen-year-old Mags was kidnapped by Emerson Bartlett; he was near-paralyzed by terror, then later by loss of blood and trauma after he rescued her. Even the slightest chance it might happen again seized him with crippling fear—an alien emotion for Bane. He was thankful he had brought ten of his own men from Turtle One, although it had delayed him to get them cleared with their guns. In the end, a favor from Scotland Yard got his men through with side arms only. Even now, they spread out around the library building.

Was he over-reacting? As he ran up the steps to the grand library, he found himself doubting his hunch that the girls were in danger. Bane had learned never to doubt a hunch. He'd followed them since his FBI days, trailing Hayden from Florida to California where he finally crucified the serial killer. Never once since had he doubted a hunch. Until now. He'd look awfully damn stupid if Khan escaped while he chased a goose across the ancient greens of Oxford.

And there was Jen, sitting at one of the carved desks beside a veritable mountain of texts, so engrossed in her studies she didn't look up as he crossed the marble floor, his footsteps echoing off the vaulted ceilings of one of the world's finest libraries.

She caught even Bane offguard when she said, "Hey, Pops, is it Christmas?" She hadn't even looked over her shoulder. She turned, laughing. "You have that unmistakable Bane smell. Manly and woodsy."

He swept her up in his arms. "That's my girl. See, I'm thinking Ph.D. for you, with that amazing brain."

She kissed him on both cheeks then pushed him away, giggling. "This is Oxford, Pops. We don't hug here."

He studied her. She still wore braces, soon to come out, and she was a stunner. At just under twenty, she was beyond a heartbreaker, so much like her mother. Bane felt a sharp pang of nostalgia. Jen could be Susan Bane's younger sister with her long, fine blond hair, bright green eyes and a smile, braces and all, that could move any heart. She didn't get her looks from him, that was certain. "I missed you, Jen-Jen."

"Missed me enough to call? To visit?" She continued to smile, the small remaining brace glittering like a jewel. Unlike Mags, Jen carried no resentment for the only life Bane could offer his girls in a world gone crazy. She didn't approve, but her complaints were always light and joyous. "So, bad guys after us again?"

"Something like that, Jen." He patted the heavy oak desk. They sat beside each other on the desk tops. "Do you know anything about this biker dude Mags is seeing?"

Jen laughed. "Only that he has more piercings than she does, and he's a big guy. Into leather and handcuffs."

"How do you feel about a quick flight to Italy? Or Greece?"

"Somewhere safe?" She shook her head. "Mid-terms, Pops. I'm not starting the term over."

"Jen—"

"I'm happy to see you, Pops. Mags may not show it, but she will be too. But neither of us is about to leave Oxford."

"I'm serious, baby."

"I am too!" She said it so fiercely, Bane recoiled. Jen was Jen, but she was a young lady now, with a strong Bane will all her own.

"The only time we see you is when you think some thugs are after us. And why are they after us? Because of you, Pops. How often can we move? How often can we start over."

Bane stared at his daughter's smiling green eyes. She hadn't spoken from bitterness. He saw only fearless determination. "You're as stubborn as—"

"You?" She placed her hand on his.

"I was going to say your mother. Or Mags."

"It's a Bane trait."

"Sadly. Just you make sure I don't end up with stubborn grandkids."

"Pops!"

"Any new boyfriends, Jen?"

"I'm all about studying."

He kissed her lightly on the cheek. "I'm glad, my bonnie lass."

And that was when the security alarm sounded.

53

Mountain View Hospital, Las Vegas

Nam stirred, shook her head, fought back the nausea. What had hit her, a tractor trailer? Floaters hung suspended in her vision. Then Panji's face.

Nam struggled to her feet with Panji's help.

"Kenji went up the stairs!" Panji said.

Nam took a few hard breaths, then ran for the stairwell. "Stay here!"

She didn't wait to see if Panji complied as she charged up the stairs. She heard the door slam behind her, glanced down, and saw Panji six steps behind her.

"Go back!" she shouted. When Panji didn't stop, Nam swung around and blocked her. "Panji, if you come, I can't go up there!"

She had to understand!

Panji set her mouth in a scowl. Nam didn't hesitate and bounded up the stairs.

At the top she halted, listening, her Glock cradled in two hands. She pressed her bicep into the door release and slid out onto the rooftop.

Immediately her gun came down. "Freeze!" She wouldn't have bothered with the warning if she had a clean shot.

Nam appraised the situation: the giant in breather mask held Kenji, dangling like a puppet in front of him, his feet off the ground, massive forearm wrapped around Kenji's neck. Kenji was naked and bleeding, but alive. Nam couldn't shoot clean, although she had a good chance of hitting the giant. But with Kenji swaying and struggling, chances were good Nam might hit him.

Without hesitation, she made her move. She slid lower, anchored and aimed for the attacker's thigh. She fired.

The giant spun with a speed that seemed impossible for his size, tossing Kenji as easily as he might a sack of flour. Nam lifted her finger from the trigger as Kenji landed on her, throwing her back. He fell into her like a limp crash test dummy. The gun clattered from her hand.

Nam pushed Kenji off and he rolled with a thump to the concrete tiles. The assassin walked towards them, his boots clopping. Kenji moaned, and attempted to stand. Nam tried to breathe. She clutched outward, reaching for her Glock.

But a hand reached her gun first.

A small hand.

Nam got up on her knees, gasping. "Give me … Give me the …"

She sagged and watched, astonished, as Panji knelt in a shooting position, both hands on the big automatic Glock eight. She shot. And shot. And shot again. Nam saw that her hands were steady and her breathing regular. Panji was clearly experienced with guns.

The assassin jerked, and jerked again. He fell to one knee. She shot again.

"No! Panji, stop!" Kenji reached out his hand.

But she didn't stop. She shot a fourth time, and the giant sagged forward and fell hard.

Panji wore an expression of horror. Her hand shook. She stared at the dead assassin and burst into tears.

Nam touched Panji's shoulder. "I know. I know. You had to do it." She slid her hand down Panji's trembling forearm and gently took the still-hot gun from her hands.

Behind her, three LVMPD uniforms ran onto the roof.

Panji sagged to her knees, crying.

The Peet Library, Oxford

Bane grabbed Jen's hand as the alarm wailed.

She didn't resist or question him. They ran, hand in hand, across the marble floor past shouting students who sprinted for the exits. She was a better runner than he was, on the track team for Oxford, a daily runner since she was sixteen, and it was Bane who lagged behind.

One of the students who reached the door ahead of them screamed.

Bane slid to a halt, pulling Jen with him.

Winston, one of Gregor's bobbies, lay on the floor in a widening pool of blood. Jen looked at him, her eyes unblinking, but she remained controlled. She didn't scream. She was a Bane girl.

Bane glanced up at the security camera over the door. The LED was turned off.

Alarm sounding, man down, broad daylight, cameras turned off. Someone had planned this, and they were damned good.

"They're expecting us to go for the main entrances," Bane said. Without another word, he led the way to the front quad, through the wide lobby and to the right, toward one of the smaller libraries.

"The Peet Library is card access," Jen said.

"No problem." Bane's shoulder drove hard into the old wood of the door, and suddenly the famous Egyptology library was open to the public.

He closed the door, jamming the lock with his pocket knife. It wasn't much of a barrier, nothing at all really, but it might fool someone into believing the door was locked. He held a finger to his lips and led his daughter into the stacks. The Peet Library smelled musty and old, the delightful aroma of ancient books bound in leather.

Bane tried his radio but the only answer was static. He punched speed-dial on his satellite phone, but there was no signal. Without being asked, Jen handed him her cell phone, but it was dead too. If someone had taken the time to bring jamming equipment, this was a well-planned operation, almost certainly a trap. They didn't care about his daughters, but they knew he'd come for them. This was all in honor of crucifying Bane. That Domergue had hinted so broadly was the lure, and that he'd dare to reveal himself meant he believed Bane had no hope of surviving this.

"What about Mags?" Jen said quietly, nearly whispering. Her face was oddly calm, flushed with excitement but not terrified. The Bane clan had been through so much, it would take the end of the world to frighten them, and even then, their natural reaction would be to survive.

"I pity the creep who goes after Mags," Bane said, meaning to reassure Jen, but from Jen's quick smile he knew she believed it too. After Mags's ordeal four years ago, she had plunged herself into martial arts, self-defense of the deadly kind, and she carried a gun in her sling bag; she was beyond formidable. It was one of the reasons he could deal with her rough taste in boyfriends. If anyone would end up bruised and battered, it would be the thug, not Mags. "Besides, I think this is all for me."

"Good thinking, Pops." She stared at him with those incredible green eyes. "My knight in shining armor brings death and destruction down on the fair maiden."

He winked. "You said I never visit."

She smiled.

"The only death and destruction here, Jen, will be for anyone who tries to touch you."

They flattened themselves against the stacks as the door flew off the frame with a loud crash.

Bane peered through the old volumes.

At the door stood the unmistakable hulking silhouette of one of the Twins. The man wore a mask, but his six foot six size, the cowboy boots and the shoulders that filled the door frame made it a certainty.

Bane looked around. There was only one other door. He nodded and Jen moved towards it.

Bane drew his revolver and stepped out from the stacks to face the assassin.

55

Las Vegas

Ciro Benetiz accelerated the coroner's van onto US-95 S. He stifled a yawn, taking his time. The *rigido* in the back wasn't in any hurry—the stiff was a cadaver not some zombie—so why rush? With five kids and two mortgages, Benetiz needed all the overtime he could accumulate, even though it had been a busy week. He had made the run from Mountain View to the Clark County Coroner's Office more than ninety-six times in four days, a record even for Vegas, and he knew the other drivers were just as busy.

This epidemic had backlogged both the Metro Coroner's Office and Clark County Coroner's Office, now overflowing with gurneys that lined the chill hallways.

This new victim would be stacked, racked and packed and had a long wait for an autopsy, even though he was a probable homicide. The stiff, Ernest Gies, would be waiting a few days in refrigeration as the four medical examiners and six forensic pathologists tried to clear the case load of hundreds left over from the epidemic.

Thank God the City Health Office had given Benetiz vaccinations against this new TZ-4. Not that Benetiz took any chances. He had three boys and two girls, and a needy wife, so he wore protection on his body and over his face.

Benetiz fumbled with a thermos of coffee as he drove to the second army barricade. They waved him through because of the coroner's seal but the slow speed gave him a chance to pour a cup of double strength java. The heady scent of coffee perked him up even before the caffeine hit his system. He wondered if Gary in receiving would log a delay if he took a five-minute break on the side of the road sipping coffee. Unlikely, and he could always blame it on army check posts. A frigging coffee on the side of the highway didn't exactly break the evidentiary sanctity of the direct-transport directive did it?

Of course it did, but Benetiz could barely keep his eyes focused on the road and he badly needed a perk-me-up.

In fact, he was so dopey with fatigue that he thought he imagined the moan that came from behind him.

He slurped more coffee, cursing as he spilled hot brew on his overalls. He started to pull off the empty highway.

He heard it again: more of a groan this time.

Benetiz braked. He had driven a thousand cadavers, but none had ever moaned before.

Could the doctors at MountainView have made a mistake? Or the coroner's investigator?

Benetiz tilted his rearview mirror for a better view of the back.

The corpse moved.

56

The Peet Library, Oxford

Bane's tiny chromed Smith and Wesson seemed entirely inadequate against the hulking blond assassin, especially with only five shots. Bane had always relied more on his wits than guns, and his little Air Light titanium revolver was more a memento than a devastating weapon. It was engraved personally from Director Harris of the FBI. This big assassin could probably take all five slugs and still lumber on.

"Hello Austin," Bane said.

Austin Bartlett peeled back the filter mask on his face, his smile Hollywood handsome as always. He tucked the mask into a small, open pouch on his belt. "G'day old friend," the man said cheerfully. "Same tiny thirty-eight?" He took one long stride into the room. "You'd think by now you'd invest in something bigger."

"It's not how big it is, but how you use it."

"A lie perpetrated by small people." Austin's grin was infectious, almost hypnotic, making it difficult to believe he was the definition of a sociopath.

"You'll leave my daughter out of this?" Bane said, poking his snub-nosed revolver at the giant.

"I'm here for you, Alban Bane, not for your daughter, and not for your autograph."

"I know." Bane found himself remembering that night at the Pantages theatre, the night Kenji Tenichi celebrated his win of *Haunted Survivor*. That night, Bane wore bandages and bruises from his encounter with Bartlett's father, and had escaped the gala party of movie stars and autograph-seeking crowds to a private room. He had nearly lost Mags, he had lost a lot of blood and the tip of two fingers to the sadistic caresses of Emerson Bartlett. That night, he had been confronted by Austin Bartlett—son of the psychopathic Emerson Bartlett, twin brother of the monster Sampson, and brother of the sociopathic serial killer Tyler Hayden.

Now Bane stared into Austin's face. If anything, in the last four years his muscle mass had increased. "You know I'd be more impressed if you had a gun."

Austin lifted his baseball glove–sized hand. He held an automatic weapon.

"Oh." Bane said. "I'm wearing Kevlar."

"So am I."

"At this range I can hit one of your eye sockets."

"Can't we just be friends, Alban?" Austin winked.

"I'm the guy responsible for having your brother executed by lethal injection."

Austin shrugged. "He was an asshole."

"So what is it you want?"

"You should know by now it's all about the Game."

"So you're not here to make me bleed?"

"Oh yes, I'm here to make you leak. Shame, though. I like you, Alban."

"Hey, I won't tell. Just tell Dad you popped me."

"Father's too smart for that."

"Don't worry, Mommy will protect you."

"No doubt."

Bane squeezed the trigger, diving to one side as he fired.

As Bane rolled to his feet, Austin's automatic pistol flashed in a hot burst.

57

Clark County Coroner's Office

Medical Examiner Doctor Joel Webley made his twenty-second Y incision of the shift. On a busy day, the forensic pathology teams might autopsy six and examine fifteen, but since the epidemic began, each shift and each team had averaged dozens. They only autopsied suspicious death cases, but Vegas had exploded in violence since the quarantine.

Oddly, the last week had been light on "typical" homicides: suicides, accidents under suspicious circumstances, gang-related deaths, ordinary domestic disputes—although there had been hundreds of domestics related to the "rage" symptom now known to be a side effect in survivors of the TZ-4 epidemic. Today he had autopsied three citizens shot dead by army personnel, people who tried to run the barricades. He had also examined nine "unresolveds," the new term for violent homicide believed to be related to the epidemic of rage. At least today there had been no terrorist-style bombings. Webley had handled three bombings yesterday, always a messy business more akin to putting together a jigsaw puzzle. And there had been one real "saw" puzzle yesterday when a lawyer went berserk on his family with a chainsaw.

Webley paused the digital recorder and turned away from John Doe nine-six-three. He played with the controls on his isolation suit, turning up the ventilation rate. The damned suits made autopsies nearly impossible, and it didn't take long for Webley to work up a sticky layer of sweat. He found he was drinking twelve bottles of water a shift, and he had lost twenty-two pounds since this all began. TZ-4 had turned into the ultimate diet for him, a non-stop sauna and water diet. His wife wouldn't recognize him, if he ever found time to go home for a few hours.

Webley swayed for a moment, feeling ill. He felt like he was running a fever. But that was unlikely. It was the heat of the suit.

"Web?"

Webley looked up. WART's Deputy Director, Armitage Saulnier, was at the observation glass, his forever-smiling face for once scowling. Arm had become a regular visitor as he coordinated army, FBI, FEMA and WART activities.

Webley shuffled to his side of the glass and tapped the intercom key. "Hey, Arm."

Arm finally offered one of his trademark smiles. "You look like shit, bro."

"That's what my wife says," Webley said.

"Y'all got a moment?"

Webley shrugged. "I've got a stack in the fridge, and they're packed in the halls."

Arm nodded, nervously swiping back his spiked orange dreads. "I know. But this is important."

"Kay." Webley yawned. "But we have to talk like this. Isolation protocol."

"No problemo, bro."

They stared at each other for a long moment, sharing their fatigue. Since this all began, both had been shift on shift, so there was no point chit-chatting about work. Work was hell.

"We're missing a vic, Web."

"I wouldn't notice."

Arm laughed, but it came out more like a grunt. "I know it."

"So who's missing?"

"We had a homicide at MountainView. A Doctor Ernest Gies, pronounced at the scene. But your driver never made it here. His van's missing, too." He sounded really on edge about it.

"You're kidding."

"For true, bro."

"How does a coroner's van go missing?"

"You tell me, bro."

"I can't. Especially with the army on the streets. Makes no damned sense."

They stared at each other for a long time. Then, Web said, "What the hell's going on in this city?"

"It's not just this city, bro." The unusual scowl returned. "This man's important."

"They're all important. But we're knee deep in bodies, Arm, what's one more?" He didn't mean to sound flip, but exhaustion made him a little giddy.

"This one's wrapped up in all this, Web. You just put the word out. Arm is lookin' for this coronor's van."

"Can't you put the army on it?"

"They're on it. Everyone's on it."

"It's that important?"

"For true, bro. For true." Without even a wave, Arm turned and left the observation lounge. Even through the glass, Web felt the door slam.

58

The Peet Library, Oxford

A bullet in the leg had barely slowed Austin Bartlett. Bane ran between the stacks, weaving as bursts of automatic gunfire spat at him, thunking into thick antique books. Bane only had four more shots in his for-show revolver, and his speedloaders were in his bag.

"That hurts, Alban."

"Ah, don't be a baby," Bane shouted back. He tried pushing on one of the stacks, hoping he might be able to topple a pile of books on Bartlett's monster son. "I'd let you cry on my shoulder, but I'm busy right now."

Another burst of bullets and priceless reference books bled for Bane.

"These books are hundreds of years old. Have a little respect!"

Austin paused only long enough to replace a clip. More books flew off the shelves in tatters. It broke Bane's heart.

Bane led Austin to the north side of the room, away from the room where his daughter was, towards the only other room branching off the main chamber. When Austin hesitated to follow, he shouted, "Stop playing! You can't be that bad a shot!"

Bane paused, peered tightly between two angled leather-bound tomes, and aimed at Bartlett's right arm. He saw a light spray of blood as he took a slice out of Austin's bicep. "I always say, if you're going to get shot, do it in a library. You die in good company."

Austin might be a terrible shot, but he was impossible to stop. Between the Kevlar and the sheer magnitude of the man, only a bullet right between the eyes would slow him down. At this range, Bane doubted he could manage it. He squeezed off one more shot.

This time, instead of firing back, Austin Bartlett dove toward the shelves, shoulder turned, like an offensive tackle at a desperate sudden-death Superbowl. Bane could only watch in shock as the monster crashed through the wood and the heavy books. Bane flew back, his gun spinning across the floor as hundreds of pounds of killer landed on top of him.

59

Wynn, Las Vegas

Abbey Chase paced her suite like a caged lioness.

Set up in a circle around the salon were six monster LCD panels, each with different feeds to a different executive. On monitor one was Jim Platt, president of Real TV; monitor two, Jerry Howarth, representing the network affiliate; on three their legal watchdog Herman Blackwood of Blackwood, Hargood and O'Shea; Public Relations Senior VP Eaton 'Bigmouth' Beasley on four; five revealed a weary Hilde Amund, Real TV's

Chief Financial Officer.

Monitor six worried her the most. Saffa Ibrahim said nothing throughout the virtual meeting, always watchful and silent, occasionally stroking his beard but otherwise revealing nothing. He represented KDS, the consortium who quietly bought up Real TV stock and now owned forty-one percent of voting shares. She knew, through various asset groups, fund managers and shadow corporations they were still buying trading shares in her company. The share values were a good buy now, with analysts downgrading Real TV from "outperform" to "sell" since the quarantine and news of *Superstar*'s woes in Vegas.

"Abbey, if you can't get this quarantine lifted, we'll be bankrupt in six weeks," said CFO Hilde Amund. "We're losing contracts, sponsors, even syndication deals."

"I'm more worried about the lawsuits," Blackwood snapped.

"Who the fuck cares about lawsuits? If we're bankrupt, we're already ruined," Hilde shouted back, tossing her long strands of grey hair.

"There can be personal liability for the directors, Hilde. Are you ready to lose your houses?"

Abbey Chase held up one of her manicured hands. "Both of you, shut up." They did, instantly. "The bigger problem is the international leg of the tour."

"There won't be one," Blackwood said.

"Why do you say that, Herman?"

"Countries are closing their borders. You'll never get the visas now."

"Leave that to me." Abbey continued pacing.

"What are you going to do?" Herman Blackwood looked nervous.

"You won't want to know about that, Herman."

"Oh." Blackwood looked uncomfortable, squirming in his tall-backed leather chair.

"I have a call in to the president."

"Of the United States?" asked Howarth, the network president. He looked relieved—probably delighted she was using her influence.

"Of course." Abbey forced a smile. "Gentlemen, and lady, leave this to me."

"We always do," Hilde said.

"The investors will want assurances," said Saffa, speaking for the first time, his voice rich and deep and only slightly accented.

"My word is all the assurance anyone needs," Abbey said, staring at monitor six. "Actually, our ratings are up. People are staying home, nervous about the plague, and we're up record share points, even if they are special epidemic broadcasts. And the scandal is making us headline news—again. Just like before, in Vermont."

Heads nodded on all monitors except number six. Bane had made her rich beyond her dreams with his bloody pursuit of the killers on her set of *Haunted Survivor,* broadcast live. He made her ever more notorious with each new epidemic headline. She might be reviled throughout the civilized world, but she would soon be one of the richest women in that same stinking world.

"KTN doesn't care as much about the ratings in America," Saffa said, his voice stern. "We care about viewers in China, India, Europe. So far, you have minimal ratings in these places. We care about the tour."

"The tour will happen. We go to Venice next week."

"If the quarantine is lifted," said Blackwood. "Abbey, it's not realistic to assume you can manage that. Even if you can—"

"I can," Abbey interrupted. She didn't like Blackwood much, and let it show in her glare and her sharp tone. "Herman, just leave all that to me. We tour, no matter what."

"No matter what worries me," Blackwood said, his voice equally angry. "That's the Abbey Chase mantra. We all know that. But we're not talking about hurting a few competitors or ruining someone's career here. We're talking about a virus which threatens the international community."

"Humanitarian that you are," Abbey said, not hiding her sarcastic tone.

"Fuck you, Abbey. Just listen for once. Even if you don't care about the millions of people who could be infected—"

"Fuck you back, Herman. Maybe you've forgotten, I employ you?" She put on her best scowl, but she was worried now. Herman was spineless, and his show of strength in front of the others meant he was worried. "I care about one thing. Real TV's return on investment."

"As it should be," Hilde said.

"Fine, Hilde, Abbey. Fine." Herman Blackwood tapped the camera on his desk, making the image sway. "But listen to me, folks, because we are talking about Real TV's return. Billions in liability, not millions."

"Oh, come on, Herman! Christ, you're a melodrama queen. We're not liable for anything. We didn't start this plague." Abbey stomped her designer heals. Something had to be done about Herman Blackwood.

"It will cost tens of millions, maybe hundreds of millions to defend the litigation," Blackwood shot back. "If we lose, billions. Okay, probably we won't lose, but we still have to front the legals."

"Call it a PR budget, then," Abbey said sharply.

"Do not worry about costs," Saffa of KTN said. "We can absorb such costs. The important thing is the tour."

"Why? Why is it so damned important?" Blackwood said. "We have eighty million viewers in America already."

"KTN did not invest for American viewers. We want worldwide audiences." Saffa's voice remained eerily monotone. "Will that be a problem?"

"No," Abbey felt her calm returning. "No problem at all."

"Even you, Abbey, can't open up international borders if these countries don't want your infected crew," Blackwood said.

"Oh, but I can, Herman. You should know me better than that." She smiled. "Now, gentlemen, and lady, I have the call from the White House on line three. If you'll excuse me?"

She didn't wait for an answer. She sliced her hand in front of her throat and her assistant Nancy killed the secure feed.

Abbey Chase walked quickly to the mirror, straightened her collar, freshened her makeup, then returned to her makeshift conference area. She nodded at Nancy. "Put the president through."

No matter what, the Chase mantra. She liked that. She put on her best smile for the president. *Superstar* would tour to Venice, London, Paris, Delhi, Taiwan, Moscow, Singapore, Hong Kong—no matter what. Even if the virus hadn't burned out, there was a vaccine. Blackwood, Bane, Kenner and the world be damned.

60

The Peet Library, Oxford

Bane stared up into Austin Bartlett's face. He ignored the explosion of pain, the immobilizing weight, and focused on survival. Austin was only human after all. The man was in as much pain as Bane, except he didn't have a crushing weight on top of him. A veteran of several past broken ribs, he was fairly sure Austin's tackle had given him two or three more impact fractures.

Bane brought his knee up hard between the man's legs. Though he meant it to hurt, it didn't seem entirely according to Hoyle, and Bane felt manly guilt as Bartlett's eyeballs rolled up to whites.

Bane pushed the beast off him and lay amongst the splinters and ruined books, desperately sucking air, grateful lungs burning. He stared up at the vaulted ceiling, barely able to breathe or move. His gun was thirty feet away, nestled in a pile of books with broken spines. It might as well have been a hundred yards.

Austin groaned, his big wounded leg trembling. Bane pulled himself to his knees. He could try strangling the monster, but he doubted he could get his hands around the man's tree-trunk neck. Woozy, he fumbled in the assassin's pouch, assuming he must have another weapon. Weakly, Austin's big hand batted at him, hard enough to fling Bane back. But in Bane's hand was the only weapon Austin carried in his belt pouch.

A hypodermic gun.

The only sound was the eerie wail of the security alarms: "Wee-eee-eee, Wee-eee-eee..."

Then, before Bane had fully recovered his own wind, Austin snapped up from the waist. The trademark grin returned. "Ouch. That hurt."

"Good to know you can be hurt," Bane wheezed.

"You're out of shape, old man."

"By your big standards, maybe." He held up the hypo. "How's this for irony?"

For the first time, Bane saw a glimmer of fear on Austin's genetically perfect features. "Careful with that, old man."

"A dose of Braxis' best?"

Austin stared at the chrome and glass pneumatic hypo gun, unblinking, a cobra watching for the moment to strike.

"I suggest we just wait here for my men," Bane said.

"I think not." Austin began to rise, Godzilla rising from the waves to terrorize Japan, elegant and monstrous. "Give me the hypo, I leave your daughter alone."

Bane managed to slide his elbow up and under, levering half to his feet. He was still dizzy and felt as if a piano had fallen on him from a third floor window. He nearly dropped the hypo gun. He made it to his knees.

Austin was on his feet.

Bane didn't think. Instead of trying to wobble to his own legs, he dove forward, like a prostrating monk, his arms reaching out, aiming the hypo at the man's Mr. Universe calf

He pressed the hypo trigger. The gun hissed as it injected into Austin's calf. Before Austin pulled away, Bane managed three quick trigger pulls. The sweet smell of Phenol made him wince just before Austin kicked him, but Bane was sure it had gone into his ankle flesh.

Austin stared down at Bane. "I had the vaccine, Bane." But he didn't sound convinced.

"I'm sure that'll be protection against three injections." He wielded the hypo. "Care for another dose?"

Austin's face was uncharacteristically damp with sweat, his features deathly pale.

The giant turned and ran from the library.

Bane tried his radio again, but again there was only static. He pulled himself back to his knees, managed to stumble across the floor to recover both his small revolver and Austin's fallen automatic. All the guns, including the hypo, went into Bane's shoulder bag.

Limping, hurting, he made his way back to Jen's hiding place.

The door was locked.

Dizzy, he called out to her. "Jen? Jen, honey?" Then he passed out.

61

Situation Room, The White House

The National Security Council rose as President Donald Radford entered the situation room.

Terrorism Task Force Chairman Franklin Farrier instinctively joined the chorus, "Mr. President," even though he was a guest of the NSC, invited because of the Khan incident. Two other members from the Council of Ten, so called by the press, were permanent members of the NSC: Vice President Samuels and CIA Director Lambert.

"Thank you, gentlemen and ladies," said President Radford. He looked more fatigued than usual. He appeared as tired as the unimpressive Situation Room, a wood-paneled basement room that felt crowded and retro with its low-back chairs and 1980s table.

Radford stooped a little and he didn't look well. Farrier knew rapid aging went with the job, one reason he never felt the urge to run for office. He had served three presidents in different roles, and all aged at least five years for every one in office.

The usual suspects were in attendance—secretary of state, chairman of the joint chiefs of staff, secretary of defense—but also Gilbert Domergue, the president's science advisor, another member of The Ten—although he joined them by secure link from Midi, France, his face pixilated as always on the screen.

"Let's start with an update on the containment," the president said.

Domergue leaned closer to the camera, a murky sillouette. "The actions of USAMRIID and WART have proven effective, sir. We now have seventeen hotspots, all under quarantine. Vegas and LA have stabilized. No new cases in five days. The fast quarantine seemed to make the difference."

The president nodded. "That's fine, then. I propose we lift the containment on those cities."

"Isn't that premature, Mr. President?" asked General Gledhill, chairman of the joint chiefs.

"Not really, sir," said Domergue, staring now at Gledhill. "Frankly, full blown quarantine was extravagant, given a working vaccine and the economic hardship imposed on those cities."

Angelina Hoek, secretary of state, shook her head. "Economic hardship is an understatement. We may have to underwrite this disaster."

"What do you mean, Angie?" President Radford asked.

"The stock market panic has created a precarious situation for everyone, but airlines and exporters are very hard hit, especially in the quarantined cities. Retail took a very large blow. We may have to bail some companies out. Or let them sink. To the tune of billions, Mr. President."

"Some industries are doing well," said secretary of the treasury Ian Seagrave. He stared a little too thoughtfully at Domergue on the LCD screen. "Genetics, for example."

President Radford waved his hand. "Casualties?"

"Let's break this down," Norman Chambers, secretary of homeland security answered. "Direct casualties of the virus, current count fifty-seven thousand, nine hundred and six."

"Good God," Radford said, although it sounded more like an exhalation of breath.

"Amen," Chambers said. "Equally worrying, the violence. We can't necessarily attribute it all to the rage symptoms so daintily described in the press, but if we take normal statistical norms, we can extrapolate a number."

"I probably don't want to know this," said Radford.

"Understandable, sir. Six thousand, three hundred and sixty-two percent above average violence resulting in homicides. Translates into tens of thousands of victims."

"Jesus Christ Almighty," said Angelina Hoek.

"Yes," said Chambers. "Quite. But there's some good news."

"There's goddam good news in there?" Radford shouted, and Farrier noticed everyone sat straighter. Radford never swore.

"Yessir!" Chambers tapped the keys on his laptop and the flat-panel screen at the end of the long table dissolved to a chart. "The incidents of violence have declined precipitously in the quarantine areas."

"Thank God for the army," said Radford, rubbing his temples.

"Actually, sir, thank goodness for Ada Kenner and Alban Bane," said Angelina Hoek.

Farrier glared at Angelina. "It was a cooperative action."

"Hardly, Franklin. You know as well as I that no one would have acted if these two hadn't demanded the quarantine. When the CDC ignored the threat, Doctor Kenner went straight to USAMRIID. She even drafted FEMA. All with Director Bane's support and usual bluster."

"Who is this Ada Kenner?" Radford asked.

"Doctor, Ph.D., expert virologist," said Domergue, his voice somewhat unenthusiastic.

"More than that," said Angelina, her voice crackling with energy. "She was coordinator of emerging viruses at the CDC. But they fired her shortly after this all began. The rumor mill says it was because she wanted a quarantine and her director disagreed. Bane picked her up immediately."

"Damn stupid," said Radford. "The CDC might have saved a few thousand lives."

"Yes, Mr. President." Angelina smiled.

Goddamed sisterhood, Farrier thought, glaring at Angelina, the secretary of state. "I think this Doctor Kenner overreacted. A lot of casualties and economic chaos because of the headlines—this Doctor Kenner caused."

"As it turned out she didn't over-react," Angelina snapped back.

"In any case, I think it's safe to lift the quarantine," Farrier said. "Before we bankrupt the country."

The president stood up and circled the table, an old habit. Everyone knew that if President Radford circled the table like a shark, watch out, he was ready to bite.

"Well, we lift quarantine, then, before it's too damn late," Radford said. "But we remain vigilant."

"Yes, sir." Farrier was exuberant.

"But this Doctor Kenner," Radford added. "I'd like to hear her opinion."

"She works for Alban Bane, now," CIA Director Lambert said.

"Bane always was smart," Radford said.

"So we remove the FAA no-fly restrictions?" Farrier asked.

Radford paced faster now, visibly disturbed, angry. "I don't see we have any choice. I'm getting calls from industry leaders. I just got off the phone with Abbey Chase an hour ago."

"Bet she was livid," Lambert said with a smile.

"Understatement," Radford said. "She tore a strip off the President of the United States."

"She's got balls," Farrier said.

"Iron balls," Radford said. "Well, there we are, then."

"Sir, for the record?" Angelina stood up and Radford stopped his pacing to face her. "Sir, I think it's too soon, frankly. Shouldn't we talk to Ada Kenner? Get her opinion? All respect to our science advisor," she nodded at Domergue, "but I think the risk is too high."

Radford shook his head. "I can't stop the nation's economic engine. The repercussions of economic stall at this delicate time are far greater than a few sick people."

"Germany has an outbreak, sir. India, as well. China, from what I hear. If we open our borders, we may be exporting more of this virus."

Radford shrugged. "Chance we must take. We have the vaccine."

"And to hell with the rest of the world?"

"Not how I'd put it, Angie." But he sat down in his chair, looking defeated.

Farrier knew he had to act now. "Sir, I have to ask one thing."

"Go ahead, Franklin."

Farrier stood up, eyes fixed on the great seal of the president of the United States. "Actually two things. First, we should stay on heightened terror alert."

"Tangible threat?"

"Khan escaped, sir. We'll find him. All our agencies are trying. But we know he already moved a lot of the virus and vaccine. So, we believe North Korea, Iraq, Iran—at least seven groups on our watch list have it."

"Shit, Franklin, you people are supposed to be stopping this sort of thing!" President Radford erupted from his chair again, a sudden bundle of energy.

Farrier didn't correct him. He was homeland security, not worldwide security, but these days it all overlapped. "We'll find Khan, sir, but it might be too late to stop these groups."

"It's one big fuckup after another!" Another swear word. Radford was beyond pissed off.

"Yes, sir, I agree sir. It's a shame Bane didn't take out Khan."

"What do you mean?" Radford stared at Franklin.

"He had Khan's yacht in sight. Let him get away."

Domergue intervened. "Bane rescued four Braxis employees, attacked by Khan."

"Noble," Farrier said. "But Khan escaped."

"Fine, we remain red status" said Radford. "What else?"

"I suggest we take Ada Kenner into custody, sir."

"Pardon me?" Radford stared at Franklin. "Isn't she the hero in all this?"

"Hero or not, sir, she's a problem."

"How?"

"She's speaking to the press, sir. That was one of the reasons USAMRIID jumped into quarantine. Hugh King published an exclusive interview with her. General Stouffville was nervous."

"She acted with good intentions."

"Yes, sir. But good intensions can damage our security."

"You exaggerate," Angelina said, her voice loud.

"She's dangerous," Farrier insisted.

"You're making her sound like a terrorist," Angelina said.

"The reason she was fired is that she can't keep her mouth shut. On red terror alert, it's important all our assets follow instructions."

"That's no basis for detention," said Radford.

"No, sir, it's not. But this is. I have evidence that she spread the virus to Canada."

"Oh for Christ's sake!" Angelina threw her pen across the room. "Franklin's full of ..." She trailed off under his glare.

Farrier smiled. "Plus she attacked two federal agents in the hall of a hospital, when all they wanted was to debrief her per your directive seven-twelve-five. At least we should question her, sir?"

Radford nodded. "That seems reasonable." He looked around the table. "Anything else?"

As they broke up, filing out the door, Angelina caught Farrier by the arm.

He tugged his bicep free. "Congratulations, Franklin."

"What?"

"You've convinced us to go from a necessary quarantine of cities to the quarantine of the one person who might have stopped all this."

62

MAID USAMRIID Lab

Ada buried herself in her work. What else could she do? A madman apparently wanted to kill her, the same maniac who killed Caff and now her favorite professor, Doctor Ernest Gies, the same crazy assassin who tried to kill Panji, Hugh King, Kenji and others. An even more terrible killer, invisible to any without a microscope, swept America with devastation. Behind them both there seemed to be some vile purpose, but Ada couldn't fathom it. To her, viruses had always been mutations of nature, simple clusters of proteins that held more power over life than the complex two-legged creatures who dominated Earth. They were scary enough. One of the simplest organisms in the universe had caused her child to be born without legs, had driven Ada's entire life's mission.

Ada's throat was suddenly dry. Again she felt the tears threaten to spill, forbidden tears. Quentin. Her poor Quentin, the legacy of her intellectual snobbishness, her ego and her negligence. Sweet, helpless Quentin was a testament to the power of that cluster of proteins that ruled the world. Man would never dominate Earth. The simple viruses would always surive, deadly, remorseless, the most terrible and devastating life forms in the universe and something she had dedicated her life to controlling—because she knew they could never, ever be destroyed.

That someone was trying to manipulate and use them terrified her. Even the simplest viruses could never really be controlled.

Ada made a new pot of coffee, careful not to wake up BB, bruised and asleep in one of the cots over the galley.

She heated concentrated milk, poured it over extra strong coffee, and sat back in front of her workstation.

Who had sent this assassin? Why? What was so important about her that she must die? What did she know—that she didn't know she knew?

Her head pulsed with ugly migraine pain that ripped down her left temple. She felt her cheek twitch. The dim light of her computer monitor brought pain, and she dimmed it until it was almost impossible to see the 120,000 magnification of the virus.

It was here. Caff had seen it, and for that he had died. Doctor Gies had been about to tell her. He had been killed. She had what she needed. Somewhere.

She leaned back in her chair and closed her eyes, half hoping she might finally drift off into sleep. Sleep terrified her. How could she sleep when thousands died each day around her.

She lost the battle, fifth cup of coffee and a bottle of stimulants notwithstanding, and her eyes rolled shut, gluey and heavy. For a moment there was peaceful gray, disturbed only by darker floaters. Then, slowly, the images came as they always did. Only this time it was Doctor Ernest Gies's face she saw. What had he been trying to tell her? There were just too many damn questions. And what had been in the hypo that the assassin had used to kill her old professor? She had asked for a full-spectrum screen for hundreds of known poisons, spinal taps, ocular fluid tests, and an aggressive autopsy that included flaying. She had to know what killed Gies.

Ada's eyes snapped open, bringing an instant needle of pain. She swayed in the chair, almost fell as blood rushed to her head. She snatched up the phone. "Outside line, please," she said.

"Yes, doctor. Who are you trying to reach?" The administrator corporal's voice sounded tired, but eager to please.

"The Clark County Coroner."

"No problem, doctor, I can connect you. Who did you want, Ma'am?"

"The on-duty medical examiner for last night."

"That's easy, Ma'am. He just called you. Doctor Joel Webley. I told him you were busy, Ma'am, but I'll get him right back." He laughed. "Great minds, hmm?"

"Tired mind on my end, Corporal. Thanks." She waited, sipping her too-sweet coffee, breathing in the invigorating coffee aroma.

"Doctor Kenner? This is Joel Webley. Thanks for calling back." He sounded even more tired than she felt, his words slurred like he had a mouth full of peanut butter.

"Coincidence, Doctor. I was just calling you."

"Huh. How about that?"

"I was calling to ask you to put a priority on the autopsy of Ernest Gies.

He would have come in last night."

"He would have."

"Sorry?"

"He never arrived. Neither did the coroner's van. Both gone. It wouldn't have something to do with USAMRIID? National Security or something ominous?"

Ada stood up, no longer struggling to stay awake. "You're telling me Ernest Gies's body was kidnapped?" Why would someone steal his body? She could think of only two possibilities: someone didn't want an autopsy, didn't want them to discover what killed Gies, or ... no, that couldn't be right. Ada put aside the impossible and stayed with the probable: someone didn't want them to know what killed Gies.

"I really don't know. I'd call Detective Ludwig Kraft at Las Vegas Metro. His case, now. I'm backed up down the hall and out to the parking lot with your bodies."

"My bodies?" Ada knew he was joking, but couldn't help the rise of anger in her voice.

"Medical Examiner humor. Sorry."

She shivered. She suddenly didn't like this man. "I'm tired."

"Was there something else?"

"Well, yes, Doctor Webley, there is. Have you been documenting stats on this epidemic?"

"Where we can. What stats are you looking for?"

"Actually, I need anything you've compiled. But I'm curious about something, even if it's just your impression."

"Shoot."

"How many mortalities have you documented where the victims were treated with the vaccine. The vaccine from Braxis."

Webley paused, and she heard clicking on a keyboards. "Huh," he said. "How about that."

"What?"

"I've been so busy with end-to-end 'knife and sews' I didn't really notice."

"It's high, then?"

"Over twelve percent."

"That can't be right."

"Oh, it's right."

"Shit."

"Yeah, I'd say. Shit's hitting the old window air-conditioner on this one. I was told three percent mortality in your briefing."

"Oh, you were there?" She tried to sound polite, but her mind raced ahead: twelve percent, not three percent, Braxis had lied, someone had lied, Gies had misled her, or … She nearly dropped the phone. Worst case scenario: the virus had mutated.

"Viruses rule the world," Gies had told his students in his Viral Mutations lecture in her first year at Harvard. "They rule the world because they mutate so quickly. Here we are debating evolution, the slow progression of complex life forms, but look at the humble virus. It never stops mutating. It's what makes it the most powerful and dangerous life form on earth." The auditorium had filled with appreciative laughter, but he had held up his hand and said, "I'm serious, people. Viruses will always rule this Earth."

"Doctor Webley," she said, her voice freshly urgent. "I need new blood samples, stat."

She hung up the phone, and sat for a moment in numb, lonely terror. Finally, she knew something! But it was a discovery that threatened to crumble the last remaining walls of self-control that held her together. Viruses will always rule this Earth. This news meant that this particular virus might very well change life forever.

London, England

Lionheart, the musical, opened to sellout crowds at the Royal Opera House in London. Only society's cream, and the very affluent, could afford tickets, a by-invitation event that included the Prince of Wales, the Duchess of Gloucester, and the Duke of Kent.

Beha-ed-Din watched from his comfortable perch on the gangway over main stage. He watched all the performances from here. His skills with aerial effects were famous in the theatric circles of England, but he was loyal to the Opera House.

He watched the flow of gowns and tuxedos. He studied the royal box, already occupied by the Duchess of Gloucester and Duke of Kent. Beha-ed-Din knew that some, such as the Prime Minister, had refused to attend despite soaring reviews. *Lionheart*'s previews made page one of *The Times*, right below stories on the epidemic in America: Rage Virus Sweeps America as Thousands Die. The Prime Minister refused to attend because Muslims all over Britain protested parliament and the theatre, calling *Lionheart* inflammatory and anti-Islam.

"The dripping evil presence of Saladin, beautifully played by John Harper, is nevertheless provocative," wrote *The Times* reviewer, after attending the dress rehearsal. "Richard the Lionheart, played in corny Arthurian style by Colin Rutherford, portrays the massacres of Saracens as noble and glorious." In spite of thumbs down, the performances were sold out.

Beha-ed-Din, like his namesake in 1191, was a witness for his people. Unlike his ancestor, the hero who reported on the historical massacre of his people at the hands of Richard the Lionheart, Beha-ed-Din the descendant would act.

The fury had smoldered as he participated in choregraphing and managing the flights of theatrical angels who came to the aid of Holy Richard the Lionheart and his Crusaders against Satan and Saladin. He had cried at the first dress rehearsal of the massacre at Acre, when Lionheart—portrayed as the brave liberator—killed three thousand of Beha-ed-Din's people, on stage to the beat of heroic drums and angelic choirs.

"Just theatre," his friends had told him. "Forget your anger."

Few in the cast and crew thought of the feelings of good people everywhere, affronted that the Lionheart could still be portrayed as a hero instead of a mass murderer. Beha-ed-Din's people had been butchered as unarmed hostages, simply because the great Saladin had been unable to raise enough ransom. And his distant relative, Beha-ed-Din, had written the eye-witness account, widely accepted as the truth of that bloody day: "In the afternoon of Tuesday, 27 Rajab, about four o'clock, the king rode out on horseback with all the Frankish army, knights, footmen, Turcoples, and advanced to the pits at the foot of the hill of Al 'Ayadiyeh, to which place be had already sent on his tents. The Franks, on reaching the middle of the plain that stretches between this hill and that of Keisan, close to which place the sultan's advance guard had drawn back, ordered all the Musulman prisoners, whose martyrdom God had decreed for this day, to be brought before him. They numbered more than three thousand and were all bound with ropes. The Franks then flung themselves upon them all at once and massacred them with sword and lance in cold blood."

Beha-ed-Din sat alone in the gangways, watching Lionheart portrayed as a hero liberating Acre, fighting armed soldiers rather than unarmed prisoners.

The crème of society now filled the glorious theatre for the first public performance, silenced by the first curtain. The protesters outside the theatre were no longer heard over the swelling magnificence of the orchestra.

It was time. Beha-ed-Din moved across the gangway to the fire systems backup. He waited for Richard the Lionheart to ride onto stage on his white steed, singing his grand aria.

Beha-ed-Din had already cleansed himself. He had prayed twice. He began to chant: "Allahu Akbar, Subhan Allah, Al-hamdu Lillah ..."

As he prayed, he triggered the sprinkler system.

Immediately, the alarms rang out and the sprinklers came to life, drenching ladies in their evening gowns and men in tuxedos.

The orchestra bravely kept playing at the urging of the conductor, as screaming women and angry men headed for the exits. The crowds surged up the aisles while water continued to spray.

Beha-ed-Din watched, himself sprayed with the TZ-4 virus. He knew there was nowhere to run. Everyone in the Royal Opera House, cast, crew, audience, the Prince of Wales, himself—all were infected.

64

The Porker, Oxford

Bane watched the flow of customers, mostly punks, skinheads and toughs, from the front seat of Gregor's Mini. Jen sat in the back, her hand thrust forward and resting on his shoulder. Even as they watched, two skinheads tumbled out of the shadowy front door, trading punches under the lopsided neon sign of a decapitated pig that simply read, Porkers.

"Mags is in there?" Bane felt a different sort of anxiety. Suddenly he was the father of a rebellious daughter.

Jen sighed. "It's her place, Pops."

"And you, Jen?"

"I never come here. Too rough a crowd."

Gregor lit a cigarette. "I've heard of this place. Not wholesome."

Bane plucked the fag from his friend's mouth. "Speaking of wholesome." He threw it out the window.

He no longer felt woozy and had recovered from the crushing tackle from Austin Bartlett, but he wasn't sure he was ready for Porkers. "Gregor, you stay with Jen. I'm trusting you with her safety."

Gregor looked relieved that he wouldn't have to go inside. "No one's touching Jen on my watch, MacBane."

"And no smoking."

"Crikey. You're worse than my wife."

Bane loosened his revolver in its holster, stepped around the brawling skinheads, and strolled casually up to the towering, shaven bouncer. "Not your problem?" He jerked his head in the direction of the street brawlers.

The bouncer folded his arms on his tattooed chest. "Them? 'Alf the time I kick it off mysel'." He sneezed. "I know you. You're Bane, 'rn't you?"

"In the flesh."

"Loved the game show, dude. You go real knackers. You're in." He gave Bane a thumbs-up and what must have been a smile, although it appeared more a growl. Bane nodded and slipped in to the smoky pub. There were some advantages to his notoriety.

The place wasn't really big, and at one time was probably your standard steak-and-kidney pie suds pub, but it had been taken over by the skinheads and bikers. It felt odd to see a biker crowd in Jolly Old England, although here the skins were called "krauts." True to the bouncer's prediction, there were several ongoing brawls amid broken glass, laughter, and a fog-like veil of smoke. Mags' favorite place, Jen had said. They might not talk anymore, daughter to father, and she had every right to hate him, but this was too much even for him.

"Look at the codger!" shouted one of the big skins at one of the two billiards tables.

"That's Bane!" shouted back one of the bimbos. He didn't know what else to call them besides bimbos, with their practically non-existent low-cut tank tops and leathers. No doubt Mags was one of them.

"Nach, it ain't Bane. He's seven feet tall," someone else barked.

Meanwhile, another two brawls broke out, with mugs smashed on shiny heads. Worse, more than half of the thugs in the pub were sneezing, hacking, coughing or rubbing their heads. He doubted it was just a common cold doing the rounds. Where was Mags in all this?

And Bane—tired, angry, wounded, feeling a sense of worldly doom—did something he'd always wanted to do. He slid his revolver from its holster, pointed it at the ceiling, and fired. Even with the shockingly loud discharge, the brawls continued for another moment. He fired once more. This time, there was stunned silence. A chunk of plaster landed near his feet.

"Would all those with sex organs that dangle please move to this side of the bar?" Bane grinned, taking perverse pleasure in his bad boy tactic. "That's right. All those without danglers, you can stay on that side." Not everyone complied, but about half of the crowd divided the pub into sexes. "Thugs and thuggettes. Yes, I am Bane. And today I'm a pissed off and sore Bane. So no autographs."

"That isna Bane!"

Bane held up one of his hands. "See? No fingertips."

"That is Bane!" Anyone who was anyone, whether they admitted it or not, had watched the "game show" torture scene on Abbey Chase's reality show as Bartlett severed Bane's digits.

A few thugs and thugettes laughed, and a low rumble of excited gossip cascaded through the bar. "Not a social call!" Bane barked out. "Looking for my daughter. I'd describe her for you, but half of you look like her."

"Landlord, this isn't funny!" shouted Mags. He couldn't see her, but her voice was unmistakable. Then she stepped out from behind a burly skin at the far end of the bar. "Who asked you to invade my space?" Her tone said it all: I hate you.

"Invading runs in the family, hon." He tried to give her a quick hug, but she ducked away. "Ah, see, a tender family moment." He holstered his gun. "Don't you people believe headlines? Even I can see most of you are sickos."

The skins just stared at him.

"I'm not talking VD or even something lightweight like SARS, my freaks and follies. I'm talking this whole TZ-4 thing. You don't watch TV?"

A tense two hours later, Bane had made a whole room full of new friends. The skins brought him pint after pint, crowding around Jen, Gregor, a few of Gregor's men, and a glowering Mags. The entire story about Bartlett in the library became pub talk, and only a silent and simmering Mags didn't laugh as Bane told of pumping the giant with his own hypodermic. It was Bane's way of keeping a captive crowd until the health unit finally arrived with their syringes of TZ-4 vaccine. When some of the skins tried to slip out, Bane shouted, "Scared of a needle, you rat-arsed rabbits?"

The near-escapees halted, angry and red-faced at being branded cowards, then relaxed and rejoined the tables as Bane launched another fun Bane story. He had them captive until each and every one of them had their shots, courtesy of WART's discretionary budget.

A few hours later, everyone was so drunk even Mags allowed Bane to slip his arms around her shoulders. Mags never loosened up, but he saw her smile a few times when she thought he wasn't looking.

"Your old man trashed the Peet Library," roared one skin, spitting warm malt as he laughed yet again. "Prof will freak."

"Landlord trashes everything," Mags growled.

"Mags, your geezer's the dog's bollocks," said her boyfriend, a tough-nug who turned out to be an all right kind of kid if you got past the skin-tight leather, tattoos and piercings on every inch of his anatomy.

Just after midnight, after Bane had crammed down more bangers and mash and pints than his poor stomach could keep down, his satellite phone rang.

He shouted over the laughter in the pub. "Bane!"

"Bane? Bro, it's Arm."

"Arm, buuuu-ddieee!"

"Bane, where are you?"

"With my daughters, buuddieee."

"You're smashed!"

"Totally snoogered. Corked. Falling down drunk." And some how he managed to squeeze out all that happened in Oxford, to the ongoing cheers and chants of a crowd of his new friends.

"Say hi to my goddaughters, bro." Arm paused, as if deciding if he should tell Bane anymore. "Bro, there's been a big bloody problem."

"Arm, buuuddieee, in our line of work someone's going to get a little bloody." He shouted out to the pubmaster. "Another jug!"

"Bane, I need you to listen."

"And I need to have sex with a spectacular goddess with gigantic chesticles."

"The Feds have lifted the quarantines."

"Party poopers."

"There's more. Another terrorist release of the virus. This time, with the group claiming credit. A group linked directly to Khan."

Bane sobered instantly. "Where?"

"Right where you are. England. London. The Prince of Wales was infected."

"I'm sure he'll get primo care. How many others?"

"A whole theatre."

"You're rushing in vaccine?"

"The Brits have a stash."

Bane scanned the pub, the empty tankards and his new friends, and his daughters who were practically strangers to him, and suddenly he realized he didn't have a life outside of chasing terrorists and maniacs.

"On the bright side," Bane said, "I doubt anyone will object too much if I sink Khan's ship and let him feed the sharks."

Arm laughed. "Bro, I think they'd pin a medal on you."

"Screw the medal. I want some overtime."

He shoved away the new pint. He hadn't relaxed like this in years. Or seen his daughters in months. All because of Khan and Bartlett.

It was time for them to take a little of their own MADicine.

65

Mountain View Hospital, Las Vegas

Panji stared in at rows and rows of babies, crying and wriggling and wrinkled and tiny. Panji pressed her face so close to the transparency of the maternity ward that she fogged the glass. "Oochy poochy, kooky, wookie." she gurgled.

"No, no, no—that's goo goo, ga ga," said the all too familiar voice of her ex-husband. He laughed. "I knew I'd find you here."

Panji didn't turn. She kept her eyes fixed on one stoic and dry-eyed Asian baby whose little hands were curled into fists. He seemed to be staring at her. "What are you doing here, Mac?"

"That's some greeting."

"You'd prefer goo goo, ga ga?" She turned but when she saw his worried frown she slipped under his outstretched arm to hug him—a quick squeeze and then fast retreat. He'd aged in the five months since she last saw him, although he'd evolved from drop dead sexy to cozy sensuality. His tanned skin was stretched too taut over high cheekbones, and the kinky mess of grey streaked hair gave him a nutty professor meets the handsome football jock look.

"I came as soon as they lifted the quarantine." His face was pale and his eyes shot with an impressionist painter's brushstrokes of mad red. "I've been worried to death."

"It's your fault I was in Vegas to begin with." Panji leaned forward again, gave him another kiss on his cheek. "How did you know I'd be here?"

"How else?" He stared down at her, his tired eyes full of emotion: jealousy, despair, sympathy, a little of each—or something else? Panji was too tired to care. "Abbey Chase called me. She complained you hadn't been on set yet since the quarantine lifted. She told me about Kenji—that he was here at Mountain View."

Panji turned away and lost herself in the room of babies. "I meant, how did you know I'd be here? In this ward."

"I was your husband for four years."

"Four years, three months, four days—three years too many."

"Ouch."

Panji reached out her hand and he took it. She squeezed. "I'm joking. I'm glad you're here."

"I know."

"So how is Kenji?"

"Discharging today. They tell me that those who will recover already have." Mac moved close to the glass and made funny gestures at the babies. "When are you going to report in? They're still filming the auditions, you know."

"That's your segue to business?" She folded her arms across her chest. "You know about the attack? About this killer in the mask?"

He nodded. "It worries me because I know you. I know you're like a pit bull with stuff like this."

"He attacked my friends."

"Let the professionals take care of this mess," Mac said

"Mess? That's what you call thousands dead—in Vegas alone—and ninety-two thousand infected but recovering? Just—a mess?"

He sighed, a long windy and artificial sound. "If you don't get on set today, Abbey's going to sue our asses. In fact, she's here, looking for you."

"She doesn't stop the auditions in the middle of a disaster? With her host in the hospital? Who does she think will watch her stupid show now?"

"Abbey stops for no one," Mac said. "And there are a lot of people sick at home."

"But who'll audition?"

"The lineups formed this morning. Over a thousand, and growing."

Panji shook her head. The show must go on? Did people care so much about being the next world superstar when there might not even be a world?

She pressed close to the glass, peering at the only baby not crying, the Asian boy. "There's something going on here that is purely hideous. And I'm not talking about Abbey Chase."

"I want you to leave this to the police, the army, anyone but you. Promise me."

"I can't."

"I'm worried about you."

"Mac. Don't."

"There's a lot at stake."

Panji waved at the baby. Not her baby, some stranger's. Mac and Panji had never been able to conceive. The baby almost seemed to wave back, his little hands and feet swaying back and forth. "There's more to life than reality television, Hollywood and the next platinum."

Now the silence went too long. An old-style sweep clock ticked, punctuating Panji's discomfort.

Mac came close to her and leaned into her ear. "There's an FBI man downstairs, looking for Ada Kenner."

"She's in MAID."

"Pardon?"

"I don't know. Stands for Medical Army Infectious Disease lab or something like that. She hasn't come out since the attack, her eyeballs stuck to her electron microscope. Why tell me?"

Mac shrugged. "I don't know about this one. He looks sneaky."

"Sneaky?" Panji swung around. "What do you mean, sneaky?"

"Like—like, he didn't mean her well. He was snappy. Pissed that I didn't know. Almost cross-examined me." He smiled. "No one, none of the doctors, cops, no one is talking to him."

"Take me!" Panji grabbed Mac by the arm and pulled him towards the elevators.

They found the FBI agent in the isolation ward. He wore a two-for-one suit and bad haircut. "Looks like a Fed," said Panji as she marched up the hall. "Excuse me," Panji called out as she approached. "Are you looking for Doctor Kenner?"

The man turned on the toes of his shoes, rather than his heels. Panji didn't know the significance of a toe-turn, but it struck her as oddly dangerous, like the move of a trained martial artist. A moment later, the man smiled, but it was the unfriendliest expression Panji had ever seen, more like something she expected from a journalist. "That's right."

He flipped open his badge. "Special Agent Newell."

Panji took the badge, weighed it in her hand. It felt real.

"And you are Panji Maingan," he said. It wasn't a question. He flashed her another phony smile. "My daughter's a fan."

"I get that a lot."

"You know where Doctor Kenner is?"

"Yes. Yes, I do. In fact, I just came back from the airport."

"I see." He didn't move, staring hard at her, as if appraising her honesty. "And where did she go?"

"Why should I tell you?"

"Because I'm FBI."

"Yes. Yes, I see that. But this hospital is full of FBI, CIA, Army Intelligence, police." She handed back his badge. "Doctor Kenner's a friend. I don't think I should tell you where she went."

"It's a matter of National Security, Miss Maingan," he said, and the way he emphasized the words, she understood it as National Security in caps. Meaning, cooperate, or go to jail.

"Ms. Maingan, it is very important."

"More details please."

"Look, I can detain you as well."

"I think you'd want to talk to Alban Bane about that first."

The special agent frowned, and two quick blinks of his eyes revealed surprise. "Why would this concern Director Bane?"

"Because both Ada Kenner and I work for him."

Agent Newell swallowed, his eyes darting left then right. "Well, Ms. Maingan, my orders come from the director of the FBI personally. And his orders are from the president of the United States."

Even though Panji was nearly a foot shorter than the FBI agent, she fixed him in her most menacing gaze. He pulled back his ninety-dollar department store jacket to reveal handcuffs. "Whatever way you'd like to do this."

Panji held out her hands.

"Panji!" Mac snapped, and he stepped between them, physically pushing down her hands. "She didn't mean anything," he said over his shoulder to the Fed.

Panji turned her head and smiled at him. "Don't worry about me, Mac. I'm due on Abbey Chase's set. I think I'd prefer this gentleman's company."

"But Panji, you—"

Panji shook her head once, but she cocked her eyes up and right. Could he still read her, like she could read him? Go warn Ada. When he didn't move, she mouthed it.

He nodded with his eyes. "I'll get our lawyer." He mouthed back: I'll tell her.

"Good idea, Mac." Panji turned, shoved out her wrists. "Take me away, officer!"

And she wasn't surprised when Agent Newell snapped the cold cuffs on her.

66

Wynn, Las Vegas

Ada flashed her new WART badge, feeling wicked as she did so. Armitage Saulnier, Bane's lieutenant, had given it to her only yesterday, a crisp new leather folio with a heavy gold badge. She was impressed by the title: "Chief Science Investigator." It sounded good, anyway, and she thought it was awesomely funny. "What am I supposed to do with this, Arm?" she had asked.

Her favorite hunky agent winked, an elaborate slow motion roll of one of his sexy green eyes, and said, "Well, you be my boss now, I think, sistah." They had laughed, but Ada felt more confused than ever. She liked Arm a lot, his easygoing Cajun charm, the total opposite of Nam's crisp, cool persona. But her new title gave her no insight into how things worked at the World Advance Response Taskforce.

Abbey's sentry examined her badge, nodded and opened the door to the vast suite. Well, so far the "badge" worked miracles, much more so than her little laminated ID from the CDC ever had. She felt naughty now, as if she were a con artist.

Ada was surprised that Abbey Chase met her, alone, in the foyer.

"Nice to see you, Doctor Kenner," Abbey said, holding out a long-fingered hand.

Ada shook the cool, sweat-free hand. "I've come for your help."

"Well then, we'd best be friends. Call me Abbey, please." Abbey Chase gestured with an elegant wave of her hand and led Ada to a study with windows more than twice her height that revealed views of the strip. "Of course, anything I can do. I'm just about to head over to our set, though."

"About that," Ada said, sitting on an overstuffed chair. "Your judge, Panji, might not be there."

Abbey's smile faded. "It seems quite impossible to control Panji Maingan."

Ada nodded. "I'd say that's true. But right now she's being detained by the FBI."

Abbey leaned forward across her desk, tenting her perfectly manicured hands in a pyramid shape. "Well, then. She found another innovative dodge. But I think you want me to exert some influence."

"If you can." Ada didn't try to mislead the Real TV CEO. It was unlikely she'd be able to fool her for long. "I assume it's in your best interest to have Panji released to your custody."

"Perhaps." Abbey stood up suddenly, and in spite of the abruptness of the move, she remained elegant and upright. Ada could only assume she practiced her every move. "Coffee?" She didn't wait for an answer and moved quickly to an elaborate brass cappuccino machine. As she steamed milk she said, "Perhaps I'm tired of Panji's shenanigans."

"Her antics might improve your ratings."

"Our ratings are grand. I don't know why it is, but every time there's a world disaster, our ratings go up." She handed Ada a foamy coffee. "Anyway, tomorrow we fly the crew to Venice."

"So soon?" Ada put her cup down on the birch-wood desk.

"Yes. We're behind schedule with this entire fiasco."

"Abbey, I hope I can exert some of my own influence."

Abbey Chase returned to her desk with her own cappuccino and studied Ada with cool grey eyes. In spite of Panji's harsh criticisms of Abbey, Ada found herself admiring the woman. She admired any woman who could achieve all that Abbey Chase had accomplished. The power and influence she wielded was inspirational.

"I assume you want to discuss delaying the tour."

Ada nodded, feeling suddenly dispirited. "Yes. Yes, I do. Viruses can go dormant. Mutations of viruses can exhibit differentials in incubation."

"Translation, please?" Abbey smiled. "Actually, I understand. But Ada, unless you can give me concrete evidence, I can't delay. We've lost nearly three hundred million dollars already."

Ada didn't know what to say. It seemed like a lot of money.

"We'll survive," Abbey said. "Although I've had to take on new investors, and they're people I'm not entirely comfortable with."

"Who's that?"

Abbey smiled. "Been taking lessons from our dear Alban Bane, I see." She shook her head, tossing long strands of perfectly coifed hair. "No, Ada, that's not for you to know. I can manage them."

Ada saw a crack in the hard façade, a flash of worry. But it passed so quickly she couldn't be sure. "So your first stop is Venice?"

"That's right."

"My favorite city."

"You're a romantic."

Was she? Ada had wonderful memories of Venice with her ex, long walks through narrow streets, feeding the pigeons in Piazza San Marco, the spice markets on the Rialto Bridge. "I guess I am." She sighed. "But it's a tourist city. The risk of worldwide vectoring of this virus is too great. From Venice, imagine a spider web of vectors spreading out in every direction."

Abbey stood up, moved to the windows and looked down on Vegas. "I certainly wouldn't want to cause a disaster. Not after what we endured here." She turned and shrugged. "But you've given me no reason to believe we're not clear of this epidemic. The CDC itself has certified our crew clean."

"I know, but—"

Abbey Chase held up a hand. "I assume if you could stop me, without asking politely, you would."

Ada nodded, pressing her lips together in nervous anticipation.

"I'm sorry, Ada. I really am. But we stand to lose too much. With or without Panji, with or without WART's approval, we fly to Venice." She picked up the phone on the desk. "But as to the other matter, let's see what we can do." She dialed the hotel desk. "This is Abbey Chase. Yes, thank you. Please connect me with the Special Agent in Charge Susan Wiltshire at the FBI Las Vegas Field Office. I'll wait."

Ada watched the change in Abbey Chase's posture. Her shoulders drew even more upright, the smile disappeared, and suddenly she appeared scary efficient. Her nails drummed on the desk, the only sign of impatience. "Hello, Susan," Abbey said. "Yes, I'm well. How are John and the kids, after this awful incident? Oh, I'm so glad. Susan, I'll make this short. I know how busy you are. You're holding one of my judges. That's right, Panji. I need her released." She smiled at Ada, nodded once. "No, Susan, that won't do. If you like, I can call your director right now. Fine. I'll wait."

Abbey Chase covered the receiver. "It's done." She frowned, listening. "Ada Kenner? The doctor?" She stared hard at Ada. "How could I know where she is? Well, yes, if I hear from her I'll let you know right away." She nodded at Ada. "I'll send a car over for Panji, all right Susan? Fine. Give my best to the family. Bye, now."

Ada realized suddenly that the little gold badge in her Fendi bag meant nothing in a world full of powerful people like Abbey Chase. And she realized the only thing she could do now was to follow *Superstar* and Abbey Chase to Venice.

67

Gulf of Aden, Near Yemen

Alban Bane grabbed the arm of the gunner's chair as the Seahawk helicopter dove towards the Gulf of Aden. Even though he had flown hundreds of helicopter missions as a Marine, Special Ops Colonel, later in WART, the pilot of the advanced new MH-60S was a real hot-dogger, and although he was no longer hungover, enough of the lingering bile was with him to make him feel ill.

Bane focused on the tiny sliver of grey below. "Is that it?" Bane asked.

"That's her, Colonel," came the reply on his headset.

"Director. Or Bane. I'm not in the marines now, lieutenant."

"Yes, Colonel."

"Can we land your hotrod on that tiny deck?" The hotrod was the navy's finest and deadliest attack helicopter, and the only craft assigned to USS *Flying Cloud*.

"Yes sir. I've practiced my landings a bit, sir." Pilot Tomlinson sounded sarcastic even over the headset radio, and as if to teach Bane a lesson, the Seahawk plunged towards the tiny ship below. It looked like a long, sleek toy.

"Is she as fast as they say?" Bane had read the gists, knew that the Lockheed LS Littoral Combat Ship was the fastest military vessel in service, but this sharp sliver of a vessel seemed more boat than ship, even though he knew she displaced 500 tons, weighing in at frigate size. She also cost a cool half-billion dollars with her shiny attack helicopter and modules. *Flying Cloud* was named after one of the most famous clipper ships of the tall ship era, and she looked as if she could live up to her reputation for speed, but could she catch Khan's speedy yacht, the *Hanu*?

"The fastest ship in the navy," Tomlinson said. "*Cloud*'s lean and mean and you'll be sick as a dog if you get motion sickness—sir."

"Great," Bane said. Could he be any sicker than now? He had spent most of the trip thinking about Mags and Jen, and how he was a crappy dad, and how much he liked their skinhead friends, and a whole lot of tired-ass nonsense. But he made two decisions in the last thirty-six hours, jumping from flight to flight: Khan would die on this trip; and Bane would quit as Director of WART. He wasn't a quitter, and he loved his job, and he'd miss the ability to be a jerk whenever he wanted, but he needed his daughters to remember him, and he was tired of the headlines.

The hot-dogger pilot dropped altitude too fast, leaving Bane's stomach somewhere up in the clouds above *Flying Cloud*, but he felt better as the slip of a boat grew into the long arrow-like shape of a small ship. He saw that she had a full helicopter landing pad back of the aerodynamic wedge-shaped bridge. She now appeared wickedly advanced.

"Is she armed? I don't see any weapons." They'd need plenty if they wanted to stop Khan.

"She has plenty of fire power, sir. A fifty millimeter deck gun—retracted sir, that's why you don't see it—torpedo launcher—the new hunter-seeker mini torps, four NLOS container launchers each system containing fifteen missiles."

"Oh. I think my penis just grew ten inches," Bane said.

The pilot laughed.

Bane didn't remember hunter-seekers in his gists, but it sounded like they were set. And they'd need to be, with Khan sitting on the best and newest stolen military equipment.

"What happens if you run into a submarine?"

"There's me, sir." Commander Criscione laughed. "Seahawk's our best helicopter. Hellfire missiles on board, sir."

"Can you outrun a stinger missile?"

"Not really sir, no." He laughed, not sounding overly confident. "Once a stinger locks on, we can only rely on countermeasures. Are you saying the *Hanu* has stingers?"

"Son, I wasn't speaking in metaphors. Khan loves his manly toys."

"Shit popsicles."

The approach seemed fairly routine until *Flying Cloud* pitched into a swell and Criscione pulled up. He hovered a moment, nose tilted down so that Bane hung on his belt straps, dangling over the sea. To Bane, they seemed so close. One moment there was a deck, marked with a circle and cross, the next moment they were over swells of water, then they were facing ass-wards. Finally the helicopter spun around, matched the deck's tilt, and they landed.

After the wrenching landing, Bane took a long breath, eyes half closed. As soon as his non-slip boots hit the helo-pad, he felt the violent motion of the ship. The small ship was made for high speed, not comfortable sailing.

He met the commander of the *Cloud* on the bridge. Commander Norman Pierce held out his hand and Bane shook firmly. "Welcome aboard, Colonel Bane." Commander Pierce seemed young to captain even a small ship like *Cloud*, with a boyish face that seemed incapable of facial hair. "You are a man of immense influence."

"That's news to me." If only Commander Pierce knew the ass-kissing he had to engage in to get this mission approved, Khan notwithstanding. His nose was still brown after three showers.

He studied the small control center of the ship, barely larger than a jet cockpit, jammed as it was with men and equipment. He had never seen so many LCD panels on a naval bridge before.

"*Cloud*'s still classified, on shakedown."

"So, first blood for the *Cloud*, Commander?"

Pierce stared at Bane, apparently not sure how to take the remark. "I suppose so. If it comes to that, sir."

"It will."

"How you got her assigned is beyond me."

"Ah, I have an admiral drinking buddy with a few secrets. Of course I'll never tell you that he has three wives in three ports. Oops. There I go again. That's why I never get to read those nifty Top Secret files." Bane stared at the shocked commander's too-young face, willing him to smile. Nothing. What happened to military manliness, bravado, a joke between comrades? Oh well. "Have you located the *Hanu*?"

"Yes, sir. Reconnaissance has her steaming towards the Port of Aden."

"Jetting actually. I'd rather not let her dock in Yemen, Captain." The idea of a hold full of virus and vaccine reaching another uncontrolled port known as a hub of terrorism scared him.

"Yes, sir. We'll catch her."

"I don't want to catch her, Commander."

"Sir?"

"I want to sink her."

Obviously Commander Pierce was shocked. Bane knew what the young commander was thinking. *But that's piracy. Or murder.*

"Yes, I'm an evil, cunning man. Yo, ho, ho, Blackbeard Bane. But one thing to keep in mind, Captain. Khan is worse than Osama Bin Laden."

"He might surrender, sir."

"About as likely as Castro giving up the export of cigars, son. He'll run. He'll fire his missiles. He might sink you. It would never enter his head that he couldn't escape. So don't you let him, Commander. Because if you do, chances are we're both swimming home. And if we make it, you'll be on toilet duty for the rest of your career."

Pierce stared at him.

"What's *Cloud*'s top speed?"

"About fifty-nine knots, sir. She was built for fifty, but we've had her touch sixty." The baby-faced captain sounded like a proud first-time father.

"That's not fast enough. *Hanu* can make seventy-five with her jets."

"So I've heard, sir. But they can't outrun our Seahawk."

Bane smiled. "They downed a Sikorsky helicopter, well armed, not long ago." He saw the moment of doubt on the captain's face. "They have stingers."

"Ouch-a-doodle," Pierce said.

Where was this kid from?

"You saw how Criscione flies."

"Yes, captain, I did." Bane rubbed his stomach. "But we'll need all his skills, all your weapons, and a big heap of luck." He could tell by Pierce's face that the captain didn't believe him. The cockiness of youth. He captained the navy's most advanced ship and the fastest.

What Pierce didn't understand was that Khan had defeated the best the world had to throw at him, surviving to the ripe old age of seventy-two on a heap of corpses that would stack higher than most skyscrapers.

Venice, Italy

Ada hunched over her computer in her hotel room instead of sitting canal-side at her favorite café on Rio Di Ca' Foscari, sipping red wine.

At least she was in good company. Best friend Barbie had insisted on coming. "Haven't been to Venice in five years, sweet-buns. You can't stop me." He had flashed his gold Visa. "This is my badge. Not as pretty as yours!"

She was glad to have him and he shared her suite, taking the larger bedroom of course. Little Nam and Big Arm occupied the rooms flanking the suite. Panji stayed in a different hotel on the Grand Canal, with the cast of *Superstar*.

"I'm going out for lunch, honey," Barbie called. "You coming?"

Ada closed her eyes, shutting out blurry visions of stained virus on the wide screen of her laptop. "No, Barbie. Don't want to cramp your style. You might meet some hot Italian stud."

"I'm not into Italians." Barbie laughed then threw his arm around her and rocked her back and forth. "I'm Italian honey. Give me a hot black guy anytime. Come on! You're so stiff, baby. You've slept one hour a day for weeks, right? Time to shake the cobwebs out."

Ada's eyes fluttered open. Of course he was right. She couldn't think anymore and she felt on the verge of some important discovery but was too tired to allow it to click. She kept coming back to the same files over and over, the files they found on Caff's laptop: a side-by-side stain that indicated two slightly different viruses. Two viruses! The second virus was not a natural mutation of the original TZ-4 because there was only a single protein differential, as if it had been artificially point-mutated. Ada doubted any other virologist would have noticed it, not because of a vain belief in her skills, but because of Caff's studious notes. He had found it; she had understood it.

And it scared her to death. Who would engineer another virus, one for which there might be no vaccine?

She had first realized it on the flight to Italy. On her first day in Venice, she sent off a report to USAMRIID and the CDC, plus the Pasteur Institute and other Level Four bio labs. "If I'm right, we have a big problem, BB," she had said on a secure line to Fort Detrick. "The first virus is responsive to the vaccine. The other virus only differs by one protein, and it's related. But my guess is that it'll be non-responsive to the vaccine from Braxis."

For two days she sequestered herself in the grand suite of the Hotel Gritti Palace, ignoring Barbie's frequent comings and goings as she ran simulations and waited for BB's preliminary tests in his Level Four lab. If she was right, and this was some new resistant virus—and the new virus spread—and assuming it was as virulent and deadly as TZ-4, then they faced a disaster that would make the tragedies back home seem like an easygoing pre-game warm-up.

Barbie threw his arms around her shoulders and pressed his face to hers. "Just an hour, baby-cheeks, then you can come back to this crummy room."

"Nothing crummy about this room."

Barbie laughed. "Rooms are only good with company. And I don't mean best friends." He winked at her. "Maybe we can convince that hot number Arm to come along."

"He's not gay, Barbie."

"For you, hot stuff, not me. Come, on, honey, he's a hunky, hung dude. Those baggy jeans can't hide his assets."

"Caff was trying to fix me up with Bane. Now you're trying to hitch me to Arm. What's up with that?"

"Bane, Arm, what's the difference? You need to get sexed, sweetie."

She laughed in spite of herself. He was right about the lunch, not the sex, and she was sure BB wouldn't get back to her at least until tomorrow. "Okay, okay. Lunch. Just lunch, right? No devious bedroom maneuvering."

"Right." He sounded unenthusiastic.

Thoughts of a fresh loaf of bread, a couple bottles of Sangrantino and a light pasta with aioli made her salivate.

Nam and Arm objected to "a stroll" around the city, but fell in step beside them as they wandered through the crowds on the glittering Mercerie. The throngs on the street reminded her of her last visit to Venice with ex-husband Devon, but with a significant difference. Many among the street horde wore breather masks, the cheap disposable kind, given out at clinics or sold by the box at pharmacies. Ada felt an odd twinge of anxiety. It was scary not to be able to see expressions, to see only a set of eyes over a starkly white filter held in place by four white elastics, overtop the tourists' colorful t-shirts and shorts. Did they take off their masks for family photos? Ada felt suddenly naked without hers. She had been inoculated with the Braxis vaccine, but now, it seemed, the vaccine might offer little protection, assuming her theory on the second virus held up.

She sighed. She couldn't even enjoy a stroll in the winding blind walkways of Venice without stressing over the virus. Fear ruled, even in the streets of the old Serene Republic. She wasn't the only one with fears. Nam grumbled constantly as they walked: "Not the best idea, no. Too crowded. Too many masks. Not good, no." But she followed along, watchful and disapproving. "I did your I-Ching, Ada Kenner. Not good. Not good at all, no."

"Isn't that jacket too hot?" Ada asked. Both Nam and Arm wore jackets, hiding holstered guns.

"For true, Doctor, for true."

They continued to wind through the crowds in the medieval markets, and Ada felt a little over-protected. Bane had insisted both Nam and Arm guard her and none of her objections made a difference. Ada felt smothered.

Finally the crowds thinned after they crossed the bridge to Dorsoduro, her favorite area. It was genuine Venice, away from the tourist attractions and crowded markets. They reached the Rio Di Ca' Foscari, then walked along the canal admiring the old houses that leaned over the waters. "There's my café." It was just how she remembered it, tables pushed right out to the canal-side, busy but not jammed with tourists. They waited ten minutes for a table, her stomach grumbling at the wonderful aromas of olive oil and garlic.

Arm pulled out the chair for her and she sat, aware of Barbie's elaborate winks at her, and his expression that said: He's got your number, sweetie.

Ada spoke fluent Italian and ordered for all of them. The sun was hot and pleasant, the canals didn't reek as they had on her last trip, and the wine was sublime: sumptuous with the faint aroma of violet, and a bouquet reminiscent of blackberries. Arm and Nam were alert, eyes moving in every direction, but at least Arm laughed at her tired jokes, and she noticed he often appraised her with his green marble eyes. Were they colored contact lenses? She had never seen such green eyes, especially in a man with such dark, luscious skin.

"Not liking this place," Nam said, drinking espresso instead of wine, her hand never far from her gun. "Too open."

An hour stretched to three and Ada sank into a rare relaxed moment as Barbie cruised guys, Nam scowled and watched, and Arm smiled at her and told her all about New Orleans and how his family survived the hurricane. Three bottles of wine and a round of *gelati* later and Ada realized she really had to get back to work. She felt guilty, even though this was her first three-hour break in weeks of twenty-two hour days. The wine made her sleepy.

Her satellite phone woke her up. She saw the Fort Detrick ID and answered, "Hi BB."

"How's Venice, A.K.?" BB said. "Bet you're working hard."

Ada felt a stab of guilt. BB slaved over his microscope in a hot containment suit while she sat watching gondolas drift by and sipping wine. "What have you found, BB?"

"You were right. The second virus is not a mutate. It's too precisely differentiated."

Ada felt the weight of the epidemic coming back. "And responsive?"

"No." He sounded nervous. "The vaccine has no effect in straight lab work on this virus."

Ada said nothing for a long time, listening to the happy chatter of tourists around her. Would they be so happy if they knew there was the chance of a terrible worldwide pandemic? "Have you notified Health? And the CDC?"

"Yes to both."

"And?"

"And they're going to study it."

"Bureaucrats."

"You were one yourself once."

"Never." He laughed. "Thanks, BB. Keep me informed. Send your analysis and raw data to my email, okay?"

"Yup. Already done."

Ada terminated the call. "Back to work," she told her friends.

"Maybe," Nam said. "Maybe not. I think we have company now."

Ada glanced behind her. Two Asian couples had arrived at the café. They looked like typical tourists, with digital cameras around their necks, touristy t-shirts, laughing and chatting behind their masks. The only odd thing seemed to be that they wore light jackets over their t-shirts. "Tourists?"

"Pretend to be Japanese tourists," Nam said, frowning, her hand creeping down to her holstered Glock, hidden under her own jacket.

"Why pretending?"

"Speaking Japanese, but with accent."

Ada listened. It sounded Japanese to her.

"And tourists from Japan, they do not act like that except in bad American movies."

Ada shrugged. Nam was being overly alert. "So they're speaking Japanese. Maybe two of them are Japanese and the other two are trying to speak their language."

"No. They are all Korean."

Ada stared at the couples, trying not to appear obvious. "How do you know?"

"I know. I was stationed in North Korea for three years."

"Still ..." Ada trailed off as she realized one of the tourists was staring back at her and his furrowed forehead made it clear he was not smiling under his mask. Had she stared too long and made the man angry?

"Not tourists. They try too hard to look like tourists." Nam shifted in her chair.

"And four more," Arm said, his eyes darting left.

Two more couples took a table by the entrance. Even to her untrained eye, they were conspicuously staring, although they could have been staring at Barbie, an odd sight in his full black biker's leather, at least on a hot late October day in Venice.

"By the bridge. Two more." Nam scowled with an I-told-you-so intensity.

The two at the bridge were kissing. "They're tourists for sure," Ada said, certain Nam was just paranoid.

"No. Who kisses like that, hey?" Nam flipped the safety loop on her holster and shifted her big automatic weapon.

"You're a Buddhist, remember?" Ada patted the table. "No killing, right?"

"Defense okay, hey?" Nam was serious.

Ada found herself staring at the couple on the bridge. It was true, there was no passion in the kiss. This passive a kiss would be normal, say, for a long married couple comfortable in their relationship, but they were playing at newlyweds. Nam was very alert.

"So what do we do?" Ada didn't challenge Nam or Arm's professionalism, and she didn't take the time to wonder who these strange people were. She felt suddenly naked and stupid.

"They just look like tourists to me," Barbie said. "Let me go see." He bounded from his chair and glided with youthful athleticism to the table with the Japanese-Korean faux tourists. "Can you take a picture of me with my girlfriend?" he said loudly, his voice sounding strangely butch-straight.

The "tourists" stopped chatting, looked confused, then one smiled, and said "Sure, sure, sure. I do it."

Arm shifted, pulling his long legs up and under him, his relaxed demeanor sliding slowly into an alert stiffness.

Nam slid to the edge of her seat.

Barbie led the "Japanese" man back to their table. "This here's Jiro, honey," and he slipped beside Nam. "Nam, babe, let's have our picture, okay?"

Nam nodded, smiling with sudden brilliance. The expression startled Ada. She hadn't seen Nam smile for quite some time, and it transformed her from harsh tomboy to a cute girl in a flash. She sprang up lightly and allowed Barbie to put his arm around her. Ada thought they did look like a couple, although he was a gay man and she was apparently a gay woman.

Ada glanced over her shoulder. The other three "tourists" were half out of their seats, as if ready for action.

"Where's our camera, Ada?" Barbie said.

Ada tried to force a smile. She couldn't play these games. Barbie, on the other hand, was a natural. She fished in her Fendi bag until she found the wallet-sized digital camera.

It was Nam who snatched the camera from Ada. "Thank you."

Ada felt confused in the moment. Everything around her seemed alien and slow. She heard the sluice of water as a gondola slid under the bridge. A waiter served flat bread slathered in oil and basil to a pair of chubby Americans at the table next to them. The couple on the bridge continued to kiss, but with their faces conspicuously turned towards the café.

Nam leaned forward. "The camera," she said, holding out her hand with the camera. As the tourist reached out for the camera, Nam's hand flashed like a striking serpent, catching the man hard on his Adam's apple. Nam spun around and caught the man hard with her knee. She reached under his jacket and pulled out a gun—with a silencer.

A gun terrified Ada, but that silencer changed everything. Nam's suspicions had been correct.

Arm leaned forward, caught Ada by the elbow, and said, "Move, my love!"

Ada felt herself lifted from the chair, but she pushed with her own legs, the paralysis leaving her, and Arm folded his big body in front of her, shielding her from the two on the bridge. Ada saw them move now, breaking their kiss, guns coming out, also with silencers.

She heard the 'pphhtt, phtt!" of gunshots, and the empty bottle of Sangrantino exploded on their table.

Venice, Italy

Panji managed a smile for contestant three hundred and eighty-three. Though these were the semi-finals, he sang sharp, and his voice reverberated annoyingly off the magnificent frescoed ceiling of the Sala del Maggior Consiglio in the Doge's palace, yet for some reason his enthusiasm charmed her. He sang with more spirit than any before him, bold in front of the cameras, his pockmarked face lighting up with real joy. Unfortunately, this kid's voice made her want to put her hands over her ears. The audience politely applauded.

After only a few sessions as a judge, Panji found it impossible to concentrate. She kept thinking about the epidemic back in North America. What really scared her was that the virus had jumped to England according to the latest news.

In lighter moments, when she tried to forget the plague, she daydreamed about Kenji, remembering their first day in Venice as they floated down the Grand Canal in a gondola, tacky but nice. Sometimes, she pondered her new friendship with Ada and the mysterious Nam. In dark moments, she had nightmares about the masked assassin who had nearly killed them all. The only thing she was not able to focus on was the budding stardom of contestants on *Superstar*.

It wasn't so much the show, or even Abbey Chase. In some ways the producer was a wonder. Who else could have obtained permission to shoot the semi-finals in grand style in the Doge's palace, disrupting and adding to tourism at the same time? She even had the Prigione Nuove, the Doge's old prison, closed down; it served both as a set for the show and a private entrance, away from the fans.

The Great Council Hall was a magnificent coup for Abbey. Nearly three thousand tourists crowded the seats on the vast floor of the council chamber that had once hosted grand balls for the Doge of Venice and visiting royalty. The *Superstar* stage was set up against the incredible backdrop of Tintoretto's Paradise, one of the largest paintings in the world.

Who else but Abbey could have pooh-poohed Alban Bane's stern recommendations to various governments that the *Superstar* tour be cancelled or postponed? Who else could turn a trivial and overdone idea—making ordinary kids prospective stars—into the highest rated show on television? But the price for her genius was a caustic personality and total lack of regard for feelings.

The prospect of four months of *Superstar* semi-finals loomed dark enough in Panji's busy life, but her constant companion now was fear. She wasn't afraid for herself—Ada had insisted she take the vaccine, and she had already been exposed to Kenji—but she felt a terrible certainty that they had brought this virus to Europe. Was anyone infected on this tour? Every sneeze made her wince. All of the crew wore face masks. Only the cast—and Kenji, the host—didn't wear protective masks. They passed out masks at the door as the audience entered, next to signs in English and Italian that said: Protective masks must be worn. Officials had insisted. In spite of the atmosphere of fear, Panji had to acknowledge Abbey Chase's skills because all of the three thousand seats were filled with eager people—every day of the semi-finals. An American reality show had become a tourist attraction in Venice. An Abbey coup.

Abbey Chase stared at her now, her toe tapping the ancient floor. The format required that Panji comment first on the kid's performance. "That was very creative," Panji said, at last. "A fun song."

As expected, Abbey Chase interrupted. "Fun? It was torture. You're the worst we've heard since New York." Some in the audience cheered Abbey's insult. It was all part of the fun of the show.

Through the exhaustion, Panji managed to rise to his defense. "No, you just need some practice. Don't give up."

"You go, Panji," a tourist in the audience shouted.

Abbey laughed, a harsh sound, and the kid winced as if she had struck him hard in the face. "Give up. Trust me. You won't have a career as either actor or singer. Garraty?"

The third judge, record producer Garraty, had long ago fallen into a hazy agree-with-Abbey routine and was dozing. He nodded. "Yo, yo dude. That wasn't right for me, man."

Unlike a hundred others, this kid didn't turn and run from the room. He stepped closer to the judges' table, his buck teeth fixed in an endearing smile. "Can I try again?"

"No," Abbey snapped.

"What was wrong with my performance?" He spoke in perfect accented English.

"Out of tune. Forgotten lyrics. Spastic dance routine. Forget it."

The audience was hushed, waiting to see what would happen. The boy still didn't move. "I will try again."

"You're embarrassing yourself," Abbey said.

Always supportive, Kenji crossed the stage. "A round of applause for Fausto Bolino." He put his arm around the bucktoothed kid. He patted his shoulders and led him towards the stage entrance, the door to the left of the Tintoretto masterpiece.

The audience came alive as Kenji returned to center stage.

"I want your baby," a girl near the back shouted, loud enough to be heard.

"Kenji's the superstar!" another girl screeched.

Kenji held up his hands. He launched into a prepared wrap up, inviting the audience to join the winning and losing auditioners in the courtyard. With a smile, and a wave, he finished the day of Panji-hell.

Panji fought her way through the crowds on the Colonnade, signing occasional autographs, then pushed her way down the Giants' Staircase, between the towering statues of Mars and Neptune, and finally caught up to Kenji in the courtyard. Young girls swarmed poor Kenji.

"We must go back inside," Kenji said, smiling. He had a peculiar way of politely pushing through the grabby crowd without jostling or hurting. "We can not go out in the Piazza!"

A small crowd of screamers, handful of paparazzi, and two Real TV cameras followed them back up the Giants' Staircase.

At the top of the stairs, one fan threw herself at Kenji, knocking him back. She tripped and fell into Panji, knocking her to her knees.

The fan's face mask had slipped off her face. Her face loomed over Panji's, inches away for a moment, her nose running snot.

She coughed.

Spittle struck Panji's face.

70

Rio Di Ca' Foscari, Venice

The Korean couple crouched behind their toppled table as patrons screamed and ran from the café. All of the Koreans carried large silenced pistols.

Big Arm pulled Ada hard towards another table. He fired, three sharp cracks that echoed on the palazzo walls. One of the four "American" tourist-assassins fell, the gun clattering from his hand.

Ada had no weapon, but instinctively grabbed a sun umbrella, yanked it from its stand and swung around. One of the assassins aimed his long silencer-equipped pistol at Arm.

"Arm!" Ada shouted.

Without thinking, she lunged forward with her umbrella, thrusting with it like a javelin. The assassin's gun fired at the same moment the umbrella hit him, and the bullet flew wide, sending shards of stone flying.

"Thanks, sistah!" Arm said as he shot three more times in succession. Two more assailants fell.

"More coming, now!" Nam shouted.

Ada felt a light wind and a paving stone cracked into two pieces ten feet from her. The new shooter was at the windows above them.

Nam rolled across the stone, firing at the window.

Ada heard a shriek as Nam's bullet struck home, but there were two more at the windows in his place.

They were pinned between crossfire from the bridge and the window marksmen.

"Only one way to go!" Arm backed her to the pavement's edge and without hesitation threw Ada into the canal.

Ada shouted out as she splashed in the murky canal water alongside two tied gondolas. The smell of stagnant water hit her a moment after the shock of the cold.

Above her, patrons screamed as they ran for their lives amid the spit-spit of silenced guns and the louder roar of Nam and Arm shooting back.

One of the Koreans stood at the canal's edge and looked down at her. He aimed his gun.

Barbie tackled the shooter from behind, knocking him into the canal. Barbie and the Korean both landed near Ada with loud splashes, Barbie on top. With no hesitation, Barbie pressed his advantage and held the attacker's head under water. The man's hands flailed as he tried to knock Barbie off him.

Ada swam to Barbie. Her friend's face, normally calm or smiling or full of good humor, was a mask of loathing. She tried to pull him off the assassin, but the Korean's hands went slack.

Barbie pushed the assailant out into the canal. The body floated for a moment, rolled over, and revealed a face frozen in a moment of anguish.

Barbie pulled her. "Swim. Swim, damnit, swim!"

"Arm and Nam!"

"They can look after—"

Shots splashed all around them. He flinched and his leather tunic tore away as if by invisible fingers. A plume of blood shot from a graze on his shoulder.

"Come on!" He dove beneath the waters.

Without hesitation, she swam deep into the foul canal.

71

Caffé Santa Margherita, Venice

Nam wanted to dive into the canal after Ada, knew her duty required it, emotionally she felt driven to it, but her partner Arm was pinned down.

She found cover under the stone bridge but it meant she had no clear shot at the two attackers on the bridge. She saw Arm's shirt in shreds and knew he had been hit. His Kevlar vest had stopped the bullet, but now the attackers knew where not to aim. She fired in full automatic mode on her Glock 18, chanting silently an old Tibetan mantra of forgiveness. Shooting came easy, killing did not, but there was no hesitation when her friends' lives were the stake. She tagged two of the Koreans and one of the Americans, relieving some of the crossfire on Arm, but now there were more men, all with guns, running from both directions up the paved sides of canal Foscari. She dropped a clip and slid in a new nine millimeter by eighteen magazine and continued firing until her Glock grew hot.

She saw Ada and Barbarino come up for air, then dive again as bullets splashed around them.

It had to be the two on the bridge! Her priority was to take them out.

Nam took a long breath, then flung herself outward and into a roll. She spun on the paving, her left shoulder taking the worst of her landing, and came around firing up at the two on the bridge.

Both fell into the canal.

But now the snipers in the palazzo windows had her. She felt a light burn on her bicep as a bullet creased her, a shock like electricity in her good shooting arm. With a howl of rage she came around, shooting again, blindly this time in a spray of fully automatic fire. The acrid sting of exploding barrel gasses brought her to life, the incense of gunfire that made her feel alive.

"Arm, down!" Nam was the better shot, and faster than Big Arm, so she swung hard to her right, came up to one knee, cradled carefully with two hands, and aimed for the muzzle fire in the upper window. Arm dove flat to the stones as she fired.

A woman crashed through the shutters, rifle clutched like a crutch as she fell to the paving stones below. Nam heard the crack of bones but no scream.

Nam and Arm swung into a back-to-back position. Arm felt like a wall behind her. All of the would-be assassins seemed to be down.

"Where's Ada?" Arm asked.

"Swimming towards grand canal!" Nam answered.

They both turned as a Venetian water taxi gunned its engine. Three men, all with guns, pursued Ada and Barbie up the canal.

There was no need for words—or thought. Nam sprinted, trusting Arm to cover her back, ran up the arch of the bridge, vaulted hard, touched the stone railing with a hand and pivoted through the air, landing hard in the back of the water taxi.

She slammed into the feet of one of the men, a numbing bolt of energy paralyzing her left side as nerves registered the shock, her gun flying loose and clattering into the bow of the old wooden boat.

Nam lay there for a moment, trying to breathe. The men were as shocked as she was and didn't move at once. They seemed Italian, olive-skinned, swarthy and muscular. One brought a big semi-automatic down, aiming at Nam's head. Nam spun hard, her foot catching the bottom of a wooden bench seat, but she yanked it back, rolled, and brought down the man with the gun with a scissor grab of both legs.

Behind her, she heard more shots. She could only spare a quick look, and saw Arm under siege again, all alone and without backup. But he had found cover under the bridge and fired rapidly. Both of them knew Ada was the most important asset and that they were expected to die to protect her.

Nam focused on her own situation. No one moved in the boat. Their guns were aimed at head and heart. She didn't move. The third man drove the boat.

"There's the doctor!" the man shouted in Italian.

"Run her down," snapped the man with the gun aimed at Nam's head.

Nam knew that she had seconds. Her own life was meaningless. Bane had told them Ada was all that mattered. No sacrifice was too great. Ada was the key.

Nam hoped it was true, because she was about to die.

72

Rio Di Ca' Foscari, Venice

Arm had only two clips left. He couldn't help Nam beyond keeping the remaining assailants busy. He tried twice to move from his shelter, only to be forced back into the damp shadows under the arched bridge by a welter of fire. His shoulder burned from the graze.

He was too big to crouch for long in the small v-crease where bridge met roadway and his big feet kept slipping on the slime on the half submerged ledge. He tried to slip out the other side, but they had him pinned from both directions.

He checked his load.

It was time to roll the dice. He doubted he was fast enough, or lucky enough, to escape a wound or two, but he could hope to survive long enough to take down the remaining four gunmen. He thought about slipping into the water, but he'd likely drown with his clumsy swimming skills, and he'd have to take off his Kevlar vest to swim. It came down to luck.

He steadied his breathing and concentrated on re-energizing cramped muscles.

It was eerily silent. Everyone was saving loads, no one firing. He heard only the whimper of one of the café guests, still cowering near one of the tables.

The next few moments would decide if this was a shit-I'm-dead kind of situation or a thank-God-and-all-the-saints sort of day.

Arm said one Hail Mary, and dove out of his cover.

He spun on his toes, both arms coming up with his Glock in a steady grip.

Then the fallen tables of the café exploded in a barrage of fire. He felt the wind knocked from him as high caliber bullets hit his Kevlar vest again, burrowing deep enough to leave welts.

Arm continued to mouth a Hail Mary and fired back at a full run, emptying a clip before he made it over the bridge. Then, a bullet tore through his left bicep. He spun around with its force, not feeling the burn of pain as he fired back. Only when his own blood splashed back into his eyes, he understood he had a bleeder.

73

Prigione Nuove, Venice

Panji followed Kenji up the worn stairs of the bridge of sighs, her enthusiasm for their escape from the fans gone as she realized that their escape took them through the old prison of the Serene Republic. This place gave her the creeps.

In ancient times, the Bridge of Sighs had been a famous one-way trip: you entered the Prigione Nuove after your torture and trial, but you didn't ever leave except sewn into a burial sack. One last look out the window on the bridge at the Grand Canal, a sigh, and you went to your tiny hellhole prison cell never to return.

Panji halted. The dank air of the old prison bridge freaked her out. She felt the death and suffering all around her: the screams of the abused tunneled through history, haunting the present. She could no more enter the dungeons of Venice than she could step barefoot in human scat.

She stopped. Kenji didn't press her. He probably felt her reluctance; he was very sensitive that way.

Panji stared into the shadows, felt a shiver, pulled back.

"We can go back. Wait for the crowds to leave." Kenji put his arm around her, making her feel warm and secure.

She stared up the haunting stairs to the Bridge of Sighs. Whenever she traveled, she never visited places known for death, torture or injustice; in San Francisco she refused to ferry over to Alcatraz; during a visit to the Vatican she left the bus tour at the notorious Castel Sant'Angelo; on a tour of London she loitered on the Thames while her friends visited the Tower of London. She found nothing fascinating or educational in such places. Her ex-husband had once taken her into the mountains of Albi to visit the burning fields at the memorial of the massacre of Montségur. "Your hero is the Lady Esclarmonde," he had insisted, and because the Dame d'Esclarmonde was a personal hero, he convinced her, but she hadn't slept for a week afterwards, tormented by too-real visions of the faces of the dying, women and men thrown into a pit by the hundreds to die in flames for nothing more than "heretical" Christian beliefs. Panji could feel the ghosts of past abuse.

She slipped hard against Kenji's body, shivering. He put his arm around her. "Are you all right?"

She nodded. "I'm not a flake, Kenji," she said as they climbed steps so worn by the dead and dying, and tourists, that the old stone bowed down. "Well, all right I'm a flake. But I hate places like this."

He kissed her cheek. "I feel it too. A place of despair."

She felt a hotness in her face, turned, saw his big smile, and impulsively leaned forward. Their lips met. She closed her eyes to the ghosts around her and felt only him, his hard body against hers, the warmth of his full lips, the taste of his salty tongue. She flew to another place. He turned her now, and their bodies met in a gentle tangle, his hands stroking her hair. She lost herself in Kenji, in his heat and his strength.

"Nice," said a voice.

Panji pulled away from Kenji's long kiss. A fan had followed them, or worse, a paparazzo. Pictures of their kiss would be all over the papers and news.

"I've always liked this place," said the voice.

Panji went rigid.

"Run!" said Kenji, and he pushed her behind him.

Panji stared up the stairs. The low archway at the top was entirely blocked by the hulking figure of her angel of fear, shrouded in shadows by a black robe, but floating in the dark, the terrifying golden mask.

74

Rio Di Ca' Foscari, Venice

Ada and Barbie hid behind the slick lacquered sides of a moored gondola, wrapped in the long shadow of the hull and the smells of sewage and silt, as they clung to the ornate mooring posts. The water was filmy, layered with the oily discharge of motor launches, and they were cold.

The gunshots were close. She wanted to slip out of the canal and run back to help her friends. Or find the police. Or do anything but hide.

A motor launch roared by, throwing the gondola against them in the rising swell of its wake, and she swallowed more sour water. Ada grabbed the mooring line and pulled herself around the sweeping stern of the gondola.

The water taxi moved erratically, slamming against first one side of the canal, then the other, running into a wooden motorboat moored in front of the door of someone's residence. Then she saw why. Nam struggled with the driver. As she held the man pinned to the wheel, her feet flashed out and kicked another man with a gun. More shots echoed off the three-storey palazzos along the canal.

"Nam!"

Barbie's hand clamped over her mouth.

The boat was well past them, roaring down the canal towards the Grand Canal.

"We have to help them!"

"We need police!" Barbie struggled with his leather shirt, pulling it over his head.

Ada used the side of the gondola to pull herself higher. She peered over the stone curbing. The café was around the bend, out of sight. She heard no more shots.

In the other direction, the water taxi ran out into the Grand Canal, Nam still struggling with three men. The taxi rammed the side of a gondola full of passengers, and they heard screams and shouts of anger, then a single gunshot.

"Let's get out of the water!"

She pulled herself up by the gondola's ornate rowlock, and the sleek black boat rolled towards them, its gunwales awash in canal water. She managed to get one leg, then the other onto a ledge just below the water level, then helped Barbie.

They remained crouched behind the cluster of mooring posts and the tall raking ferro of the gondola's prow.

It seemed they were alone.

The water taxi with Nam had drifted out of sight behind a row of palazzos. Which way should they go? Right, to help Nam, or left, to help Arm? Or to get the police?

"Why are these people shooting at us?" Barbie asked as he threw his leather shirt to the stone.

"I don't know." And she didn't. Why were so many people trying so hard to kill her? Because it was clear that they were targeting her. What did she know? Were they afraid of what she knew about the second virus? Or was this about Domergue and Braxis and his threat? "Let's get back to the café."

"We're not armed, sweetie."

"No, we're not. But Arm's my friend."

Barbie wrapped his arm around her. "It's dangerous to be your friend, baby." But he kissed her lightly on the cheek. "Let's go rescue hunky dude."

As they ran along the narrow ledge in front of private canal-side homes, she prayed Nam would be all right.

75

Gulf of Aden

The smoke whipped clear of the scudding waves over the gulf of Aden, swept away by a high north wind. *Flying Cloud*'s big fifty millimeter deck cannon fired again, but the only sign of damage on the *Hanu* was the charred scar and two jagged holes.

Criscione's Seahawk helicopter darted in and out like an angry hawk, spraying *Hanu* with .50 caliber gunfire, but stinger missiles and standing orders from *Cloud*'s captain kept her from seriously engaging with her Hellfire missiles. "Just keep her from getting away," Pierce had told the helicopter pilot. "I don't want to fish you out of the ocean."

Or us, Bane thought as he watched helplessly. He had nothing to contribute here, beyond his firm orders, "No matter what the cost, Khan cannot reach port." Earlier, before they sighted the *Hanu*, he had asked, "Can I steer this puppy?" They stared at him like he'd lost his mind. Then he looked for a steering wheel. Where the hell was the wheel? "Okay, at least you've got to let me fire a torpedo. Or a missile?" More stares. These guys were too damned serious for Navy men. Now he kind of wished he was up there with Criscione. He was sure the young pilot would have let him fire a few rounds.

Still, it was a serious business. He joked to take their minds off his standing orders—Khan goes down, no matter what the cost. Twenty-three crew members and the helicopter pilot and gunner, plus the Navy's prized high-speed half-billion-dollar Littoral ship—all could easily be lost. Stinger missiles did not miss. *Hanu* had torpedoes. She was faster. And Khan was more dangerous than a hungry shark in bloody waters.

Bane suddenly visualized himself bobbing in the ocean, surrounded by sharks, the smoking hulk of *Cloud* sinking amid screams of dying men. Only two things in the world terrified Bane: the ocean and closed spaces. And it made Bane admire these brave men even more. They were willing to risk sinking their cramped little ship to stop a dealer in mass destruction. They knew what was at stake, they were willing to die, and that made them heroes.

Bane didn't like feeling helpless. His little five-shooter revolver and his smart mouth could contribute nothing to this. He had brought them to this, but now he had nothing to offer except orders that might mean their death.

Khan was too dangerous to let him get away again.

"She's getting away," Bane said. He leaned on the riveted sill, pressing his face to the safety glass. He felt the hard vibration of *Cloud*'s twin engines. *Hanu* was pulling away. She was dramatically faster than *Cloud*, and only the Longbow helicopter's dance with stinger missiles had slowed her down.

"I could order Criscione to deploy Hellfires," said the captain.

Bane scanned the bridge. Five officers stared back at him. He didn't want anyone dead, least of all the hotdog pilot of the Seahawk.

"Tell my buddy up there to fire everything he's got. Then you sink her, son."

Pierce didn't answer. He studied the fleeing ship through a permanently mounted binocular telescope. "Right full rudder, steer course two-three-two."

Twenty-three brave navy officers and crew was a small price to pay to save perhaps millions of lives.

76

Grand Canal, Venice

Nam fell hard against the gunwales as the water taxi rammed the gondola in the grand canal, throwing the two remaining assailants sternwards. Killing the pilot wasn't such a great idea, she decided.

Nam saw the startled look of the gondolier, his face red, fists raised as he yelled, then the man jumped into the water. The tourists screamed as the rear half of the gondola tipped up and sank instantly.

Nam flew forward with an outward crescent kick, catching one of the two remaining assailants hard on the chin. He flew from the boat to join the tourists and the gondolier in the choppy water. But the third man came up, firing.

Nam dove low, then flung herself forward onto the bow of the driverless water taxi as it lunged forward at full speed into the grand canal. The man with the gun fired one more time, then hesitated. Instead of shooting at her again, he tried to pull the dead pilot off the throttles.

Nam turned her head. She heard the shouts behind her.

She had a momentary glimpse, something tall and white, probably one of the two-tiered ferries that plied the grand canal.

She heard the crash, a loud whomp, a scream, the shriek of tourists.

77

Rio Di Ca' Foscari, Venice

Arm tumbled backwards into a café table, scattering loaves of bread and glasses of wine. A bottle of red wine shattered, staining his leg, mingling with the blood.

He lurched sideways on the stone, ignoring the searing pain in his thigh. Something struck his face hard, probably flying stone shards.

His clips were all empty. He tried for the canal, a quick dive into the dirty waters of the Foscari. A second bullet shattered his scapula, and he fell hard, three feet from the water, screaming his rage.

He heard the roar of automatic gunfire, felt the blows on his Kevlar, and multiple impacts in his thigh, calves, shoulders.

Something wet struck his face. More of his blood.

Arm coughed. Tried to roll the last three feet. If he could just tumble off. Fall into the water.

Dizziness took him now. Probably loss of blood. He felt a buzzing in his ears.

Through the ringing in his head, he heard three quick thumps. Then there was no more pain.

78

Rio Di Ca' Foscari, Venice

Ada watched Arm die. The tears came on her suddenly. Only minutes ago, Arm had been sharing a bottle of Sangrantino with them, and she had been laughing at his easy humor, listening to his harrowing tale of Hurricane Katrina, talking about his son the budding football player and his twin brother and his ex-wife. Now his son would have only a widowed mother and an uncle.

Barbie put his arm around her. There could be no doubt Arm was dead. She saw his body flinch with each bullet, but they were lifeless movements, no more than reactions to the force of the impacts. Big Arm lay in a kidney-shaped puddle of his own gore.

Big, smiling, easygoing Arm was dead.

The rage and grief rose up in Ada. It would have burst from her in a wild shriek except that Barbie's hand squeezed her shoulder, reminding her they were not safe yet.

Tourists and café patrons were dead as well. Six patrons lay in an untidy heap in the doorway to the café. They had tried to escape. A waiter had fallen across one of his tables, his hands still clenching a bottle of wine.

Where were the police? How could war break out along the canals of Venice without someone calling the police? Her own bag with its phone lay on the pavement near Arm's cooling body.

Barbie held her close, and for a moment she almost cried. They shared their grief in silence.

Then he whispered, "Babe, we must go."

But Ada didn't move from the corner of the old palazzo. She stared at the carnage, struggling with a fury that threatened to control her. How could she be strong in the face of this bloody massacre? Arm had been a living, cheerful person. She hardly knew him, but she counted him a friend: he had a son, a mother who survived Katrina, a twin brother he loved to death, a best friend Bane, and he was the nicest person she had ever met. He had saved them, saved all of them. But it cost him his happily-ever-afters.

"Ada! Please!"

Ada gained control. Tears flowed down her face. It was an alien feeling. She had not allowed herself tears since Caff's death, even through all the horror of the virus and violence. And before that, not since Quentin's birth.

She wiped away the tears. She wouldn't cry again. Not again. Not until this was all over and she could mourn fallen friends.

"Let's go. Let's get the hell out of here."

Ada and Barbie pressed back against the worn old stone of the palazzo and moved slowly back around the corner.

They were waiting there, three of them with guns, in the Campo Santo Margherita.

79

Gulf of Aden

Bane watched the Seahawk helicopter explode. At first he didn't realize what had happened. The stinger flew so fast he had time only to register the burst of smoke from the deck of the *Hanu*. Criscione's helicopter veered, blowing countermeasures and flares, but an instant later there was an orange plume, a burst of flame, a ball of smoke, then long seconds later a reverberating barhooom!

"Christ," Captain Pierce said and he stared at Bane. Your fault, sir, his eyes said.

Everything seemed to happen slowly then. The smoke cleared, blasted by a fierce wind, the carcass of the helicopter staggered, the clap and then mushrooming roar of the explosion reached them, and helicopter debris rained into the Gulf of Aden.

Bane closed his eyes for a moment and said a quick prayer for Criscione. A good young man.

Pierce snapped. "Steer oh-two-six!"

Bane felt the glares of all the bridge crew in *Cloud*'s command center. They had lost two friends. They had lost two friends because of Bane and Khan.

Screw this.

Bane stared at the *Hanu*. She was turning back to her original course and increasing speed. If she got out of range now, without the Seahawk, they'd never catch her. "It's now or never, Captain," Bane said, trying to sound cold and detached, but his voice caught with emotion. He hadn't realized how much he had cared for the hotdog pilot. "Blow her the fuck out of the water."

"Your honor, sir." Pierce pointed at a flashing red button. "Fire the torpedoes, sir."

Bane didn't hesitate. He nodded, and slammed the button with the flat of his hand. "Up your jets, Khan."

He watched the twin hunter-seekers surge from their bows, carving an instant turn in pursuit of the *Hanu*.

"Her jet propulsion is her weakness," Pierce said, watching through binoculars.

"The heat."

"Yes, sir."

They watched the torpedoes' deadly trails. The concussion when it came seemed delayed and for a moment *Hanu* roared on at high speed. Then she staggered, her stern lifted, a flash of heat, a moment later twin booms.

"She's crippled," Pierce said. "They may surrender."

"They won't," Bane said, through clenched teeth. "I know Khan. He'll fire every missle until we're sinking too. Finish it, commander."

"Sink her?"

"I'd prefer you blow them out of the water."

Pierce said nothing.

"Your silence is very eloquent, Commander," Bane said, grimly. "But I want no chance of this monster escaping."

They watched the listing ship. It was clear she was already going down. *Hanu*'s crew launched lifeboats and some men jumped into the water.

"Are you sure, sir?"

Bane stared at the flashing red button on fire control. Finally, he said, "Naw. Saw it in a John Wayne movie. Prepare for survivors, Captain."

Pierce smiled for the first time.

80

Prigione Nuove, Venice

Panji and Kenji ran down the stairs. Kenji held her hand hard, refusing to let go.

Behind them came the clop, clop, clop of booted feet on the old prison stone.

The prison was deserted, closed to the public at the request of Abbey Chase with her damnable influence. The old *stanza di tortura,* the torture chamber, was a set for *Superstar,* but there would be no crews there now. The gloom was illuminated by the occasional hot circle of sunlight from low arched windows—windows that could not open.

They turned at another stairway, wide enough for one person, the steps worn into dips from the trudging steps of prisoners across centuries. She could feel them everywhere, the ghosts of those imprisoned souls, in the chill of the dank air, in the screams she heard in her head, in the graffiti scrawled on the walls.

"We're going too deep," she whispered.

The assassin herded them, like a dark shepherd. They were below the canal level. The stones wept moisture and they slid on the slippery stone. The smell of death was all around them. She could taste the decay of centuries of dying on her tongue.

Dead end.

They had escaped to a wet lower cellar, well below the waterline, the lowest of basements, where the public was never allowed to come.

Clop, clop, clop. The relentless boots of the angel of death.

Kenji moved in front of her, facing their only escape. A spear of light tumbled down the one-way staircase. He held her hand.

Panji saw first the boots, then the tight form-fitting black pants, monster legs and tree-trunk thighs, then the hands, fists the size of a baby's head, and an expansive chest. Finally the golden mask, the leering, smiling, too-beautiful mask.

"There you are," the voice said.

Panji ignored the creature. She squeezed Kenji's hand, moved beside him, looked into her Kenji's face. "I love you."

He smiled, leaned forward and kissed her lightly. "I love you."

"How delightful. How touching," said the angel.

The boots stepped down to the slick basement stone.

And Kenji attacked. He pushed Panji back, spun into a low whirl which lifted like a tornado. His heels caught the assassin hard on the face, and the creature stumbled back.

The mask flew away, shattering into three pieces on the steps.

Kenji was a blur, dancing around the giant, his fists pummeling. He stomped hard on the assassin's instep.

The man stepped back into the long finger of diffuse light.

Panji saw his face.

She stiffened. She had perhaps expected some tormented, twisted wreck of flesh. But the features were a near clone of the mask, beautiful, smiling, intense. But—but there was something else. Something familiar. She knew that face.

"Do you like my beautiful face?" the assassin asked.

Then he was on Kenji. Kenji flew back hard into a low stone arch that swept up from the wet floor.

Panji looked around for a weapon. Her hands were nothing but insect-like nuisances to the giant. She needed something. Anything.

As Kenji deflected hard off the arch, a wedge of centuries-old stone fell away. Kenji fell with a grunt to the floor, his cheek landing in a slimy puddle.

Panji ran to him, ignoring the hulking beast that stood over them.

The killer batted her aside as if she were a buzzing mosquito, but as she tumbled away she grabbed the wedge of stone Kenji's feet had knocked loose.

As the killer leaned over him, Kenji rolled over, spun on his back like a child's top, his legs reaching out like a vise. The giant swayed for a moment, like a tree in an insignificant wind, but Kenji kept turning, bending his body.

The tree toppled. The killer fell first to his knees.

Panji ran up behind him. On his knees, the assassin was her height now.

She swung the rock with all her strength.

It made a wet, sickening thunk.

"Oh." The killer grunted, swayed forward again.

She struck a second time, turning the sharp wedge.

This time it struck with a sickening crack, like stone breaking.

The old stone flagging from the dungeon broke into two more pieces. But the assassin fell forward, his nose grazing a stone footing, his face scraping as he slid floorwards, leaving a dark smear.

The monster bled. He was human after all.

Kenji caught Panji from behind, pulling her close. She felt his heat. Felt his face on her face. He kissed her all over her cheeks, her chin, her nose, distracting her from the carnage she had wrought.

"Come. Let us get out of here."

He kissed her again.

"That hurt," said a voice behind them.

The monster sat up, his face a mask of blood. One of his perfect teeth was gone.

Slowly he stood up, appearing to be only a little bruised.

Kenji bent his knees, ready to leap again into action.

But the killer shrugged. His big hand reached into the fanny belt on his waist and he pulled out a gun.

"Enough play for today," the killer said, and he laughed.

He pulled the trigger. Panji heard a light hiss of air and a bitter gassy smell. Kenji's hand flew to his neck. He sagged to his knees, his eyes wide open in surprise.

81

Site P, Paris

Doctor Gilbert Domergue handled the emergency board meeting from the conference room two levels down into the limestone bedrock of Site P, Braxis's primary facility. The Paris facility employed nearly four thousand in various manufacturing facilities above ground, but the secretive underground research facility was home to only three hundred of the elite researchers.

He was alone in the room. He never attended board meetings in person, except the annual meeting, and relied instead on elaborate secure conferencing. He preferred the Site P conference room, with its elaborate setup of twelve sixty-inch monitors, each with camera links to the other board members. Their chairwoman was in Rome, the other board members scattered from Japan to America—a who's who of world corporate executives, most of them CEOs of their own companies.

As always, he allowed just a hint of arrogance into his summary. "Finally, ladies and gentlemen, sixty-two countries have placed substantial orders for the vaccine," he said in English, the language of their company's international board. "Analysts have moved our rating to 'outperform' and our stock has trebled since last month. We are all very rich, gentlemen and ladies."

Their chairwoman, Nicia Napoli, CEO of the wildly successful Napoli Cosmetics, was not so easily mollified. "I am concerned, Docteur Domergue, about several things," she said, not smiling, her voice halting though her English was excellent. "Six class action lawsuits have already been launched in various states."

"Inconsequential," Domergue said, offering his best political smile. "We will settle, only because of the Begley incident, but it will cost us barely one billion American. We have already realized orders close to one point one billion doses. Ninety dollars for American orders per dose, nine hundred elsewhere. Basically ..." He paused, allowing a moment of drama. "Basically, a trillion dollars. With a *t*, gentlemen and ladies." More money than the economies of many countries of the world, and nearly all of it profit.

There was a moment of stunned silence. Even Napoli was taken aback by the number, he could see it on her elegant, aging face. "But Docteur, if we set a precedent, if we settle, we might realize further, ah, further lawsuits, yes?" But even she sounded unconvinced. If they lost a hundred billion in lawsuits, it hardly impacted the profits.

Domergue nodded, pausing long enough that he didn't look as if he hadn't planned his response. "Nicki, I assure you we've accounted for all these variables. Worst case scenario, with our monopoly and patents, we realize seven hundred billion in profit." He smiled.

"And how much, Docteur, would we have realized had Begley not been so careless?" asked Director Drummond, CEO of Drummond Petroleum.

"Perhaps three billion, Iain," Domergue admitted.

"How fortuitous," Drummond said, the sarcasm evident.

"Yes. Quite so. But there we are." Domergue allowed himself a moment of triumph and lit a Cuban cigar, drawing on it as he watched their faces.

"Are you aware, Docteur, that Ernest Gies petitioned the board?"

Domergue coughed, choking in mid-draw. "Ernest? No, I was not aware of that."

Nipoli waved a sheaf of papers. "He builds a convincing case for negligence on your part."

Domergue stubbed out the cigar on the stainless steel tabletop, missing the ash tray. "On my part? What are you saying, Nicki?"

"These are copies of all your signed authorizations on Protocols two-ninety-two through four-sixty-one. Including authorization of testing on dangerous offenders."

"All properly approved by the health department and—"

"Yes, yes, Docteur, we are quite aware. Quite aware indeed. The lobbying. The bribes. Very aware."

"What are you implying, Nicki?"

"That you have been grossly negligent as CEO of Braxis. Grossly negligent."

"Nonsense!" Domergue leaned forward on the table, felt the coldness of the steel tabletop. "Everything here, everything about Braxis, is me. I have built it all."

"The good and the bad and the ugly," Napoli said. "Your favorite movie you once told me, no?"

"This is no laughing matter, Nicki." Domergue had not expected another board revolt. Now that he held only eleven percent of voting stock—a ploy that allowed him to expand, to develop facilities around the world, to compete in the trillion-dollar playground—his position as CEO was never secure. "Braxis has never performed so well, Nicki. The shareholders will not stand for an executive shakeup."

"Possibly, Docteur." She smiled, and her expression told him: we are watching you, Domergue. She was enjoying this. Damn the woman, she wanted him gone. She always had.

"Just in the last three months, our net worth has quadrupled."

"Yes, Docteur. And people around the world are sick. Hundreds of thousands have died. Some people who have taken our vaccine, they have died in rather messy fashion."

"Our disclaimers protect us!"

"Yes. Yes, they do. But the cost of litigation cannot be ignored."

"We can afford it." Domergue felt his old confidence returning. "Hollow gesturing does not impress me, Nicki."

Napoli shook the papers, purportedly from Ernest Gies. Had the scientist conned Domergue with his mild manners and kowtowing? What had Gies sent them? "We shall see how hollow the gesture is."

"Be plain, Nicki."

"I intend to move an immediate motion of incompetence."

"Pardon?"

"I intend to see you removed."

It had been a long meeting, and Domergue's weariness made him impatient. "Nicki, analysts are now predicting we will hit seven hundred and eighty per non-voting share. A ten-fold increase."

The silence was complete. What could they really say to that? They could hate him all they want, despise his arrogance and his dominance of the board, but they would make more on their Braxis stock options than they could ever make as CEOs of their own companies.

"On that note, I take my leave. I am called to an urgent meeting."

In classic Domergue-style, he disconnected the links before anyone on the board could object.

What the hell? What the fucking hell had Gies done? He would have to get that report. With Gies dead, it would be easy enough. Domergue's people were already decrypting Gies's hard drives.

Domergue paced the room. Gies knew too much, that was clear. The entire protocol had been his initiative, his project. Domergue had lobbied, secured funding, approvals, handled congress, bribed officials, wined and dined the president, used his influence with the *Decemviri*, the much vaunted Council of Ten, but ultimately it had been Gies's research, Gies's project, his brilliance. Begley and Gies. Now both were dead. Thank God.

The intercom on the table chirped. "Bonjour, Docteur Domergue," said the voice of the Site P coordinator, Yvette Rabaud. "I have an urgent call for you from Site X, sir."

"Site X?" Domergue felt his face tighten. Site X was the most secretive lab, the place where Braxis was free to experiment without governance, where unauthorized "human" trials were often conducted. Only Domergue and a handful of scientists were aware of Site X's true ungoverned purpose. Site X was a four-hundred-and-thirty-acre island off the coast of Brunei, in the South China Sea. In Braxis, no one talked about Site X. It was the wild west of pharmaceutical facilities, where no laws applied.

"Put it through, Yvette, thank you."

Monitor one dissolved to a smiling face.

Domergue stared. He felt his own control slip.

"Hello, Domergue," said the dead Doctor Gies.

82

Site X, Near Brunei

Ada stared at Ernest Gies through the shatterproof glass wall, managing barely to control a flurry of emotions. Panji held one hand. Kenji the other and they all stared at madness.

Ada—and her friends Panji, Nam, Kenji and Barbie—had been drugged, bound, hidden away in the hold of an old wooden motor launch in Venice, dragged unceremoniously on board a sleek yacht and drugged again. They had awakened on an aircraft, evident by the thrumming and vibration and the sound of engines. They were drugged a third time, and—it seemed days later—awakened in this glass menagerie. Even after they woke, they were so dopey that hours passed before they were able to put together all that had happened: Arm was dead, and they mourned him in their own ways; they had been attacked in different ways, captured, drugged, brought somewhere by someone.

And that someone was Ernest Gies, mild and easygoing ex-Harvard Professor, eminent virologist, godfather to Ada's son Quentin.

Ada prided herself on control, on never showing her emotions, but her untarnished armor threatened to crumble with this latest revelation. She had suspected Gies wasn't dead from the mysterious report of his "missing body." She had even known he bore most of the responsibility for the world pandemic, and part of her had always known he was more involved in all of this than everyone guessed, but it still hit her hard as she stared at his grandfatherly face. Why would he do all this? Insanity seemed the only plausible explanation.

She hadn't trusted him since Site F, but she still found it hard to accept Gies as Dr. Frankenstein. Three days ago, Ada had even sent an encrypted message to Bane after she came to suspect he was alive: Doctor Gies's body disappeared. Probably alive? I highly recommend he be apprehended. A.K.

What had happened to Ernest Gies?

"So," she said, trying to sound calm, trying not to show the anxiety that was evident by the pumping of her heart, the rise of heat and sweat. "So. I was right."

"Right?" His fatherly face showed kindness.

"That you were alive."

"Yes, kiddo. I am alive. Are you happy?" His voice sounded mechanical through the two-way radio system.

"Don't give me kiddo." Ada said, controlling her anger only barely. She put aside memories of Gies the father-uncle-mentor; this man was a mass-murderer, kidnapper. "Why are we in here, Gies?"

"Doctor Gies."

"How did you manage your death? A paralyzing neurotoxin?"

He nodded, smiled. "In the correct dose. Puffer fish venom."

She frowned. "Zombie medicine." In Haiti, puffer fish venom in the right dose had been used to simulate death, to create the zombie illusion.

"That's right, kiddo."

"Don't call me that. I might have been your kiddo once, but spare me your paternal drama. If you cared, I wouldn't be in here. Wherever here is." She felt her own blush. Panji and Kenji and Barbie and Nam stared at her.

"Site X. It's an island we own, near Brunei." He smiled. "So no one knows you are here. This place—it doesn't exist."

"And this?" She rapped on the glass barrier.

"Level 4 bio containment cell."

"There's no such thing."

"There is now. We test viruses here."

She stared at the furniture bolted to the wall. "On people? You test on people?"

"Human trials, yes."

"This isn't about human trials, Gies. This is human torture."

"You don't understand, kiddo. We're going to save many people."

Ada stepped back, unable to comprehend Gies's madness. This was a man she knew, once loved. Panji put her hand on Ada's shoulder, then Kenji, then even Nam. They all stared at Gies, the madman.

"You look well, for a dead man," Ada said finally.

"But you knew I wasn't dead."

"I knew."

"How?"

"I spoke with the coroner in Vegas."

"Always the smart one, kiddo."

Her control slipped. "Doctor Kenner to you."

Gies stared at her for a long time. "Ada. Ada, you're like a daughter to me."

Ada kicked the shatterproof glass and it reverberated with a low musical hum. "Do you always lock up your daughters?"

"The naughty ones."

Ada placed both her hands on the glass, facing out and up and leaned her face close enough to fog it. "Besides, you have a son."

"Oh." He blinked several times, his face pale. "Oh. You know about Conner."

"You always told me he was dead. But that's not true, is it?"

"What do you mean?" His lip trembled.

"I mean I got curious when you started acting odd about this virus. You know, 'cure for violence' and all that rubbish. In honor of your son. Except, until recently, your son was an inmate at a Paris institution for the criminally insane."

"He's not insane!"

"It's genetic, I'm sure. The crazy gene came from Dad, no doubt."

"You are here, kiddo, because you left me no choice. I tried—you have no idea how I tried— to warn you off without hurting you."

"You hurt us plenty."

"No. Not you. The mouse was just to scare you off."

"He killed my friends!"

"Oh, let's be grown up about this, kiddo. People die. We did the minimum possible to scare you off. The problem is, you don't seem to scare."

She turned away, unable to look at Gies. "No. I scare plenty."

He sighed. "Oh Ada, you force me into this. I really, really wanted you to back down."

"That's why you got me fired. Why you tried to scare me off."

"Clever girl. As always."

"And now what, Gies? You play the mad scientist? Christ, Gies, you're a walking cliché." She gave him the universal "screw you" sign. "You'll give reputable virologists a bad name."

Another sigh. "You don't understand. I can cure violence."

"Cure violence with violence?" She showed him her fist. "I'll show you violence if you let me out."

"Not with violence, Ada. We can vaccinate against—"

She knocked on the glass with her fist. "I've heard this before. You're smarter than this, Gies. You should have known there is no cure for the madness." She smiled. "You're a living example that there's no cure."

"You don't understand." He seemed to be crying, tears abruptly launching down his cheeks. "Ada, I'm so sorry."

Gies left the outer room. The door slid closed.

Ada stared at the door. The tears came, and then her friends hugged her, all of them in one group hug. Even Nam.

"This is crazy," Panji said.

"It has been from the beginning. We've been manipulated." Ada felt tears in her eyes. "Even Bane was a puppet."

"That old man he is nutty," Nam said.

"Nutty, but brilliant, Nam."

"No one can find us here. Ever."

"I know."

Kenji spoke for the first time. "Which means we have to get out of here ourselves."

They fell silent, staring at the unbreakable glass wall between them and freedom. They had no time to mourn Arm or think about how crazy the world was, or how insane Gies was, or even if Bane could possibly find them on this hidden island. They started to plan their escape.

83

Midi, France

The helicopter disturbed the peace of Domergue's thirteenth century Abbaye du Midi. Workers in the vineyards looked up, pointing, as the armed helicopter dove towards the turreted tower. It landed on the pea gravel driveway, beside a powder blue Bentley Arnage T.

Bane waited until the blades spun down. Two large Newfoundland dogs bounded around the old stone wall of the tower, shaggy and gigantic. They barked fiercely, but their big cuddly bear faces made a lie of their growls.

Bane jumped out. The big dogs pressed close, but their bushy, upright tails wagged. He reached out his hand and one of the Newfies licked him, the tail batting faster. Sentries with automatic weapons surrounded him, but he ignored them.

"Alban Bane," said Domergue, stepping out of a shadowy archway. "Always a flair for the dramatic." He looked exhausted. His classically handsome face sagged, as if tailor's pins had been pulled out and released all the crispness from his features. "I should have you killed."

"You tried that once, Emerson." Bane grinned. "I take it my visit is not a real surprise."

If Domergue registered the use of his real name, he didn't show it, nor did he bother trying to hide his face. Emerson Bartlett, a.k.a. Doctor Gilbert Domergue, smiled, but it was a fleeting expression. "No, you're one of the men I keep a watch on."

"Likewise, buddy."

"How long have you known?"

"Since just before this mess began." He had suspected Domergue was his old nemesis Emerson Bartlett before the near-tragic flight 411. He had confirmed it in London after speaking with two Braxis shareholders and tracing a small line of credit through several blind corporations back to Boston, to an account owned by Emerson Bartlett, a.k.a. Jonathon Wingate, a.k.a. Doctor Domergue, a.k.a. serial killer, maniac, psycho, father of mass murderer Tyler Hayden and the murderous giants Sampson and Austin, the Twins.

"I see. And you did not try to arrest me, why?"

"It is easier to watch you this way. If I tried to extradite you, you'd go into hiding."

"Ah. But a real cowboy would ride in and challenge me to a—how it it called—a shoot-out?"

"Too good for you. You thrive on your reputation. I want the world to know how ugly you are. I want the world to see you as you really are—one big lump of nasty, stinking shit that your Mama wiped off her ass and tried to flush."

"How terribly rude of you, Alban."

"Chicks dig insensitive macho types."

Bartlett's sudden tight lips conveyed danger. "So why are you not reaching for your trusty revolver, Inspector?"

"Later. Right now, we have a world to save."

"Oh dear. Such melodrama."

Bane smiled. "Although I am tempted to take a moment to blow out your knee caps." He held up his shortened fingers, memories of his past games with the psychopath Emerson Bartlett.

"Oh, fabulously histrionic. You know you would make a wonderful Mafioso."

"Yes, wrong job. They would have called me Al the Knee-Capper. Or Bane the Basher."

"Yes, that suits you fine."

"Just so you know, I'm still going to kill you. Rather painfully, even by your standards."

"Oh, now, my dear boy, let us not get corny. What is it you need from me, old friend?"

"A scream, some suffering, maybe a little pleading for mercy."

"Later, correct? We don't have the luxury or our little games, yes?" He gestured towards a path. "Walk with me? It's more private." He held his hand up to his sentries, indicating they stay behind.

Bane fell into step beside Bartlett, and the two enthusiastic Newfs padded alongside. Somehow he managed to resist the urge to pound Bartlett's head into the nearest elegant garden statue. He needed the bastard. It took all of his control to keep his hands in his pockets, away from his revolver. Just a quick shot or two to the foot, or the thigh, something for Emerson to remember. But there was no time.

"I have a company to save. You have a world."

"Yes, I understand you're fighting your own battles."

Bartlett's stride didn't falter. He walked on for a long moment, winding down the path towards the vineyards, under a grove of olive trees. "Yes. Yes, I'm no longer CEO of Braxis. Gies exposed my fraud, it seems." He shrugged. "Between my identity issues, the question of my original capital, and your recent blunders, they decided to remove me. No matter. I have a solid power base."

Bane felt no satisfaction at the news. "I hear Sampson's dead," he said, watching Bartlett's reaction. "Ordinarily, condolences would be in order. Under the circumstances, the world's a better place without him."

Bartlett shook his head and looked away. "His mother is quite distraught over losing her angel. And now my other dear boy has deserted dear old Dad. Austin works for Gies now."

"Austin isn't sick?"

Bartlett stopped, turned to face Bane. They stood alone in a vast formal garden, surrounded by the pleasant music of ancient fountains and birdsong. "Three injections, Bane? Luckily the vaccine was effective. He's a strong boy."

They glared at each other for a long moment, the hate rearing up between them like mythical beasts, all flames and teeth.

"I guess your malpractice insurance doesn't cover mad scientist syndrome?" Bane said, with an effort again not to dive for his gun. How much he wanted to blast the smugness from Bartlett's handsome face. That he was no longer CEO of Braxis didn't make him any less dangerous. He was still a psycho, a billionaire many times over, and connected around the world.

Here was the man who had strapped his baby Mags to a gurney, Mags and Arm, and played a reality TV show with their lives. Before this week was out, Bane would be back to do worse to Bartlett. But for now, he needed the monster. A demon to fight another demon.

"Truce, yes?" Bartlett smiled. "I guess congratulations are in order?"

Bane stared at the man, always the enigma, always segueing in some unexpected direction. "How so?"

"I heard—my network's still intact, you understand?" He smiled. "I heard you took care of Khan."

Bane folded his arms on his chest. "Not happy news for me. He's dead."

"And you hoped for information."

"That's right."

"And you are here for information."

"That's right."

Bartlett sighed. "I guess we have always been adversaries."

Bane put on his fiercest scowl. "You're being too polite. When this is over, I plan to chop you into little pieces and fertilize your vineyard with the remains."

"How thoughtful." Bartlett bent to stroke the big head of one of his Newfies. The dog licked his hand. "You'll need to go to Site X. Near Brunei. And you'd best hurry. I believe your friends, such as they are, will not survive long."

Site X, Near Brunei

Ada sat in one of the plastic molded chairs, facing her friends Panji, Kenji and Barbie. Nam circled them like a hungry shark, pacing the sterile room at a dizzying pace.

There wasn't anything new to say, but the silence wasn't comfortable. What could they do but wait? Days had passed, and they had no idea what was happening outside of their twenty-by-twenty-foot prison. Was the virus controlled? Had the new mutation vectored? Was Gies profiteering from the vaccine? Where was Bane? It was useless to think of these things in their silent sterile white-on-white world, a place with walls that didn't yield to kicks, glaring lights behind screened cages, and one wall of thick bulletproof glass and triple seals designed to keep in viruses, and the eye of a single camera in a corner, always watching. The only furnishings were molded plastic bunks bolted to the walls, and the plastic chairs.

The hush was deafening. Ada found the long hours of silence, broken only by meals brought by armed guards, allowed her time to brood on her mistakes. And she didn't like brooding. Mostly she found herself thinking of Quentin. Of how she'd never have a chance to say, "I'm sorry" to her son, to explain why she blamed herself, how it wasn't his fault that she was never around, that she loved him. More than anything else, she wanted to live long enough just to tell Quentin that he was a beautiful human being.

Angry at herself, she focused on her friends. "I'm sorry about this."

Panji, who had given up on singing light pass-the-time ballads, leaned forward and touched her knee. "How is this your fault?"

"It seems I was the threat. You were—"

Nam stopped her pacing. "No time now for this. Now is the time to escape."

Ada smiled, in spite of their situation. She had developed quite the affection for Nam. "Okay, we escape. But how?"

"There's always a way."

Panji smiled. "She's right."

"I agree," said Kenji.

Ada noticed the electrical connection between Kenji and Panji. At any other time it would have been adorable. Now it was bittersweet. They might not live to enjoy each other. "Of course she's right. But we're in an empty room. Plastic chairs that weigh three pounds each, bulletproof glass, a negative pressure ventilation shaft large enough for a mouse. We tried everything."

"No, not everything," Nam said, her voice ferociously loud in the small room. "If everything, we would already be out of here." She glared at Ada. "You're the big science person. Think."

"I am! Nam, it's an empty room with plastic chairs."

"We could start a fire," Kenji said. "Places like this must have alarm systems."

"Electrical fire, maybe." Ada pointed at a caged electrical receptacle. "But there's a sprinkler system." She nodded, feeling energized by her friends' enthusiasm.

"Maybe the doors unlock in a fire?" Barbie pointed at the lock. "Magnetic locks."

Ada shook her head. "No. This is a level four facility. If anything, backup systems kick in and lock us in permanently."

Ada joined Nam in pacing the room and soon all four of them were orbiting the cluster of white chairs, studying every inch of the place. But the room was designed for bio-security. The doors slid pneumatically, the locks were magnetically sealed, the ventilation system was powerful, the kind Ada was used to seeing in isolation units. "If this is a bio-isolation unit, it's hermetically sealed."

"What else?" Nam asked.

"These are painted walls, probably over a triple layer of poly." Ada rolled her neck, until a bone cracked.

"Ouch," Barbie said, rubbing his own neck.

"The finish is not totally smooth," Panji said, rubbing the white walls with her hand. "It feels chalky."

Ada touched the paint. "You're right." She closed her eyes. There was something about paint in the isolation wards at hospitals, something she knew, something important. She almost had it.

What? "Wait. Wait. The paint will contain a high concentrate of calcium oxide."

"What's that?" Nam stared at her.

"It's lime."

"Lime? Like lemons and limes?"

Ada smiled. Nam was adorable. "No, no. Like lime chalk. Only they call it burnt lime or quick lime. It has a permanent disinfecting quality, that retains it's qualities over years."

"That's true," Panji said. "My people used to sprinkle lime on the bodies at burials."

Ada put her hand on Panji's shoulder. "Because it's known to be anti-bacterial, even anti-viral. Your people came to understand that it prevented plague as bodies decompose."

Panji smiled. "And what does that give us?"

"Lime burns. Calcium oxide is very painful. It can—"

"It can blind!" Nam snapped. "I remember."

"Mixed with water it can burn." Ada nodded.

"Maybe we can scrape the paint into a powder," Barbie said.

"Use these plastic chairs?" Panji picked up one of the chairs.

"But the camera," Ada said. They'll see what we're doing."

"There's only one camera," Panji said, stubbornly. "We can work in the far corner."

"Okay. And do what?"

Nam was already scraping the paint in the corner hidden from the camera, with the sharper edge of the plastic chair.

"Careful, Nam. Don't get it in your eyes," Ada said.

"But what do we do with this?" Panji asked.

"Maybe we blind that big fucker," Nam said. The eagerness of her voice made Ada pause. The big fucker was one of the Twins, the one called Austin they now knew, a nearly impossible man to stop. "That fucker, he'll be easy to handle if blind."

"Doesn't help us get out of here, though," Barbie said, sounding a little despondent. Obviously he had hoped the lime could be used to dissolve the glass wall or something more dramatic.

"No, but it is a weapon," Panji said. "At some point they have to come get us."

"Maybe they'll leave us here forever," Nam said, still scraping fiercely on the wall.

"Or maybe they turn off the ventilation and we suffocate," Barbie said.

Ada frowned. "We can't wait for either."

"Then we start a fire," Barbie said.

Ada stared at the sprinkler nozzle. "If we're trapped, we won't last long. The smoke will kill us in minutes."

"How many minutes?" Panji asked.

Ada shrugged. She was caught up in the excitement of action too, but the idea of choking to death was not appealing.

"After the room's full of smoke, maybe we last three minutes."

"I used to dive the nets, back in Hong Kong," Nam said, and a smile broke out on her round face. "I can hold my breath a long time."

"How does that help us?" Ada asked.

"Maybe if one of us can survive long enough for the big guy to come see what happened—" Panji said.

"And they'll open the door when they see the fire," Ada finished.

"Right."

Nam laughed. "I can hold my breath for a long, long time. Dive very deep. Maybe close to fifteen minutes."

"Fifteen minutes!" Ada could see Nam was wiry, strong, fit, but how could anyone live that long without breathing?

"Anyway, we're going to die so why not try?" Nam made a swiping motion in front of her neck.

"You don't know that," Barbie said. "That old codger likes Ada."

"No," Ada said. "The answer to this virus is out there, in the computers of this facility. We have to get those answers!"

"I thought there was a vaccine," Kenji said.

"There's a second virus. A mutation."

"Of course there is," Barbie said, the sarcasm thick in his voice.

Ada smiled. "Anyway, we can't ever be released, not unless Gies wants to go to prison forever ..."

"So we start a fire," Nam said, sounding eager to get started.

"The smoke will kill us," Barbie said.

Ada laughed.

"That's funny?" Barbie stared at her.

"No. Not funny. I just visualized your reaction to what I'm about to say," Ada said, still smiling.

She felt mad and wild, and it gave her strength. "In World War One, soldiers survived gas attacks by urinating on their clothing and wrapping it around their faces."

Barbie laughed. "I'm not into watersports, honey."

Ada shrugged.

"How can you laugh, now?" Panji said.

"Why not?" Kenji said, with a smile. "Why not die laughing? At least we will have good karma."

"Oh, Great Maker."

"So you want us to pee on our shirts and wrap them around our heads?" Barbie said it, in between fits of laughter.

"So we're doing this?" Ada stood on one of the plastic chairs, leaning close to a caged receptacle. "Yes, we can start a fire. I think I can."

"Well girls, what do you say?" Panji smiled at Barbie, then Kenji. "Sorry—guys, too."

"Just think of me as one of the girls," Barbie said, and he flexed a bicep, revealing a bulging muscle.

Kenji shrugged and managed a smile.

"Okay, girlfriends," Panji said. "Let's do something."

85

The White House

Doctor Ernest Gies shook the chief of staff's hand, his grip sincere and strong. "It's good to see you again, Barney."

Barnaby Godsafe had aged since their last meeting nearly a year ago. His hairline had receded markedly, his eyes were shot with red and he smelled of stale coffee and cigars. "Anything for you, Ernest. Congratulations, by the way." Gies feigned confusion. "For what, Barney?"

Barnaby gestured for Gies to take a chair and sank back into his Chippendale armchair. "Who would have believed you'd become CEO of Braxis. Damn it all, well done, my man. I hear your stock's at six hundred."

"That may change, tomorrow," Gies said tightly. It would likely hit two thousand before the week ended. "But thank you for the good wishes."

"Came as a surprise to me. I thought you loved your lab."

"Necessity," Gies said, trying to sound mysterious. "I fought for control of the company because I disagreed with Domergue's—opportunism. And he was a fraud." He hoped he didn't sound too clever.

"Coffee?"

Gies shook his head.

"What do you mean, disagreed?"

"Domergue is a French national. He doesn't feel as I do. I believe, in this emergency, the TZ-4 vaccine should be available to all Americans. At the true cost, not some inflated book value."

The chief of staff snapped forward in his chair, fatigue dropping away. "Meaning?"

"Meaning, seven dollars a dose."

"Christ, Ernie, that's incredible."

Gies smiled. This was his country. He was not about to see his own people dying. The rest of the world, well fuck them. They could make up for the loss, pay to save their own. Those who could afford it would survive.

"The president will give you the Medal of Freedom for this!"

Gies shrugged. "I just want every American to have this vaccine." He didn't care about a Medal of Freedom. He cared about obliterating violence in America. He knew, with certainty, that the survivors of the plague would be violence-castrated. That was the entire purpose of TZ-4, a purpose

Domergue had stripped away in his quest for money. A world without violence. A world without violent urges. A virally lobotomized world. Heaven. There would be no more kids as aggressive as Conner. It was too late for Conner, but it wasn't too late to save America from spiraling into a hell of gang violence and terrorism. The new TZ-4F had been point-mutated to target the production of the "violence gene" as it had been dubbed by Braxis. Could there be a more noble cause, a more perfect world? If a few hundred thousand, or even a few million, had to die to ensure the perfect world, it was still ideologically sound.

He felt a momentary pang of guilt, not for these thousands, but for Ada Kenner. She was like a daughter to him.

"You'll get the Nobel Prize, too. I'm sure of it."

Gies liked Barney's enthusiasm. "Now you're talking." A Nobel laureate. That would mean something. "Barney, I've authorized the diversion of all international destination shipments to the health department. We'll have enough doses for every single American. Maybe even Canada—if you care."

Barney shrugged. "Our little brothers, I guess."

Gies smiled. "And those in Europe and parts of Asia who can afford the fair market price—six hundred a dose—will have protection as well." He scrupulously didn't mention any Middle Eastern countries, India or Pakistan. They wouldn't have the vaccine at any price. It was his gift of peace to the world.

"That's seems very fair."

Gies frowned as his phone rang. "Sorry, Barney. I didn't turn it off."

"Go ahead, my friend."

Gies answered.

"Sir, this is Teng," said an excited voice on his phone.

Gies heard alarms in the background. "What's happening, Teng?"

"We have a fire! In the isolation ward."

Gies snapped out of his chair. He mouthed "Sorry" to Barney and slipped out into the hall past the assistant. In a quiet voice, he said, "Teng, this is a ruse. They're trying to escape."

Ada. Ada was too smart, by far.

86

Site X, Near Brunei

Nam lay on the cold laminate floor, cheek numb, eyes nearly closed, holding her breath. Her friends lay on the floor, faces low, their coughing stopped, faces wrapped in wet clothing.

There had been no coughing in long minutes. It meant her friends were unconscious—or dead. She felt the wetness on her face, the tears, an alien feeling, but she was sure it was the smoke, not some weak, whimpering sympathy for dead friends.

Even if they were dead, she must live. She must survive long enough to escape, to let Bane know. She focused on her meditation, on her silent chanting to Tara the Savior Buddha. Tara saved from all the dangers of the world. Nam put her entire faith in the silent chant, in her mental picture of the female Buddha, glowing and serene. She wrapped herself in this protective glow.

The tears came faster and hotter now. So much smoke.

The white room had been transformed into a grey hell, angry swirls of acrid smoke. When the sprinklers finally came on, drenching them, the smoke stung and then there was churning steam, and the crackling sound of sparks as Ada's jury rigged electrical fire drowned. The lights flickered off and they were plunged into darkness. The harsh emergency lighting didn't cut through the dark cloud that hung over them. The loud wail of the alarms made it nearly impossible to concentrate on holding her breath.

Nam fought the urge to move, to check her friends, to help them. She focused all her will on not moving. The smoke stung her eyes, but now the water from the sprinklers helped with the burning, washing away the betraying tears.

Under her chest, she clutched the blanket of dust, the crumbling dust they had laboriously scraped from the walls. She protected it from the sprinklers with her body and two layers of clothing. It had taken hours to painstakingly grind the paint flakes into powder using the sharp corners of the plastic chair. Burnt lime Ada had called it. Ada told her it must be dry at all costs.

She reached out her hand and tried the door again with her knuckles, not revealing too much movement in case the Braxis people were watching on the security cameras. The door had not unlocked with the fire alarm.

The smoke began to clear, but it was too soon to breathe.

She focused on controlling her heart rate, just as she had as a child diving in the murky waters of Cheung Chau. Tara had helped her then. She helped her now. Tara would help her save her friends.

Finally Nam heard voices. The outer door slammed open and through half-closed eyes she saw men rush into the room. Most of them carried fire extinguishers. Two had guns. Only six men. No problem.

Nam felt lightheaded. She had to assume she had been breathless for more than ten minutes. That's when the euphoria of oxygen deprivation usually hit her when she free-dove. Through squinted eyes, she saw shadows, floaters, blurry motions. It became difficult to concentrate on the sacred chant: Om Tare Tutare Ture Soha. She became acutely aware of not moving, of not breathing, and sounds became louder, muffling and echoing at the same time in her air-starved delerium. In this state, she often had visions.

She tried to concentrate. As a teenager, fifteen minutes was possible, just barely, but she would burst through the water surface on the edge of death, in the hold of a special kind of ecstasy that only came from suffocation. She beat the best boy in the village with his time of twelve minutes by three whole minutes. Her father had boasted about it for weeks. Her aunty had tried to get it recorded in the *Guinness Book of World Records*. Now, twenty years later, she knew she'd never be able to hold that long. With the smoke clearing, she probably could take air between clenched teeth. But still she waited; if she coughed, the guards would be alerted.

She heard the hiss of the door.

She waited. She waited, and prayed that her friends would live. They might need artificial respiration, or treatment, but she begged Buddha Tara to rescue her friends.

She almost passed out.

The booted foot of a guard bumped against her forearm.

Now was the time!

As fast as a striking viper, she wrapped her arms around his calf and pulled him down. She heard his grunt of surprise, but already she lunged upwards, her elbow crushing his windpipe. She saw the look of terror, the blood seeping into the corneas of his widened eyes, and she knew he would die. She rose, breathing in short breaths, holding the precious lime powder against her chest.

She focused on her training, shallow breaths, shallow breaths. The men cried out an alarm. But she turned lightly on her toes and her elbow drove hard into a second man's solar plexus. He fell hard against the glass. The transparency thrummed and vibrated but held. He left a red smear as he slid down the glass to the floor.

"Shoot her!" one of the guards shouted.

Nam swung around, knee cocked, right leg spinning up and around, and her heel connected with his chin. He flew back into a plastic bunk, breaking the frame off the wall. She breathed fast now, and the euphoria of air, mixed with an epinephrine high, gave her strength like she had never felt before.

Her hand dove into the cloth and pulled out a handful of lime. Without aiming, she threw it in the direction of the nearest armed guard just outside their prison door. He stepped back, surprised, brought down his automatic weapon. Suddenly he screamed, his hands flew up to his face. He clawed at his eyes.

Nam relied on speed to give power to her blows, and she launched through the door, pushing off with her hands, her fists catching the man on both cheeks in book-ended blows. She landed hard on his chest, her knee driving into his crotch, snatched his gun, and spun around. As she came back to her feet in a low crouch, she was already firing. She wasted no time with "don't move," or with warning shots. She shot to kill. Tara would forgive her in the circumstances.

She fired three quick bursts, and the remaining guards fell back in a welter of arms. One man shrieked. The bullet had torn through his abdomen. Without treatment, he would die a slow and lingering death.

Nam turned quickly. All the guards were down. More would come, she knew that, but she ran to her friends in the isolation room. Kenji had already stirred awake. He coughed, yanked the urine soaked cloth off his face, and bent over in a fit of wrenching heaves. Nam rolled Ada over. She wasn't breathing! Instantly, she pushed Ada's head back and opened her mouth.

Nam calmed herself then began mouth to mouth. Ada's lips felt cool, and there was no response. Nam's fingers felt for a pulse. Nothing!

Nam alternated between artificial respiration and cardiopulmonary resuscitation. As Nam pressed down on Ada's breastbone with the flats of her hands, her friend remained limp, eyes open.

Barbie coughed and stirred. Kenji tended to Panji who was already coughing. Coughing was good; it meant life. Kenji elevated Panji's head, resting her on his lap as she gasped for air, stroking her long hair with the affection of a long-time lover.

But Ada didn't cough. Her heart was stopped. She was dead.

Nam continued artificial respiration and CPR even as a wailing klaxon reverberated through the facility.

"Security breach, level four," a toneless voice announced on hidden speakers.

Red and amber alternating lights flashed, reflecting eerily on the remaining filaments of smoke and steam.

"Ada!" said Panji, now sitting up. She coughed some more, and came up to her knees.

"Guard the door!" Nam shouted, handing the gun to Panji, then turned back to alternating chest massage with her small hands and mouth-to-mouth. Already a minute had passed and Ada remained lifeless, her legs and arms as limp as cooked noodles.

Barbie snatched up one of the fallen weapons, an M4 Carbine, but stood staring at Ada, his face frozen in a wax-museum expression of horror. Kenji stared down at Ada and Nam. Neither of them made for the door. Finally Kenji touched Barbie's arm and said, "We guard the door."

The alarm stopped its wail, but the amber and red lights continued.

"Guards coming!" shouted Barbie.

Nam heard gunshots, the rhythmic play of automatic fire.

Barbie shot back, spraying the hall. Nam paused only for a moment. Barbie was not good with a gun, jerking back and nearly dropping the powerful M4. He half closed his eyes as he fired.

"Kenji, a gun!" Nam shouted.

Kenji stared at her. He shrugged. "No gun. I cannot shoot a gun."

She remembered he was once a Buddhist monk, then quickly forgot him as she took a long breath and brought her mouth back to Ada's cool lips.

Panji put her hand on Nam's shoulder, making her jump. "I'll take over."

Nam continued massaging Ada's chest for a moment, staring at the lifeless face of her friend, then let the anger take her. She nodded, snatched up the second M4, and ran lightly to the door. She glanced back and saw Panji administering mouth-to-mouth, then focused on the hallway.

The long hall swept around in a curve, disappearing left. She saw six guards, not well sheltered but firing a steady stream of cover as two others moved from doorway to doorway.

"Amateurs," Nam said, referring both to Barbie and the guards in the hall. She put Ada out of her mind for a moment and focused totally on the enemy. Ada would live or die. Nam could do no more than keep the rest of them alive. This was her strength. Killing. The Art of Death.

Three quick bursts from her expropriated M4 Carbine and three men fell. None were incapacitating wounds. Nam always shot to kill if she shot at all.

The remaining three guards fired back, providing a hail of bullets as cover. Nam ignored the men providing cover fire. She waited. Three doorways down the hall, a man ran from his cover as the guards fired. Nam aimed at the running man. He fell hard to the floor, sliding in the blood of one of the other guards.

Nam spat a big gob of saliva. Her father had taught her to spit at enemies for luck. She lobbed a good one into the hall. These amateurs were no match for her at all.

Then she heard the sound of hope, a wrenching cough behind her.

All of them turned to look.

Ada levered up in a spasm of coughing. She gasped for air, clutching her chest. But she was alive!

Panji grinned, holding her friend by the shoulders.

Nam turned quickly back to the hall situation, the professional in her not allowing for moments of happy distraction. Two guards had moved up one doorway.

Nam ignored them.

Standing in the center of the hall, as if immune to bullets, was the giant assassin, the man she now knew as Austin Bartlett. He smiled as he walked up the hall.

"Shoot him," Nam shouted. "He's just human." She fired a long burst of automatic fire at the hulking man with the angelic face, but had to pull back as the Braxis guards aimed at her muzzle fire. Austin sprinted ahead and dodged lightly to one side with speed that seemed impossible for such a large man. Then he ran like a train engine, chugging at full speed as Nam and Barbie both fired.

Nam was sure she caught his shoulder with a bullet, as he flinched to one side, but the maniac kept running, straight at them, harder and faster and weaving like a receiver making for a touchdown. The two Braxis guards fired again, and Nam dove to the floor as bullets thudded into the walls and door, scattering splinters and debris. She came up, fired a round and took out the two remaining guards, then aimed at Austin again and—a hollow click.

"Any more clips?" she shouted.

Panji shook her head. "Half a clip."

Barbie held up his M4. "Almost out. Save it."

"Hand to hand, then," Nam said. She glared at Kenji. "You monks aren't afraid to fight hand to hand?"

Kenji smiled. "I am no monk."

Nam spat again out into the hall, this time a primitive challenge. Let them come. She'd kill them with her bare hands.

Austin Bartlett must have realized they were out. He stopped running. He put his hand to his bloody shoulder then smiled.

As he walked towards their doorway, she felt grudging admiration for the monster. She had been assigned to take out many targets, many men and women, but never had she faced one so formidable.

Austin stood alone in the hall, his gun lowered.

"Use the lime," Ada gasped behind Nam, her voice low and raspy.

Nam nodded. Ada had read her thoughts. She held the shirt loosely. She had to do this right. She had packed the lime carefully into Kenji's shirt, tying the shirt sleeves. She held the cuffs of the shirt with one hand, careful to hold it turned up. If she did this wrong, all their efforts scraping paint was wasted. She needed to use a whipping snap, and only when they were close.

"Go out there with arms up," Nam said to Kenji and Barbie.

They stared at her for a moment, as if not understanding, then Kenji nodded. He stepped out in the hall, his hands held up as if in surrender. After a moment, Barbie followed.

As if surrendering herself Nam stepped behind them. Panji and Ada followed. All held their arms up, but in one of Nam's hands was Kenji's shirt, and about two pounds of finely ground lime.

"Do not shoot," Kenji said, his voice calm.

Nam stepped between Kenji and Barbie.

They walked slowly.

Austin the giant grinned at them wolfishly, a hungry look.

Nam waited. She tightened her wrist, but tried not to tense her body. Austin might see her tension.

"That's fine," Austin said. "No closer."

Nam pretended she didn't understand, kept walking.

"Stop!"

No more waiting. Abruptly, Nam tensed her legs and flew into a long roundhouse kick, but her heel missed and as she spun completely around, her arm snapped out, hand releasing one of the tied cuffs of Kenji's shirt.

A white cloud, driven by the force of her spin, flew straight into the face of Austin Bartlett.

He swayed for a moment, startled. His big hands came up to his eyes, brushing away powder.

Nam didn't wait, She continued her spin, like a mad dance, and the ball of her foot caught Austin on the chin.

Then Austin Bartlett, the angel of fear, screamed.

Austin tore at his face, raking his eyes with long fingers, clawing at the burning lime.

"Bitch blinded me!" the angel shrieked.

They ran past Austin as he scratched at his bloody eyes, Panji half supporting her, and Ada found herself looking back at the giant, squirming on the laminated floor, feeling sorry for his agony. But her friends swept her along.

"Computer," she said, hoarse. "Need a computer."

The second virus. Its secrets lay here somewhere. Somewhere in this Braxis hell.

Panji pressed her cheek close to Ada's. "What?"

"I need a computer!" The words exploded out of her.

Nam, Kenji and Barbie continued to run up the hall, not realizing Panji and Ada had stopped.

The hall was a long, curving sweep, with glass-walled rooms on both sides. Every room was a lab, most of them with computers. To their right was a bio-hazard four containment area for handling dangerous viruses, recognizable by the universal warning symbol, the equipment and the airlocks. "In there, Panji."

Panji hesitated only for a moment, shouting after Nam. As Panji helped Ada through the door, Nam, Barbie and Kenji came back.

"No time for this, Ada."

"Have faith, Nam," Panji said, giving her hard-assed friend a quick look. "Ada knows what has to be done." She helped Ada to a chair in front of a large monitor.

As Ada clicked some keys, Nam said, "More guards coming. No time!"

It didn't matter. There were things more important than life. And yet life was more important than anything.

The screen flashed a message: Secure access only.

The keyboard had a biometrics scanner. "We need someone. Someone has to unlock this terminal!" She looked at Nam's sweat drenched face. She could smell the stench of death on Nam, the killer; how different from Nam the pacifist Buddhist. Could both exist in one body "Nam, it's important! People are dying all around the world!"

Nam spat then turned and ran back into the hall.

She came back a moment later, bent over the keyboard, pressed something to the scanner.

Ada didn't understand at first. The screen unlocked. How did Nam do that? Then she saw the bloody stub of a finger in Nam's hand. Nam tossed it across the room as if it was garbage. It bounced off the wall and knocked over a centrifuge tube, shattering it.

Ada stared at the shattered tube, the discarded finger.

"Hurry now!" Nam shouted, and she took up a position at the lab entrance.

Ada focused on the monitor. She became very conscious of her own fingers as they stumbled on the keyboard. Who's finger was that? A sentry? A scientist? Nam knew it had to be someone with clearance. Had she killed someone just to take his finger? Ada shivered, tried to focus.

She scanned the directory.

The directory listed protocol numbers. Hundreds of them.

"Oh no," Ada said.

"No oh-nos," Nam snapped. "We will be dead soon. So, no oh-nos!"

Panji put her hand on Ada's shoulder, a calming influence "What?"

"Too many files."

Panji squeezed. "Just remember. You told me you talked to Gies. More than once right? Did he say anything?"

The alarms, the ugly smear of blood on the biometrics, the tingling in her own fingers, the pain in her lungs—all the physical sensations made it impossible to remember anything.

"Remember," Panji whispered in her ear. She massaged her shoulders. "You know."

Ada closed her eyes, sank into Panji's fingers and soothing voice. The alarms and sounds of running feet and lingering itch in her throat from smoke faded. She focused on Panji's voice, whispering over and over: "You know."

She remembered, then, in a sudden flash. Gies talking in the lounge at Site F. The protocol number. Gies had told her, all those weeks, months—all that time ago, back at site F. "An accident in Protocol 440," Ada said out loud.

She typed in: 440.

"Hurry!"

Ada heard nothing more. She jumped through the files, reading quickly. Oh God. They had played God. They had even experimented on ...

"I need a DVD!"

Panji, Kenji and Barbie tore through the lab, opening drawers and cabinets while Nam watched the entrance.

"He's coming," Nam said.

"Who? Who's coming?" Barbie joined her at the door. "Oh shit. This guy never stops."

Ada didn't have to look up. She knew. Coming up the hall was the angel of fear, Austin Bartlett. Nothing stopped him.

The glass wall of the lab shattered, exploding inwards. The bullets deflected off the laminated glass of the bio-containment area, obliterating lab equipment. Nam and Barbie fired back.

"I have a disc!" Panji shouted

She handed Ada a DVD.

Ada ignored the guns, the shattering world of the lab. She inserted the disc, calm, still reading the file.

Gies was insane. There could be no doubt. He had played with BDV, sacrificing rats, monkeys, then people in his pursuit of a cure for violence. And in doing so, he had created violence. He was mad.

The files began to copy …

The monitor flew across the room in a flurry of bullets.

Panji grabbed Ada, pulling her to the floor.

"The disc!" Ada snapped.

She ejected the disc with fumbling hands. Her fingers tingled. Was it fear, excitement or a neuropathy caused by oxygen starvation. It burned. She shoved the disc into a pocket.

Another burst of machine gun fire rattled the bio containment shield.

"He's firing blind!"

A klaxon sounded, and a synthesized voice announced: "Warning. Outer seal breach, bio-containment lab sixteen. Warning …"

A red light flashed over the airlock to the bio-hazard area.

"We have to get out of here," Ada said, staring in through the thick glass at the inner lab. Steam poured from the inner vents. It was refrigerated in there. She shivered. A room full of death. Bio containment level four labs only handled viruses and bacteria that were fatal to human life, that had no known cure or vaccine. What horrors lay beyond that wall? She had spent all her life in labs such as these, and they had never frightened her. But now she felt a chill of certainty. Behind that wall was death. Death for everyone she knew and loved.

Outside the lab, the mad angel continued to fire.

"Stop him!" Ada shouted.

"We're trying," Nam shouted back.

The alarms continued to sound. "Warning! Ventilation systems malfunction! Evacuate Level four immediately!"

Nam threw her gun across the room "I'm out! Clips!"

Barbie held up his gun. "Half a clip!"

Nam held out her hands. "Give!"

He handed her the gun.

Panji grabbed Ada's hand and pulled her down behind a steel counter. They watched as Nam rose up, aimed carefully, and fired. She fired a steady burst until the chamber clicked empty.

They waited. The only sound was the klaxon.

Nam peered out. "He's down." She stepped out into the hall.

"Be careful," Panji shouted. "He's been down before."

Nam shook her head, and dropped her weapon with a clatter to the floor. "No. This time he's down."

Ada followed them out, stepping on broken glass, her hand wrapped around the disc in her pocket. Nothing else mattered but that disc.

Nam was right. The angel of fear had no angelic face. No face at all. No demon would rise from the bloody wreckage in the hall.

A new alarm shrieked, louder than before, it filled the halls, so loud Ada covered her ears. "Warning, bio containment breach. Incendiary protocol activated."

"What's that mean?" Panji asked. But the horror on her face made it clear to Ada she understood.

"They're using explosive chemical heat to destroy the viruses," Ada said. "This whole level will be vaporized!"

They ran. The floor was deserted, full of sounds and light, but empty of people. They found an elevator.

"We use stairs," Nam said. "If there is an explosion, not good to be in an elevator!" She pointed at an emergency exit sign.

Ada found new wind. She found she wanted to live. As close to death as she came, as peaceful as it seemed, she wanted to live. To bring the disc to Bane, or the CDC, or USAMRIID, or anyone who could act on the data. She wanted to live, to see Quentin, sweet beautiful Quentin. She had let him down all these years, afraid of him, afraid of facing what she had done, but now all she wanted was to see him. To touch his face. To kiss him. To tell him all the things a mother should tell a son. And if he shoved her away, even if he spat in her face, she would be happy.

They ran up the stairs, passing other scientists, technicians, even guards with guns. No one cared about them anymore. Everyone ran for their lives. Above them, Ada saw a bright square of light. The emergency staircase went right to the surface.

They followed the crowd outside. Her eyes hurt for a moment as she pushed through the men and women in white coats. It was oppressively hot, and she saw stunted Nipa palms and lush tropical vegetation. She smelled salt and heard ocean surf and monkeys.

Nam led the way to a sandy beach, away from the bewildered scientists and guards. Seabirds swooped down, screaming at them. And in the distance, Ada heard a thrumming sound, mechanical, almost ominous. She turned south, shading her eyes, and saw the dark smudge on the horizon. A helicopter.

They felt something like an earthquake's aftershock. Ada turned back towards the Braxis facility. A black cloud erupted from one of the surface buildings, a moment later, smoke gushed from all the exits. She hoped everyone got out. Seconds later, their world erupted. A small building launched skywards like an old Jupiter rocket.

Ada fell to the sand, they all did, covering their ears. The hollow booming became a higher pitched screech.

The first helicopter landed.

Alban Bane jumped out, his shiny little chromed revolver in his hand. And to Ada, he was a true angel.

Manifesto Club, Washington

Ada followed Alban Bane and six of his agents, including tough little Nam, into the Lincoln Room of the Manifesto Club, a discreet building that reeked of old pipe tobacco, drenched in prestige. The cherry-wood alcoves in the octagonal foyer displayed famous American masterworks that belonged in an art museum.

"Would you wait here, sir?" the doorman asked with a tone that really said: You don't belong here, go away.

"No," Alban Bane said. He held out the warrant again. "We are not here as guests."

"That is evident, sir."

"You will take me immediately to Doctor Ernest Gies. Or you will be arrested for obstruction." Alban smiled as he said it, and Ada felt the stir of something. Pride? She was proud of Alban Bane, as much as he was apparently proud of her.

He always made her feel that way now. Mr. Dependable. She had known it was Alban in the helicopter as she lay on that beach on the tiny nameless island off Brunei. As the world erupted around them, she kept her eyes focused on the helicopter, knowing, somehow certain, it was Alban Bane. And it was. He had found them. He had begged a helicopter from the Sultan of Brunei, and flown to the rescue. Who said there were no knights in shining armor? To her, it was no cliché.

The disc she had copied from the computer at Site X was hard evidence that would convict not only Gies, but Braxis. The files also contained information on a workable vaccine for the mutated second virus, already released to Braxis competitors for rapid development.

Ada had insisted on coming with Bane to "confront" Gies. It seemed important after all they had been through.

"This way, sir," the doorman said, finally.

"You will not announce us."

"The secret service will do that for you, sir."

"Fine." He leaned close to Ada and whispered, "The entrances are all covered."

Ada nodded. She felt a thrill in all this, and a little shame at the surge of pleasure she felt. That feeling intensified as they followed the curt doorman up a long pillared hallway. Twenty-foot-high statues of angels faced in, glaring down at them. Ada flinched under their gaze, remembering Sampson, the angel of fear.

They passed a library, crowded with men smoking cigars. "Was that the chairman of the joint chiefs?" Ada asked.

"Yes," Bane said, but his answer sounded like a sigh.

"Why do it here, Al?" Ada asked again.

"To make a point."

"Is that why the reporters are outside?"

Bane smiled. "Too many good people died. A lesson must be learned."

She nodded. "And it feels good, too?"

"Yes, it does." He winked at her.

Ada walked fast beside him, confident in his strength. She could hardly believe she had accepted his invitation to dinner tomorrow night. Did that work? Dinner with the boss? It didn't matter. She liked Bane, and they deserved at least a quiet dinner at Primi Piatti.

Two blank-faced secret service agents stood at the double-arched doorway to Mensa Hall. They stepped in front of the doors, eyes fixed on Alban Bane, each almost indistinguishable from the other, in square-cut blue suits, with nearly identical haircuts, frowns and glaring eyes.

"You can't enter, sir." Agent A said.

Bane showed the warrant.

"That's not relevant, sir," Agent B said. "The vice president is in a closed-door session with CIA Director Lambert and—"

Bane stepped closer, eye to eye with the secret service agent. "You know who I am?"

"Yes sir."

"This warrant is signed by a supreme court justice."

"You'll have to wait, sir."

"No. I won't have to wait." Bane nodded, and his six agents spread out in a V formation around Bane and Ada.

"Don't create an incident, sir."

"I didn't create the incident," Bane said. "Step aside."

By now Ada saw that a crowd had gathered in the long hall of the Manifesto Club, a veritable who's who of Washington, all of them men, all of them watching the spectacle. Many powerful witnesses. Did Bane really want to press this? But then Ada realized she did, and that was the point of doing it this way. She wanted to see their damned faces. She wanted the vice president and CIA director and the entire cadre of power to know they might be next. She wanted it as much as Bane. Somewhere, she hoped the ever-smiling ghost of Doctor Cafferty Toy was watching. Somehow, she felt he must be.

Secret Service Agent A tilted his head to the right, the side with the earpiece. Without a word, he stepped aside.

Bane reached for the door, but the doorman intercepted him and pushed open the great doors.

Inside, six men clustered around a cheery fire, all holding brandy snifters, and none of them looked surprised: Vice President Samuels, CIA Director Lambert, FBI Deputy Director Kaplan, CEO Jerry Staughan of JSE, and Terrorism Task Force Chairman Franklin Farrier, and the new CEO of Braxis Genetics, Doctor Ernest Gies.

The stoop shouldered Director Lambert of the CIA walked quickly towards the door. He stepped in front of Alban. "Director Bane. Do you know what you are doing?"

Bane smiled. "Director Lambert, I know exactly what I am doing. When there's this much mud, you get out a hose."

Lambert's tired face twitched just for a moment. Anger or fear? Ada couldn't tell. She felt a chill, either way. He stepped aside.

Bane moved quickly into the room, the inner sanctum of power, the room where the power élite met. Ada, Panji, Nam and the other agents followed, creating a tight phalanx around their director.

"Ernest Gies," Bane said, his voice clipped and serious. "Ernest Gies, you are under arrest on multiple counts of homicide, multiple counts of kidnapping, multiple counts of assault with a deadly weapon, multiple counts of extortion. You have the right to—"

"I know my rights," Gies snapped, stepping forward.

Bane snapped on the cuffs and finished reading Gies his rights.

"You can't do this, Bane," Vice President Samuels said, putting down his cognac. "This man was just awarded the Medal of Freedom by the president."

"Yesterday. I know. I would have arrested him then, but I didn't want the president to look bad."

Samuels winced. "You can't do this," he repeated, as if he couldn't think of anything else to say.

"Yes. Yes, I can." He lifted Gies cuffed wrists. "And I've only just begun."

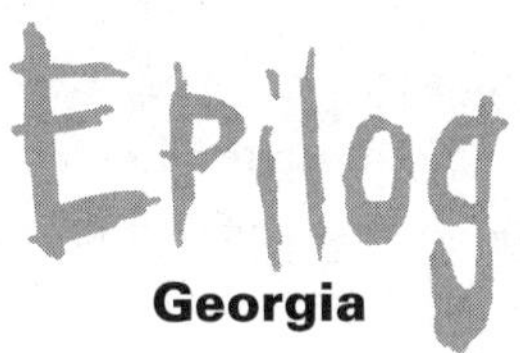

Epilog

Georgia

They were all there, standing by the magnolias—all her friends: Panji and Kenji, Nam and Barbie and Arm in his wheelchair. And holding her hand, Bane. It was strange how they had become so tight in so few months, as if they had always been close, and always would be. Earlier that afternoon, they had even visited the Caff at Oak Lane Cemetery. Panji and Kenji were soulmates, that was clear. Panji, Ada and Nam, new friends, clicked into a zone reserved for natural sisterhood. As they sat on the stone bench by Caff's tombstone, Panji named the trio: "NAPsters, get it? N.A.P.—Nam, Ada, Panji? I'm going to write a song."

The biggest surprise in the last few weeks had been the discovery of Arm in a hospital in Rome. Ada had flown in with Bane, and both of them had cried at his bedside as he grinned at them and said, "Naw, none of this now. For true, I be fine." Then he cried too. Doctors said he would walk again after months of physio. A happily-ever-after for Arm.

Of all the battles—invisible viruses that devastated people's lives, corrupt politicians who even now clung to their careers, mad assassins, and, saddest of all in some ways, the insane Doctor Gies—none of it compared to the terror Ada now felt.

The exhaustion of the last few weeks fell away. The pandemic was under control, quarantines were lifting, the vaccine had helped manage the spread. Ada hadn't slept, watchful for new hostpots, even flying to Peru when a new outbreak occurred in Huras. She rarely slept. She fought battles in a dozen countries, and now, thank God, the plague was controlled. And through it all, what kept her going—aside from the steady friendship of the NAPsters—was this anticipated moment.

She couldn't do this alone. She thought she could, after all she had faced, but she always found a reason not to face Quentin. An emergency in the lab. Another outbreak. But all her friends had shown up in her lab, dragged her out to a van, and driven her here.

She stared at the ominous blue door. She had painted that door herself. Devon had refused to sell their little bungalow, even through their divorce, even in the years that followed. She saw that her camellia bushes were out of bloom, but they reached up to the eaves of the house. She had planted them with Devon, laughing about their future together, one sunny spring afternoon. They had grown from barely a foot tall, to car-sized bushes, lush and green, the autumn blooms dried but left unsnipped.

Panji put her hand on Ada's shoulder. Bane held her right hand. Nam, always the charge-ahead leader, walked up the pea gravel path, turned and looked back.

"It's time," Panji whispered.

Bane squeezed her hand one more time.

And they left her there at the bottom step. All of them, as if they had practiced it, gave her a thumbs-up sign. Kenji's smile was sunshiny and nearly as wide as Arm's smile. Barbie giggled. Nam frowned but nodded. Panji mouthed, "Go on." Bane blew her a kiss.

Ada took the first step.

The bottom step squeaked. It had always squeaked. Devon and Ada had pulled it apart, renailed it, screwed it down, braced it, but always that step squeaked. She almost turned back. A flood of bittersweet memories took her. She'd rather face the ghost of Sampson Bartlett than this.

She made it to the door through a force of will she didn't know she had.

She stared at the doorbell. It would ring a classic ding-dong, she remembered. She had personally picked it out.

The door opened before she could ring the bell.

Devon stood there, looking as terrified as she felt.

"Are you ready?"

Ada shook her head. But she was. It was all that mattered now.

Devon took her hand and guided her into the haunted home of her memories.

"Quent," Devon said, his voice trembly. "Quent, this is your mother."

Quentin stood in the living room—he stood!—on prosthetic legs, supported by a cane in each hand.

His smile was devastating. He was crying too.

Ada fell to her knees in front of her son.

About the author

Derek Armstrong

He loves the provocative, controversial and unique.

What the critics say:

"Armstrong's abundant enthusiasm for his material, combined with the semi-satirical plotline, compel us to keep reading, and his prose style keeps us chuckling." David Pitt, *Booklist Magazine*

"Derek Armstrong is good," Michael Korda, *Simon & Schuster*

"Gruesome, suspenseful, and rich with dark humor, Armstrong moves the reader through time and space with a keen sense of momentum and dash. His characters are diverse, bold, unforgettable ..." *ForeWord*

Armstrong focuses on "high concept" but with a key difference. Black humor, edgy dialogue and "broad swipes at the zeitgeist" are integral to Armstrong's unique writing. Armstrong is as likely to make fun of his own "thriller" genre as reality television—the target of his attack in ***The Game***. His historical thriller, ***The Last Troubadour,*** makes light of both the Catholic Church and the latest passion for the Holy Grail. He has been called "cheeky" and "daring" and "provocative." Derek Armstrong writes thrillers because, according to him, "they're entertaining and you can be ridiculous and serious at the same time. Thrills and laughs belong together. Really."

Derek Armstrong has won many awards for advertising copywriting Internationally and wrote ***The Persona Principle*** (Simon & Schuster) with co-author Kam Wai Yu, now translated into six languages.

Forthcoming titles include ***The Last Quest***, the sequel to ***The Last Troubadour*** and ***Blogertize—A Leading Expert Shows How Your Blog Can Be A Money-Making Machine***.